THE AVON ROMANCE

Four years old and better than ever!

We're celebrating our fourth anniversary...and thanks to you, our loyal readers, "The Avon Romance" is stronger and more exciting than ever! You've been telling us what you're looking for in top-quality historical romance—and we've been delivering it, month after wonderful month.

Since 1982, Avon has been launching new writers of exceptional promise—writers to follow in the matchless tradition of such Avon superstars as Kathleen E. Woodiwiss, Johanna Lindsey, Shirlee Busbee and Laurie McBain. Distinguished by a ribbon motif on the front cover, these books were quickly discovered by romance readers everywhere and dubbed "the ribbon books."

Every month "The Avon Romance" has continued to deliver the best in historical romance. Sensual, fast-paced stories by new writers (and some favorite repeats like Linda Ladd!) guarantee reading *without* the predictable characters and plots of formula romances.

"The Avon Romance"—our promise of superior, unforgettable historical romance. Thanks for making us such a dazzling success!

BY LOVE ALONE

JUDITH E. FRENCH

AVON
PUBLISHERS OF BARD, CAMELOT, DISCUS AND FLARE BOOKS

AVON BOOKS
A division of
The Hearst Corporation
1790 Broadway
New York, New York 10019

First Avon Printing: April 1987

AVON TRADEMARK REG. U.S. PAT. OFF. AND IN OTHER COUNTRIES, MARCA REGISTRADA, HECHO EN U.S.A.

Printed in the U.S.A.

K-R 10 9 8 7 6 5 4 3 2 1

To Gary—for today, tomorrow, and all the yesterdays

Chapter 1

England 1754

By the faint light of a pale hunter's moon, Lady Kathryn Storm waited impatiently beside the Oxford Road, pistols primed and face swathed in highwayman's black silk. The ebony stallion trembled beneath her, and she laid a practiced hand on his arched neck. "Shhh," she soothed. "Be still." A twig snapped to the left, and Kate shivered. "Is that you?"

"Who else would it be?" Geoffrey cursed softly.

Kate strained her eyes in the darkness and made out the form of her brother on a ghostly gray wending through the thick trees. "You picked the spot," she reminded. Geoffrey's temper was short and as soon appeased.

"The Earl's coach has to slow to make the hill. It's the best ambush for miles. I know my business, Kate, and it's my neck if anything happens to you. I must be out of my mind for agreeing to this in the first place." He reined in beside her and the two stablemates nickered a friendly greeting.

"It's Father's neck, you mean. Nothing will go wrong. How can it? You've been doing this long enough."

For nearly seven years Lord Storm's estates had been financed by a toll taken at the muzzle of a highwayman's flintlock. Queen's Gift and the lesser manors belonging to the Storm family required a fortune to maintain, a fortune Edward Storm no longer had. Rather than see his land confiscated, his children stripped of their belongings and hauled

1

off to debtor's prison, he had followed the example of many desperate men before him.

The deception had come to an end when a sniveling informer had roused suspicion against Lord Storm and he had been taken into custody by the High Sheriff. Geoffrey had been in London, at the home of a friend, and had luckily missed arrest. It was Kate's scheme that had brought them to the Oxford Road on this particular night.

"Two men are accused of the robberies," she'd explained to Geoffrey. "One on a black stallion, the second on a gray. The leader on the gray never speaks. He carries a pair of double-barrel flintlocks with gold-inlaid stocks. The smaller highwayman always repeats the same words."

"God's teeth, Kate! Spit it out! What are ye aiming at?" he fumed. "I say, 'Stand and deliver!' "

A trace of a smile tugged at the corner of Kate's mouth as she watched her handsome brother. Geoffrey was the image of their father, blond to her own brown tresses. They shared only the startling blue eyes and the Storm nose. Two years younger, Geoffrey had been more like a twin. They had learned to ride together, to shoot, and—to Geoffrey's anguish—to execute the finest dance steps. "The bandit who speaks carries Scottish pistols, single-barrel with silver stocks. The description given by the victims seldom varies."

"And? Out with it or I shall strangle you with my own hands!"

"And our solution is simple, little brother. You shall take Father's place, ride his gray and carry his weapons, and I . . ." She paused and grinned. "I shall ride your Lucifer and shout, 'Stand and Deliver!' "

"The hell you will!"

It had taken the better part of a night and day to convince him. If another robbery was committed, a robbery so bold that it could not fail to arouse public outcry, then Lord Storm would be proved innocent and must be released. Kate had long experience in contesting the stubborn will of her men. Her mother had died in childbirth when she was nine; since then, Queen's Gift had been a male stronghold.

Only those bold and high-spirited had any chance of commanding respect.

It was that boldness and a sharp, witty tongue that had kept Kate from the marriage bed of men old enough to be her grandfather. She had been betrothed at sixteen to a second cousin, a man she liked and respected, if nothing else. Lord DeCheyne had been taken ill and died of smallpox before they could be wed, and Kate had dodged marriage and its restraints ever since. She had her hunting dogs, her horses, and the companionship of a doting father and brother. If she must forgo children to keep her own freedom, so be it. Kathryn Storm would be no man's docile possession.

The Earl of Westbrook would be leaving his country house this night to journey to London. Kate knew because he had confided his plans to her over dessert at Saturday's dinner party. He had pawed drunkenly at her knee beneath the table and burped out his departure, along with the request that she accompany him. She had blushed prettily, hid her calculating blue eyes behind a feathered fan, and moved her knee out of reach. The Earl was a perfect candidate; he would be carrying a large sum of money on his person, and he was cousin to the King himself. It had been an evening well-spent.

An owl hooted and Kate shifted in her saddle. Her throat felt tight and her breath sounded loud in her ears. The smell of danger was like a fine French perfume in the night air. She had secured Geoffrey's promise that there would be no violence. "We don't want any trouble," she added. "Even if we fail, we will have accomplished our mission by being seen." Lucifer tossed his head and she reined him tightly. "Shhh, easy boy, just a little longer."

She had no fear of the animal; her riding was the equal of Geoffrey's, the equal of any man she knew. She had ridden astride since she was five years old, privately and publicly. Sidesaddles were dangerous, fit only for fools. She'd no wish to end a cripple like Lady Satterly by falling from one of the ridiculous contraptions. Lord Storm had upheld her in this, and the gossips be damned. "Shameless!'' they'd whispered, and Kate had only laughed. This night would prove the wisdom of her choice.

A slight rumbling noise signaled the approach of a vehicle. ''Wait,'' Geoffrey cautioned, ''until I give the signal.'' He crossed the road to the deep shadows of the oaks beyond. Kate wrapped the reins around one gloved wrist and took a firm grip on the Scottish pistols.

The massive coach horses pounded into view, slowing even now on the grade. Two figures loomed from the driver's seat. A sharp whistle from the oaks cut the air and Kate set her spurs into Lucifer's taut black sides. There was a brilliant flash, a shot exploded in the night, and the coachman sawed at the reins.

''Stand and deliver!'' Kate shouted in her deepest voice, and trained the Scottish flintlocks on the coach window. ''Your property or your lives!''

A bewigged head appeared in the door opening. ''B'God! Do you know who I am?'' The Earl swore foully and Kate lowered one flintlock until the muzzle centered on his bulbous red nose.

''Out!'' Kate ordered. Lucifer danced nervously and twitched his ears. One by one the passengers climbed from the coach: the Earl; his brother, Lord Thomas; a daringly gowned woman of dubious reputation; and an older man Kate had never met. She motioned them to the side of the road. The moon passed behind a cloud and the horses' breathing was the only sound in the night stillness.

Geoffrey waved the coachman and footman from the seat, then dismounted to collect the loot. Kate had been instructed to stay in the saddle no matter what. The passengers were her responsibility and she watched intently for any furtive movement. Her brother moved quickly to strip the victims of jewelry and watches. A small metal box inside the coach yielded heavy coin. Kate held her breath. Another moment and they would be riding safely away. Suddenly there was a rumble of hoofbeats on the road.

Geoffrey turned to mount and the coachman lunged at him. Geoffrey's double-barrel flintlock spit flame and lead. With a cry, the man pitched forward into the dirt. Geoffrey swung up onto the big gray, and the passengers scattered as shots rang out from the approaching riders. Kate heard the faint buzz of a musket ball as it passed her head. "Get the hell out of here!" Geoffrey yelled. He slumped forward slightly in the saddle and Kate hesitated for a fraction of a second. "I'm all right! Go!" She set spurs into Lucifer's side and drove for the forest road as her brother's horse veered off in another direction.

Lord Ashton noted with satisfaction that his second shot had drawn blood. The rogue was hit, certain. He waved Giles and some of the men in pursuit of the wounded highwayman and led the chase for the second. A quick glance as they thundered past the coach told him that his uncle, the Earl, was unhurt. Giles's mount had thrown a shoe as they rode out of the courtyard and he'd had to find a replacement. The delay had placed Pride Ashton and the men-at-arms a good half mile behind the coach's progress. A damn good thing it wasn't farther, or the highwaymen would have pulled off their robbery and escaped before he could reach the scene.

Lashing his horse, Ashton galloped after the outlaw. He'd been spoiling for excitement for weeks and the bay was the finest animal in his uncle's stables. He'd run the thief to ground in no time.

Kate lay low over the black's neck as branches whipped at her face and head. It was too dark to see the path; she must trust Lucifer's instincts. Another shot passed over her head and she spurred the stallion on. Ahead the trees thinned and the uneven ground opened onto a low meadow. The black sped across the soft ground, tearing up clods of earth with his pounding hooves. "Faster," Kate urged. "Faster." She ventured a glance over her shoulder. A horse and rider broke from the woods behind her.

A four-rail fence loomed before them. Lucifer soared over it, found the harder ground beyond, and scrambled onto a dirt farm lane. The stallion had the bit in his teeth now; there was no stopping him even if she'd wished to.

Ashton's bay took the jump evenly. A cry behind him and the sound of an animal in distress proved that one of his men hadn't been as lucky. He couldn't suppress the surge of admiration for the black-garbed figure ahead. Damn, but the bastard could ride like a cossack! Still, he was human, and no man or horse could keep up the pace. Ashton would see the scoundrel jailed and hanged or know why.

After dreary sessions in dusty law offices and smoke-filled drawing rooms, this manhunt was almost a relief to Ashton. England was maddeningly boring. Pride's father, an earl, had passed away last fall, and Pride had made the journey from the American colony to settle the estate. For the only son and heir to his father's titles and vast wealth, it had been a necessary if time-consuming task.

There had been no love lost between Pride and the haughty Lord Ashton. His romance with Pride's Shawnee Indian mother had probably been the only reckless thing Lord Ian Ashton had ever done. Pride had spent years in his father's care, but England was never home. His obligatory visit to his uncle had finished the duties. In a few weeks he would be on the open sea, bound for the Maryland colony and his plantation, Ashton Hall, due west of the Chesapeake.

As she galloped ahead of her pursuer, Kate's nerve was fast dwindling. She would not be caught; she couldn't. Geoffrey and her father would both suffer if she didn't make good her escape. Lucifer was slowly pulling away, but not fast enough. The village of Beauford Downs lay just ahead.

She chanced another look back. The single rider was still far ahead of the rest. If she could lose him, it would be easy to evade the others and double back toward Shepton Abbey. Perhaps Geoffrey was already there. No, he'd ride far afield before returning to the rendezvous. Shepton Abbey was no more than a pile of ruins. The country folk believed it haunted by the ghosts of long-dead monks. She and Geoffrey had played there as children. It was a stroke of genius to pick the Abbey, even Geoffrey had agreed.

"We split up after the robbery," he'd ordered. "Follow the plan, no matter what. Alfred will be waiting at the ruins with a change of clothing and a carriage. He'll take Lucifer and Gray Boy to the farm.''

"If he's not scared off by the ghosts."

"And you, sister, are you not a wee bit nervous to be there in the dead of the night?''

"It's the living I fear and few of them!''

Kate wondered if she'd spoken too rashly. The rider on the bay was out for blood. She wondered if she dared risk a shot herself. It might discourage him, although her chances of hitting him were ludicrous. Kate eased the right pistol from her belt and fired off a shot in his direction just as Lucifer's hooves struck the wooden bridge that crossed Beauford Run.

Pride cursed and ducked as the pistol roared. His own was empty; he could not fire again until he stopped to reload. Straight through the village the highwayman thundered. The nerve of the bastard! ''Giddap!'' he urged, raking the bay's sides with his spurs. The hairs on the back of his neck raised as he thought of possible ambush ahead. He was as lost here as that scoundrel would be in the wilds of Maryland.

Lucifer's neck was soaked with sweat. Kate could feel his breathing deepen. ''Good boy, good Lucifer,'' she encouraged. The gate beyond the village was closed. Kate caught her lower lip in her teeth, but the big black cleared the obstacle with a foot to spare. ''Now! Go!'' She brought the whip down hard on his flanks and he gave every ounce of reserve in a great burst of speed. Why in God's name had she ever gotten into this?

The road led into Beauford Wood, a narrow rough trail. For nearly a half mile they galloped down it, then Kate pulled hard on the reins and wheeled the stallion into a break in the trees. Sliding off, she led him down a steep hill and into the shallow water of a wide stream. Her boots were instantly soaked, but the trees were too thick overhead to ride. Lucifer tried to drink, but she twisted his head up firmly. ''Not now, darling,'' she whispered. ''Not while you're sweating so.'' She scooped a little water in her gloved hand and moistened his velvety nose.

As he reached the forest, Pride became aware of the

silence and reined up. No sound of hoofbeats behind or before. He leaned against the puffing animal and reloaded his pistol. "So it's a hunt you want," he murmured softly. Patches of moonlight filtered through the trees overhead, barely enough for him to see the path ahead, let alone to track. He'd have traded his best riding horse to have his half brother, Tschi, here. A Shawnee brave could track a rumor through a snowstorm. Well, Pride was half Shawnee himself and he didn't do bad, by his own reckoning.

On the third pass he noticed the broken seedling. He knelt on the leaves and traced the outline of the horse's hoof in the damp earth. Good enough, as long as the quarry kept running and didn't lay a trap of his own. The trail to the stream was easy enough to follow. The hoofprints didn't come out the other side, so it was anybody's guess which way the highwayman had gone. Away from the village would make sense; it would also be what the thief would be expected to do. Had he played the fox and turned back? Pride turned upstream. If the highwayman was as smart as he figured, he might be too smart for his own good.

Kate, still plodding along in the stream, had lost track of time, and the cold water was numbing her feet. The boots were surely ruined, and they were Geoffrey's favorites. It would require some explaining. Norseman's Hollow lay somewhere to the right; she would chance it. Carefully, she led Lucifer out of the stream and through the soft ground that led to the sheep meadows. At the edge of the open, she mounted and kicked the big horse into a trot. She'd be lucky to get back to the abbey before dawn; it was miles in the opposite direction.

A cold trickle of doubt invaded the corners of her brain. Had Geoffrey made good his escape? Then she remembered the coachman; pray God he wasn't hurt too badly. The gun must have gone off by accident. Geoffrey couldn't have fired on an unarmed man. Tears threatened to fill her eyes, and she brushed them away. Father would be released; that was the important thing. She'd make discreet inquiries into the fate of the coachman and whether he had a family. It had all been a game—a serious one, of course. But if the man had been maimed or, God forbid, even killed, she must bear the responsibility as much as Geoffrey. Kate shook the damp leather reins and clicked to the stallion. The sooner she reached the ruins, the sooner her questions would be answered . . . for good or evil.

Pride grinned wolfishly as he spotted the muddy prints leading up out of the water. There would be no ambush. If the highwayman intended to stand and fight, he would have picked a spot along the stream and taken his pursuers unaware. Most of the gentlemen of the road were alike, brave enough when facing unarmed prey, but yellow when it came to a real fight. He swung up and set spurs to the horse, pausing only long enough to fire several shots in the air. It would let the men-at-arms know his direction and also put a little pressure on the outlaw.

Halfway across the meadow, he spotted a horse and rider crossing an open stretch of road. The clouds overhead parted, illuminating the landscape in an elusively golden glow. Both horses broke into a gallop almost as one.

Kate lashed Lucifer unmercifully, fighting his head to keep him from the road. A crossroads lay not a mile away; it was much too dangerous. She forced the black into the woods and lay low over his plunging neck as branches raked her head and arms.

"Bloody fool!" Pride swore. The forest under these conditions could break a horse's leg as quick as not. "I'll have every strip of hide off the beggar's back, then draw and quarter him myself!" Without hesitation he followed, trusting the bay not to run headlong into a tree.

Lucifer found a game trail and turned onto it. Stubbornly, Kate clung to his neck. A branch had struck her face and her left eye was swollen and weeping. Blood trickled unheeded from her forehead. Still the devil followed! She could hear his mount crashing through the woods behind. By moonlight, she glimpsed a fallen log across the path and braced herself for the jump.

Lucifer rose to meet it, struck his front left shoulder on a protruding branch, and went over off balance, landing heavily and falling to his knees. Kate felt herself falling, then cried out as she hit the ground hard. For a moment, she lay there stunned, every ounce of breath knocked out of her. Dazed, she brushed at her face; Lucifer stood head down breathing heavily, favoring his right foreleg.

Painfully, Kate got to her feet and walked toward the stallion. "Whoa, boy, whoa." He shook his head and stepped out of reach, the leather reins dangling. "Whoa, Lucifer," she pleaded. Her mouth tasted of blood and dirt and she spat, suddenly becoming aware of the approaching rider. One pistol lay in the path; she seized it and flung herself behind the log. "Halt!" she cried. "I'll shoot."

Pride's flintlock roared an answer as he flung himself from the saddle. Kate squeezed the trigger of her own pistol, the flash near-blinding in the semidarkness. She dropped the weapon and fumbled for the mate at her waist. In seconds, the man was upon her. She backed away, pistol at arm's length. "Don't try it," she warned.

Pride stared into the muzzle of the Scottish flintlock, expecting to feel the shock of lead. For an instant, the pistol wavered and he lashed out with one foot, kicking it free. He drove forward with his fists, striking the highwayman squarely on the jaw and knocking the scoundrel senseless into the dirt. Instinctively, he knelt to search the limp form for hidden weapons; his practiced hands moving up from the waist to encounter small but well-formed breasts. "By God, a wench!"

From far off, Kate felt the strange hands on her body. With a cry she brought her knee up and twisted away, flailing her fists with all the strength she possessed. Rude laughter sounded in her ears as an iron hand dragged her upright and shook her as a terrier would a rat.

"Put me down!" she screamed. He released his grip, and Kate tumbled to the path, scrambling back and putting up her hands to defend herself. "If you come near me, I'll . . . I'll . . ."

"You'll what?" Again the laughter. "This is a pretty mess! Am I to tell my friends in Annapolis I captured a Turpin of the road, and it turned out to be a sniveling wench?" He stood before her arrogantly, legs apart, arms folded on his broad chest. "On your feet, girl, I've no need of you on your back tonight."

"You colonial louse! I should have blown your grinning head off!"

"You had your chance, lass, and you'll get no more. This is an odd occupation for one without the nerve to pull a trigger." He took another step closer and Kate caught a faint scent of toilet water.

"You fancy yourself gentry, do you, you craven coward? How much courage does it take to strike a lady?" She was shaking now, not with fear, but rage. Why hadn't she pulled the trigger?

"I see no lady! A highwayman's strumpet is more like. I'll admit you ride well enough, and fill a man's breeches sweetly." He bent and retrieved Kate's pistols and tucked them into his belt. "I'd best keep these. We want no accidents."

Kate judged the distance to Lucifer. Her head was still ringing from the blow, but she knew she could ride if she could only reach her horse's reins. "Have you a name?" If she could distract him, perhaps . . .

He picked up Kate's torn black tricorn and handed it to her mockingly. "Lord Ashton at your service, madam." An eyebrow arched. "Eighth Earl of Ashton. And your own name?"

"Molly. Molly Wiggins." Let him think her a village wench. It mattered not. "Please, sir, for pity's sake. I'm not a bad girl! I've three hungry children to feed. The tax collectors have squeezed us until we must steal or starve." Kate deliberately roughened her speech as she warmed to the lie. "I'm no slut, but a goodwife. He forced me to it, did my Harry. They'll hang me, sir, if ye don't let me go."

Pride threw back his head and roared. "So first it's a noble lady and now a poor country milkmaid. Methinks you are a strolling player, girl, so sweetly do you give the lie. Thief and liar you are, but I like your spunk. Give us a kiss, do." He took her in his arms and kissed her soundly.

Kate stomped hard on his instep with her boot heel and struggled free, running for Lucifer. Pride caught her round the waist. Wildly, she struck at him with fist and boot. They fell to the ground, and he caught her wrists and pinned her back against the damp earth, the length of his hard body pressing against hers. "Let me go!" she screamed. He brought his mouth down to hers roughly, and Kate caught his lip in her teeth and bit hard.

"Damn you!" He slapped her, and she began to weep. Ashamed, he loosened the pressure and allowed her to sit up.

Kate choked back angry sobs and wiped at her nose. "I'll not be raped! I'm no whore!"

"I'm sorry. I thought you willing, if a bit shy. I'm not a man to force his women."

"Please, you must let me go."

"Who are you? Give me no tales about innocent girls led astray." He lifted her chin with one hand and tilted it in the moonlight. "You're no girl, you're a woman grown—and one with some claim to gentility."

Kate slapped his hand away. "I don't like to be touched."

"Damn it, woman, what am I to do with you?" His gravelly voice softened. "You've led me a merry chase and I—"

The sound of a hunting horn and men's shouts broke the forest stillness. Pride stood and pulled Kate to her feet as a party of horsemen rounded the bend, single file. Pride recognized Giles's lanky form among the group.

"Damn you to hell," Kate said, and straightened her weary shoulders. "If we meet again, let it be there."

"Are you all right, sir?" A man hastened to catch Pride's bay and lead it forward. "You're hurt," Giles insisted.

Pride waved him away. "It's nothing."

The men-at-arms stared at Kate and murmured among themselves. A stranger came forward with a torch and thrust it into her face. "You've done well, Lord Ashton. Do you not recognize her? This is Lord Storm's daughter, the Lady Kathryn." He seized Kate roughly and began to bind her hands behind her back.

"Is that necessary? The woman's no danger to you now."

"With all due respect, Lord Ashton. I am Hugh Mercer, the High Sheriff. I have known Lady Kathryn since she was a child. She is a Storm and as good a shot as her brother. I will risk none of my men to play gentleman." He turned back to Kate. "This will go hard on you, m'lady. You'll join your father in Newgate Prison."

An underling brought Lucifer and reached for Kate. "No!" Pride shoved him away. "I'll seat the lady." White-faced and silent, Kate allowed herself to be lifted onto the saddle. "I'm sorry," he breathed.

"Come down to Tyburn, sir," she spat. "I'll give you an even merrier show at my hanging."

Chapter 2

Rain beat through the open barred window and ran down the crumbling stone walls to the dank interior of the cell. In the far corner a woman coughed incessantly, and the idiot in the other corner kept up her infernal wailing to the thing in her arms. Kate stretched her hands up as far as possible to catch the rain and wiped futilely at her grimy face. Another month and she would go as mad as the dummy. She looked down at her hands; the nails were broken and dirty, the knuckles bruised and swollen. Newgate Prison was worse than an asylum; it was a zoo, a zoo where the animals had to fight for daily survival.

Eleven women shared the fetid cell, a rectangle, six paces by seven, not counting the sunken alcove that held the honey buckets. Filthy rushes covered the stone floor, sticky with grease and human vomit, a virile breeding place for fleas and other vermin. Twice a day the iron-barred wooden door was opened and a bucket of swill passed in. Bread and water came each morning. Kate thought the bread fit only for pigs, and the water . . . The best one could say about it was that it was wet.

No lady of Kate's position should have been thrown into the common side, treated with such indignity. But Lord Storm's estates and investments had been seized by the Crown. In Newgate, one must have funds, supporters on the outside to provide decent food. Kate had none. Her initiation into the subhuman world of London's poor had been a bitter one.

Kate had only the clothes she had been wearing the night

of the robbery, and those were now foul and threadbare. Had she not fought like a caged lioness the morning they had dragged her in here, she would have been left as naked as she was born. Fat Meg, the whore, had advanced on her menacingly, two crones on either side, spewing obscenities. A strong right to the slut's jaw had broken one of Kate's knuckles, but she'd dropped the poxed slattern like a poleaxed ox. The others were on her like a rat pack, but she was young and strong and well-fed. They retreated grudgingly, leaving Kate in peace, except for an occasional taunt. She gave as good as she got, and the flung curses became a welcome break in the monotony of the long days.

The only light in the room came from the single window that was partially below street level. Nothing was seen but the shod feet of passersby and the wheels of official carriages. Almost daily, they heard the slow creak of the cart that carried the condemned to Tyburn Gallows, but they never saw it. The air in the cell was thick and malodorous. The opening of the cell door only brought waves of stench from the passageways.

Kate's place was near the window. She had a blanket, claimed from a dead woman. Wrapped in the thin plaid, she spent most of her days remembering. Within the confines of her mind, Kate escaped the horrors of Newgate to happier times. Memories of summers in the highlands of Scotland, wandering through the green glens, or frosty autumn hunts across the broad fields of Queen's Gift beside Geoffrey and her father, brought a smile to her lips. Memories of newborn pups and yuletide gatherings in the great hall were so close she could almost smell and touch them.

Geoffrey and his friends spent long winter hours at the card table in the east wing. Lord Storm had taught his daughter hazard at the age of ten. Often she would join them, and once she won a fine bay hunter from young Lord Darcy. She could see the look on Darcy's face now as she raised the bet and took the hand. Yes, and she'd joined them in a round of spirits after adding yet another tale to the outrageous reputation she enjoyed.

Kate was worried about both her father and her brother. Geoffrey must be free; she'd not seen or heard of him while she was in the custody of the High Sheriff. In fact, he'd questioned her closely about Geoffrey's whereabouts. If he were in hiding, it was strange he'd not arranged for a friend to carry some message to his sister.

Kate supposed there would be some sort of a trial, but what or where she didn't know. One thing she did know, her father would find some way to free her from this cell. She must keep her sanity until he did.

The poor mindless woman in the cell sidled close to Kate. Her hair fell in greasy blond strings and spittle drooled from the slack mouth. Grinning, she held out her bundle for Kate's inspection. The woman's smell was overpowering. Kate's stomach lurched and she fought to keep from gagging to the uncontrolled glee of Fat Meg and her allies. The woman's empty blue eyes filled with tears as the bundle fell to the stone floor, and a large beef bone clattered away.

"Crimey!" Fat Meg cackled. "Her babe's a marrow bone!"

Terrified, the woman crouched, arms over her head, rocking back and forth, a wordless wail issuing from her misshapen bosom. Kate retrieved the polished bone, wrapped it carefully in the rags, and tucked it into the woman's arms. "It's all right," she soothed. "Here's your poppet, safe and sound." The wailing stopped and a toothless grin spread over the snotty face, the sounds of pain replaced with happy chuckles. "She just had a tumble, but the baby's fine. Give her a hug," Kate continued softly. "It's all right." She turned a cold eye on Fat Meg. "Leave her be. She hurts no one, and she's got nothing worth your while to steal."

The obscenely fat woman put both hands on her immense hips and stuck her chins forward. "She's an animal, that's what she is! Murdered her own babe, drowned it in a keg of ale, she did! She's Tyburn bait, same as you, bitch!" she screamed.

Kate's temper rose. "She's not got the mind of a poor dumb beast! Leave her to God. Are you so daft you don't know such folk are God's chosen? Touch her and you'll bring down a curse on yourself!" Kate warned. "You've more nerve than me," she lied, "to tempt fate. Treat that kind soft, I say. Who needs more bad luck?"

"Amen to that, yer ladyship," chimed in a new voice. Fingers Nettie, the pickpocket, deftly caught a flea and cracked it with her narrow teeth. "We've enough bad luck to go round! Any what wants more can 'ave mine!"

"Aye, leave the dummy be," another agreed. "Would ye spoil tonight's dinner party wi' the Lord Mayor?" Howls of shrill laughter pushed her farther. "And King George 'imself may pardon us all, right after we entertains 'im royally!"

The sound of bolts being drawn silenced the laughter. There was no reason for the guards to come at this time of day unless a new prisoner was being brought in, or someone taken away. The women backed away from the door warily. The door creaked open. "Lady Kathryn Storm," a gruff voice called. It was the jailer himself. "Yer to come wi' me, yer ladyship. Now!"

Kate's heart quickened. She was being released. Somehow Father had managed it. Head high, she walked across the cell. "Mind what I told you about the dummy," she warned. "Leave her to God."

"Good luck to ye," one called. "Ye might remember us with a pint o' ale some cold night."

Kate followed the jailer and a second man with a torch down a narrow corridor and up a twisting flight of steps. They passed through an iron gate opened by an equally impassive guard, then across an open courtyard and into a brick building. The halls here were wider and swept clean. Another iron gate led to an office and guardroom. A pot of soup was bubbling over an iron stove, and Kate's mouth watered at the delicious smell. How long had it been since she'd had anything decent to eat? Father would be furious when he found out how badly she'd been treated. And Geoffrey! He'd be fit to have the walls pulled down!

"Is my father here?" Kate asked.

The jailer frowned. "My orders is to move you to these apartments, not to answer questions." He disliked dealing with nobility, troublemakers all of them. A man could do his job and still come out wrong!

Another flight of stairs led to a short hallway and a locked door. The jailer took a large key from the ring at his waist, unlocked the door, and ushered Kate into a small but pleasant room with a fireplace and curtains at the window. "Yer to stay here now," he said. "Someone will be up wi' water fer washing in a bit." The door closed firmly behind him and she heard the key turn.

Water! Maybe enough for a bath! Kate clapped her hands and twirled like a child. Pray God there'd be clean clothes to put on after. Trust Father to know she'd not want to face him looking like a street beggar. She glanced about the room. Before the fireplace was a round table and two straight-backed chairs. There was a settee and even a small bit of carpet before it. An open doorway showed a smaller room containing only an old-fashioned draped bed and another chair. Kate flung back the shutters at the single window. Barely six inches away was a blind brick wall. She heard the door open and hurried back to the sitting room.

A young girl stood just inside the doorway. She bobbed a curtsy. "I'm Janet, yer ladyship. I'm 'ere to 'elp you." A bucket of water stood by her feet. "I've some pretty clothes too, m'lady." She held out a rose-colored dress. "I can help wi' yer hair. I does it fer all the fine ladies, I does."

"If you're to do anything for this lady's hair, I hope you brought some strong soap. I swear my head's full of lice. I'll need more water than that." Kate tested it with a finger; it was lukewarm. "You tell the jailer I'll need three more buckets of hot water and some clean undergarments. The ones I have on are not fit for the rag merchant."

The girl nodded, big-eyed. Janet's father had said the lady was to have what pleased her, within reason. "Yes'm."

"And some of that soup I smelled in the guardroom. And fresh bread and cheese. Hurry now, before this water turns to ice." Thank God, Father had thought to provide some decent clothing. Kate began to strip off her filthy rags. The boots would have to do for now, but she certainly needed clean stockings. These were more holes than cloth. "Step to it, girl! What are you waiting for?" Janet stepped.

An hour later, Kate sat in a straight-backed chair as the girl brushed out her soft brown hair until it shown with warm auburn highlights. The borrowed gown was a little large and plunged shockingly at the neckline but at least it was clean. Janet chattered on as she brushed and then pinned the hair deftly into place.

"Beautiful!" she declared. "I'm so glad to have you here on this side. That other side's bad, my da says. I never been there, but you can smell it, beggin' yer pardon, m'lady. Ladies don't belong with that street trash. Quality belongs here. You can have a fire whenever you want, jest ask."

"Thank you," Kate laughed, "but I doubt I'll be here long enough for that. Do you know when my father will be arriving?"

"No'm, nobody tells me nothing. Go help the lady, Da said. Sometimes I get something extra for meself." She looked hopeful.

"I won't forget you, Janet, I promise." Kate finished off a morsel of cheese. "I've no coin on me, but when my father gets here I'll have him reward you suitably."

Silently, Janet gathered up the buckets and towels. Promises bought nothing. She'd had promises before. Still, this one seemed nice. Perhaps she might keep her word. Janet picked up the man's coat Kate had worn. It was beyond use, but the buttons could be sold. "I'll be back in the morning, m'lady." She rapped three times and the door opened.

"But I won't be—" Kate stopped in mid-sentence. As Janet ducked out, a tall figure filled the doorway. "What are you . . . ?" She felt an angry flush rise through her face. "Where is my father? I demand to see him! I've nothing to say to you!"

Pride Ashton inclined his head slightly and grinned. "You've improved, greatly improved, since our last meeting, Lady Kathryn."

Speechless with rage, Kate stared at him. From the tips of his shining black leather boots to the ruffled lace at his throat, Ashton was the epitome of a court dandy. His powder-blue velvet coat covered a white silk waistcoat stitched with silver thread. The gray breeches were indecently tight over muscular thighs. Fawnskin gloves embroidered with precious stones dangled from one powerful hand, a hand that Kate remembered had struck her roughly. All that was lacking was a powdered wig. Instead, his raven-black hair was drawn back and caught at the nape of his neck with a blue silk ribbon. His shoulders seemed too wide for a gentleman; they must belong to some country blacksmith! But it was the face that held her, a rugged face with high cheekbones and dark compelling eyes, eyes that mocked her.

"You are pale, I hope you've not been treated too badly."

"You scrofulous knave! Treated badly! Not as badly as I'll treat you if you don't get out of my sight!" she lashed out.

"So I didn't dream you." He laughed. "I'd begun to believe you were only a nightmare."

"What are you doing here?" she demanded. "My father will have you—"

"Lord Storm has quite enough trouble of his own at the moment. I doubt if you are his top priority. Stop that screeching, you sound like a village fishwife. I did expect some sort of thanks." He dusted off a chair with his gloves and sat down. "You're not an innocent girl, and Lord knows you're not stupid. Who do you think provided these quarters?" He waved a hand. "I've lost a lot of sleep over you, and I still don't know why."

Kate dropped into the opposite chair. "You? You paid for this? But why?"

"I should think that would be obvious."

Kate's hand shot out and caught him full in the face. "What do you take me for? Do you think I can be bought like a street slut for a dress and a bowl of soup?"

Pride caught her wrist, a hard mask dropping over the handsome face. "Don't do that again." Kate tried to twist away, but he held her effortlessly. "I allow no man to strike me and I'll be damned if I'll permit it from a wench." He brought her down firmly on his lap and pinned her against him. "You have a foul mouth for a gentlewoman,

Kate. Whenever I meet you, you keep protesting you are no whore. I never accused you of such. No, sit still, stop squirming, and listen to me.''

"Let me go!"

"To hit me again? I'm not a fool. You'll listen."

"I won't."

"I'm not your enemy. If I'd known you were a woman, I doubt if I'd have chased you." Kate kicked hard at his shin with her heel and he crossed one leg over hers to hold her. "Stop it, you're behaving like a child!"

"I won't be handled!" she protested breathlessly. "You're no gentleman!"

"Gentleman? A Shawnee brave would have every strip of skin off your back by now. And you're hardly in any position to be calling names. You, Lady Kathryn, are not only a thief but a murderess."

"Murderess? I'm no murderess!" Kate stopped struggling. "Why . . . ? The coachman? Did he . . . ?"

"Dead as a post. This is no prank, woman. They'll hang you. Don't tell me it never occurred to you?" He released her and she jumped up.

Kate's eyes misted and the words seemed to choke in her throat. "It was an accident. We never meant to . . ." She turned her head toward the window. "God save us," she whispered. "I never thought the man dead. I knew he was hit. He leaped for—" She straightened her shoulders. "I meant only to scare him when I fired. It was an accident."

"Liar. It wasn't you who shot the coachman but your accomplice. There are witnesses. It will do you no good to lie. In the eyes of the law, you are both equally guilty of murder."

"If you think me no whore, then why this?" She shrugged. "Why are you doing it?"

"For some stupid reason, I feel partly responsible for you. I know what the poor side of Newgate is like. You deserve better."

"Can you tell me anything of my father?" Kate took a deep breath and tried to regain her composure. The nightmare wasn't over; it was just beginning.

"Only that he is still being held for trial." Pride stood and folded his arms across his broad chest. "I want to be your friend, Kate. I think you could use one now."

"I've behaved badly." She colored. "I do owe you thanks. But I still don't know why you're doing this. You don't even know me. Why would you befriend a thief and a murderess?"

"My uncle, the Earl, will probably ask the same thing." Pride grinned. "He probably won't ask quite that calmly, but . . ."

"Why?"

"You're an attractive woman, Kate. Surely men have shown an interest before."

"Interest? To what end? Surely you must have something in mind? Is this to be a purely Platonic friendship?" Her voice sharpened to a cutting edge. "And what, Lord Ashton, am I to contribute to this friendship?"

Pride's hands tightened into fists. "Damn it, woman. Must you have everything spelled out for you?"

"Does this friendship include the physical expression of love?"

"It might."

"Then you do take me for a whore!" Kate seized a brass candlestick and hurled it at him. He caught it in mid-air and threw it back. It struck her shoulder and she let out a yelp of pain. "Ouch!"

"I said I'd take no more from you, woman!" Pride lunged for her and she dodged away, drawing back her right hand into a fist. "I've laid out good silver for your welfare and I'll take my payment now."

"By hell, you won't!" Kate backed away. "I'd sooner spread my legs for the devil!"

"Doubtless you soon will!" He grabbed at her arm.

With a curse, Kate ducked behind the table, overturned it, and dashed into the adjoining room, slamming the door. There was no lock so she leaned all her weight against it and reached out for the chair. The door splintered as the full force of the man's shoulder hit it. Kate seized the chair and held it before her. "No! Damn you! No!" Tears of rage spilled down her cheeks.

Pride flung back the ravaged door and snatched the chair from her numb fingers and threw it against the wall. "Enough of this cat-and-mouse game, Kate. You push my good temper beyond its bounds!"

Kate backed toward the curtained poster bed until the edge struck the back of her legs. "I have pushed your temper? Well then, let me push no farther. I will pay my debt to you, colonial! Let it not be said that a Storm cheated anyone of his just due." She began to tug at the back laces of her gown. "Give me leave, sir, to remove the garment you so graciously provided. You may yet have the use of it when I am hanged!" In her haste, the ribbons tore and she tugged the dress off over her head, leaving herself in chemise and petticoat. "Patience, m'lord. I'll have this out of your way in a second." She ripped at the thin muslin underbodice, exposing her small breasts. "They are not large, but I think we can consider them well-formed," she sobbed.

Pride stared at her trembling flesh for a long moment, then removed his coat and wrapped it about her. "I meant to take only a kiss, fair Kate," he murmured hoarsely.

His lips brushed hers tentatively. His breath was sweet and Kate's mouth softened to the kiss. She felt her heart beating faster and she rose on tiptoes to savor the tenderness of his kiss. Of their own volition, her arms stole around his neck and her lips parted. Pride's body molded to hers as the kiss deepened, and Kate's brain was filled with the rich smoky scent of him. His hand stroked the hollow of her back and eased up to caress her neck and then her bare shoulder. "No!" she cried. "Don't, please." She pulled away, breaking the spell. "Please, don't."

Visibly shaken, Pride ran his fingers through his dark hair and sat down on the bed. "I meant you no harm, Kate, you must know that. For God's sake, put your dress back on!"

Weeping, she gathered up the fallen gown and pulled it on, fumbling at the laces. "I didn't mean . . ." she sobbed. "I . . . I just . . ."

"I was wrong. It was a rotten thing to do. I assumed because you rode the highway as an outlaw that you . . .

that you could be had. The rest of what I said was true. I am attracted to you. Dry your eyes, you're safe enough now, as long as you keep your gown on. I'm half Shawnee—that's an American Indian tribe. My savage half has better morals than the civilized gentleman. The Shawnee never commit rape. It's bad medicine."

Kate's tears had turned to hiccups.

"You don't have to do that; I feel bad enough already."

"I can't help it; when I cry, I get hiccups. I always have," Kate protested. Pride stalked into the sitting room and returned with a goblet of wine.

"Drink this."

She took the pewter vessel and sipped. The wine was sweet and its warmth crept down her throat and heated her stomach. "Thank you." She wiped at her eyes. The hiccups seemed cured. "Are you really an Indian?" she queried. "You don't look like a redskin."

"More like a Welshman? Aye, I'm Shawnee, more red than white I think, most of the time."

"I'll go back to the other side."

"Don't be a fool. It's little enough I can do for you. Keep the room. I'll leave and trouble you no more, though I dearly wish you'd take me up on my offer."

Kate smoothed her gown into place. "And if I quickened with your seed, what then?" she challenged. "Would you see your own child go unborn to the gallows?"

"For one in your occupation, you know little about the law, woman. A bearing female may claim her belly and receive mercy from the court."

"What mercy? To be sold into slavery as a bond servant? To be shipped off to the ends of the earth? I'd sooner be dead!"

A shadow passed over Pride's countenance as he followed her back into the sitting room. "You'll be long enough dead, woman. Don't seek it out."

Kate scoffed, "What would a dandy like yourself know of death? Or of violence? You've been coddled all your life. Some things are more valuable than life, m'lord. Freedom is one of those things!"

"There are bond servants aplenty in the Colonies. It's

not a bad life. They work hard, but there's a promise of better things to come."

"I was born Lady Kathryn Storm and I shall die so. I'll be no man's servant. The rope, they say, is quick."

Pride took her hand and raised it to his lips. "God be with ye, Lady Kathryn. If your father yet has friends in high places, it may be that the trial will go well. If we do not meet again, I ask your forgiveness for my behavior and wish you only the best."

"Oh, we'll meet again, sir. Did you not consign me to the fires of hell? I doubt not you will take the same path, sooner or later. I'll save a place for you near the flames!"

The room echoed with emptiness as Pride's footsteps receded down the hall. Kate caught her lower lip in her teeth. She'd spoken rashly, bitterly, to the only one who'd shown her kindness in the godforsaken place. She'd called him no gentleman, but he was a most attractive gentleman. "Bloody colonial!" she hissed to the vacant chamber. If it weren't for Pride Ashton, she'd have won free. She'd be safe and laughing with Geoffrey at Queen's Gift.

Arms folded, she began to pace the confines of the room. Where in God's name was Geoffrey? He'd have more sense than to wait to be captured. He was in hiding, certain! But where? Why hadn't he found a way to let her know he was safe? Anger flared within her as she remembered the dead coachman. There'd been no need to shoot the man. Geoffrey was ever a hothead. Father would be furious. In all his years upon the King's highway, there'd been no killings. He would never forgive Geoffrey, or her. She must share in the guilt. It had been a fool's game from start to finish.

Ashton's obsidian eyes haunted her. Damn him! The man was a devil. She licked at her lower lip, remembering the kiss they had shared. He had experience enough in that, she'd vow. And he'd believed her an easy piece! Kate hugged herself nervously as she walked to the window and gazed at the courtyard below, gray and empty like her own soul. She drew the curtain and poured herself another goblet of wine. Spirits, Geoffrey said, were a great healer of foul moods.

She slept fitfully that night on the clean sheets. Dreams of Fat Meg and slamming iron doors brought her bolt upright in the twisted quilts. Once she saw her father, face swollen and blackened in death, swinging from a rope while a crowd of jeering faces roared approval. Sweating, Kate got up and drained the last of the wine. Her throat felt raw and scratchy. She slept again at dawn and woke shivering. Her head ached and the room was spinning. Too much wine, she thought. It was too much of an effort to get up so she lay there, dozing on and off until a girl's voice wakened her.

"Yer sick!" Janet accused, throwing up her hand in a sign to ward off evil. She backed away. "You got the fever! I'll leave your breakfast by the door. You can't expect me to stay round fever!"

"Wait," Kate protested. "I'm not . . ." She buried her face in her hands. The pain in her head was devastating. "Water, please. Just a little water. I'll be all right." The door slammed loudly.

Hours later, thirst drove her from the bed. She was so weak she could hardly stand. Foot by foot, Kate made her way into the sitting room. The tray sat on the floor by the door beside a bucket of water. Gratefully, she plunged her face into the water and drank from her hands.

Reason asserted itself from deep in her brain. Save the water! Janet might not come again. Kate took the mug of ale from the tray and sipped it slowly. It was cool and yet it stung her sore throat. She dipped a bit of bread in the ale and tried to force it down, but she couldn't eat. Sitting on the floor, she edged her way back to the bedchamber, dragging the water and tray with her. If the fever got worse, she might not be able to reach the sitting room.

In bed again, Kate wrapped herself in the quilts and fell into a deep sleep. It was dark when she roused enough to seek out the water. After that she lost all track of time.

It was the second day, or perhaps the third, when a frightened Janet hurried Kate into her clothes and smoothed the tangled hair. The girl wore a bag of garlic around her neck and the strong smell caused Kate's stomach to churn.

"You must help me," Janet urged. "You go to trial today and you must look yer station."

The gown, Kate noticed foggily, was blue; a new one then, with many petticoats and a wide hoop. "Where did this come from?" she asked. "It's not mine."

"The lord, 'e sent it, with a bit of silver for me." Janet jerked at a tangle in Kate's hair and she flinched. "He's a gent, 'e is, wanted you to look fine for the court."

"Pride . . . Lord Ashton? Was he here?" Kate tried to clear her thoughts. "Does he know I was sick?"

Janet shrugged. "A footman brought the gown and me coin. He's not been near Newgate to my knowin'. 'Andsome footman he was too, black hair like 'is master." She brushed at Kate's waxen cheeks with rouge. "You needs color, m'lady. You look like death's-head if I might say so, poor thing."

The silver seemed to have gone a long way toward easing Janet's fears of the fever, Kate thought as she allowed her face to be painted. Perhaps she'd feel better if she got out in the air. She wondered if Pride would be at the trial. "Not likely."

"What, lady?"

"Nothing, you needn't be afraid. It's just an ague, not the pox. I took cowpox as a girl. Those who have it never get smallpox. I'll be fine in a day or two."

"I did hear such, but they's other bad fevers, ma'am. You can't be blaming me for being afeerd."

The courtroom was crowded and noisy. Kate was unsteady on her legs and leaned on the arm of a man who introduced himself as her barrister, William McNicholls. Later, she would try unsuccessfully to recall all the events of the afternoon. Now the voices seemed overloud and the colors too bright. The chambers were suffocating.

"Kate!" A familiar voice broke through the blur. Warm arms clasped her against a hard chest. "Courage, Kate," her father urged. "Show them all what stuff a Storm is made of."

"Father, why are you here? Where's Geoffrey? Is Geoffrey here, too?" She clung to him, dry-eyed, burying her face in his ruffled shirt. He would never forgive her if she wept in public. "I'm sorry, Father. It's all my fault."

"Hush, girl. I'm reaping the harvest of my own sowing. Chin up. I've been prouder of you than any man his son, remember that."

Then rude hands pulled her away. "Father?" A grip tightened cruelly on her arm and she found herself before a polished wood railing. A white bewigged figure was saying something, but his words were jumbled in her fevered brain.

The man McNicholls nudged her. "Answer. Can you not say something in your own behalf?"

"Speak now or forever hold your peace!" a voice thundered.

Kate stifled a giggle. Was someone being married? She shook her head. Whatever they wanted of her, she would tell them nothing. She would not inform on her brother, not on Geoffrey. Must not even say his name. Whatever they did to her, he was free.

". . . to be carried from this place on the first day of May to Tyburn Gallows. And there, for the high crime of robbery upon the King's road, to be hanged by the neck until dead. God rest your soul."

"Father?" Kate looked about, but the faces were all strange. There was no one she knew. "Father?" What had the judge said? Tyburn? To be hanged by the neck until dead? Then a pair of dark eyes caught hers, not taunting but sorrowful. Pride Ashton. He made his way through the milling crowd toward her.

"Kate." Pride's rugged features were twisted with an inner pain.

She straightened her aching body. "Damn you to hell, sir!" she cried, then turned away to follow the barrister, her eyes bright with unshed tears.

Chapter 3

The days following the trial were confused. Kate was vaguely aware of Janet coming and going and of a man who claimed to be a surgeon. Someone forced water into her parched mouth and soothed her burning head with wet cloths. Gentle hands changed her soiled bedclothing and sweat-soaked sheets. Was it her father? She remembered seeing her father and asking about Geoffrey. She hoped she hadn't spoken his name aloud. Was there a trial . . . or had she dreamed the witness box and the red-faced judge? No, it was real. She had seen her father, but not Geoffrey. Of that she was certain. Her father had spoken to her . . . her father and someone else . . . Pride Ashton. Him she would never forget or forgive!

It was late afternoon when Kate finally woke with a clear head. Her throat was still sore but she was ravenous. The brisk sound of a broom and a female voice singing came from the adjoining room. "Janet?" Kate called hoarsely. "Is that you?"

Her round face appeared in the doorway. "Yes, ma'am, it's me. Feelin' better today?"

"Yes, yes I am. Is there anything to eat?" Kate sat up. Lying across the chair was a green velvet dressing gown. She reached for it, noticing the delicate table and fine leather trunk by the window. The room had changed noticeably since her illness. Kate lowered her bare feet to the thick rug and slipped into the soft wrapper. "I'm starving."

"Stay there, m'lady. No need for you to get up yet. I'll

fetch it in to you.'' She carried in a tray loaded with food, curtsied awkwardly, and set it on the table. ''Drink this, ma'am, it'll give you strength.'' She offered a goblet of wine. ''They's white rolls an' some fish. Cheese an' apple flummery. If they's anythin' else you want, ye've only to ask. The gentleman says yer to 'ave whatever you wish.'' Janet grinned shyly. ''He sent the pretties an' the sittin' room's fancy as any lord's castle. I never seen such fine things, let alone to have the carin' of 'em.''

Kate paused in mid-bite. ''Lord Ashton? He paid for this too?'' For an instant she considered flinging the goblet aside, then drained it. He'd have no pay for his trouble! And if he came here again . . . ''I'm to have what I wish, those were his words?''

''Yes, m'lady, 'Twas him what paid for the surgeon too. You woulda died without him. He let yer blood. I seen it. Three times he come, an' you know what they cost.''

''Then what I want is to never lay eyes on Lord Ashton again. He is not to be admitted to these rooms. Do you understand?'' Kate's eyes were hard.

''But, m'lady?''

''I will not see him,'' Kate repeated. She took a deep breath. ''I'm to die, aren't I? The judge sentenced me to Tyburn Gallows, didn't he?'' Janet stared at the floor and twisted her apron into a knot. ''When?''

''Mayday, m'lady.'' Tears welled up in the serving girl's eyes. ''But some are pardoned by the King. You could be, m'lady.''

''Do you know where Lord Storm is being held?'' Janet shook her head. ''He's not in this building?'' The girl shrugged. ''Are there any you could ask? It's very important.''

''Me father brings me to work in the mornin' and me brother, John, he sees me home. I'm not allowed to speak to no one, just the ladies I care for. It's not fittin' that I talk with these others at Newgate. I'm a good girl, ma'am. I'm sorry. But I know nothing about his lordship.''

''You've heard nothing of Lord Storm's case from your own father?''

"No, ma'am. But if I do, I'll tell you first thing, I promise."

"You do that. And when I . . . when I leave here, what's mine shall be yours. I don't know if Lord Ashton will send his servant to collect his belongings, but if he doesn't, keep them for your dowry."

"Oh, thank you, ma'am." Her eyes widened with excitement. "I knew you was a fine lady the first time I seen you." She poured more wine. "We must put roses in yer cheeks. Such crowds come to watch the hangings."

Day by day, Kate's hope faded as there was no word from her father, no message from Geoffrey. How bright the sunlight glowed, spilling through the windows of her apartment; how fresh the air, even laden with the smells of London and the smoke of a thousand chimneys. Each hour was precious to her, and each slipped away like water through her fingers until the date of her execution arrived.

A red-eyed Janet appeared earlier than usual with a new gown in her arms, a gown of lavender-and-white satin with a décolleté neckline edged in lace. There were high-heeled slippers to match, in the latest Paris fashion, and an exquisite white lace cap with lavender silk ribbons. "From the gentleman, m'lady, with his love. He asks will you agree to see him and he sent you this note." Hesitantly, she held out a creamy beige envelope.

Kate snatched the paper away and crumpled it into a ball, then threw it into the farthest corner of the room. "I've made myself quite clear on that, Janet. I do not wish to see Lord Ashton again on this earth. You may repeat my words to him."

"But you will wear the gown, won't you, m'lady? It's so beautiful." Kate sniffed noncommittally. "Oh, mistress, do wear it! The men will weep to see such a vision go to the gallows and the ladies will turn green with envy. The gentleman sent this too." She produced a velvet bag and poured silver coins into her hand. "To pay the executioner."

"I'm supposed to pay the bastard for stretching my neck?"

"Yes, ma'am, it's the custom. Only those what ain't got pay naught. They say it promises an easy death. They's ways to make it painful if he wants." Janet clapped her hand over her mouth. "Forgive me, m'lady. I talk too much." Huge tears spilled down her scrubbed cheeks.

Kate turned to the window, suddenly chilled. *I don't want to die,* she screamed silently. *Not this way!* She forced back the tears. Her father had reminded her of her duty. She was a Storm and must face death as one. "I'll wear the dress," she said. "If the mob wants a show, we'll not disappoint them."

Janet ducked out again for wine and bread. Kate's throat was like stone. Nothing could force her to swallow even a bite, but she downed the wine. Instant courage, she thought wryly. She hoped it would be enough.

A few minutes alone with a starkly dressed man of God, and Kate was escorted down the hall and through the passageways and down the outside steps to a waiting open carriage pulled by two ebony coach horses. The coachman and footmen were also garbed in jet-black livery.

Light-headed, Kate allowed them to assist her into the vehicle. Across the court, a narrow door opened and she saw two guards shadowing a pale figure toward the carriage. "Father!" she called. Lord Storm looked up at her cry, his face pinched and drawn, the color of tallow. Kate caught her breath. Had he been ill too?

Lord Storm threw off the hand that held his arm and quickened his step. His wrists were bound with crude iron manacles, but otherwise he was dressed as befitted his station. The steel-gray of his coat only accented the pallor of his complexion.

"Father, are you all right?" She stepped from the carriage and hurried toward him. "Father?"

A spasm of pain passed over his face. "Kate?" His eyes widened in shock and he clutched at his chest. "Kate." he crumbled and would have fallen but the guards caught him.

"Father!" Kate threw her arms around him as they lowered him to the damp cobblestones.

"Forgive me," he murmured. "I . . ." His voice trailed off.

The guard shoved Kate away. "See here! This ain't no
. . ." He held his hand in front of the prisoner's mouth.
"He ain't breathin', Jake. His lordship's dead, that's what!
He cheated the hangman. Damn me! Didn't he swear he
would!"

"No!" Kate protested. "No! It can't be! Let me to
him." She fought her way to his side, raising his manacled
hands to her lips. "Please no," she begged. "Father, don't
leave me. I can't do it alone."

The older guard motioned to the footmen. "Sorry,
m'lady. He can't hear ye now. He's cheated the hangman,
certain. Maybe it's for the best." The footmen took Kate's
arms. "Go along, ma'am. It's time. He'll be looked after.
A Christian funeral's been paid for. Go along."

Stunned, Kate allowed them to walk her back to the
carriage. Father was dead. He was dead. Was it God's
mercy? Would that she had gone with him. So quick the
light had gone from his eyes, so quick. Even now, his face
looked gentler, the lines of pain and worry erased.

The jailer waved and the carriage, flanked by four prison
guards on horseback, lurched ahead across the courtyard
and through the open iron gates. Kate sat erect, frozen, her
eyes wide, seeing nothing. The coachman whipped the team
into a gallop and the carriage careened through the twisting
cobblestone streets toward Tyburn.

Pedestrians scattered, horsemen veered aside, cursing the
carriage and its occupants. Soon the coach horses were
forced to slow to a walk by the sheer number of people,
farm animals, and vehicles clogging the street. Dirty-faced
urchins darted behind the wheels, shouting and catching
hold of the rear of the carriage. The coachman was forced
to clear a path with his whip, cracking it menacingly over
the heads of those who hindered passage. The tip of the
leather caught the ear of a beggar and he howled in indig-
nation as he scrambled to safety, seconds before he would
have been crushed by the carriage wheel. In his haste, he
bumped into a baker's apprentice who dumped a dozen
fresh loaves of bread into the street.

Passerbys grabbed at the bread and in the confusion a

ragged pickpocket snatched the purse of a fat woman.
"Thief! Thief!" the goodwife bellowed.

Kate stared straight ahead, oblivious to the pandemonium. She should be crying. Her father had died before her
eyes. Why wasn't she crying? Nothing in her sheltered life
had prepared her for the brutality of this day. Fear the
rope? No, she welcomed it to end this waking nightmare.
Her pain was so deep and all-encompassing that nothing
could frighten her further.

Just ahead of the carriage was a two-wheeled cart bearing a wooden cage containing two prisoners. "Tyburn fodder!" someone cried, and the chant was taken up by the
street brats. Overhead, a pox-faced maid emptied a chamber pot onto the cage from an upper story window.

"Tyburn! Tyburn!" the mob shouted. Three apprentices
began singing a lewd ditty about a hangman and a whore.

The jeering pierced Kate's stupor and she looked about
anxiously. The boys were throwing stones at the cage now
and one bounced off the carriage. Kate flinched.

"None of that!" a guard threatened, wheeling his horse
in the boy's direction. "If it's a split head ye want, I'll
give it to ye!" Laughing, the stripling ducked into a narrow
alley. "Don't worry, yer ladyship," the guard promised.
"We'll not let them turn ugly."

The prisoners in the cage were not as fortunate. Rotten
vegetables and fish pelted the bars. A half-grown boy had
climbed to the top of the cage and was poking at the men
with a long stick. "Hangman! Hangman!" he shouted, and
the crowd roared its approval. Kate watched helplessly. No
matter what they had done, the prisoners were human. They
deserved to be treated like men, not beasts.

"It's the lady highwayman!" a woman called. "They're
hangin' the lady highwayman today!" The mob crowded
close around the carriage wheels and the footmen paled.

"Are ye the one?"

"Be ye the Mistress Turpin that robbed the King's highway?"

"Aye!" Kate answered boldly. "Toss me a flintlock and
I'll teach the executioner a new dance!"

Loud laughter and cheering came from the onlookers. "She's a game cock!" one cried.

"No cock, but a hen!"

Kate clung to the edge of the carriage as it rolled on, thankful for the solid wood. She could not have stood up to save her life. Sensing her safety depended on the goodwill of the hecklers, Kate traded jest for jest and forced herself to laugh at their crude humor.

A florid-faced loafer pulled himself into the carriage and grabbed Kate's arm. "Gi'e us a kiss, wench! Them red lips will be cold soon enough!"

The sot smelled of sweat and stale ale, and Kate's stomach lurched as he brought his leering face close to hers. "Take your filthy hands off me!" Kate demanded, raising her fist to strike him.

There was a clatter of horse's hooves on the cobblestones and the crowd scattered. A horseman brought his mount close to the open carriage and leaned from the saddle to seize Kate's assailant by the shirtfront. "Back to the gutter where you belong, scum!" He dragged the man across the pommel of his saddle, then dumped him headfirst into the street. "Be glad I don't run a sword through yer stinking ass!" With a cry the man scrambled to his feet and ran. The horseman turned back to Kate.

"Nothing more's hurt than your pride, I trust. Sorry we couldn't get here sooner. There was a fire on the bridge and we had to come the long way." Pride Ashton removed his feathered hat and nodded a greeting. "My men will see there are no more incidents." He indicated the dozen armed riders in green livery that surrounded the carriage.

Kate struggled to regain her composure as she straightened her gown. "For your rescue, Lord Ashton, I thank you." Her tone was strangely chilled. "I do not appreciate being mauled by strange men, as you should remember. But that man has hardly humiliated me more than you have done. Am I to show public gratitude to the man who has caused the death of my beloved father? I can only believe that you are here today to take some enjoyment from my execution."

Pride flushed crimson. "So, I am a sadist who finds

perverse gratification in a woman's suffering? Very well, you are entitled to your opinion. My condolences on the death of your father. I will trouble you no longer with my presence." He brought his riding crop down hard on the bay's rump and the animal leaped ahead. "My men will see you to Tyburn, Lady Kathryn."

Kate stared after him until horse and rider disappeared around the corner. Why? Why was he doing this? What did he have to gain? Without his testimony, she would not have been convicted and her father might still be alive! Pride Ashton was her executioner as much as the black-hooded figure waiting at Tyburn. And yet . . . yet she could not deny the thrill that coursed through her veins when she caught sight of him. She was losing her mind! Well enough that the hanging be today, before she turned into a raving lunatic!

The open square at Tyburn was so crowded that the carriage could inch forward only a foot at a time. The citizens of London had turned the executions at Tyburn into a fair. Sweetmeat sellers and prostitutes were elbowed aside by uniformed soldiers of King George. Red-cheeked country girls traded glances with apprentices and drunken sailors. Barking dogs and screaming children scampered underfoot and added a note of innocence to the scene.

In the center of the square loomed the gallows, a raised platform occupied by several figures in black, a bewigged official, and a hanged man. Kate averted her eyes. Death came to all mankind, but to provide sport for this blood-thirsty mob seemed sacrilegious. How could a loving God permit such awful things to happen?

Kate descended from the carriage unaided and made her way through the passage which opened in the human mass. She tried to pray, but her mind was blank. She could remember nothing but a bedtime prayer her father had taught her when she was a child. By sheer force of will, Kate straightened her back and walked toward the gallows. If Geoffrey was there in that vast crowd, he would feel no shame in her death. Her foot found the first step and she began the climb.

There was the loud crack of the trapdoor and the second

man dangled kicking from the gallows. The assemblage roared their approval. Kate closed her eyes for a fraction of a second and uttered a silent prayer for the prisoner. Would anyone do as much for her? What did it matter? She was a Storm. She could do without their prayers. Her chin went a little higher and she continued up the wooden stairway.

"She's a bloody tough'n!" a woman cried.

"Aye, the wench! See the nerve of 'er!"

"A spine like hickory!" yelled a one-eyed sailor.

" 'Tis the female highwayman!" came another cry. "She's got pluck! Here's to ye, darlin'!"

Kate flashed a false smile and waved light-heartedly to the onlookers, then held up the bag of coins Pride had sent her. "I'll not waste this on the hangman," she declared, tossing the silver high over the heads of the cheering multitude. "Take it and welcome!"

"You're mad, child," a black-frocked clergyman said, taking Kate's hand. "Your thoughts should be on your immortal soul and confession, not on jests with that rabble."

Kate pulled her hand away. "Let God judge my sins, not you."

Two guards took her arms and pulled her roughly forward. Kate's breathing became more shallow. She bit the inner flesh of her lip until she tasted the warm salt of her own blood. She'd not faint and be dragged like a sack to the rope! Dimly she was aware of the roar of the crowd in the background. The sheriff unrolled a scroll and began to read her sentence.

Just behind him stood a tall figure in black. Only his eyes showed, large and unblinking like those of some hooded bird of prey. Kate stared into them boldly, until the gray inhumanness flickered to pity. He's just a man, she thought, a man like any other. Man or demon from hell, he had no power to frighten her. She . . . What was the sheriff saying?

". . . the mercy of the King. That the prisoner, Lady Kathryn Storm, sentenced to death, shall be spared the finality of the rope. It is the decision of this court that the prisoner be transported to the colony of Maryland and there be sold as a bond servant for a period of not less than twenty years.''

Kate's eyes widened. ''What? What did you say?'' Not to die? To be sold like an animal? A slave? ''No!'' she protested. ''No.'' But the guards were already hustling her from the platform and down the steps.

Pride Ashton waited at the bottom. ''Ah, Katy. You'd have saved yourself a lot of grief if you'd only read my note. I persuaded my uncle to have your sentence commuted to transportation. I've known since yesterday.'' He took her in his arms and kissed her soundly to the delight of the onlookers. ''God, darling, but you've got nerve. A man would think you were going to a ball, not a hanging.''

Kate stared at him, speechless. Again he'd interfered with her life. Her lips stung from his kiss; her legs felt unsteady. His strong arm supported her as blackness invaded her brain.

''None of that now! We'll have no fainting!'' Pride brought his hand sharply down on her backside. ''Keep your wits about you, girl.''

''You bastard,'' she uttered between clenched lips.

''That's my girl.'' He laughed. ''You'll like Maryland, I promise.''

''I'd have rather gone to hell!''

''Wait a bit, Kate,'' Pride cautioned. ''In time we may make that trip together.''

Chapter 4

Kate was carried back to Newgate, riding pillion behind a silent guard, with another riding close beside. There was no chance for escape; neither cruelty nor kindness was shown by her escorts. Within the gates, she was taken once more to the common side. Again, she thought, and steeled herself for the filth and terror of the satanic cells.

At the guardroom, a jailer handed her a brown homespun gown and indicated a narrow door. "In there wi' ye and take off yer finery, miss. Ye need ha' no fear, I'm past the age of lechin'. Yer fine gown would only cause ye trouble wi' the other women. I'll sell it for ye and split the profit."

Kate shrugged. She'd see no coin from the beautiful lavender dress, but it was senseless to make protest. The homespun would give better service where she was going. She stepped into the inner office, closed the door, and stripped off her dress, vowing to have the eyes of the first man to stick his head through the doorway. None did, to her relief, and she pulled the scratchy brown gown over her head and tied it at the waist. The fit was not bad, if a little short due to her own height.

A rap at the door hurried her along and she handed over the satin garment and matching high-heeled slippers. Barefooted, she followed the man down a flight of stairs and through a shadowy corridor. At the bottom of the steps, he paused to take a torch and light it. Kate coughed at the thick smoke but kept her peace.

At an iron door, an old woman ladled out bowls of soup. She offered one to Kate, who refused. "Thank you, no. I'm not hungry."

"Yer missin' supper, there be none till mornin'," the matron warned. "A drink of water then. This'n's good, I bring it from me own well daily."

Kate nodded gratefully and sipped from the wooden dipper. The water was warm but clean and it eased her parched throat. She took also the half loaf of bread, stuffing it in the bosom of her dress.

"Smart, ain't she," the woman cackled. "Been here before, I reckon." She patted Kate's shoulder. "Ain't too bad where yer goin', sweetie. Bond slaves is prime goods. No use to nobody if they be weak or dead. Bond slaves is treated like regular gentry round here."

Through the doorway and then another hall and the guard paused to lift the bar on a low wooden door. "Here ye be. Don't worry yer head 'bout the fine gown. I'll see to it."

The room was dimly lighted by two barred windows. It was small but dry, with four sleeping shelves along the two side walls. On the nearest bunk, a weeping form lay crumpled. Another woman lounged under the window, smoking a long-stemmed clay pipe. "Another mate for ye," the man called.

"Did ye bring my 'bacco?" the smoker asked. The weeper only wailed louder.

"Tomorrow."

Kate carefully skirted a water bucket and stepped to the center of the narrow room.

"You know when they're shippin' us out of here?"

"Don't tell the likes of me." The door shut and the bar dropped into place.

"You bound for the Colonies?"

Kate nodded. "Twenty years. I'm Kate Storm."

The girl took a last puff and carefully laid the pipe on the window ledge. "Maggie. Jest Maggie. Though I been called a whole lot worse." The girl grinned impishly and tilted her head to one side, regarding Kate quizzically. "You a thief?"

"Highwayman."

"Well, just don't try snitchin' nothin' o' mine and we'll get on right enough. You got anythin' on you?"

Kate pulled out the flattened loaf. "Hungry? I'll share."

"Righto." Maggie held out her hand for the bread.

Kate tore it in three pieces. "Who's that?"

"No need to save her any. She'd just chuck it up. She's got a bun of her own in the oven. She don't do nothin' but bawl from morning to night. She's about to drive me crazy. Glad to have someone chipper to talk to. Her name's Nell. She was a joy girl over to the Blue Goose Tavern till she fleeced a gent. Her belly kept her from the rope. You?"

"Just missed it, a pardon. I was only at the dock this morning." Kate sat down on the edge of a sleeping shelf, pushing aside the dirty blanket. "At Tyburn. I was that close to the hangman."

"Crimey! Figures you'd get transport. You got the look of a lady. Stared Old Nick right in the eye, did you? I'd have wet me drawers, I would. My mam says them hangmen ain't human. Sold their souls to the devil. Lots o' girls won't take their coin, not even when they offer to pay double."

Maggie sat on the bunk across from Kate and pulled her dirty bare feet up under her. Some attempt had been made to keep her face and hands clean, and her blond hair was caught at the nape of her neck with a faded red ribbon.

"No use to glare at me so fierce. I ain't no whore. Not that I ain't got an eye for the lads, I do. But I make my way on my feet, not on my back." She paused in her breathless chatter. "What's the matter, luv?"

Kate buried her face in her hands and began to shake. The other girl slid off the bunk and came closer. "I . . . I forgot. My . . . father, my father died this morning. It was only this morning and it seems like years ago."

"Before the hangin'?"

Kate nodded, her face ashen in the semidarkness of the cell. "He's all I had, except for my brother Geoffrey. I loved him so much . . ." Dry-eyed, she rocked to and fro like a sorrowing child. "How could I forget?"

"The rope puts a powerful fright into a mortal, my mam

says. If we had a drop, we'd drink to him. But he's gone an' yer here. Don't be blamin' yerself. A few prayers is all you can give him now.''

"I can't. I can't pray any more than I can cry. I'm just numb.''

"Never knew me own dad, not fer certain anyway.'' She laughed. "Who does? Where I come from there ain't many who bother to get married. But if you had a real father and he was good to ye, then you've more than most. That oughta count for something.''

"What will it be like, do you suppose . . . the Maryland colony?'' Kate's voice sounded strained and far off to her own ears.

"Not much like London, I vow. A fella come in the pub once said he'd been across the sea to America. He had a hunk of hair he claimed was a red savage's scalp. Fierce them redmen be and bloodthirsty, he claimed. Course most sailors is all liars, so who knows. I do hear tell there is Indians and woods so deep no white man has ever found their way out of it. Not much of a place for a lady like you, but better than being in a hole with dirt shoveled over it.''

"I wish I could believe that.''

"What you need is a good night's sleep. Things always look better in the morning. Why, when they first carried me to Newgate I was fair daffy. Course I knew I was being transported from the first. It's thieves Old Bailey is hard on. All I did was kill a fella. He tried to hurt me and I fought back. Didn't mean for him to die, just wanted him to go away.''

"But if it was self-defense . . . Didn't you tell the judge what happened?''

Maggie laughly wryly. "Judges don't listen to such as me.'' She paused thoughtfully and then went on. "Course it might not be so bad. They got rules, and when my time is up, I get a cow and kitchen stuff fer me own. They say women is scarce in the Colonies, and a pretty girl can pick and chose.''

Kate lay back on the bunk and closed her eyes. She was

too tired to think straight anymore, or even to listen. She fell instantly into a deep and dreamless sleep.

Four days later, the three women were led from their cell to join with two dozen other female prisoners in the yard. Manacles were locked on their wrists and they were instructed to climb into open wagons. Cries of bitter protest greeted the manacles.

"Just till ye reach the ship, *ladies*," the guard assured them. "So nobody tries to run off. Ye'll be well treated on the ship."

Maggie elbowed a fat woman aside to squeeze in beside Kate on the wagon floor. It was a bright fresh morning with a breeze to blow away the London smog. Kate's heart beat a little faster just to be out of the confining cell.

"It won't be so bad, luv," Maggie said. She reached over and pinched the weeping Nell. "Cut it out. You'll get us all in trouble with yer wailin'. The Colonies are short on women, my mam says. If ye don't ruin yer looks by bawlin', ye might get a father fer yer young'n."

Nell wiped at a drippy red nose and sniffed. "Do ye think so?"

"I aim to marry me a rich squire, I do. Then it'll be Mistress Maggie this and Mistress Maggie that. No more carryin' slops an' chamber pots fer me."

Kate laughed. "You're an optimist, Maggie."

Her friend wrinkled a pert freckled nose. "Is that good?"

"It is."

"Then I am."

Two guards climbed into the front seat, the driver slapped the reins over the horses' backs, and the wagon lurched off across the cobblestones. Kate laid her head against the rough wood and tried not to think of her last ride from Newgate. Whatever lay ahead, it couldn't be worse than what she had already faced.

The air became fresher as the wagons moved toward the docks. Seagulls flew overhead, diving for scraps of rubbish in the street, screaming and fighting among themselves for choice bits. The smell of fish invaded the air, fish and tar and spices and all manner of strange raw odors. Sailors in striped pants called out to the wagons and a few women shouted back boldly.

Maggie contained her excitement by whispering to Kate whenever she spied a good-looking man. "Lookee at that'n, Katy. 'Andsome as a lord, 'e is."

A tall, dark-haired man shouldered his way through the crowd, followed closely by two burly companions carrying a heavy, iron-bound trunk. The gentleman was elegantly dressed in spotless fawn breeches and tan coat. All three had pistols thrust into their waists.

"Ain't he somethin'! Must 'ave sewed 'im into them breeches." Maggie giggled and the man glanced toward the wagon.

Kate caught her breath. The stranger was Pride Ashton. Quickly, she turned her face away, not wanting him to see her. She'd not provide more sport for his amusement. Was he to haunt her footsteps to the end of her days?

"Good day to ye, sweet," Maggie called. "Lord, but a girl could lose her good name over such as that'n!"

When Kate ventured a glance again, he was gone, lost in the crowd. Good riddance, she thought, and turned accusing eyes on her friend. "If you want to marry well, you'll have to mend your manners. You can't be calling out to every man jack you see like a streetwalker."

Maggie visibly drooped. "Yer right, I know. But Lord, that were prime cut o' beef! He'd raise the dead, he would." She sighed. "Yer a lady, so right actin' comes natural to you, Kate. But fer me, it takes some doin'. Don't be mad, now. I'll try, I promise. Fer I'm bound to raise me station in the world. It's a solemn vow!"

"I imagine there'll be few ladies in the Colonies. With hard work and luck, we may just pass you off as one. We'll practice on your speech first. It'll give us something constructive to do during the voyage."

"My, but them fine words just roll off yer lips. If I ever got to sound like you, my own mam wouldn't know me."

Kate rubbed at the raw spot on her wrist. "The important thing is not to let them separate us when we board the ship. My father . . ." She paused and then went on. "My father said conditions aboard the vessels bound for the New World are deplorable. Together we stand a better chance of arriving there alive and in decent health.''

"Righto. It's you and me, Kate, chums no matter what!''

A red-cheeked woman in starched mobcap and apron ducked from the doorway of a shop and ran along side the wagon. "Get away from there!" the driver warned. "No talkin' to the prisoners!"

"Mam!" Maggie grabbed the bundle thrust over the side.

"I said get away!" The guard raised a threatening fist.

"God bless ye! Send us word if ye can." The driver's whip cracked over her head and the woman threw him an obscene gesture. "Don't be forgettin' us!" She scrambled out of the way of an oncoming team. "Give 'em hell in the Colonies!"

"Bye, Mam," Maggie called, blinking away tears. "Don't worry about me! Bye!"

A skinny redhead reached for the oilcloth bundle and Kate brought her manacles down across the woman's knuckles. Maggie jabbed her sharply with an elbow and she let out a howl, burrowing through the closely packed prisoners to safety. "Let that be a lesson to the rest of you sluts," Maggie snapped. "Me an' Kate's a team! Stay away from us if ye know what's good for ye!"

The team rounded a sharp corner and slowed to a walk on the steep cobblestone hill. Dozens of ships rode at anchor in the muddy harbor at the end of the street, ships of all sizes and purpose. Foreign flags flew from the masts of most of them. Kate stared wide-eyed. The dock was a pandemonium of stacked bales and barrels. Sweating, swearing men unloaded the nearest vessel, jostled by ships' captains and richly dressed merchant princes. Orders were barked in strange tongues and accents, reinforced by the crack of a leather cat.

"I hope they don't expect us to unload their damn ship," Maggie said.

The driver shouted back a coarse innuendo.

"Yer not man enough! You wouldn't know a woman from the back end of a sheep!"

The man's neck turned beet-red and he slunk within his shirt as the prisoners jeered. "Sheep lover!"

Kate kicked Maggie's ankle in exasperation.

"Sorry, Kate. But 'e did ride me. I ain't one to take tongue from such as 'im."

The wagons halted and were immediately surrounded by armed soldiers. A bewigged magistrate waved the guards down importantly, and they dropped the tailgate of the wagon. "Be quick about it," he called.

A clerk checked names off a list as the women climbed out. "Over there. Line up there."

The soldiers closed ranks tightly to hurry the prisoners in groups of six to waiting longboats. Awkwardly the women scrambled down a ladder and into the boats. Kate clung to the side as the sailors began to row. Water lapped about her bare feet.

"Crimey, the tub's gonna sink," Maggie cried.

A rower leered. "Not to worry, dolly. If it does, I'll carry you on my back."

"Stow that talk," the one-eyed bosun ordered.

Kate pulled her skirts high over her ankles to avoid the dirty water. The bloated carcass of a cat bobbed alongside the longboat, then vanished in the murky waves. Kate tried to breathe through her mouth to avoid the smell. London's waterways were little more than open sewers, flushing out the filth of the city with every outgoing tide.

Maggie nudged her friend, then reached down and pulled her skirt up between her legs and tucked it into her waist. Kate followed suit. A rope ladder was being lowered over the side of a matronly merchant vessel just ahead. Any unprepared female climbing up would provide the same show for the sailors they had undoubtedly given boarding the longboat.

Yellow-haired Maggie was the first woman up the ladder. She was rewarded with catcalls and admiring scrutiny from the crew as her bare feet touched the deck. Kate was close behind, followed by the others. An officer waved them to an open spot on the deck, while the other longboats were unloading.

Kate looked around; the ship was old but clean and seemingly sound. The sailors seemed well-disciplined. There was no sign of the captain, but the two officers kept order with quiet military precision. The worst of her fears gradually subsided. Perhaps the old woman at Newgate had told the truth. Bond slaves were valuable property. They would be well-treated until they reached America and their indentures were sold.

"Keep yer eyes down, Kate, fer God's sake," Maggie whispered. "It don't do to be noticed by such as these. Sailors ain't none to mess with. Play stupid if ye can. We've got a long voyage ahead of us an' it's a small ship."

The younger of the two officers, a freckle-faced redhead, was reading off names and assigning groups of ten. As their names were called the prisoners stepped into lines and their manacles were removed. Kate waited anxiously for her name. Suppose she and Maggie were given different quarters? In the short time they'd known each other, she'd come to rely on the good sense of the gutsy Londoner and didn't want to be parted from her if she could help it.

"Storm, Kathryn." The officer looked up from his list. "Storm?"

"Here." Kate glanced sideways at Maggie and stepped forward.

"Follow this man." He indicated the grinning bosun.

"Why?" Kate demanded. Why separate instructions for her?

"Ye'd best foller me," the bosun said as he unlocked the heavy iron at her wrists.

The officer gestured impatiently. "Do as you're told, woman."

"Not until I know why and where I'm going!"

"Go on, Kate," Maggie hissed. "Won't do no good to throw a fuss here. Yer temptin' the cat."

The bosun took her arm roughly and she jerked away. "Keep your hands off me."

"You'll walk or be carried," the redhead threatened.

Reluctantly, Kate followed the burly seaman across the deck and down a steep flight of narrow steps. They passed several doors, then he stopped and opened one, revealing a small cabin. "Inside."

Kate froze.

"Ye'd best not turn up yer nose at this, *yer highness.* Ye've not seen below decks where the others be stabled."

"I'd rather be with the rest."

"Ye've no say in the matter." He shoved her inside and slammed the door behind her. Kate heard a key turn in the lock. When his footsteps receded, she tried the brass handle. "Damn." When were they going to stop locking her in little cages? She paced the confines of the tiny room. The only light came from a minute porthole with glass so wavy she could hardly see a thing through it.

There were two bunks, one over the other, and a desk built into the wall, a single chair, and barely a square yard of floor space. A pewter ewer and bowl stood on the desk. She used the water to wash her face and hands, then sat down on the lower bunk. There was nothing to do but wait, wait and try to keep the ghosts of panic banked.

Minutes passed into hours. Bored, she combed out her hair with her fingers and rebraided it, pinning it up as neatly as possible. There was nothing to be done with the gown; it was all she had to wear. She washed the rest of her body a little at a time without undressing, and finally her feet. The water was black. Whoever belonged to the cabin would have to find their own fresh water.

Sounds of running feet and creaking ropes startled Kate out of a half doze. The ship was moving. She swallowed hard. Somehow, even until the last moment, she had believed that Geoffrey would come swinging aboard, an army of Storm retainers at his back, to rescue her. America, the Maryland colony . . . they were at the other end of the world. How would he find her? "Damn it! Damn it! He can't . . . I know he can't!" She would have to find him. She'd gotten herself into this and she'd have to get herself out. Somehow, someway, she'd win her freedom and return to England and Queen's Gift and find Geoffrey.

He'd been hurt in the fight, maybe worse than she'd realized. Then, by the time his wound had healed, it was too late to help her. That's why he hadn't been at the trial. If she knew her hotheaded brother, he'd be spitting fire by now. He was capable of doing anything when his fury was aroused.

Kate flung herself back on the bunk. Like a child, she'd been expecting a fairy-tale rescue. She'd show Geoffrey. She was as much a Storm as her father, as any of the rest. It made her no less that she was a woman. Her inner resolve stiffened. "I'll do it myself, I swear," she whispered. "I swear."

Kate sat bolt upright as footsteps stopped outside her door and a key rattled in the lock. The door opened wide and she stared into the smug face of Pride Ashton.

"Greetings, bonnie Kate. I hope you're a good sailor. I'd hate to share a cabin for months with a seasick wench."

"You bastard."

He threw back his head and roared. "Didn't I tell you she was a game one?" Pride stepped aside as two men carried an iron-bound trunk into the room. "You can bring the rest down later. The lady and I will have words now in private." The men withdrew and Pride entered the cabin, closing the door behind him. "Well, you could look happy to see me."

"I'd sooner look into the face of hell."

"Don't be bitter. I've saved your scalp and the sooner you realize it, the better for both of us." He folded his arms and leaned arrogantly against the door.

Kate jumped up. "And what makes you think I'm any more willing to be your doxy here than I was in Newgate?" Her hand ached to smack his grinning face. "You'd have done better to let them hang me. I'll be no man's slave, sexual or otherwise."

Pride lowered his arms and the grin vanished. "I've no wish to have you as a slave, Kate. I want you, hell, yes. I'd be a liar if I said otherwise. But I want you willing. There's little joy to be had in a whore."

"And none at all to be had from me. Send me back with the others. I won't stay here."

"You don't know what it's like down there. It's not safe, and certainly no place for a lady, not even your breed of lady. You'll find me better company than the rats." She tried to duck past him to reach the door handle and he caught her wrist. "Stop that. Don't be a fool, Kate. Where would you go if you get out? You can't walk around a ship like this without protection. If you're afraid of rape, have sense enough to be afraid of it beyond that door."

"Rape is rape." She pulled free of him, trying to deny the inner trembling his touch had precipitated.

"No, Katy. It's not and you know it," he said hoarsely. "I'll not see you handed from man to man in the fo'c'sle and then dumped overboard to the sharks when you're used up." He pulled her tightly into his arms. "Now listen to me, damn it. There'll be no rape from me." She turned her face away and struggled to escape. "Stop that wriggling against me or you'll make a liar of me yet." He kissed the soft tendrils of hair that escaped her crown of braids. "I'm your friend, Kate, whether you believe it or not. And I'd like to be more." He caught her chin in his callused hand and gently tipped her face up to meet his penetrating gaze.

His eyes were black, blacker than any human eyes could be. Unconsciously, Kate found herself drawn into the bottomless depths of those obsidian pools . . . down . . . down.

Suddenly, she became aware of his mouth on hers. What began as a tender exploring kiss grew into a ruthless assault, an assault all the more deadly because it held no violence. She was defeated not by his strength but by her own weakness, as her defenses were swept away in a tide of swirling emotions. Her arms encircled his neck, pulling him down to meet her own growing passion. Her body strained against his, reveling in the hard masculine strength of him, in the iron thighs, the broad chest . . . in the whispered, honeyed words of love.

With an anguished cry, Kate wrenched away. He made no effort to hold her and she backed as far as the tiny cabin would allow. Her eyes sparkled with unshed tears as she raised a trembling hand to her bruised lips.

"Can you still deny you care for me?"

"Yes! No." Kate turned away, pressing her face against

the damp wall. "You're a devil, Pride Ashton," she whispered.

"You're not the first to say so."

"But why?" She turned to face him, keeping the small chair between them, ashamed of the body that betrayed her. "Why me?"

"Damned if I know." He laughed. "You've been nothing but trouble since I first laid eyes on you." The dark eyes twinkled with mischief. "You're too skinny, too. The Shawnee in me prefers a woman with more meat on her bones."

"Then go below decks and pick out someone more to your liking! Or have I been bought and paid for?" The anger rose within her, blocking the soft weakness. She welcomed it, forcing her voice to a shrew's whiplash.

"In a manner of speaking. What I paid for was the service of a servant for the voyage, a private financial matter between the ship's master and myself. Your indenture will be auctioned off in Annapolis with the rest. There's nothing I can do about that, believe me. It's King George's law and not subject to bribery."

"You paid for my services? And what of my reputation—an unmarried man and woman to share a cabin? What will the crew think? The other bondwomen?"

Pride shook his head in exasperation and ran a hand through his thick black hair. "Can't you get it through that stubborn brain? Lady Kathryn Storm is dead! She may as well have swung at Tyburn! You are a convicted criminal, a bond servant. You have no reputation!"

"And you, sir, have no honor!"

The barb struck home and he flinched. "Your tongue, wench, is too sharp. You speak of what you know little." A flush burned his cheeks as he put his hand on the door. "I'll leave you to cool your ill temper." How could he explain to her that he meant her to be a servant and nothing more, that he'd put down good coin just to save her from dishonor? The words stuck in his throat. She'd not believe them anyway. "My men will be coming with my luggage. You may unpack and stow what there is room for. The chest you are not to touch. There are some things in the baggage for you too.''

''And am I to provide your gentlemen with services also?''

The black eyes hardened. ''No, m'lady, that pleasure is mine alone.''

Kate threw an oath at his departing back. She'd be no whore, not for him, not for any man. She'd die first. ''You may unpack,'' she mocked his voice. Pride Ashton would rue the day he crossed paths with her.

Chapter 5

There was a loud rapping at the cabin door. "Jonas, ma'am, wi' the baggage." The colonial accent was so heavy Kate could barely understand him. "Make yerself decent, we're comin' in." A short wait and then the door was unlocked.

It was the same two servants who had carried in the iron-bound trunk for Ashton. They were much alike, broad and sandy-haired, with thick muscular arms and necks and washed-out blue eyes. Both seemed to have had their noses broken repeatedly. They looked more like dock workers than honest retainers.

The first man touched his forelock. "Jonas Bennet, ma'am. An' me brother Bill. He don't talk much to females." Bill's ruddy face flushed, and he nodded respectfully as they brought in the luggage.

"Two will slide under the bottom bunk, the other we'll have to put against this wall. Not much room to spare in these cabins, is there? Pride said—"

Kate stiffened. "If you're referring to Lord Ashton, you'd best show more respect to your master."

Bill guffawed. He elbowed his brother and howled with glee.

Jonas swallowed a chuckle and tried to keep a straight face. "You got a lot to learn 'bout the colonies, ma'am, and Maryland fer sure," he drawled. "Me an' Bill, we work fer Pride. He's a good man an our friend. But you can't rightly say *master*. Me an' Bill, we ain't got no *master*."

"Master," Bill echoed. "That's a good'n." He pulled the

battered cap back on his head. "Not since we cut loose from
our pa."

"He said to tell ya, he was takin' supper wi' the captain.
I'll fetch ya somethin' from the galley myself." The amusement was plain on his broad face.

"You needn't bother."

"Now, don't be like that, miss. You got nothin' to fear
from me an' Bill. We wouldn't mess with Pride's woman.
Just struck us funny what you said. Comin' from London ya
couldn't expect to know no better. Just not used to hearing
Pride called Lord Ashton."

Bill chuckled from the hallway.

"I'll fetch ya some vittles. You'd best eat now. Food gets
kinda rank after a few weeks at sea."

"I don't care what he told you. I'm not Pride Ashton's
woman. Do you understand? I'm not!"

"Whatever you say, ma'am. But I'll bring the food jest
the same."

They closed and locked the cabin door and she heard their
laughter as they went down the hall. Kate kicked the nearest
trunk. There was nothing she could do but wait.

Jonas returned a short time later with bread and cheese and
a mug of ale. "Not the fare they're havin' at the captain's
table, I'll warrant. Oh, he said yer to have this." Jonas tossed
Kate an orange. "And this." From inside his shirt he took
an oilcloth bundle and unwrapped it carefully. "It's a book,
ma'am. He thought maybe it would help to pass the time."

When he was gone, she picked up the book from the desk
and examined it curiously. It was entitled *An Account of the
Settling of the Chesapeake Bay Area and Its Original Inhab-
itants,* a history of the Maryland colony. Kate scanned a few
pages. The more she knew about America, the easier it would
be to make her escape and return to England. The light in
the room was fading, so she took the book to the top bunk
and began to read in earnest, but soon she drifted off to sleep.

"Do you do anything but sleep?"

Bewildered, Kate opened her eyes. Where . . . ? Pride
Ashton's mocking face was illuminated by a ship's lantern.

"Did they leave you no candle? I'm sorry. There were after-dinner drinks and then a few hands of cards. I meant to be here sooner. Did you read any of the book? What did you think of it?"

Kate drew her legs up under her modestly. On the top bunk, she was as far away from him as the cabin would permit. "Yes, I did, some of it, before it got dark. Thank you. I'm surprised a gentleman of your background would know anything of reading, let alone a book of such obvious merit."

He chuckled, a deep and warm sound. "Yes, Katy, I do read. As a matter of fact, not only have I read that particular history, but I wrote it. I'm glad to know you approve."

"Liar!" she protested, feeling childish in her response. "There's no need to put on an act, I know what you're here for." Now that the words were out, the fear began to creep quickly up her spine. She shivered. "I meant what I said. I'll not be your whore." He was too powerful to hold off physically; she'd have to depend on her wits. Trouble was . . . Trouble was her mind was blank. She didn't know what to do.

"If you know why I'm here, then put on a wrap. It's a damp windy night. I'm taking you for a walk on deck."

"I have nothing else, just this dress." Her voice sounded small and far away.

"Sweet Jesus, woman! Do ye listen to nothing I say? If I didn't know better I'd swear you were Shawnee. I told you there were clothes in the baggage." He fumbled with a trunk, pulled it from under the bed and opened the lid. A woman's cloak lay on top. "I hope the things fit. I said you were tall. I thought ye'd have little enough for the voyage."

Kate allowed him to drape the soft wool cloak over her shoulders. It was teal-blue and fit perfectly. She followed him wordlessly down the narrow passageway.

"Be careful," he warned. "The stairway's steep."

" 'Tis called a ladder."

"Damn you for a shrewish wench! I know what it's called."

"Am I to be paraded now, like a prize cow?"

"Do you think of yourself as bovine?"

"What makes you think I won't throw myself overboard?"

"Suicide? I hadn't thought you were that stupid. Do so if you wish, but the sea is a cold grave." He took her arm and tucked it under his. "Truce, Kate. Whether you believe it or not, I mean you no harm. I brought you up for fresh air. I couldn't stand to be locked in a close place myself. I apologize for the cabin. It's the best to be had." Better for them both, he thought, if he could have had a larger. It would be agony to be this close to her without wanting more.

"Best would be my own cabin with a stout lock on the inside."

"Sometimes we have to settle for second best."

Suddenly, Pride pulled her into his arms and covered her surprised mouth with his own. She tasted the faint sharp bite of rum on his lips as she struggled to pull free. The touch of his hands sent warm chills through her body, and her limbs felt strangely weak.

"No, Kate, not yet," he murmured, kissing her again, lifting her from the deck against his body. She kicked uselessly with her bare feet against his high leather boots. One of his hands slipped inside the cloak to fit against her bottom and she gasped. Pride's tongue slipped between her teeth and she bit down hard.

"Damn it!" He pushed her away and spat blood. "You nearly took my tongue off."

"And so I will if you try that again." She tried to still the trembling, tried to convince herself that she hated him . . . that she hadn't liked his touch.

"You warmed to me before."

"I did not." She turned away, moving swiftly toward the rail. He followed. "I promised no truce," she said stubbornly.

Kate looked out over the water; the ocean was dark. The waves are like black furrows, she thought, stretching to the edge of the world and off, to the boiling chaos where the sea monsters breed. She gripped the worn railing. *I should jump*. Do it, an inner voice urged. Kate sighed. Not this way, not until every bridge was burned. The wind whipped at her cloak and she pulled it close. Pride's arm settled securely about her shoulders.

"I'm sorry," he admitted reluctantly. "London's manners must have rubbed off on me more than I care to admit." Kate held her tongue.

After a long silence, Pride began again. "Can we not stroll the ship like friends? I promise no more advances until they are welcomed." He grinned boyishly.

"Then you will have a long wait." Kate turned away and began to walk down the deck. He caught her hand and she let it lie limp in his, not willing to risk another physical encounter.

"Friends only, for now. But a friend may hold a lady's hand." His touch was gentle but firm.

"I don't consider you my friend, Lord Ashton. You were the instrument of the destruction of my life and of the loss of my father."

Pride released her hand. "Unwittingly, perhaps. But you and your father must bear the greater responsibility. You are too intelligent to deny your own guilt in the matter. I regret the death of your father, but he did die of a heart condition. Have you considered that he could have met the same fate in his sleep? The Shawnee say our days are numbered from the first, and what will be, must be."

Kate dropped onto a coil of rope and covered her face with her hands. The simple truth of his statements pierced her mind like a sharp knife. Pride had come to the aid of his uncle during a robbery. He had fought and pursued the highwayman. His behavior was without fault.

"You're right," she said hoarsely. "What happened after we stopped the coach . . . my being sent to Newgate . . . my father's—my father's death. You were never to blame. It was wrong of me to accuse you." She looked up at the dark silhouette standing over her. "But your actions in the prison were unforgivable! It was an assault on my honor that I shall never forget or forgive."

Wind-tossed clouds parted and a brilliant saffron moon briefly illuminated the deck of the *Maid Marian*, bathing the huge masts and railing in a soft golden glow. The black furrows of the sea dissolved into frosted swells and Kate's heart thrilled to the wonder of it. For an indescribable time there was no reality; she was caught up in a translucent crystal of beauty that shut out all else.

Pride's voice shattered the crystal. "Am I the first man to desire you?" His eyes were pits of blackness beneath the craggy brows.

"No," she stammered. "No . . . but . . . there are other ways of—"

"There are no other ways! You are a woman grown! A woman who has never known the joys of love. I want to teach you those joys, Kate. I won't apologize for that." He took her hand and pulled her to her feet. "If only you knew how beautiful you are, with the moonlight on your hair." He held her at arm's length. "Kiss me, Kate."

"I want none of your kisses," she lied. "Or your honeyed words. Doubtless you've said the same to many a woman."

He laughed. "True. But I never knew they were false until tonight."

"Then you admit you lie," she dared, only too aware of the smoldering sensuality he held in check. She stilled an inner trembling. Pride Ashton was no savage predator of women, despite the taut wild look that flickered across his chiseled features. He was an English gentleman, with a gentleman's code of honor.

"I don't lie, Kate. " The voice was low and controlled. "To a Shawnee, a liar is not worthy of being counted a man. If I say my words to other women were false, it's only because I never felt this way before. You are a very different breed of female. It's a little unnerving."

Footsteps on the deck invaded their isolation. Kate looked up to see a cloaked figure approaching. Pride's arm dropped possessively around her shoulder.

"Evening, Lord Ashton. I'd have thought you'd be abed."

"Captain Reynolds. We thought we'd get some fresh air

first. May I present Mistress Kathryn Storm. Kate, the master of the *Maid Marian,* Captain Joshua Reynolds. The captain is a colonial by birth, he hails from Boston Town in the Massachusetts colony.''

The captain's walking stick tapped the deck impatiently as he cleared his throat. ''Hmmpt. *Mistress Storm?* I must say, Lord Ashton, I am unaccustomed to being introduced to barefoot wenches on my own ship.''

Kate felt her face go crimson at the insult. A ready answer rose to her tongue, cut off by Pride's forbidding glare and tightened grip on her arm.

''That she is barefoot is my own oversight. Mistress Storm is under my protection, Captain Reynolds. I would hate to see any unpleasantness spoil the good feelings between us. I'm certain my uncle, the Earl of Westbrook, would agree.''

''Hmmpt.'' A sharp nod of dismissal, and the walking stick rapped out disapproval as the caped figure continued on his rounds.

Kate giggled.

''You'd be wise to keep your amusement to yourself. Captain Reynolds is a dangerous man, more so on the deck of his own ship.''

''You were quick enough to remind him of your relationship to the Earl,'' she challenged. ''Are you afraid of him?''

''The Shawnee fear only ghosts, and I gave up believing in haunts when I was ten,'' he answered sardonically. ''I think we'd better go below. The wind's rising.''

''I prefer to stay on deck.''

''I prefer you to return to the cabin, out of the captain's sight and mind. My uncle owns the *Maid Marian,* but the farther we get from England, the more his influence dissipates. It will be a long voyage. This is neither the time nor place for your mischief.''

Kate scoffed. ''He reminds me of a toad! And I haven't been frightened of them since I was a babe. For a man of action, you seem somewhat timid, m'lord. I hardly think the captain would risk offending the nephew of his employer. Doubtless you're safe enough.''

"It wasn't me I was worrying about, you silly chit." He motioned toward the hatch. "Below. Now."

"Yes, m'lord. Whatever you say, m'lord." Kate mocked.

"There is a chamber pot beneath the bunk, and I presume fresh water in the pitcher. I'll allow you privacy to do whatever women do when they prepare for bed. There is a sleeping garment in the trunk."

"If you think I'm taking off my clothes for you—"

"Don't tell me you intend to wear that one dress until we reach Annapolis," he chided. "Please yourself. But if you begin to smell, I'll wash you in lye soap, dress and all."

Kate's cheeks flamed and she bit back an oath, nearly missing her step as she reached the passageway at the bottom of the ladder. Pride caught her arm and she jerked away. "I've no need of your help, Lord Ashton."

"As you wish," he replied patiently. He unlocked the door and handed her the iron key. "I have another. Keep the door locked whenever I'm not with you. Open to no one but the Bennet brothers. No one, do you understand?" The gleam from a swaying ship's lantern brushed across Pride's upper face, highlighting the Mongolian cheekbones and wide brow. An amused chuckle escaped the narrow lips. "Retract your claws, she-cat. I've no intention of ravishing your tender flesh on the other side of this door. When we make love, you'll do the asking."

"You smug bastard! It'll be a cold day in hell when I do."

Pride laughed. "For a lady, your vocabulary is strangely lacking. Bastard is incorrect. I am most definitely legitimate. My parents were married three times; once according to tribal rites, again in Philadelphia by a bishop, and finally in London. The King himself was witness to the ceremony. My mother was quite the toast of London that season, a genuine novelty. Would you care to know where I was baptized?"

"No, I wouldn't!" Kate slammed the door in his face and jammed the key in the lock. His laughter crept under the door.

"I'll be back in a few moments. The bottom bunk's mine."

Kate threw the cape on the floor and kicked it into the corner. If he was telling the truth about leaving her alone sexually, it should make her feel better. It didn't. Pride Ashton was a swaggering, swelled-up, arrogant colonial! There were no words to express her contempt. She wished she'd spent more time in the kitchen at home. The cook had had a flaming temper and a tongue that would do honor to a wagoner!

She dropped to her knees and pulled the trunk out from under the bunk. Hastily, she rifled through the contents, astonished at what she found. There were dresses and petticoats, fine linen undergarments, and a pair of kidskin slippers that looked as if they would fit. The gowns were plain but of good quality, fit for a prosperous tradesman's daughter. There seemed to be clothing for both summer and winter wear. Someone had gone to a great deal of trouble and expense to fit out a complete wardrobe.

Kate puzzled over it as she drew on a soft nightdress that reached modestly from neck to toes. Why had Pride shown so much consideration? Surely he considered her no better than a light-skirt, no matter the fine words. Taking a leather case and clothing for the next day, she closed the lid and replaced the trunk, then retreated to the top bunk.

Cross-legged, she opened the red leather case. Inside was a sterling silver brush and comb, a mirror, needle and thread, scissors and pins, and a variety of hair ornaments. A muffled cry of delight escaped before she clapped a hand over her mouth. How lovely they were. She fingered the beautiful brush. "Books and oranges and geegaws," she murmured. Admittedly, Ashton was a dangerous adversary, a man who knew her weaknesses.

A tap alerted her to Pride's presence. "Coming in," he called. He filled the small cabin with his muscular frame.

Unwilling to let him see her face, Kate turned her back and pulled the blanket up around her. Something about this man was overpowering; she knew in her deepest soul that she did fear him—not for what he might do to her body, but for something even more frightening she could not put into words. Her muscles tensed, and she caught her lower lip between her teeth.

"A pleasant night's sleep to you, too." Pride blew out the lamp. "If you snore, I'll kick the bottom of your bunk. I can't abide snoring females." He undressed quickly and folded his large frame into the bunk.

The room smelled of woman, not a perfume but a clean, fresh woman smell. Pride lay on his back and closed his eyes, willing himself to think of something else . . . anything else. It had been too long since he'd shared the pleasures of a blanket with a woman. He chuckled. He was thinking in Shawnee again. He'd never cared for the services of a paid whore; usually the smell would be enough to make a man think of other things. The tightening in his loins reminded him that this soft armful was only a few inches above his head. The fact that she was totally in his power only made things worse. She'd accused him of having no honor. Pride let out his breath with a whoosh and turned over. It would be a hell of a lot easier if he didn't have any.

Kate stuffed part of the blanket in her mouth and bit down. She'd not give him the satisfaction of knowing how annoying he was. She'd be silent if it killed her, and it probably would!

"My pistols are under my pillow, but I warn you, I'm a light sleeper. If you lay hands on me while I'm sleeping, I'll accept it as an invitation to play." He chuckled. "Sweet dreams, Katy."

For nearly an hour she lay tense, hardly daring to move a muscle. Pride's steady, even breathing infuriated her. Either he was trying to trick her, or he had fallen instantly asleep. Gradually, Kate relaxed, lulled by the gentle rocking of the ship. When she woke, it was morning.

With a start, she sat up, clutching the blanket tightly against her throat. Pride was seated on the lower bunk pulling on his boots.

"Did you sleep well?"

The tenderness in his voice disarmed her. "Well enough," she stammered. "Thank you for the clothing . . . the brush and comb. I had nothing." A tightness filled her throat. *I'm alone, really alone.* Realization flooded through her brain. She was tired of pretending a toughness she didn't feel.

Pride stood up, his face inches from hers, and a broad smile lit the dark eyes. "That's probably the most pleasant thing you've ever said to me." His pleasure was tempered with doubt. Why was she being pleasant? Kathryn Storm was not to be trusted, not for a minute, but yet . . . He deliberately made his voice light. "I consider my money well-spent. You are most welcome, Kate. I thought of sending for some of your own things, but I'm afraid they'd be of little use to a bondwoman."

Kate slid her legs over the side of the bed. "You do well to remind me of my position." Her trembling voice betrayed the words.

"Your position will be what you make it." God, but he wanted her! If he had any sense at all he'd get out of this cabin and up on deck. Instead, his hands closed about her waist, and he lifted her down from the bunk, pulling her against him and bringing his head down to kiss her tenderly.

Kate stiffened, trying to deny the delicious sensations that spread through her body. His hands slid down over her hips to caress her bottom. Somehow, her arms went around his neck, and she found herself returning the kiss, surrendering to his touch.

"Katy," he murmured hoarsely. "You've got to stop this if you want it stopped." His hand cupped her breast beneath the soft gown, and she gasped with delight as his fingertips stroked the hardening nipple. The tightening in his loins intensified, and he caught his breath sharply. He wasn't certain he could stop if she asked him to. "Katy?"

His lips traveled down her cheek to the base of her throat, igniting sparks of throbbing sweetness. She lifted his face to look into the ebony eyes. There was no taunting there, no arrogance, only tenderness. She pressed her lips to his, and when his tongue sought the warmth of her mouth it seemed natural to welcome it eagerly. Natural to seek comfort in his strong arms.

Pride dropped to the lower bunk, pulling her into his

lap. "Do you understand?" he pleaded. His breathing was ragged and uneven. "I'm promising nothing, Kate."

"I don't care." She clung to him, meeting kiss with kiss, sliding deeper and deeper into a dream world as he continued his ever-deepening kisses. His hands on her breasts were maddening, and tiny moans of joy escaped her lips. He pushed her trembling back against the wool blanket and knelt beside the bunk.

"I'm scared," she whispered. Her eyes glistened with tears.

"Shhh, shhh," he murmured. "It's all right, darling. I won't hurt you." Gently, he kissed away the tears and began to undo the buttons at her throat.

"I . . . I've never done anything like this before," she sobbed. "I . . ."

"Shhh." His lips silenced her with a kiss as his fingers traced a pattern on her neck and exposed shoulder. His tongue brushed the hollow of her throat.

Kate's eyes widened with surprise as he slipped a warm hand inside her gown to caress her breast. The gown parted and he took her nipple in his mouth, sending spasms of exquisite sensations through her body. Time seemed to lose all meaning. There was nothing but the two of them, nothing but the wonder of these feelings as he touched her body in all the secret places, nothing but the kisses Kate wished would never end.

Then suddenly she was aware of his weight pressing her back against the mattress. He caught her hand in his and laid it against the throbbing length of his passion. "I want you, Kate," he said hoarsely. "I want you . . . but you must want it too. Tell me, Kate."

Shaken, she buried her face in his hard shoulder, unable to think, unable to speak.

"Kate," he insisted. "Kate?"

"Yes," she whimpered. "Oh, God help me . . . yes."

He kissed her gently and she felt the solid thrust of his flesh between her legs. There was a sharp pain as he drove deep inside. Kate caught her lip in her teeth as he moved rhythmically and the pain receded to a raw aching. The intensity of his thrusts increased, and she found herself caught up in a current of something . . . something she couldn't describe. She rose to meet his demand, as her blood heated, seeking, searching for some unknown goal.

Suddenly, Pride gave a cry and relaxed against her, his breathing harsh and ragged. He whispered her name and rolled off, cuddling her against him.

She buried her face in his shoulder, unable to deal with her own emotion. She lay almost without breathing, letting the current slow and finally go slack, regretfully releasing the excitement that had possessed her in the last few moments of his lovemaking.

"I'm sorry if I hurt you." She'd been a virgin. Damn. If he'd known that . . . "It will be better next time, Katy, I promise. He felt like the worst kind of blackguard. He'd been certain she was lying about her innocence as she'd lied about her presence at the robbery. He kissed the crown of her hair. All he could do now was to try and undo what damage he'd done.

Tears rolled unchecked down her cheeks; she felt strangely empty. Her sobs changed to hiccups and he began to chuckle. He kissed her and rocked her gently.

"Hush, now, *ki-te-hi*," he murmured. "Did I hurt you so bad?"

"No. Oh, damn it, I can't do anything right. I told you I wasn't that kind of woman." She raised her head to look into his eyes. Would he shame her now?

"What kind of a woman? You were a virgin. No one expects you to know how to make love. It's a thing to be learned, like riding a horse. It's a gift, Katy, to give to a man. Your first time." A wave of protectiveness swept over him, and his arm tightened about her. He forced a chuckle. "You've a natural flair for it, I can tell." He bent his head to kiss her lips. "Now," he whispered. "Tell me, did you like it?"

"The first," she admitted. "The kissing and . . . what you did . . . But . . . the rest. I just . . ." How could she put into words what she didn't understand? "I hurt, and I feel like a fool."

Pride sat up and pulled her into his lap. "For a woman

there is pain the first time, but that won't happen again. You're a passionate woman, Kate, and it's nothing to be ashamed of, ever. Now, dry your eyes.'' He kissed the tip of her nose. ''What happens between a man and a woman is a natural thing, a thing to take joy in.'' He traced her eyebrow with the tip of his finger. ''I'm the one who should feel the fool. I took my pleasure and didn't give you the same. It won't happen again, I promise.'' His voice thickened. ''I'll leave you to bathe in private. Don't be frightened if there's a little blood.''

''What did you say to me? Before?'' she asked shyly. ''You said a word. Kiy . . .''

''*Ki-te-hi*. It's Shawnee for *heart*.'' With a final hug, he got up and began to dress. ''I warn you,'' he teased, ''in times of passion, I revert to my savage upbringing.'' He sighed reluctantly. ''That will be lesson enough for this morning. I'm breakfasting with the captain, and I'm sure they're waiting for me. Jonas will bring your breakfast. If you want to go topside today, just ask him. He and his brother will watch over you. You're safe enough with them as long as you don't draw attention to yourself. I'll have a special supper brought down tonight so we can dine together.'' He grinned boyishly. ''Have a good day.''

Kate curled into a tight ball and pulled the cover up over her. ''*Ki-te-hi* . . . heart.'' She smiled and burrowed sleepily into the mattress. Next time, he'd promised. Next time it would be different. Her heart thrilled. There would be a next time. She didn't regret what had happened. She'd needed someone desperately, and Pride Ashton had been that someone. Beneath that exasperating exterior was a sensitive, gentle human being. No matter what happened when they reached America, she would not regret giving herself to him. It had gone a long way toward filling the emptiness. She might be ignorant about the act of making love, but this much she knew. A woman could be initiated by someone far worse. She smiled sleepily. Far worse.

Chapter 6

The days and nights that followed were to be forever engraved upon Kate's heart. The tiny cabin was her world; she and Pride were the only humans that existed in it. As Pride had promised, the pain was gone from their love-making. And he was a man well-versed in the arts of love, a man who knew well how to stoke the fires of her passions until they flamed out of control, until they reached heights she had never dreamed of.

In all her life, this was a part of her being she had never conceived of. She had seen herself as a modern woman, independent and strong, needing no man to feel whole . . . complete. But now . . . Now she counted the seconds he was gone from her side, thrilled to the sound of his footsteps in the passageway. She was hopelessly, head-over-heels in love with this mysterious half gentleman, half rogue of a colonial.

Kate dared not question if she trusted him. How could you trust someone so totally alien? He was unlike any man she had ever known before. After the robbery, when he had chased her on horseback, she had seen a fearless rider, a tough, angry adversary. And yet he had saved her from hanging, treated her with respect and tenderness. He had shied from trouble with the captain of the *Maid Marian* like any milksop court dandy, but claimed intimate knowledge of the savage wilderness. Who and what was he really? Her eyes traveled over the sleeping form sprawled on the bottom bunk.

One arm was flung across his rough-hewn face, younger-looking in sleep. His naked chest was almost hairless, marked here and there by old scars and glistening now with a faint sheen of moisture, evidence of their fervent union. His breathing was light and steady; she wondered if his pillow concealed a loaded pistol.

Kate moved slowly to a half-sitting position. A circle of lantern light spilled over Pride's narrow waist and taut, hard belly. The blanket only half-covered the dark nest of hair at his groin. Kate felt the flush of blood flame her cheeks as she remembered the pleasure his engorged manhood had given her only minutes before. Lust, she knew, was a grave sin. It was one she must plead guilty to. She stifled a chuckle. Would that all sins were so sweet.

A deep twisted scar ran down his exposed thigh, a scar put there, Pride had said, when he tangled with a female black bear. Kate doubted the tale, but admitted its color. Surely any man who had battled such a beast with only a knife would have come away with more than one such token, if he lived to tell the story at all. Gentlemen, she knew from experience, were inclined to embellish their narratives and to take credit for heroics performed by others. Why should Pride Ashton be any different?

His legs were long and tanned and corded with muscle, his bare feet well-formed and clean as usual. Cleanliness was another of his habits, unusual to the point of eccentricity. The man bathed all over daily, requiring buckets of sea water to be heated and carried to the cabin every afternoon. It was a performance that drew amusement from the crew and passengers alike. Too much bathing was detrimental to a man's health; anyone knew that.

It was a habit Kate found endearing, even when he forced her to follow suit. "I can't believe it's an Indian trait," she'd protested, shivering, as he'd poured water over her naked body. "I've always heard them referred to as filthy, stinking savages who smear themselves with paint and animal fat."

"Your own British ancestors, Kate, were running about stark naked and painting themselves blue in Roman times," he said wryly. "Not only are the Shawnee scrupulously clean but they can trail a European in the woods by his unwashed scent. As to the paint, any visitor to the royal court is in no position to comment on the makeup of an Indian. At least war paint doesn't cover a season's worth of accumulated grime.''

It was another of Pride's tales she doubted. Cautiously, she pulled up her legs and tried to climb over him to the floor. A strong hand captured her and pulled her down on top of him.

"Don't go," he whispered, nuzzling the silken texture of her bared breast. "Lie here beside me, so close I can feel the beat of your heart."

Kate sighed and snuggled down, laying her head against his chest. Already the glow was beginning in the warm places of her body. They would not lie still long. She flicked at Pride's left nipple with the tip of her tongue, and his moan of pleasure brought a moistness to the source of her womanhood.

"Witch," he teased. "A man's nipples are not to be toyed with. What do you take me for?"

A growing hardness pressed against the base of her belly and Kate giggled, moving suggestively against the pressure. "I am but an innocent maid," she murmured. "How do I know what is proper with a man?"

"You are insatiable, wench. Have I not serviced you twice already today?"

"Once," she corrected.

"Then let me remedy the oversight."

Pride pulled her face up to his and covered her mouth with his own in a kiss that swirled her down and down into a bottomless pool of desire. His hands explored the curves of her yielding body; his growing rod of passion found its way into her slick passageway of love. They coupled quickly, fiercely, seizing the joy of willing flesh against flesh until they collapsed, panting, exhausted by the utter abandonment of their lovemaking.

Kate awoke to darkness, then realized she was alone in the bed. "Pride?" There was no sound in the cabin above the beat of the waves against the wooden hull. The door latch turned and Kate threw up her hand to protect her eyes from the bright light of the ship's lantern in the passage-way. "Pride?"

The dim figure emitted a harsh laugh and held the lantern higher. Captain Joshua Reynolds leered as the light spilled over Kate's naked form. "As pretty a sight as these eyes have seen in many a voyage," he taunted.

Kate seized the blanket from the floor and pulled it protectively over her body. "Get out of here! You've no right—"

The cruel features hardened. "This is my ship, woman! Don't you forget it! I've every right." The walking stick tapped the deck menacingly, then raised to push the door open wider. "Especially to a toothsome whore like your-self." The lantern swung to and fro as he lounged against the hatchway.

Kate gasped at the vile obscenities that spilled from the tight-lipped mouth. "You filthy bastard!" she spat. Her hand slid under the pillow and emerged brandishing Pride's flintlock pistol. With her left hand she eased the cock into full position. "Get out of this cabin or I'll blow you straight to hell!" she threatened, all fear dissolved in white-hot fury. "Out!"

"That's your death warrant, bitch! I'll have you keel-hauled until the flesh hangs from your bones." He lunged toward her and she squeezed the trigger.

The flint struck the frizzen. Kate braced herself for the shock of the recoil but there was none. The captain grabbed for her and she brought the barrel of the flintlock down across his wrist. He let out a howl of pain and half-fell to the floor.

"What the hell?" Pride brushed past the fallen skipper to twist the pistol from Kate's hand.

Cursing, Captain Reynolds staggered to his feet and re-trieved his stick. "She tried to kill me! That bitch tried to shoot me on my own ship." He raised the walking stick like a weapon and Pride caught it firmly.

"Cannot a man even go topside to relieve himself with-out you causing trouble?" Pride demanded. Almost ca-sually, he backhanded Kate, knocking her against the wall of the cabin. He released the stick and stood between her and the captain. "My apologies, Captain Reynolds," he said stiffly. "This is a dirty matter. Rest assured that she will be properly punished."

"Me? He forced his way in here! He—"

"Shut up, you stupid wench!" Pride snapped. "You can see she's not right in the head. I'll tend to her."

"The tending will be mine." Reynolds's scarred face whitened to the color of old tallow. "I'll have her neck before the next sunset or know the reason why."

Pride scoffed. "The voyage is hardly begun. I paid good coin for the use of her body and you'll keep your bargain. The slut is not worth your anger. She'll pay for her impudence, never fear. You are no doubt aware that I am familiar with the customs of the Indians. I know many ways to cause pain without reducing the value of the merchandise." Pride motioned toward the door, and lowered his voice. "What happened here is best forgotten. Consider the rumors which could spread if she were executed . . . not only among the crew, but in higher circles. A man's career could be ruined and for what? We both know that you were never in any danger. Obviously the bitch cannot even fire a pistol."

"This is my ship, Lord Ashton, my ship! Remember that! I am master here."

"Indeed, I never thought otherwise. You have my sincere apologies and the promise that no one will ever hear of this, my word as a gentleman." Pride followed the captain into the passageway. "The ladder is steep. May I suggest that you use it only when absolutely necessary." The ebony eyes met the captain's glare of pure hate without wavering. "It is, as you say, your ship. You may go where you like. But some places are more dangerous than others."

"Lord or not, don't push me too far, Ashton."

Pride dismissed the man with a curt nod and returned to the cabin, closing and locking the hatch. "Damn you, I was gone not five minutes. You are the most self-destructive woman I have ever met!"

Kate trembled with anger. "You struck me!"

"You're lucky I didn't let him have you. I should have

left you to rot in Newgate. You're stark raving mad. I leave the cabin to take a leak and I come back to find myself involved in mutiny. Did you have to assault the captain? Couldn't you have been satisfied with the governor's aide? He's aboard ship.''

"I'd have killed the bastard if you'd had sense enough to prime your pistol. What good is an unprimed piece?''

"And am I to cavort with a naked maid with loaded pistols under my head?''

"You hit me, you coward!'' Kate retrieved the second pistol from the mattress and flung it at his head. "Go ahead, torture me if you dare! You're not a man . . . you're a . . . a . . .''

Pride caught the weapon in mid-air, examined it quickly, and laid it on the desk. "Enough of this foolishness. Damn it, Kate, you're a woman and you still behave like a child.''

"Craven varlet!''

"Like a child you throw empty taunts. How old are you anyway?''

"None of your damn business. What would you have had me do, submit to him? Do you think because I've been sleeping with you that I'd spread my legs for a man like that?'' Acid tears welled up in her eyes and spilled down the flushed cheeks. "Do you think I have no pride left?'' She wiped at the hateful tears, ashamed of the weakness they showed.

"Be logical, woman. Couldn't you have stalled him until I returned? I was only gone a few minutes. You should have known I'd be right back, that I'd protect you. Have you so little faith in me?''

"Why should I trust you? I don't know you! I know nothing about you.''

"You know enough about me to come willingly to my bed. That should mean something.'' He leaned against the door and folded his bare arms over his chest. The sleeveless vest hung open to reveal the muscular scarred chest. "What am I to do with you?'' He sighed. "Reynolds would have cheerfully sentenced you to death. You've put us both in great danger by your thoughtlessness.''

"That's it, isn't it?" she demanded "I've put *you* in danger."

Pride's face darkened with anger. "If we were in Maryland," he explained, his voice low and measured, "there would be no question of my being able to protect you. Or even in England. But this is very different. The voyage will last another six weeks at least. We could be murdered and thrown overboard, then entered in the ship's log as victims of fever. Don't you understand, Kate Storm? There is no law here but that of the captain."

"We're English. Englishmen have rights that cannot be taken away," she protested stubbornly. "Even a captain can't come in here and use me like a common slut!"

Control snapped and Pride launched into a tirade in a totally incomprehensible language. Kate stared at him as though he had taken leave of his senses. One by one, he took up the flintlock pistols and primed them. "You've assured that I'll get very little sleep for the next six weeks," he muttered. "Get up in the damn top bunk. I don't want to look at you."

She scrambled up and wrapped herself in a blanket. "Give me one of those, loaded. I'll protect myself and to hell with you!" She turned her back to him and stared at the wall, forcing back more tears. Damn! She was as weepy as the parson's aging daughter! It was her own fault for expecting more of him. He was no different from the rest. All talk and no action! The man had no code of honor. He was despicable. How could she have been such a fool as to trust him, even a little? "And you lied about the book!" she taunted. "You said you wrote it."

"I did."

"Liar! I saw the flyleaf. That isn't your name."

Powerful hands seized her waist and yanked her off the bunk. She struck out at him with all her strength, cursing under her breath. Despite her efforts, he pinned her easily against the bunk and fished the history out from under with his free hand.

"Your mouth runs constantly, like a jay," he panted. "Your brain has no control over your tongue at all. I pity the poor devil who takes you to wife; he's letting himself in for a lifetime of hell on earth.''

Kate bit his exposed forearm and he threw her facedown and sat on her back. Her head struck the corner of the bunk and one foot tangled in some article of clothing. Sensing the uselessness of further struggle and the humiliation of her position, Kate lay still, trying to slow her heavy breathing.

Pride slammed the book down inches from her nose and opened the cover. "Read it!" he ordered.

"I can't. You're squashing me."

"Read it."

"I can't."

"Chobeka Illenaqui. That's my Indian name. Medicine Bow. Say it."

Kate muttered an obscenity and he yanked her to her feet and shook her. She swung at him with all her might and landed a blow full on his nose. It began to bleed and he dropped her and clutched at his face.

"You're no woman; you're a wolverine. It's useless to even talk to you." He turned away in disgust and pulled on a coat. "You've an empty head, Kate, and that's a sad thing for man or woman."

She retreated to the far corner of the cabin, snatching up a pistol as she went. "Just the same, I'll keep this," she threatened. "Call out if you need my help."

"A dark day in heaven!" The hatchway door slammed behind him and she flew to lock it. What now? A trickle of apprehension crept down her spine. If he'd really deserted her, what then? She laid her face on the cold steel of the flintlock. No matter what came to pass, she'd be no easy prey.

Her worst fears were assuaged when Pride banged on the hatch a few minutes later. "I'm leaving the Bennets outside. I'll be topside until morning. You may as well try and get some sleep. I sure as hell won't get any tonight."

"Jonas," she tested, still distrustful.

"Yes, ma'am."

"Thank you for coming, both of you. It's good to know there are men I *can* depend on."

"Yes, ma'am."

Footsteps retreated down the passageway. There was a low murmur of voices and a weight settled against the door.

The candle burned low. Kate retrieved the book from the floor and smoothed the pages. Her eye fell on the unfamiliar name again and her finger traced the strange syllables. "Chobeka Illenaqui . . . Medicine Bow," she whispered. Was it a lie or the truth that Pride had written the book? With a man like Pride Ashton, who knew?

Kate lay awake all night, jumping at every unfamiliar sound like an untried colt.

Two long days passed before Pride returned to her bed, two days of bitter silence between them. During that time, Kate was never once permitted to go topside, to leave her door unlocked, or to be without the constant guard of one or both of Pride's men outside the hatchway.

When the reconciliation did come, it was Kate who initiated it, sliding down from the top bunk and slipping under the cover beside him. He enfolded her in his strong arms without a word.

"I'm sorry," she whispered, hours later, when their frantic lovemaking had exhausted them. He silenced her mouth with a kiss and Kate slept, the first real sleep she'd had since Captain Reynolds had broken into her cabin.

By mutual consent, they avoided discussion of the argument. Pride's good humor returned and they spent hours playing chess or just talking, whiling away the long hours until night. Then, under cover of darkness, Kate could steal a few precious moments on deck, breathing the fresh sea air.

"I've stared at the walls of that cabin until I think I'll go mad," Kate protested when Jonas reminded her it was time to go back. "Please, just a little longer."

"Pride said we're to have ya safe locked up before the card game ends."

Bill nodded. "He were plain about it." He spat a wad of tobacco over the side and motioned with his long rifle. "Best ya get below."

Reluctantly, Kate went. The sea had not provided the

mental lift it usually gave her. She was uneasy, more so than the coming of her monthly woman's cycle should cause. Something about her relationship with Pride Ashton seemed altered, something intangible.

It was not that he'd tired of her. If anything, he was too attentive, too tender of her feelings. The flame of their desire for each other still burned white-hot. No, it was not that.

Kate bid the Bennets a good night and locked the cabin door. Absently, she began to pace the small area. What was it? What was wrong between her and Pride? Had he lied about himself all along? Did he perhaps have a wife and family in Maryland? Was it the end of the voyage and the proof of his deception that he feared? Her eyes fell on the iron-bound trunk.

"Don't touch it," Pride had warned.

What could it possibly contain that he would be so concerned with? Kate nudged it with the toe of her kid slipper. If it were money, it would be locked in the captain's safe, thus insured by the ship's owners of its safety. She dropped to her knees beside the trunk. The iron lock was the size of her fist.

"What are you doing?"

Kate whirled to face him, feeling the blush rise up her cheeks. "What do you mean sneaking up on me?" She'd been so intent on the trunk she hadn't heard the key in the lock. Now she supposed he'd accuse her of snooping in his things! "I wasn't doing anything," she lied.

Pride pushed her aside and examined the lock on the trunk. "You were warned about this," he snapped. The hawk eyes were cold.

"Go ahead, accuse me of trying to steal whatever's in your precious box! Do you think I'm a common thief?" She moved to sit on the bottom bunk.

"Considering how we met, I'd have good reason to, wouldn't I?"

"I explained to you why I did it. I've told you over and over. You still don't believe me, do you?"

"I don't know what I believe," he said honestly. "And it hardly matters." He stood up and looked at her strangely.

"I'll not be throwing it in your face long. Once we reach Maryland, I doubt we'll see one another again. Ashton Hall is a long way from Annapolis."

"You mean you're really abandoning me? Letting me be sold on the block like a slave after we . . ." The words were out, the words that had caught in her throat a dozen times. "I thought you loved me," she murmured. Her eyes were blurry with tears she would not permit to fall. The new world she'd built was falling around her. "I thought . . ."

"Damn it, girl. Don't make it any worse than it is. Did you think I intended to keep you? This isn't England. It's not the custom here for a man to bring a mistress home to his mother."

She hurled herself at him, scratching his face with her nails. Effortlessly, he pinned her against his chest and she broke down in shattering sobs.

"Stop it. Stop it, Kate," he said hoarsely. "I never told you I loved you. I never promised any more than I've given."

"I hate you," she sobbed. "I hate you. Let me go, damn you."

"I'll let you go when you calm down."

"You've had your way with me, now I'm not good enough for you."

"Don't be a fool. You've enjoyed it as much as I have. And I do care for you, Kate, whatever you believe. If I were the marrying kind, I can think of no other woman I've met who attracted me so. I've paid my debt to you. Can't we part friends?"

Kate freed an arm and struck at his face with her fist. "I'll kill you!" she cried.

He grabbed her wrist and wrestled her to the deck. "Must I tie and gag you?"

"Bastard," she sobbed. "You yellow bastard."

"Listen to me. Your life's not over. Despite your foul disposition, you'll be married in three months. Hell, you'll probably be royal governor of the colony in three months. I've given you back your life, woman. Now it's up to you to make the most of it."

Kate went limp.

"Kate? Are you all right?" He rolled off her. She lay unmoving. "Are you playing possum on me, girl?" He crouched over her body and Kate brought a fist flying up to smash against his groin. Pride gasped in pain and she rolled away, leaping for the pistol on the desk. He seized her shoulder, spun her around, and swung.

Kate's jaw exploded in a shower of falling stars. She blacked out and slumped to the floor. Pride caught her and carried her, unconscious, to the bed.

Guiltily, he looked down at the bruise growing steadily darker on the ivory skin. Damn! What was he supposed to do, let her blow him away? If she'd gotten her hands on the pistol she'd have done it! He laid her gently on the mattress and then tucked both flintlocks into his belt for safekeeping. He rubbed at his aching groin. Damn, it would teach him to mess with virgins! She was right. He should have let her hang. "God knows what she'll do to the Colonies." The sooner the *Maid Marian* docked and he saw the last of Kathryn Storm, the better!

Something scurried in the darkness and Kate heaved a wooden bowl at it.

"If that's a rat," Maggie said, "take better aim. We'll get the cook to roast it fer us. It would have to taste better than this salt fish and hardtack. This stuff's hard enough to drive nails."

Kate shuddered. Even as a joke she didn't consider rats funny. The thought of eating one turned her stomach. She retrieved the bowl gingerly and examined it to see if it was cracked. If it wouldn't hold water, she'd be forced to drink from the bucket with her hands.

Mentally, she counted the days since she had returned to the other prisoners, either nine or ten. The hole she shared with Maggie and four other women was somewhat smaller than Pride's cabin. She wondered if it had been stupid to insist that he send her here. What difference would a few more days as his kept woman matter?

She bit at a ragged fingernail. Damn it, it did matter. Before, she'd thought they had something between them.

Something—hell, face it! Love. She'd half . . . no . . . she'd fallen in love with Pride Ashton and proved herself the fool he accused her of being. She could not have stayed, trading her body for a few choice rations and a private cabin.

He'd asked her to stay, with no strings. But she could not trust herself. The anger she felt over her own actions was nothing compared to the rage that blurred her mind when she looked at him. "I'll kill you if you try to keep me," she'd warned.

It had not been easy to be accepted by the others. Only Maggie had welcomed her with an easy laugh. The women had called her whore and worse, but for once Kate held her tongue. She deserved whatever they labeled her. Pregnant Nell had been the loudest until Maggie gave her a sharp slap across the mouth.

"You've no call to wrong Kate. You with a bastard in yer own belly! You'd not be fat and sassy with yer own teeth in yer head if she didn't get them Bennet boys to sneak us limes and biscuit from her own table. I don't doubt Kate went without some days to remember us."

Nell had wailed and sniffed and glared but her comments trailed off. Then one of the girls from the compartment across the passageway took to sneaking off with the sailors, and gossip turned elsewhere.

"Bill says we may be sighting land in a few weeks. He ain't half-bad for a tobacco-chewing man. Course I mean to have me a squire at least," Maggie confided, kicking a pile of straw into a passable bed. "Now when they put you up fer auction, Kate, you smile and look friendly, but not too friendly, lest they take the wrong idea. 'Twould be grand could we get a place together, but it's not best to count on such. We must find a way to let each other know where we be, luv. Yer me only friend in the New World. I'd not like to lose track of ye."

"Or me you," Kate agreed. "But if you're going to catch a country squire, we've got a lot of work to do. Not luv, but *my dear*. My dear, you are my only friend in the Colonies." Mischief lighted the blue Storm eyes and Kate suppressed a giggle at her own proper King's English. "It shouldn't be hard to find you, Maggie. I'll just inquire for the lady of the grandest plantation in Maryland.''

Maggie grinned good-heartedly. "I'll do me . . . my best,'' she promised earnestly. "For I'm that serious, Kate. I mean to be a lady.''

"Listen to her,'' Nell scoffed. "Puttin' on airs.''

Maggie raised a clenched fist. "Shut yer trap, slut, or you'll land in Annapolis with two black eyes.''

Kate laughed. "A lady, dear Maggie, does not threaten other ladies with black eyes.''

"Jest pistols?'' The two dissolved in laughter.

Kate wished all their days could be so merry. But there were violent squalls that tossed the schooner like a matchstick. Water poured through the hatchways and moans of terrified prisoners filled the fetid air. The stench was unbearable as necessary buckets overflowed and even drinking water turned stagnant. Still, even the threat of Captain Reynolds was not enough to send her begging to Pride Ashton. She was here and here she would stay until they reached land or died trying.

Somehow the journey passed. The dreaded tap-tap of the walking stick on the deck never sounded outside Kate's compartment. And then, after days of false hope, Jonas Bennet came to tell them that the vessel had entered the mouth of the Chesapeake Bay.

"Wonderful,'' Kate breathed. "Will it be long until we dock?'' Thoughts of a bath in something other that salt water were even more tantalizing than the prospect of fresh food.

"The Chesapeake's a mighty body of water, a regular inland sea, with more ducks an' geese than ya ever seen afore. Fall comes, they cover the water like a carpet. They hunt whales in here, them what's got the nerve. Course I never seen one, but I hear tell. Them that lives along the shore never wants fer food, not with fish an' crabs an' such.''

"But when do we reach Annapolis?''

"When the skipper's ready. Hours or days, jest dependin'. There's plantations up an' down the bay what pay fer cargo delivered. Don't know what the *Marian*'s fetchin' from England. Shouldn't be long though. An' you'll catch sight of shoreline when they let ya up on deck fer air.'' He touched his forehead respectfully. ''You're a real lady, ma'am. An' me and Bill want ya to know—'' he broke off, red-faced.

''We're proud to have knowed ya,'' Bill finished.

''An' you too, Miss Maggie,'' Jonas finished.

''And I'm proud to have known you,'' Kate answered. They had turned out to be more friends than jailers and she would miss the two brothers, ragged around the edges or not.

Maggie was strangely silent that night. ''I'm worried,'' she finally admitted when Kate pressed her for an explanation. ''When that sellin' of the indentures comes, I'll do jest fine. Anybody can see I'm a likely wench. I'll end up on a farm or servin' in a tavern. But what about you? One look at you will tell them yer no ordinary prisoner. You can't cook. You don't know one end of a cow from the other. You're only good fer one thing, Kate. A man might choose you fer a fancy piece, but not fer his kitchen.''

''I can read and write, and I know horses. There are rules to protect a bound girl, you said so yourself.'' Kate touched her friend's arm. ''You're not to worry about me, Maggie. Look out for yourself as best you can. Maybe Pride . . .''

''No. Not him.'' She shook her head firmly. ''He's too fine fer the likes of me. 'Sides, Kate, I wouldn't take yer man if I could get him.'' She threw her shoe at a rat scampering along the bulkhead. ''Drat! Missed him.''

''He's not my man!'' Kate protested.

''So ye keep sayin'.'' Maggie retrieved her shoe and slipped it on. ''No. What I'm lookin' fer is no lord. A squire will do just fine, and it don't matter to me how old he be. I wouldn't mind being a rich widow, you know.'' She grinned. ''Wipe that scowl off yer face. I'd give good measure fer what I got. I mean to give my little ones a name they can be proud of. This ain't England, luv. I can do it here.''

''I wish you luck, Maggie.'' Kate put down the stocking

she was trying to mend. "A girl with your looks and wits will do fine in the Colonies."

"Pray God 'twill be so."

For the first time, Maggie looked unsure of herself. Kate teased away her gloomy mood, and then lay awake through the night wondering on her own fate.

Some time during the night they dropped anchor in Annapolis harbor. The long journey from England was over. But after the waiting and watching for shore, Kate found she almost hated to leave the familiar ship.

Kate looked in vain for Pride as she and the others were brought on deck. Her legs trembled as she made her way down the narrow gangplank and onto the dock.

It was more crowded than she had expected of a colonial port. The harbor was filled with ships, mostly British, but some flying unfamiliar colors.

The prisoners were hurried down the dock to a brick building nearby. There, fresh clothing and bathwater was provided, along with the biggest meal the women had seen since they'd been sentenced. An aging apothecary gave each one a quick examination and then they were shown to clean quarters.

Gratefully, Kate stretched out on the clean straw of her bunk, ignoring Nell's loud snores a few feet away. Just being ashore was heaven. She'd survived the voyage, but what was to come might be worse than anything that had happened since she was first sentenced.

The day passed slowly. Word circulated among the women that the auction would be held the following day.

"In the courthouse square," Maggie said.

Kate swallowed hard. She had seen cattle auctioned in much the same way at home.

"Cheer up," her friend whispered. "It won't be so bad. Maybe yer friend, the Earl, will be there."

Kate knew better. Pride was gone. He had promised her nothing, and that's what she had received. She'd been a fool to believe otherwise.

At dusk, Jonas Bennet had come to the building where the women were held with Kate's trunk and belongings.

"We're headed west tonight," he told her. "Pride said I'd best fetch ya yer plunder."

"I don't want it," she'd protested. "I want nothing from that man."

"They're yers and you'll be needin' 'em. Don't be hog-stubborn."

The matron had frowned and put her hands on her ample hips impatiently. "If you don't want the trunk, girl, I know plenty who will," she said. The white starched mobcap bobbed up and down in time with her double chins.

"She wants it," Jonas said. "They be hers, sent by Lord Ashton of Ashton Hall." He winked conspiratorily at Kate. "He'd take it amiss did someone take the girl's stuff away."

"What do you take me for? I'm an honest goodwife. Be off with ya, ya woods riffraff. No one will steal the girl's things."

By the following afternoon, Kate was glad she had taken the trunk. If she hadn't, she'd be sitting on the bare dirt like the others. Slaves had been auctioned off first, mostly field hands, and then the bondmen. Kate's fair skin was beginning to burn under the hot Tidewater sun.

A girl from the inn across the way came with a tray of cider, offering a mug to each woman. Kate's mouth was parched. "I'm sorry," she admitted. "I have no money to pay you."

"Paid fer already. Drink and welcome," the girl answered with a thick Cornish accent. "Yer standing where I was last summer. It ain't so bad. I'll be a free woman in another three years."

Not me, Kate thought. What had the sheriff said? Twenty years? In twenty years she would be an old woman with gray hair, her life over. The cider was bitter and had an aftertaste, but the liquid soothed her dry throat. Who knew what cider was supposed to taste like in the Colonies?

By the time the first of the women were called, it was growing dark. Torches were lighted and the crowd gathered closer. Kate's head felt light and her stomach queasy.

"Do you feel funny, Maggie?" she asked.

"No. Yer jest scared, that's all. Chin up, girl." Her friend winked. "Don't settle fer none less than a squire."

"Step up! Step up!" the magistrate called. "Don't miss this chance to procure a fine servant! Every one guaranteed to be sound. No toothless and none feeble. Terms, seven to thirty years, a real bargain."

"Tyburn fodder," an onlooker called. "Knife ya in the back some dark night."

"No sir, not a murderess in the lot. Step closer, gentlemen, ladies. You'll not see a lot to match these lassies in the coming season."

"I'm looking for a dairymaid," a woman called from an open carriage. "Are any listed?"

He scanned the paper. "You're in luck, Mistress Longtree. Come forward, Nell, let the lady see you."

"She's in the family way."

"An honest widow, ma'am. You'd not hold that against the girl. Two for one and you'd have the child's indenture till it turned of age."

Kate was hardly aware when Maggie was led away behind a grand carriage. Her own name sounded in her ears.

"Kate Storm, over there, the brown-haired lass. Fair to be a lady's maid or child's governess. Real breeding. She reads and writes a fair hand. Who'll open the bidding on this young woman bound for twenty years?" He motioned. "Come up front, Kate, so the gentlemen can see you. Isn't she special?"

Kate tried to stand and the earth moved beneath her feet. Something was terribly wrong. The cider . . . the cider had been poisoned.

A bid was called from the rear of the crowd and then another. "She's not sick, is she?"

"Guaranteed sound by the apothecary. Gentle breeding, I tell you, just having a case of nerves."

Kate's hand went to her throat. She was unable to speak.

"Did you find the cider sweet?" a harsh voice asked.

Kate blinked. "No," she protested weakly. "Not you."

Joshua Reynolds lifted his walking stick until it touched her chin. "Fifty pounds!" he shouted.

"No."

The captain's seamed face split in an unholy grin. "I'll have you, wench," he promised. "And you shall learn to dance to a new tune."

"Fifty pounds! I have fifty pounds. Who will say seventy-five? Twenty years, gentlemen. This is truly an investment. Who'll say seventy-five?"

"Sixty."

"Sixty from Lord Terrance MacIntire. Thank you m'lord. Who'll say seventy-five?"

The bid was met and raised. Kate struggled to maintain consciousness.

Reynolds was so close she could smell his foul breath. He squeezed her arm viciously. "One hundred pounds!"

"We have one hundred. Who'll say one fifty?"

The crowd was silent.

"One hundred, going for one hundred. Last chance. Going to Captain Joshua Reynolds of the *Maid Marian* for one hundred pounds. Going . . . going . . ."

"Two hundred pounds." A giant in buckskins stepped from the shadows.

"Two hundred, two hundred. Captain Reynolds? Going . . . going . . . gone! To the woodsman for two hundred pounds! That's coin, sir. No promissory notes on this purchase. You have hard money?"

"Aye."

The last thing Kate saw as she pitched forward in a faint were a pair of knee-high, bright beaded Indian moccasins.

Chapter 7

Kate's eyes felt like someone had poured sand in them and attempted to glue them shut. Her head was pounding and her stomach was doing flip-flops. Worse yet, the earth was still swaying. Not only shifting from side to side, but creaking. Creaking? It sounded vaguely like saddle leather. Tentatively, she reached out and touched the familiar outlines of a saddle. She breathed deeply and tried to clear her aching head.

The unmistakable odor of horse filled her nostrils. She was on a horse! She opened her eyes. It was pitch-black but there were trees above and around her. She was riding through a forest and there were definitely other horses behind her. Was it a dream? No. Not she . . . they. She was sitting in front of someone on a horse. The image of Indian moccasins flashed across her mind, and then the memories came flooding back. The auction and the leering face of Joshua Reynolds . . . the bitter cider . . . an Indian. Her indenture had been bought by an Indian! She bit down hard on the inside of her lip to stifle a scream.

Not daring to move and reveal to the savage that she was awake, Kate concentrated on clearing her mind. The smell of horseflesh was familiar and comforting. There were other odors, strange but not unpleasant. Was that the smell of Indian? She was riding in front of a man, a big man, her head cradled against his chest. Soft leather fringes brushed her cheek as he breathed. She struggled to see more of her surroundings, but it was so dark that the outline of the horse's head was no more than a suggestion. How could the rider possibly see where he was going?

"Haven't you played possum long enough, Kate?"

Kate's head snapped up, clipping his chin and causing him to bite his tongue as she spun around to stare into his face. "Pride?"

"Damn it, wench." He struggled to control his rearing horse, hold her from falling off, and free his mouth of blood all at the same time. Half-sliding, half-jumping free, Pride landed in a tangle of underbrush with Kate on top of him. Loud guffaws issued from the trail behind them.

"Ya been in England too long, Lord Ashton!" Jonas roared. "Ya forgot how to set a horse!"

"Or hold on to a woman!"

Pride cursed vigorously as he pushed Kate aside and climbed out of the bushes, reins still caught firmly in his hand. He spat again and felt his tongue with a finger. "You're determined to make a mute out of me, aren't you?" Roughly, he grabbed her arm and pulled her to her feet.

Kate brushed leaves and stickers from her hair. "I didn't know it was you. I thought you were an Indian."

"Who the hell else but me would be dumb enough to pay a year's profit from their land for a woman that can't even cook?" Pride soothed the nervous horse and swung up into the saddle. "Well, what are you waiting for? Come over here so I can pull you up. Or are you intending to walk?"

Kate scrambled back up before him on the saddle.

"Damn woman," he muttered, half aloud.

Bill chuckled.

"Where are we going?" Kate ventured meekly. As much as she hated this arrogant, insufferable colonial, anything was better than the depraved captain of the *Maid Marian*.

"Home." He turned back to his men. "That's enough from you two."

They rode in silence for hours. Despite Kate's efforts to stay awake, exhaustion overcame her and she fell asleep, safely held in Pride's tireless grip.

She opened her eyes as he handed her down into Jonas's arms. "I'm awake," she protested.

Jonas sat her on the grass and she sank down. It was just cracking daylight above the high trees. They had stopped in a small clearing beside a fast-running stream. Bill brought her a tin cup of water and she drank gratefully.

"Don't wait on her; she's not a cripple. By rights, she should be waiting on us. I gave enough for her services," Pride said gruffly. He waved toward the stream. "Wash up if you want, but do it downstream from where we drink and water the horses. We'll stop long enough to cook a bit to eat. You can go off in the trees if you need to, but don't go far. I won't waste time looking for you if you get lost."

"Don't pay no mind to him." Jonas uncinched his saddle and slipped off the blanket. "He's just mad at his own self 'cause he left Annapolis without ya the first time." He examined the bay gelding carefully for any rub spots on his back and led him to water.

Bill chimed in, "Said he was glad to be shut of you. We was miles west when he changed his mind an' we turned back."

"He was shook up some when he got there and found out that old devil Reynolds almost got his paws on ya."

Kate got to her feet unsteadily and went down to the stream. The bank was smooth and sandy. She knelt and splashed the cool water on her face and arms. It felt like heaven. From the corner of her eye, she watched as Pride led his chestnut stallion to drink.

Despite the weeks they had spent in close contact on the ship and the time she had known him in London, Kate felt him almost a stranger. He looked taller, broader in the rugged buckskins. His hair was drawn severely back and caught with a beaded strip of rawhide, and he wore a hat made of animal skin. There was a wild, untamed look about him that frightened her.

It's only Pride Ashton, she reminded herself. He's a gentleman, no matter what he looks like now. He's only trying to scare you.

"What are you staring at?"

Kate's chin went up and she longed to pick up one of

these smooth rocks and heave it at his head. "What happened to your clothes? Why are you dressed like a savage?"

"We're going where there are no roads. What would you have me wear? Satins? Silk?"

"I'm sorry I bumped your chin. Thank you . . . for saving me from Captain Reynolds. I'd have killed him, you know, before I let him touch me."

"I know. You don't have much regard for your neck." He hobbled the chestnut and let him graze on the sweet, thick grass beside the stream.

Kate slipped off her thin slippers and stockings and let her feet dangle in the water. "Why did you do it?"

Pride took a long rifle from his saddle and primed it with powder from a horn container that hung around his neck. "You stay close to camp with Jonas. Bill and I will try to bring down something fit to eat." His eyes narrowed. "None of your tricks. You're out of your element here, Kate Storm. You'll have to learn to depend on us until you develop some common sense, if you live that long." He strode off into the trees without looking back.

Kate dried her feet on the grass and put her shoes and stockings back on. The little clearing was beautiful in the early morning light. The sun warmed her body and the cheery song of a bird overhead raised her spirits. She went over to where Jonas was cutting wood with a small ax. "What's that bird?"

Jonas put two fingers to his lips and imitated the orange-and-black songbird's whistle so perfectly that Kate clapped with joy.

"That's it exactly. What's it called?"

"Oriole. That's the buck; his lady wears softer colors. Pretty, ain't he?"

She nodded. "Can I help?"

"Look around an' see what squaw wood ya can pick up." He grinned. "That's little branches an' twigs for starting a fire. Dry wood's best, dead but not rotted."

"Is it safe to build a fire? Won't it attract Indians?"

"None round here. None we got to worry about anyhow. 'Nother day's ride, be a different story. Might stumble on an Iroquois war party. Only make one mistake like that.'' His eyes twinkled. ''Knew a fella lost his wig that way. Scared the brave half out of his wits, having a scalp come off in his hand thataway. Didn't even stop to tomahawk the fella. Don't guess they'd take your hair though.''

A musket shot rang out. Kate flinched.

''Easy, girl. That's Pride's long rifle. We'd better get this fire crackin'.''

The two men returned shortly, bearing a yearling doe between them. They dropped it by the fire. Pride motioned to the deer. ''Butcher it, Kate.'' He pulled a wicked-looking knife from the sheath at his waist. ''We'll broil the liver for breakfast.''

Kate backed away. ''Not me. I don't know how.''

''You never hunted in England?''

''Of course I hunted. I've killed bucks with neater shots than that one, but the gamekeeper always did the butchering.''

''Skinning's squaw's work, if there's one nearby.'' He flipped the ten-inch knife into the dirt at her feet. ''Get to it.''

Kate recovered the weapon and tested the steel's edge with her finger. It was razor sharp. ''Aren't you afraid I'll use it on you?'' she dared.

Pride shrugged. ''You can try.''

Bill and Jonas exchanged glances, then turned away to busy themselves with the packhorse. Kate nudged the dead deer with the toe of her slipper.

''We'd like to eat some time today,'' Pride said sarcastically.

Kate held her temper. ''Look, I don't know anything about this. If you'll show me this time, I'll try to learn. I don't want to ruin the meat.'' The blue eyes were innocent. ''There's a scent gland somewhere. I know if I cut into that . . .''

''This is a doe. A buck's different.'' He squatted Indian-style beside the animal and held out his hand for the knife. ''I'll show you once. Pay close attention.'' He inserted the point of the knife into the tough skin and began the bloody task.

Bill brought green branches to cook the meat over the coals. He tossed Kate a sack and she unrolled dry apples and small flat cakes of cornbread and spread them on a clean cloth. In a short time they were enjoying the fresh broiled venison. Kate nibbled at hers at first, then downed several large pieces, surprised at how hungry she was.

The remainder of the animal was cut up and suspended over the fire to cook slowly. "It wouldn't keep no time at all raw," Jonas explained.

"We'll get a few hours' sleep while the doe's roasting, then cover some more ground," Pride said, stretching out on the grass. "Jonas, you take first watch."

"Why did we ride at night?" Kate asked, as she and Jonas cleaned up the scraps from their morning meal. "It doesn't make sense."

"He wasn't sure if the captain was goin' to send some of his crew huntin' fer us. Best to put a few miles 'tween our backs an' Annapolis. Pride likes to ride at night. That's the Injun in him. Always does the unexpected."

"What's it like, Pride's home?"

"Best you wait and make up yer own mind, Miss Kate."

"He said his mother lived there," she persisted. "That she was an Indian."

"Menquotwe Equiwa. It means Sky Woman in Shawnee. She most goes by her English name, though. It's Rebecca. Mistress Rebecca is a fine lady. You'll like her."

"Not if she's anything like her son. Does she speak English?"

"Some."

Pride raised up on one arm. "How are we supposed to sleep with you two chattering? You'd best rest while you can, Kate. You'll be a long time in the saddle."

Kate retreated to a deep hollow of grass and curled up in the warm sun. The sky was a bright, brilliant blue, laced with fleecy white clouds. Small insects droned lazily around her. In a short time she drifted off to sleep.

The next two days' journey was much like the first. They traveled by night and slept in the day. On the third afternoon, Kate rode the gray packhorse, his lead strap securely knotted to Pride's saddle. The weather continued fair and clear, a welcome change from the storms at sea.

Sometimes they followed a rough track and sometimes they cut through thick forest or open meadows. The ground became more hilly as they traveled west. Kate was awed by the beauty of the untouched land; it seemed to go on forever. And never once did they see or hear another human being.

The weeks in prison had left Kate soft, but despite aching muscles she refused to give Pride the satisfaction of hearing her complain. Slowly, her body hardened to the ride and she began to enjoy the feel of the horse beneath her. Bill and Jonas were good companions, pointing out colorful birds and game as they rode. Pride, however, remained as distant and cold as he had been that first morning. Any attempt to mend the breach between them seemed hopeless.

"Send me home to England," she'd pleaded. "My brother will pay any reward you ask. I've no wish to go to your plantation, or to stay in this godforsaken country another day longer than I have to." She would not admit to him the magnificence of the wilderness or her joy in it. England was home. England was where she belonged, not here.

"In England you are condemned to death. I bought you as an indentured servant. You may as well learn to like Maryland. You'll be here for the next twenty years."

The black eyes were emotionless, so lacking in any human mercy that Kate began to wonder if the man were truly sane. "You can't keep me here against my will," she protested. "I said you'd be repaid."

"And I said you talk too much. This is dangerous country. Better to keep your eyes open and your mouth shut if you don't want to end up skinned alive by a Mohawk."

That night, Kate nodded in the saddle until Pride took her up before him again. She dozed off and on. When daylight finally came, they were alone in the forest. "Where are Bill and Jonas?" she asked sleepily.

"Gone."

"Gone where?" She looked around. The packhorse was still behind them.

"We've been gone a long time. They've got business to tend to for me." He kicked the chestnut into a trot. "Not far to the house." The stallion tossed his head, still full of spunk despite the extra weight of two riders. Pride guided the horse downhill and onto a well-worn path. "There! Through the trees."

Kate's eyes widened. Set into the hill was a rough house of logs surrounded by a leaning split-rail fence. A half-fallen barn stood to one side, together with several smaller sheds and huts. A dozen shingles were missing from the cabin and the door hung crazily to one side. The single window was unglazed and covered with a rotting deerskin. "That's your house?" she stammered. "Ashton Hall?"

"Well, what did you expect? There's been nobody to keep it while I was in England."

Kate shook her head disbelievingly. "No, it can't be. You said your mother lived here. This place is deserted."

Pride's voice sharpened. "Damn right it's deserted. I told her to put a garden in before she went off trailing her family. Just like a squaw! Come springtime they get itchy feet." He lifted Kate down and dismounted, wrapping the stallion's reins around the nearest fence rail. "Where the hell is my cow?"

"Your cow? Where are your servants?" She glared at him. "You said you owned thousands of acres . . . a kingdom. This can't be Ashton Hall!"

"I got you and the Bennets, and my mother if I can find her. That's enough of us to put in a corn crop. It's too late for tobacco this year. Bossy? Bossy!" A sorry-looking hound crept from the barn and began to bark.

"Is that your dog?"

"Red! Come here, boy!" The graying dog inched closer, lips drawn back in a snarl. One ear hung in shreds, a wound long healed. "Red! Damn you, it's me! Quit that growling." He turned back to Kate. "Just don't stand there, woman. Unload the horses."

Ignoring him, Kate walked up to the house and pulled back the door. The interior was worse than the outside, if that were possible. Something scurried into the corner of the room as she stepped into the house. It was almost too dark to see, so she took a stick and pushed aside the deerskin at the window.

One wall was dominated by a stone fireplace. A ladder and hole led to the second floor. A rough table lay on its side. The only other furniture in the room was a bench and a boxlike bed with rotting straw for a mattress. A few iron kettles and some woodenware were scattered across the floor. Kate took one look and flew out the door.

"I'm not staying in that hovel a single night! I don't know what you're trying to pull, but I wouldn't stable my horses in that hole!"

Pride pushed past her into the house. "Damn Indians stole everything again! Every time I go away this happens. When I get my hands on my mother she'll wish she'd stayed here like I told her to." He picked up a twig broom off the floor. "Here! You might as well start in. Water's down the hill that way. It's a good stream, never goes dry. We got a lot of work to do if we're going to make it livable by night."

"I won't sleep in that place! I'd rather camp out under the trees like we've been doing," Kate protested.

He spun around and grabbed her by the shoulder. "Listen, woman! I'm in no mood to take any shit off you. Take that bucket and fetch some water. Then start sweeping! I'm going to ride over to the neighbor's and see if he's got my cow. When I get back, this place had better look like you did some work, or I'll have the hide off your back."

She picked up the bucket cautiously and backed out the door. He was mad! She was stranded in the wilderness with a madman! She ran down the hill in the direction he had pointed. As soon as she could, she'd steal a horse and ride east by the sun. Anything would be better than staying here with this maniac!

An old trail led to the stream. Kate filled her bucket and started back for the house. Pride and the horses were gone. Kate's trunk sat by the rail fence along with several bundles. There was no sign of the iron-bound trunk or the dog. With a sigh, she went back into the cabin.

For nearly an hour, she swept and scrubbed, setting the bench and table to rights and carrying out the foul straw. The house was damp but she had nothing with which to start a fire. She made three more trips to the stream for water before the pine floor was clean to her satisfaction.

When the room was as fit as she could make it without soap or proper furniture, she ventured up the creaking ladder. The tiny room upstairs was lit by a single open window. The floor was bare except for a pile of acorns and the remains of a blanket. Those she threw out the window, then went back down for the broom and proceeded to sweep the room.

The sky was clouding up as Kate carried in the trunk and baggage. There was nothing left to do, so she took a clean dress and underthings and went to the stream to bathe and wash her hair. Rumbling thunder hurried her along. A brisk wind turned the leaves upward and made the farmyard seem even more wretched as she ran back into the house.

She waited, hungry and cold, as the first drops of rain began to fall. What if he never came back, if he left her here alone to die? "Bastard," she muttered. There was a neighbor; he'd said so. She'd find her way there and convince them to take her back to the coast. Just then she heard the sound of wagon wheels.

A huge farm wagon lumbered around the edge of the barn, driven by a blackamoor. Pride sat on the wagon seat and in the back were two more black men. One held a rope looped around the neck of a brown-and-white cow. The driver pulled the team up close to the cabin and they began to unload the household goods. Kate watched as they carried in a crude bedstead and bedding, two chairs, a tall butter churn, and armfuls of other supplies.

"They had my cow," Pride said, as he pointed out where to set up the bed. The sagging shell of the old bed was tossed out in the yard. "I left the horses over there until I could get another fence up. No sense in chasing them all over the territory."

The men completed their tasks quickly and silently, nodded respectfully to Pride, and then drove off in the wagon the way they had come. Kate looked about the crowded kitchen helplessly. There were piles of cooking utensils and bags of flour and cornmeal and jugs of vinegar and cider everywhere.

"That cow needs milking. You'd better get to it if you're going to put this kitchen to rights before you cook supper. I'll take Red and see if I can bag us a rabbit or two." Pride picked up his rifle. "The house isn't bad, but there are still some cobwebs in that corner."

"You want me to milk a cow?" Kate stared at him in horror. "A cow? Clean the kitchen? Cook? Who the hell do you think I am?"

"My bondwoman."

Kate's fingers tightened on a pewter mug and she hurled it at his head. He ducked and she grabbed the broom and attacked him with that. "You bastard!" she screamed. "You yellow, good-for-nothing, lying, backwoods bastard!"

Pride twisted the broom from her hands and pushed her backward. She landed in the pile of feather ticks heaped on the bed and he gave a flying leap and landed on top of her, pinning both wrists. She exploded in a spitting, biting, kicking mass of white-hot fury.

Seconds passed before he got a firm grip on her again. They were both breathless and their eyes were barely inches apart. "You will," he panted.

She glared back, the blue Storm eyes cold as glacier ice. "I won't. You can beat me, starve me, or skin me alive. But I won't be your damn kitchen slave."

The black eyes leered. "If you won't cook and clean, then I can think of another woman's chore you will do."

"I'll cook," she relented. "But I won't do that."

"Just like a female, always changing her mind." Laughing, Pride got to his feet. "We'll see, Katy, we'll see. For a woman your age, your blood's pretty hot. It shouldn't take you long to get lonely." He retrieved his fallen rifle and whistled for the dog. "Watch out for old Bossy. She kicks when you milk her."

"If she kicks me, I'll cut her head off!"

When she was sure he was gone, Kate threw herself on

the bed and cried. It was a shameful thing to do. She was a Storm and no weakling, but there were times when nothing else helped. She rubbed at her eyes and sat up. She probably looked like something that had crawled out of a rat hole. She ran back to the stream to wash her face and pin back her hair.

It would be getting dark soon, she'd have to hurry. Back in the house, she put one feather tick and blankets over the rope bed. The other two she dragged, one at a time, up the ladder to the little room overhead. She added a blanket and a candle. She'd sleep up here, as far from Pride Ashton as she could get. There'd be no opportunity for any intimacy between them.

How dare he suggest that she hungered for his body? That she would offer herself to him under these circumstances? He would learn soon what she was made of. He had met his match in her!

She went back down to the kitchen and looked for a fire-starting kit. With flint and steel she could light the wood in the fireplace. In the third bundle she found what she was looking for. Luckily there were enough dry twigs to ignite. Everything outside was dampened by the rain. Once the fire was going, she could light candles. When she was satisfied it would stay lit, Kate took a kettle and went out to confront the cow.

The animal was tied to the split-rail fence. As Kate approached, it raised its head and let out a low pitiful moo. The eyes were round and large and stupid-looking. Cautiously, Kate walked around the cow. What side did one milk the thing from? One mounted a horse from only one side, so it stood to reason that there was a proper side for milking.

She set the kettle down and picked some grass for the cow. If it was eating, perhaps it wouldn't notice she was trying to milk it. The animal reached for the grass eagerly and Kate carried the vessel to the business end. Determinedly, she reached for the nearest teat.

The cow swung her head around and made an angry noise. Kate hung on grimly and squeezed. Nothing happened. The bag swung almost to the ground, obviously heavy with milk. She squeezed again and the animal swung her tail, striking Kate in the face. "Stop it," she ordered. "Eat your grass or you'll be breakfast instead of milk." She tried again. Nothing.

The cow stepped sideways, barely missing Kate's foot. Kate butted her head into the beast's side and took a new hold on the teat. To her surprise, a little milk trickled into the kettle. "Good girl," Kate cried. "Good Bossy." Release and squeeze. Release and squeeze. Bit by bit, milk began to accumulate in the bottom of the container.

When the flow ceased, Kate reached for a new teat. It was slow, tedious work, and her hands ached. On the second pull, the cow mooed, lashed out with her tail, and stepped into the kettle with a large dirty foot. "You idiot!" Kate screamed. "Look at what you've done!" All the work for nothing.

Cursing under her breath, she took the kettle to the stream in the dark, rinsed it out, and returned to the cow. She was just finishing up when a man's form stepped from the darkness behind her. She jumped, almost spilling the precious milk.

"Oh! You frightened me!" It was Pride, making no more noise than the hound that padded beside him. "I guess you didn't get any rabbits," she chided.

"I got rabbits."

"No you didn't. I didn't hear any rifle shots."

"Killed them with a rock. No sense in wasting lead."

"You did not kill any—"

Grinning, he held out two furry bodies.

Kate pursed her lips and stomped toward the cabin. The man was infuriating! The milk sloshed in the kettle. At least the damn cow hadn't gotten the best of her!

She carried the milk inside and strained it through a piece of clean linen, then looked around for a place to put the crock.

"You've got to put it in the stream," Pride said, dropping the dead rabbits on the table. "It will sour tonight if you don't keep it cool."

"I know that," Kate lied. "But I need milk to make cornbread for supper. Get those rabbits off the table!"

"Cornbread's not enough. I want fried rabbit for supper."

"If you want rabbit, I suggest you take them outside and clean them!" She busied herself with a bowl and cornmeal. She'd watched Jonas mixing it up, but she wasn't sure how much of what went into the bread. It couldn't be too complicated. He'd just measured by eye.

"This time I'll clean them, but I'm not going to keep doing all your work for you. I'll put Bossy in the barn. You stake her out to graze in the morning after you milk. Don't forget to water her."

In a short time, water was boiling on the hearth for a rabbit stew and she'd dumped the bread dough into a Dutch oven and raked coals over it to bake. She wiped off the table and laid out the pewter plates and a wedge of cheese. This cooking wasn't as difficult as people let on.

Pride brought the rabbits in and she cut them up and dropped them into the salted water along with some dried vegetables and more seasoning.

"I said I wanted fried rabbit."

"You're getting rabbit stew."

It had begun to rain again. Pride carried in an armload of dry wood from the barn and added it to the fire. Then he mended the leather hinge on the door, closed and bolted it for the night. The room began to feel cozy with the rain drumming on the shake roof, the crackling fire, and the smell of baking bread.

"How can a man like you, an English gentleman, a lord, be content to live here in this wilderness in a hut like some half-starved peasant?" Kate asked, as she drew the chair up to the plank table.

"This is my home. I'm comfortable here, and far happier than on my father's estates in England." He sipped at the cider, grimaced, then got up and hunted down a small keg. He poured a mug of dark island rum and sipped at it slowly. "Does wealth mean so much to you, Kate?"

"I'd expected the Colonies to be backward, rustic . . . that there would be certain hardships. But this?" She shook her head. "I was not brought up to be a kitchen slavey. Surely you have responsibilities, people who depend—oh!"

The smell of burning bread became apparent and she jumped up and grabbed for the Dutch oven.

"Don't Kate! You'll burn—"

"Ouch!" Tears filled her eyes as the tips of her fingers blistered. She popped them into her mouth like a child. "Damn it." The oven was clearly smoking and the smell was no longer pleasant. With a poker, she hooked the iron pot off the coals and pushed back the lid. Smoke poured from the interior. "My bread," she wailed.

"Maybe it's only burned on the bottom," Pride sympathized. He filled a bowl with water and offered it to her. "Put your hand in this."

The stew was little better than the scorched cornbread. The rabbit was tough and the vegetables underdone. The two ate in silence with Kate blinking back tears.

"It's not so bad."

"It's awful," she admitted. "I told you I couldn't cook. I told you, but you wouldn't listen."

"At least you didn't do anything to the cheese." He sliced off a bit and offered it to her. Kate shook her head. "Next time, go easy on the salt," he suggested, refilling his mug of rum. "This stew has a real pucker to it."

Kate set her plate on the floor and the hound gulped it gratefully. "Dumb dog," she muttered.

As she cleared off the remains of dinner, Pride climbed the ladder and threw down the feather ticks. "You're sleeping with me," he said. "I don't trust you out of my sight. Besides, it will be cool before morning. I want you to keep my back warm."

"I won't. I hate you!" she cried. "I won't let you touch me."

Pride laughed and spread the feather ticks on the bed.

Chapter 8

Kate lay as far from Pride as she could in the bed. Her muscles ached from the unaccustomed work. She had cut wood, helped to mend the leaking roof, built a section of split-rail fence, and hoed a field to plant corn. And in the two weeks they had been at the plantation, never once had Pride kissed her or tried to make love to her.

There had been no chance for escape. He had left her alone only on days so miserable she could not stir from the cabin. She had been unable to learn what direction the neighbor lived in, or if there were any other human beings within miles. This place had become as much a prison as Newgate.

The bad temper and moodiness Pride had shown on the journey was gone. Usually he was cheerful, leaving her puzzled at his chameleonic behavior. Who and what was he? she wondered for the hundredth time. Was he mad or just playing a bizarre game with her?

"Katy," he murmured.

Kate stiffened. He rolled over and stretched out his hand to stroke her cheek. "Don't."

"Roll over next to me. My feet are cold."

"In June?" The hand trailed gently to her throat and brushed the pulse beneath her skin, sending thrills of delight through her body. "Leave me alone. I'm tired."

Pride rose up on one elbow. "You're the most stubborn woman I've ever known, worse than a Shawnee squaw and that's going some. You know you want me to make love to you. Why are you torturing us both?"

She pushed aside his hand, trying to slow her breathing. Even the touch of his hand against hers was a temptation. "If you have so much respect for your mother's people, why do you always insult the women? Call them that word?"

"What? Squaw? That's no insult. It means woman. The Shawnee regard their females highly. They're cousin to the Delaware and follow many of the same ways. I know of one Delaware chief that's a woman."

"I thought the savàges considered their women to be slaves, to buy and sell as they choose."

"Only white men do that. Some will, I suppose, as tribal laws weaken, and they take on European manners. But Shawnee women are the real power in the village. They own the houses, the children. They can divorce their husbands any time they please, just by saying so in public. What most whites don't understand is the payment given to a marriageable girl's family is a bribe to buy the man's way into her clan. There is no such thing as a bastard Indian child. Every babe has a mother, and an infant takes the mother's family name and clan." The hand was back, tracing down Kate's bare arm. "I've missed you, Kate . . . dreamed about you. It's not such a long way. Come over here," Pride said hoarsely.

"No." She turned her back to him, pretending an indifference she didn't feel.

"Then I'll have to come over there." He rolled over swiftly, trapping her within his arms and pressing his mouth to hers in a gentle, teasing kiss. "Ah, Katy, we could have such a pleasant twenty years if you weren't so hardhearted. Can't you take pity on a man in pain?" He cupped her chin in his hands and gazed provocatively into her eyes. "It's been a long time, darling . . . too long."

The husky voice pierced Kate's wall of defense, and she trembled in his arms, certain he would hear the frantic beating of her heart. "No," she protested faintly. "Don't. I . . ."

Pride brushed feather-light kisses across her lips and down her face to linger on the pulse at her throat. His fingers stroked her silky skin, caressing, tantalizing.

Memories of his lovemaking swept over her and her limbs went languid. "Let me go, you beast," she murmured, unable to keep the amusement from her voice. His hard body, warm against her own, sent chills of delicious sensations through her brain.

"Sweet Kate," he coaxed. His fingers moved down her neck to her shoulders, stroking and rubbing until she sighed with pleasure.

He kissed her again, a slow exploring kiss, and Kate felt a sweet tide of delight spill through her veins. Pride's lips parted slightly, and she welcomed the deepening kiss, meeting his tentative searching with her own.

"You don't know how much I've wanted you," he murmured. His fingers moved down her arms, brushing against the softness of her breasts through the thin cloth. Her nipples hardened at his caress, straining against the material. "I want to touch you. I want to feel your skin next to mine."

Kate's breathing quickened as he brought his head down to kiss her breasts, taking each swollen nipple in his mouth as his hand followed the curves of her body. She buried her face in his hair, inhaling deeply, breathing in the spicy man-smell of him, letting the enchantment wash through her mind and push away the doubts.

"Let me undress you," he begged. With trembling hands, she helped him to slip the gown off and they kissed again. Ever so gently, Pride's tongue probed the secret places of her mouth, awaking the sensual desires she had so desperately tried to suppress.

Little moans of pleasure filled her throat as she stroked the corded muscles of his neck and shoulders. Her hips moved beneath him in the age-old dance of love, teasing, tantalizing, bringing a moist sweetness to her most intimate spot.

Again and again, he whispered her name as he trailed sweet, hot kisses across her burning flesh. Their limbs entwined in a united desire to become one. With a cry, Kate dug her nails into his sinewy thighs as the white-hot flames of passion consumed her body and carried her beyond the point of no return.

Joyously, she received the evidence of his love, arching her back to meet his vigorous thrusts. Caught in a riptide of surging emotion, they became not two souls, but one; spiraling higher and higher, culminating in waves of earth-shattering rapture.

Afterward, they lay in each other's arms, not speaking, hardly daring to breathe, unwilling to risk the loss of the glorious unity and contentment each felt. Pride traced the freckles over her nose solemnly, then kissed each one and licked away the budding teardrops in the corners of her eyes. *"Ki-te-hi,"* he whispered, "how can a woman be porcelain and silk and steel all at the same time? The Great Good Spirit, Wishemenetoo, must have laughed loud and long when he, in his wisdom, created Kate Storm."

"Is that the Indian God?" She snuggled even closer, all thoughts of escape pushed to the deepest recesses of her mind. The candle had burned almost to its end, but the light was enough to reveal Pride's rugged face, and catch the gleam of the obsidian eyes that stared at her with love. She cared not whether he was Christian or pagan at this moment. And if he revealed that he worshipped a savage deity, or none at all, she did not possess the power to move from him a fraction of an inch.

"Wishemenetoo has many faces and many names, but in the end he is only one. I think it matters little to him what name he is called by."

"Do these people know of Christianity, of Jesus?"

"They have their own prophets but will accept Jesus too when they know more of his teachings. To a Shawnee, religion is something to be lived every minute of every day. Ake, the earth is sacred to him, as is Kesathwa, the sun, and Gimewane, the rain that falls from the heavens. Life is sacred to the Shawnee."

"But the tales I've heard . . . murder . . . scalpings."

"The Shawnee are no better and no worse than the English. They are very different, but different is not inferior. There is a lot the two peoples could learn from each other. Sometimes I think being of mixed blood is a blessing, and other times a curse. I'm not really at one with either world." He pulled her head against his chest. "Why do you let me ramble on? I'd rather talk of us, Kate."

"Us?" She kissed him boldly, her eyes sparkling with happiness. "How can there be *us* between Lord Pride Ashton and his bond slave?"

"I'm the slave, Kate." He rolled her on top of him. "Do your worst, mistress," he dared. She did not disappoint him.

Kate awoke with the first light of dawn and lay listening to the birds outside the cabin. Pride lay beside her, deep in sleep. Thoughts of the night's pleasures brought a deep blush to her cheeks. Whatever else this man was, he was a sensitive, virile lover. Could there be some future for them together in this wilderness? She didn't know, not her own mind or his. She wasn't sure what she wanted anymore.

Pride opened his eyes and smiled. "Good morning, sweet. Did you sleep well?"

"No," she laughed. "Not at all. You didn't let me."

"I'll make it up to you. I'll cook breakfast."

"You?"

"I'm a man of many talents." He grinned. "Turn over and sleep a little longer while I hunt up the main course." He swung his long legs over the bed and patted her familiarly on the bottom. "What have you got to lose? I can't be any worse cook than you."

Kate mumbled a reply and snuggled down in the warm spot he had left in the tick. The smell of frying trout awakened her an hour later. "Mmm," she moaned, stretching. "Is that fish?"

"It is, m'lady. *Amatha*. Fresh caught and prepared especially to tempt the palate with a secret mixture of Indian herbs. Will you come down to dine?" he teased. "Or should I have Angus bring up a tray?"

Kate giggled and reached for her wrapper. "Turn your head away." Pride gave an exaggerated leer as a bare breast flashed between blanket and garment. "Tend to your duties, knave," she ordered, catching the spirit of the jest.

The worn pine boards felt cool to her bare feet as she

crossed the room to the trunk. Taking clean underthings and the dress she had laid out the night before, she went outside. "I'll be just a minute," she called back. "Don't eat all the fish."

The dewy grass sparkled like diamonds beneath her feet as she ran toward the stream. It was a glorious morning! She inhaled deeply of the sweet smell of the forest, then paused to listen. Overhead, two squirrels chattered angrily at each other and a mockingbird echoed their quarrel. The sun laid a carpet of speckled gossamer magic through the rustling leaves, and Kate felt as though her heart would burst from the beauty of it all. "It's an enchanted morning," she whispered, and hugged herself with joy.

Hurriedly, she washed in the sparkling water, dried herself, and dropped the homespun gown over her head. She brushed her hair quickly into submission, braided it into one long plait, and tied it with a red ribbon. She was glad she hadn't paused for her shoes; the earth felt so good beneath her feet.

When she got back, Pride was just sliding the fish onto plates at the rough wooden table. Bowls of wild strawberries with cream caught Kate's eye and she clapped her hands like a child.

"Strawberries! Oh, Pride, where did you find them? I love strawberries." He slid back the bench for her and she sat down, her eyes dancing. "How did you do it all?" There was steaming hot tea and a plate of fresh cornbread.

Smugly, he lifted the lid of an iron skillet to reveal a mound of scrambled eggs. "I found the chicken," he boasted. "Thought the foxes got her."

They were halfway through the meal when the hound barked a warning. "Who can that be?" Pride's face darkened. He caught her hand and squeezed it. "Sit. I'll tend to whoever it is and send them on their way." Kate followed him to the door.

A horse cantered down the rough track and slowed as it neared the house. "Who . . . ?" Kate's hand went to her hair.

The blooded bay mare danced sideways, showing off four dainty white stockings, as the elegant rider in a red-

and-silver riding habit and feathered tricorn hat reined her in tightly. A startlingly beautiful woman stared directly into Kate's astonished eyes. "I believe, Pride, that your lark has gone on long enough." She smiled, showing even white teeth and lighting the dark almond eyes with sparks of mischief.

Kate looked up at Pride and he reddened. "What lark? Pride?"

He took a deep breath. "Kate, may I present Lady Rebecca Ashton, my mother. Mother . . . this is Kate . . . Lady Kathryn Storm, late of Queen's Gift and London."

"Your mother?" Kate flushed to the roots of her hair and sank into a curtsy. "Lady Ashton," she murmured. "I didn't . . ."

Rebecca laughed, clear and bell-like. "I imagine Pride prepared you for buckskin and beads." She held out her hands to her son. "Well?"

He lifted her down from the sidesaddle in one easy motion. "We're just having breakfast." He kissed her cheek. "Will you join us?" Taking her arm, he led her into the cabin as graciously as though they had entered a palace ballroom.

Kate stared at the olive-skinned beauty. Her face was oval-shaped and without blemish, the black hair swept into a knot at the back of her neck. She could have passed as Italian or Spanish. There was no hint in her carriage or speech that she was anything other than a great European lady, certainly nothing that even hinted of an Indian savage. As to her age, she hardly looked old enough have a son in his teens, let alone one of Pride's years.

"I'm happy to meet you, Kate. You are all Pride said you were and more. I'll make no excuses for my son; he has a strange sense of humor."

Kate looked down at her bare toes peeking from beneath the coarse gown. She must appear a common slut to this cultured woman . . . her son's whore. She fought back the salt tears of anger. "He does indeed, Lady Ashton."

"Rebecca, please. My husband's titles are of little purpose here. To my friends and family I am Rebecca, and I hope I may count you as one of those." She glanced about the cabin. "I suppose he told you this was Ashton Hall, too."

"Yes."

"Now, Mother . . ."

"Now Mother nothing. You must come home with me, Kate, at once. Pride has avoided his responsibilities long enough. I've had the managing of the plantation since he left for England. He has played, now he must return to his duties." She took Kate's hand. "You can ride behind me on Satin."

"Kate will stay here." Pride's voice tightened.

"She will not. You've had your joke. Enough is enough. Kate?" There was no mistaking the steel in the petite, erect figure.

"And did you bring a horse for me?" Pride said.

"You can walk." Rebecca turned toward the doorway. "Someday, my son, one of your games will go too far and you will lose what you reach for."

Kate bit her lip, waves of mortification sweeping through her. All this was a sham! She had been tricked again. Tricked into giving her body, her . . . No! Damn it! She would not let him see how much he had hurt her.

"I'll be honored to ride with you to your home, Lady Ashton . . . Rebecca, if my *master* will permit it." She glared at Pride.

"When he's silent, you can assume that he's given his permission, however unwillingly." Rebecca led the way outside and waited for her son to lift her onto the sidesaddle.

Hastily, Kate pulled on her slippers and Pride sat her up behind his mother.

"I'll be there by evening," he said.

"I've asked Cook to prepare all your favorites for supper." Rebecca smiled. "Try to be on time. I want to hear all the news from London. But most of all I want to see your book." She touched his shoulder gently. "I've missed you. And there's much you should know of affairs here. War drums roll to the north and west."

"Tschi?"

She shrugged. "You know your brother." Rebecca

straightened in the saddle. "Tonight then." She took the offered reins. "It *was* time." He nodded and she turned the mare's head and tapped her lightly.

The two rode for nearly an hour in silence, following faint trails and crossing several streams. The terrain was slightly hilly and Kate lost all sense of direction. "Is it dangerous to go alone and unarmed here?"

"On Ashton? I think not. This is all land deeded to Pride by his father. Besides, I am not defenseless." From the folds of her jacket, she produced a German pistol. "Pride tells me you are a good shot. It's a skill that comes in handy here."

"He told me that you were an Indian," Kate faltered.

"I am. Shawnee."

"But you don't seem . . ."

"Don't seem to be a red savage?" Rebecca laughed. "Oh, but I am. Don't be fooled by the civilized veneer. Christianity didn't take and I'm afraid many of the moral laws the English live by seem rather silly to me." Her voice softened. "You needn't feel embarrassed by your relationship to my son. If you bring each other happiness, that's all that matters. The Shawnee try not to make judgments on other people's lives."

"Make me happy? He doesn't make me happy! He makes me furious! He's egotistical, arrogant and . . . and a liar! I hate him!" Kate protested.

"Your eyes say different."

"He deceived me! Made a fool of me! Not once, but over and over! He has no regard for me as a human being! He—"

"Don't be so certain. Pride may be a rogue, but he is an endearing one. I think he cares for you a great deal."

"Please, I'd rather not talk about him. A mother would be expected to see only the best in her son, not his failings."

"Perhaps . . . but the Shawnee have a saying. 'Who knows a tree best? Ake, the earth, the mother from which it grows.' Often a mother may know the strengths and weaknesses of her children better than any."

The mare broke into a trot as they left the woods and

entered a cultivated field. Rows of young corn stretched
before them, hoed by more than a dozen blacks. "This is
the beginning of our cropland," Rebecca explained. "It's
not far to the plantation house."

"Does Ashton Hall have many slaves?" Kate eyed the
workers; they seemed young and strong.

"None at all." She waved a greeting and the men paused
to give respectful notice to the mistress. "These men are
indentured servants. We have freemen laborers and bondmen and women of black and white skin, but no slaves.
Pride is against slavery."

"Indentured blacks?"

"Bought as slaves and freed. Most have signed indentures for a number of years. At the end of that time they
may go free as any bond servant."

"You say most."

"The children are free without claim."

"Colonial society must think your son quite mad."

"Others may think what they like. Ashton Hall prospers.
Freemen do more work than slaves and with lighter
hearts."

"Yet he holds me prisoner against my will."

Rebecca turned the mare through a gap in the split-rail
fence and onto a dirt road. The animal's ears pricked up
and her pace quickened. "She's eager to reach the barn
and her new colt."

They crossed a wooden bridge and went up a hill. The
trees covered the road like a living roof, the branches in-
terwoven and bright with birds. Beyond the short stretch
of woodland, tobacco fields stretched on either side of the
road. Here too, workers, both men and women, were busy
keeping the soil free of weeds and insects.

A man rode toward them at a fast trot. He waved and
Kate recognized him. "Bill!"

He reined in and touched his shapeless hat. "Miss Rebecca, Miss Kate. Wondered when you two would make
each other's aquaintance."

"Pride would rather it had been later," Rebecca said
tartly. "He's afoot. Take a horse for him if you've nothing
more pressing to do."

"Yes'm." He grinned boyishly. "Think you'll like this house better'n t'other one?"

"You and Jonas knew what he was up to?" An acrid taste filled her mouth. Everyone had known. Everyone was laughing at her. The sweetness of the past day and night was washed away in a tide of bitterness. She was a Storm! She would be no man's fool, least of all Pride Ashton's.

"Said he wanted to see what stuff ya was made of," Bill admitted. He spat in the dust beside the road and looked at her in dumb admiration. "You'll do, I'd say." He turned his mount back to ride beside them.

A flock of sheep milled in the road and they picked their way carefully through them. A slack-eyed boy doffed his cap. "How do, Miss Becca." His patched hair was the color of straw and his nose a lump slightly off center.

Rebecca smiled. "Good morning, Robin. Are you taking good care of my sheep?"

"Robin is! Robin is takin' care of d'sheep!" he cried. His rumpled features lit and he danced a little jig. The black-and-white collie spun in circles and jumped up to lick the boy's face.

"Robin. This is Mistress Kate. Can you remember that? She belongs to Pride," Rebecca said, speaking slowly and emphasizing each word.

Kate tensed. "Hello, Robin," she said. "I'm glad to meet you."

"Uh-huh. Uh-huh. Robin don't ferget. Pride's Miss Kate. Pride's Miss Kate. See my pretty sheep! Robin takes good care of d'sheep."

"I'm sure you do," Kate replied, her voice softening. "It's a hard job. Mistress Rebecca must be proud of you."

The boy beamed and nodded his head up and down. "Robin don't ferget. Robin watch d'sheep good. Miss Becca like Robin."

"That was kind of ya, ma'am," Bill said as they rode on. "Lots of folks don't take to the boy, jest 'cause he's the way he is. No harm in him though."

"Robin earns his keep," Rebecca added. "It's hard for him to learn anything new, but once he gets it straight, he never forgets." She turned her head to look at Kate and the dark eyes filled with sorrow. "He's an orphan. His parents were building a cabin west of here on the Amaghqua. Iroquois killed and scalped his parents and three sisters. They left him for dead. He wandered in the woods for days before the Shawnee found him and brought him here."

"How terrible." Kate shuddered as she thought of the boy witnessing the slaughter of his family. "It would be enough to drive anyone crazy, let alone a child."

"Back of his skull was crushed in with a tomahawk." Bill spat again. "They lifted part of his hair. Jonas sewed 'im back together but didn't do too pretty of a job. He weren't more'n four or five year old."

"That's inhuman." Kate's eyes filled with tears.

"Iroquois ain't human."

Rebecca laughed coldly. "The British buy Indian scalps, children as well as adults. Robin's mother had black hair. It may well be decorating some mantel in London."

"It were Iroquois," Bill insisted.

"An Iroquois swung the ax, but who ordered it? It's hard to tell white from Indian when the bounty's high enough." Rebecca urged the little mare into a canter. "The house is just ahead."

They rounded a bend in the road and Bill swung open a wide gate. On a slight rise, sheltered by wooded hills, stood a two-story stone house flanked by stone and wood wings. Wide steps led to a long low porch running the full length of the dwelling. Pillars in front of the main section supported a balcony on the second floor.

"It's beautiful," Kate gasped. And it was. The magnificent house seemed a part of the landscape, the solid blocks of stone and graceful windows so natural above the sweeping green lawns, so right. Four double granite chimneys reached skyward, wisps of smoke coming from one on the far right. Kate supposed it to be the kitchens. "Did Pride build this?"

"Lord Ashton, his father, started it—the center part. It's fashioned after his childhood home. Pride designed the wings. There are twenty-two rooms in all. Small compared

to the great mansions of England, but enough for a woman
born in a wigwam to manage.''

''But here, days from anything . . . how did he do it?''

''If one has sufficient funds, anything is possible. Most
of the building materials—the stone, the wood—are local,
taken from Ashton. The craftsmen came from the Virginia
colony; the furnishings and art from England, all over Europe really. My son is quite an educated savage. Wait until
you see his library.''

Kate regarded her closely. Were the dark eyes mocking?
''I'm at a loss for words,'' she murmured. ''Nothing here
in Maryland is as it seems.''

''Nothing ever is.''

The interior of Ashton Hall was as lovely as the outside.
The heavy double door opened to a spacious center hall,
paneled in rich walnut and decorated with carvings of native flowers and leaves. An Indian motif embellished the
cornice, inlaid with various grains and colors of wood. A
wide staircase curved upward to the second floor. Kate
stroked the pineapple-shaped newel cap. The wood was
oiled to a smooth satin finish. A rare Chinese carpet graced
the walnut steps. ''I've never seen anything quite like it,''
she admitted. ''It's a mixture of—''

''Several worlds?'' Rebecca finished. ''As is my son.
Come, let me show you the rest of the house.'' She led the
way through the bright airy rooms. ''Shall we start with
the kitchens?''

Kate was bewildered at Rebecca's attitude. She was no
honored guest, but a bondwoman and her son's whore.
Why was the Indian woman acting as though she were a
member of the family? Silently, she followed, her mind in
turmoil.

Serving girls in crisp white mobcaps bobbed curtsies as
the two passed. Rebecca's manner to her servants was warm
and authoritarian, no different than that of most high-born
ladies Kate had known in England. The house was well-
staffed with mostly white bondwomen. The cook, a man,
was a Welshman and an ex-military man who ran his
kitchen with spotless precision.

''Mistress Kate will be shown the same courtesy I am,''

Rebecca warned the little man. "You will obey her instructions in all things as long as they do not counter my own."

"Yes'm." The cook glared at Kate.

Rebecca led the way outside to show off the dairy and smokehouse and laundry. "He is an excellent cook," she confided, "but inclined to be a bit overbearing. He's a freeman now and could leave if he liked." Behind the house was a kitchen garden with herbs and vegetables. A more formal garden, enclosed by a hedge, stretched behind the two-story section.

"Your flowers are lovely," Kate said. How to ask what she really wanted to know? The small talk sounded trite.

"These are mostly wild. I will have roses but they're not in bloom yet."

Kate took a deep breath. "Please! You must tell me my position here. I'm confused. Am I to be a servant or not?"

Rebecca folded her arms and sighed. "That's the problem. I'm not sure. Pride can be exasperating at times. Technically, you are his property."

"I will not be his doxy."

"Let me show you something." They reentered the great hall from the west entrance and walked to the north wing. Rebecca opened a door, revealing a charming bedchamber. There was a curtained four-poster bed, a fireplace filled now with an arrangement of wild flowers and pine, a delicate French armoire, and a small sitting arrangement. French doors on the far wall opened to a private brick courtyard. "This is to be your room," Rebecca said. "Yours alone. No one may enter without your permission, not even my son."

She caught the doubting look in Kate's blue eyes. "No, you are wrong. This is the Shawnee way. Pride's chambers are down the corridor. You may invite him here, or you may go there if you wish. But no one will force you to give your body against your will." She smiled. "My own rooms are in the south wing; you will have privacy here to fight or love as you wish. But . . ." She shrugged. "As to your exact duties, I don't know. That is Pride's decision. I understand you owe him your life."

Kate blushed. "Yes . . . more than once, I think."

"Then you must pay back the debt you owe before continuing with your life. I cannot give you advice. But I will say it is best not to reject happiness, whatever form it takes."

"You are very kind, kinder than I deserve. But it doesn't change the way I feel about Pride. He has wronged me greatly. I could never trust him again. I don't belong here; my home is England. If I can, I will escape and return there."

"You are honest at least." Rebecca waved a well-manicured hand. "Make yourself comfortable. I must give some instructions for the afternoon's duties. I'll have Mary bring you a tray. Supper will be at six in the dining room. Until then." She smiled and was gone.

Kate dropped onto the bed. The cage had gotten better, but the bird was still a prisoner. What new devilment did Pride Ashton have planned for her? She would play his game on the surface while she planned her getaway. She would spend Christmas at home with Geoffrey or know why.

Until then, she would make the best of the situation. There would be no more lovemaking with Pride. Rebecca would believe the worst of her, but that didn't matter. *She* would know different. She had learned her lesson painfully.

Kate wondered about the mysterious Rebecca Ashton. How had a full-blooded Indian woman become such a cultured lady? Pride said his mother had spent time in England, but still . . . It was almost beyond belief. Kate was curious to learn her story. She liked Rebecca and would like to have her as a friend if possible. It was something she had thought about few women before. Most of all, why did Rebecca remain here, cut off from all civilized contact? She would obviously be welcomed in the best homes. With the Ashton titles and wealth, she could be a leader of London society, even marry again if she wished. Without meaning to, Kate stretched out on the soft coverlet and fell into a deep sleep.

At supper that evening, Pride stood at the head of the table and offered a toast. "To Kate Storm. May she find true welcome and happiness in Ashton Hall.'' His mother lifted her glass and Kate stared stonily at her plate.

He was doing it again! Whenever she had him fixed in her mind, he did the unexpected. The man smiling gallantly at her was again a gentleman of the highest order. His dress and manner were without flaw. He wore the red coat and ruffled stock with ease and style. From under veiled eyes, Kate looked in vain for the rough frontiersman, the brute who had abused her on the trail from Annapolis. Was he insane? She had heard of those who exhibited different personalities in their illness.

There seemed to be nothing of a madman in his behavior toward his mother. They laughed and joked together as friends. She was eager to hear all the news of London and to have him describe the latest fashions.

Kate squelched all attempts to include her in the conversation. She would watch and study him. How else would she know how to deal with him?

The meal was excellent, as Rebecca had predicted. There were fried ham and roast wild duck, all manner of vegetables and breads served with a hearty Spanish wine. The dessert was a triumph of whipped cream and chocolate cake. Kate thought of the plain fare she and Pride had made do with at the cabin and her spine stiffened. He would find out soon enough that his jest had backfired.

After supper, the three retreated into the library for thin cups of steaming chocolate. Kate chose an imported Chinese chair as far from Pride on the settee as she could get. ''You'll have to take lessons from David in the kitchen,'' Pride said. ''She's a terrible cook, Mother.''

''I am no cook at all,'' Kate replied, stung. ''It was never expected of me before. And I have no interest whatsoever in learning.''

Rebecca stood up and kissed Pride's cheek. ''If you'll excuse me, I've been waiting to read through your book now that it's been printed.'' She nodded to Kate and swept from the room in a rustle of silk.

Pride rose and followed her to the doorway. "Let's ride at dawn. You can tell me the war news then."

Rebecca answered, but Kate was unable to understand the language. Pride returned to the settee.

"There goes a remarkable woman," he said. "She knows when to leave."

"And when to keep her mouth shut?" Kate trembled with anger. "She is a remarkable *lady*, hardly the savage . . . the *squaw* you led me to expect. Of course I should be accustomed to your lies by now." She sat the cup and saucer down before it slipped form her fingers. "Don't try to deny it. You lied to me! You made me believe that . . . that hovel was Ashton Hall. Well, I hope you all enjoyed your laugh."

"One thrust at a time, if you don't mind, Katy Storm. First. Menquotwe Equiwa is not one to keep her mouth shut. She once faced down King George himself. I did deceive you about Mother. It's a family joke. It took many years for her to acquire that veneer of sophistication, years of study and practice to perfect her speech. She speaks excellent French, by the way, and reads it. But for all her brave colors, she is still Shawnee. She lives this way by choice . . . first for my father, and then for me."

"But she seems so happy."

"She is now. But she was never happy in England. And she could hardly return to tribal life. This is a no-man's-land we've created for her. This is her world. I like to think she has the best of both."

"But if she prefers the Colonies, why here? Why not Annapolis or Williamsburg? Both I understand are lovely towns. There would be other ladies there, women of her own class. It must be so lonely here for her."

"In England she is Lady Ashton. In Williamsburg she would only be a red savage wearing the clothes of a lady. She would not be accepted there. Times are not what they were. There is bad blood between the colonists and the Indians. The Shawnee are a powder keg and the flame creeps closer."

"Your mother's position hardly explains your lies to me.

Why did you do it?'' Kate demanded. ''Why?'' She had risen from her chair and came closer to stare him in the eye.

''I wanted to have you all to myself for a while,'' he admitted. He reached out to touch her and she jerked away. ''I love you, Kate. I didn't want to share you, not even with her.''

''I believe you wanted me alone, all right, alone and scared, too confused to fend off your advances. You wanted to use me!'' Kate brought the palm of her open hand across his cheek with all her might. ''You bastard!''

Pride's face darkened with anger. Only Kate's handprint was raised in white on the tanned skin. He caught her wrist. ''Don't ever do that again!''

Kate struggled to be free and he pulled her into his lap and pinned her arms. ''Let me go,'' she spat.

''Never!''

''Will you rape me in your mother's house?'' she cried, as he forced her back and covered her mouth with his.

He shoved her aside and stood over her, fists clenched. ''I've never raped you! I didn't need to! You came willingly. Don't lay that to me!'' He touched the fast swelling cheek. ''You should learn to control your temper or be prepared for a broken jaw.''

''Oh!'' she dared. ''Will you break it?''

''Not me, but most men would. You're a shrew! A shrill-tongued, overaged, spinster shrew.''

''Call me what you will. But you'll not lay hands on me again by my consent!''

''We'll see about that, woman!'' Angrily, he strode from the room, leaving the door ajar.

Kate heard a muffled giggle. Doubtless they had provided good sport for the servants' gossip. To hell with him! She didn't care. Carefully, she gathered up the chocolate cups and returned them to the kitchen.

It was too early to sleep. Kate wished she could go outside, walk the plantation grounds, even go to the stables. But suppose she met Pride. She was not prepared for another scene tonight. She returned to her bedchamber and busied herself with unpacking her trunk, which stood at the foot of the four-poster and hanging the things in the armoire. Her garments were much more suited to a servant than a . . . a what? What exactly was she?

The last rays of sun were laying patterns on the polished pine floors as she closed the empty trunk. There was no sound but that of a dog barking far off. The hair rose on her neck and she shivered, unable to shake the idea she was being watched. She turned toward the French doors and let out a sudden scream! A feathered savage stood not ten feet away, staring at her.

Chapter 9

Kate backed away, unable to quench the terror that clutched at her brain and numbed her body. He moved into the room, not as a man would move, but like some great predatory cat.

"Silence!" he ordered. His English was clipped and precise, making the visage all the more dreadful.

His eyes narrowed and he drew closer. His near-naked form glistened with oil and Kate caught a whiff of something putrid. The man's head was shaved except for a strip three fingers wide that ran from his forehead over the top of his skull. It was streaked with red and blue. A single eagle feather dangled from the back. His face was painted black and yellow. A steel trade ax was tucked into the rawhide cord that wrapped about his lithe waist. Clenched in his dark hands was a silver inlaid long rifle.

With an evil grin, he lowered the muzzle of the gun until it menaced her breast. "I do not like screaming women."

Gathering her wits, Kate made a dash for the door. The Indian blocked her path with the barrel of his gun. She opened her mouth to scream again and a form hurled through the French doors. The savage spun to face the new intruder and Kate dodged away.

Pride crouched just inside the room, a knife gleaming in his hand. "Tschi!"

The painted warrior laughed and lowered his gun, easing down the hammer. "Ah, brother. I nearly had you that time. You should be more careful. The French will pay dearly for your head."

Pride stood and laid the knife on a table. He beckoned to Kate. "It's all right. This is my brother, Tschi."

A rush of air filled her lungs and she nodded, too frightened to speak. She backed toward the door.

The Indian spoke in his own tongue and Pride snapped back a reply. Kate's eyes flicked from one to another. They were arguing, that she could tell. Her hand found the doorknob.

Almost like magic, the door swung open. Rebecca stood there, barefoot in a silk dressing gown. "Tschi! Is this the way you come to your brother's home? Can you not wash the stench of war from your hands? Or . . ." Her ebony eyes fastened on the shapeless bundle at his waist. "Or come here without your trophies?"

Kate stared. It looked like human hair. Scalps? For a moment she felt as though she might faint.

Seeing the girl's pale face, Rebecca put a steadying arm around her shoulder. "It's all right. You're in no danger." She glared at the men. "Both of you, out of here, at once!"

"Am I not welcome here?"

"You are welcome, my son. But it was cruel to frighten our guest in this manner."

"Come then, let us go where we can talk. There is no need to frighten my brother's new slave." Tschi's smoldering gaze burned across Kate's body.

"Kate is no slave." Pride's voice was low and deadly. "But she is *mine*. Take care, Tschi."

"Ah, yes. I have taken before what was yours, have I not?" He laughed and Kate shivered. Her first impression was right; this was no man but a beast.

Rebecca watched as the two men went out into the garden, then closed the French doors and locked them. "Will you have a maid to stay with you?" she asked. "No harm will come to you here. Tschi is a dangerous man, but he knows how far to test Pride."

"He . . . he is your son? That . . . that man?"

"Pride and Tschi are born of different fathers. I was a widow when I met Ian. Tschi remained with my people. He is Shawnee."

Kate composed herself. "No, I will be fine. It's just that

he startled me. He came through the doors there. I didn't expect . . ."

"You did not expect a warrior to invade your chambers. There is no need to feel ashamed. You did not know. The fault was his." She patted Kate's arm. "I must go to them now, before blood is shed. They cannot be together more than a handful of minutes without fighting. Sleep, Kate. Tomorrow will be better."

Kate nodded, unable to hide the distress in her blue eyes.

"I will send Bill to sleep outside your door."

"No, please. I feel foolish enough. Thank you just the same."

Rebecca nodded approval. "Good. Until tomorrow then."

There was no question of sleep. Kate lay awake, starting at every creak, every rustle of leaves from the tree outside her window. Overriding the fear was shame, the shame of cowardice. She had screamed like a common tavern wench. Since when did a Storm quake and shiver at a half-naked savage? Surely they were all enjoying a good laugh at her foolishness. She wondered if Pride had been in on the joke.

It was well after the witching hour when a low voice called her name and a tap sounded on the glass of the French door. "Kate." It came again.

She crossed the room, heart pounding. "Who is it?"

"Pride. I want to talk to you. Can I come in? Unlock the door."

"Why should I trust you?"

"Because I could kick the damn thing in if I wanted to. Come out here if you'd rather."

There was no need to dress. She had never taken off her clothes. Cautiously, she unfastened the latch. "Only to talk," she warned. "I mean it."

"I'm in no mood for your body tonight if that's what you're worried about." He led the way into the boxwood garden. They followed a curving brick walk until they came to a bench.

Nervously, she sat beside him. "Well? What is it?"

"I'm sorry about tonight. I had no idea he was within a

hundred miles of here." He reached for her hand and she snatched it away.

"No, don't touch me." She sighed. "I was terrified. I thought he was one of the Iroquois everyone keeps talking about. He doesn't look much like a friendly Indian."

"He isn't." Pride's voice was full of concern. "You stay clear of him. He's gone now, but if he comes back . . . Well, it's best if you avoid him altogether."

"But he is your brother, your mother's son. Why . . . ?" The moon broke through the clouds, illuminating the garden. Kate caught the sweet scent of apple blossoms.

"Listen to me. War is about to break out between the French and the British. If that happens the Colonies are caught like a nut in a vise. The French are paying the Indian nations to kill the white settlers. Most of the tribes are allied with France. Only the Iroquois show any real interest in siding with England. The Shawnee are on the fence. They hate the Iroquois, the British, and the French. Which way they'll go is anybody's guess." He stood and faced her. "When it happens, not if, anyone with a white skin living west of Philadelphia is in mortal danger."

"Ashton Hall?"

He shrugged. "There is no reason for the Shawnee or any of their relatives to attack us. But we're well within range of an Iroquois strike. Even though their land is far north of here, distance means nothing to an Iroquois war party. It's common for warriors to run from Canada to the Great Smokies in five days and be in fighting shape when they reach there."

"You expect the Iroquois to attack Ashton Hall?"

"I believe it's highly unlikely . . . unless one of their war chiefs decides he has a grudge against me, or has a vision, or . . . You cannot predict what an Indian will do. And the Iroquois are very dangerous men."

"Your mother said the same thing about *him.*"

"She's right. Tschi's power-hungry. He has a following of young braves who will seek glory at any price. He's no fool! He's cunning and he's absolutely without fear."

"You sound like you hate him." Kate glanced over her

shoulder. The garden had suddenly become a place of shadows.

"Tschi?" Pride laughed. "No, I don't hate him. What we feel for each other is a warped sort of love. We've been rivals since we were children. But he taught me to tickle trout and to hunt rabbits with a sling. We shared a lot of good times as well as bad."

"Why did he come here?"

"He heard I was home. And he probably wanted to brag about those Iroquois scalps on his belt."

"No," Kate insisted. "Why did he come to my room? He frightened me deliberately."

"He heard I had a woman and wanted to see what she looked like. It's like him to want to scare you. Tschi has a cruel streak. But he knows better than to harm you." Pride held out his arms. "I'm sorry about the cabin. But what we had there was real enough. Kate . . ."

"No. What we had there was a lie. It's all been a lie. I want no part of you or your Indian wars . . . or your crazy brother! I want to go home." Her back stiffened. "I won't be tricked again."

"You are home, Kate." He motioned toward the house, then followed her back to her room. "Lock it from the inside."

"I will."

"Good night." He caught the door. "Wait. This is stupid. Neither of us wants to be alone tonight. Let me come in."

She forced her voice to coolness. "Once and for all, am I a slave or not?"

"What kind of talk is that?" he said scornfully. "Of course you're not a slave! Katy, please . . ."

"If I can choose, then I choose to sleep alone. Good night, Lord Ashton."

Through the long hours of sleeplessness before dawn, she wondered if she had made the right decision. She could not deny that she desired his body . . . the feel of his lips . . . his touch. But if she were ever to be free of him, it must begin here.

As the first light of morning sun touched her bed, Kate

drifted off to sleep. At noon, a maid tapped at the door with tea and toast.

"Dinner will be a little late today, mum. Mistress Rebecca's out riding with the master. Would you like water for a bath?"

"Yes. Thank you . . ."

"Mary, it's Mary, mum. I'll see to yer bath right away."

The hot water to bathe in was a luxury, but Kate hurried through and dressed in her best gown. She should not have slept so late. Rebecca would believe her lazy as well as wanton.

Lady Ashton was still in her riding habit when she and Pride came into the dining room. She greeted Kate with a warm smile. "Good morning. Sorry to have left you alone, but there was much for Pride to see and much I had to discuss with him." She pulled off her gloves. "Allow me a few moments to freshen up before we eat."

The maid carrying dishes to the table saw the unspoken order in the master's eye and hurried from the room. Kate stood waiting.

"If you are no longer willing to have a relationship with me, you must be prepared to earn your keep. There are no slackers at Ashton Hall."

"And did you think I meant to be?" Kate flushed. "Surely you don't want me here. Should I go to the scullery, or perhaps the fields?" She glared at him fiercely.

"Don't be a fool. I want you to assist my mother. There are records to keep. A plantation is a settlement to itself. You and she seem to get on well. If you will follow her instructions, I will be satisfied. You will keep your own bedchamber."

"And my bed?" she dared.

"And your lonely bed. Checkmate, Katy Storm. I hope your stubbornness will bring you pleasure."

His words echoed in her head in the days and weeks to come. There was much to do, so much that she wondered at the ability of Rebecca to manage when left alone.

First, the house servants must be instructed in the daily chores of cooking and cleaning. There was the garden to be looked after and vegetables to be dried for the coming winter. Records of seed and livestock and indentures must be constantly maintained. Squabbles must be settled between servants and illnesses tended. Sheep must be sheered and wool spun and then woven into cloth. Clothing must be sewn. Meat must be salted and dried. All these things and more fell to the mistress of a great plantation such as Ashton Hall.

Many of the duties were familiar to Kate. She had taken a woman's place at Queen's Gift for many years. But here, in the wilderness, there were far more responsibilities. Once Rebecca realized how capable the younger woman was, she was glad to share the burden.

Kate saw little of Pride except at meals. She knew he rode with his mother each morning, and she often wished for an invitation to join them. In one of her rare moments of relaxation, she had gone to the stables and asked that a horse be saddled for her.

"Sorry, Miss Kate. Can't do it. Master's orders. Yer only to ride with him." The stableboy had doffed his cap, red-faced. "I'm only follerin' orders."

It had reminded her that she was indeed Pride's possession, and must wait on his whim for the simplest of pleasures.

With the coming of full summer, Pride too was busy from early morning until dark overseeing the crops. He had shed his white shirt and rode bare-chested to the fields, tanning as easily as the laborers until he was the color of his Shawnee brothers. He seemed completely at ease on horseback or side by side with a dirt-encrusted bondman, pulling a wagon wheel from the mud. Kate found a growing admiration for the man, in spite of all her determination not to allow it.

With Rebecca she felt an easy rapport. Often they worked side by side for long periods without exchanging a word. Lady Ashton was not one to chatter on idly, but she had an intelligence to match Kate's own, and a well-developed sense of humor.

This morning they had been compiling a list of spices and household ingredients to be ordered from England. It might be nine months before they were delivered. Anything forgotten or misjudged would have to be done without for another year.

"Pride owns a ship, the *Lady Rebecca* that sailed for the Far East nearly two years ago," Rebecca said. "If it's not lost, we'll have treasures aplenty when it docks in Annapolis. He ordered a complete set of dishes and a rug for the center hall. Last time, there were beautiful silks and that hand-painted wallpaper that covers the dining room wall."

"Two years and you've heard no word?" Kate stood on a chair, peering into the the back of a cupboard.

"We lost a ship five years ago, in the Sea of the Japans. Pride can hardly ask for the *Rebecca*. She flies under Dutch colors and pays no duty to the Crown."

"But that's . . ." Kate searched for the right words. "Illegal, isn't it?"

Rebecca laughed. "Half the fortunes of the Virginia and Maryland colonies are made in smuggling. Pride says that Mother England treats us as stepchildren, and as stepchildren we must find our own way."

They continued on for nearly an hour before Kate voiced a question she had longed to ask. "You said you had to leave your oldest son with the Shawnee when you married Pride's father. It must have been very difficult for you. Surely you would rather have taken him with you to England."

Rebecca dusted off her apron and lowered the dark-lashed eyes. Kate thought again how very young and very beautiful she still was. "I'm sorry," Kate apologized. "I shouldn't have asked so personal a question."

"No, I don't mind telling you. It was difficult to leave Tschi behind, but it was the wish of my family. Clans are very strong among our people. My mother and my grandmother forbade me to take him. I could not disobey them."

"Who cared for him?"

"My mother and then an uncle. He was only two when we sailed and it tore out a part of my heart. Pride has helped to fill that hole. Later, when I returned, Tschi was with me at times. But I could not take him from his house family. He and Ian hated each other from the first."

Kate climbed down and closed the cupboard door. "Lord

Ian must have been a very special man. Was he anything like Pride?"

"Yes . . . and no." She smiled thoughtfully. "To me, Ian was very kind, very gentle. To his son, he was steel. He was not a man given to displays of affection. And despite his outrageous action in taking an Indian to wife, he was very set in his ways."

"Have you ever thought of marrying again?" Kate asked boldly.

"Never." She laughed. "I am too set in my ways. My sons are the only men I need in my life, and grandsons when that day comes."

Kate flushed. "Don't look for any from me. I'll bear no bastards."

"Are you so blind? Pride means to make you his wife."

"His wife?" Kate scoffed. "Not likely. He wants me as a whore. He has never mentioned marriage. And I'd not have him if he asked." She gripped the back of the chair tightly. "Never! I can't bear the sight of him," she lied.

Hearty male laughter came from the kitchen doorway. Pride's form was outlined in the sunlight. "Not have me? Not have me? You shall have me, Kate Storm. Not only will you have me willingly to husband, but you'll do the asking!"

"The hell I will!"

He stepped into the room and caught her around the waist, lifting her from the floor and kissing her lightly on the lips. "A fine bride you'll make, too. Shrew or no shrew."

Kate kicked his knee. "Put me down!" How dare he make fun of her? Handle her so before his mother! She looked about for Rebecca, but she was gone.

"I told you she knew when to leave." Laughing, Pride released her and reached for a sweet biscuit from the pewter plate on the table. "You're not getting any younger, Kate. We should start soon if we're going to have an even dozen children. You don't want to be gray-haired and nursing a baby."

Kate backed away, her eyes narrow with rage. "I'll have no baby of yours! And none from any other man either!

I'll not be tied to a squalling infant! I'm my own woman, Pride Ashton, and I'll stay that way!"

"Not until you've served your legal indenture," he answered smugly. "If you hold out that long, you'll be entitled to two gowns, a spinning wheel, some walking money, and a cow. The cow might be as old as you, though."

"Oh!" Too furious for words, she ran from the room. The man was infuriating. To suggest that she would ever ask him to marry her! "Ohhh!" She almost tripped over the downstairs maid in her rush toward the privacy of her own room. She must escape from here, and the sooner the better!

The next morning, Rebecca invited Kate to ride with them. It was on the tip of her tongue to refuse, but caution held her temper. If she had access to a horse her chances of escape would be infinitely better. She accepted.

"Pride said that you ride astride," Rebecca said. "I have some clothes of his that he wore when he was a boy. They'd be more comfortable than your skirts."

"Thank you." Kate smiled. Better and better. Boy's clothing would not only be easier to ride in, it would prove a disguise if she needed one. "I'd like that. And . . . I'm sorry for the scene in the kitchen yesterday. It's just that he makes me so angry."

A maid brought the loose linen shirt and breeches. The shirt laced up the front and the pants were only a little loose. She turned about in front of the mirror in delight. It was a relief to be free of confining skirts and petticoats. There was a tap at the door. "Yes?"

"Mary, ma'am. Master sent you these." The door opened and the girl offered a pair of white deerskin moccasins. "He said yer slippers was gettin' thin."

Kate examined the beautiful patterns of leaves worked into the soft leather.

"Try them on." Rebecca stood in the doorway.

The moccasins fit perfectly. Kate walked across the room, savoring the lovely new shoes. "Did you make them?" she asked.

"Pride did. I did the quill work and beading. That's dyed porcupine quilling."

"They're beautiful. Thank you." Kate could not help contrasting her own hoyden costume with the Indian woman's stylish riding habit.

"If you're ready, I think the horses are outside. We're riding out this morning to check on the lumber crews. We're clearing forest for a new field."

A surly-faced groom held the reins of three horses: Pride's stallion, the pretty bay mare, and a beautiful brown-and-white pinto with a white mane and tail that almost swept the ground. Kate ran forward to stroke the soft nose and silky mane. "He's beautiful," she cried. "What's his name?"

"Meshewa," Pride answered, coming down the steps. "I hope you like him. It means horse in Shawnee." He put his hands on her waist and lifted her into the saddle. "The Shawnee took him in trade from west of the Mississippi. They claim he was a buffalo pony."

Kate gave her attention to the animal, petting and whispering to him. She didn't want to think about the fact that Pride had chosen this beautiful mount for her, or that he had sewn the lovely skin shoes. She didn't want his kindness, only freedom.

"He's yours, Kate." Pride swung up onto the stallion beside her. "No strings."

"With you there are always strings." Kate leaned low over the gelding's neck and whispered his name, "Meshewa." The black ears flicked and he tossed his fine-shaped head. "Good boy," she crooned. "Good Meshewa."

The groom gave Kate a look that said he understood and she returned a genuine smile. The man was tall and broad-shouldered, with short-cropped brown hair. His small eyes were gray and he wore a short beard. She nodded to him as they urged the horses into a trot and away from the front steps of Ashton Hall.

"Who is that new groom?" Kate asked Rebecca.

"Pride?"

"His name's Simon. I moved him from the field to the stables last week. He had some problems adjusting to the

other men. He's bound for twelve years.'' Pride regardly
Kate closely. ''Why the interest in one of my convicts?''

''Aren't I one too?'' Kate dug her heels into the pinto
and he leaped ahead eagerly.

''Stay away from him,'' Pride called after her. ''He's
not been here long enough to trust.''

The three cantered down the open road. The pinto had
an even gait; his strong muscles moved easily beneath the
silken hide. Kate breathed in the fresh air and laughed for
joy. How she had missed riding! Since she was a child,
horses had been one of her greatest loves. Meshewa was a
beauty. It would be hard to leave him behind when she left
for home.

''Race you!'' Kate dared, giving the gelding his head.

Pride took up the challenge and galloped after her.

Hard feelings and bitter words were lost in the wonder
of the day. The bright sunshine, the soft breeze, the glory
of the wilderness stretching on and on, lent enchantment
to the day. It was difficult to believe Pride owned all this
marvelous land.

At noon they halted the horses near a running stream and
shared bread and cheese Rebecca had brought in a saddlebag, washing it down with clear cool water. The animals
grazed nearby, nibbling at the tender green shoots of grass
beneath the trees. Kate lay back and stared at the cloudless
gray-blue sky. ''Why are you clearing a field so far from
the plantation house?''

Rebecca coughed, not quite covering a stifled laugh.
''Actually, we're not that far. It's just over that hill.'' She
motioned. ''Pride thought he'd give you a tour of Ashton.''

''You mean we've been traveling in circles?''

''Something like that.'' Pride met Kate's glower with a
boyish grin. ''It was such a good day for a ride, I hated to
spoil it with work. But now we really must see to the lumber crew. They're about a crow's fly that way.''

Kate looked from one to the other. She'd been had *again*.
But she was having too good a time to become angry. ''So
actually, you own twenty acres and we've been riding back
and forth across it like bewildered tax collectors.''

''To tell the truth, I'm not sure how much I own. The

maps are all different. But we measure by square miles, not acres. A lot of the land was acquired by treaty. It's registered in Annapolis but I haven't tried to claim it.''

"Owning land is a concept I still have trouble with," Rebecca confided, "even after all these years as a civilized woman. How can any man lay claim to the earth? How far up can be sold? To the tops of the trees? To the clouds? Earth is *earth.*''

"But I don't understand. Your son, you . . . As Lady Ashton you own vast estates.''

"I follow the English customs in this as I do in many other things I don't understand. May I not honor your ways without accepting them in my heart?'' The dark eyes were compelling.

"Yes, of course. I just . . .'' Kate trailed off. The pinto nuzzled against her and she stroked him gratefully.

Pride caught the reins of his stallion and helped his mother to mount. "I think I'll go back to the house," Rebecca said. "Enjoy your ride.''

Kate was fascinated by the clearing process. They heard the ring of axes long before they could see any of the woodsmen. The tall trees were felled one by one, the branches cut away, and then the logs were hauled by oxen to the sawmill.

"You have a sawmill here?''

"These trees are old. If they die, I can't bear to see them burned uselessly. The lumber can be stored. A lot of it we use on Ashton for building. Prize wood, such as walnut and cherry, properly dried, can be sold in Philadelphia and Williamsburg for furniture-making. If we were closer to the coast, some of these oaks would become masts, but hauling them by land is too difficult.''

The lumbermen greeted Pride easily, respectful but friendly. They answered his questions fully and offered suggestions as to ways in which the land might be cleared more quickly. He introduced her to his foreman, Bo McBane.

The tall Scotsman doffed his plaid bonnet. "Me pleasure, mistress.''

His accent was so thick, Kate could barely understand him.

"You swing that ax like you know what you're doing," she answered.

McBane beamed. "Thank ye, thank ye. Should hope I do. Been twenty yare at it, man 'n' boy."

"McBane's the champion axman in the colony. He won ten pounds last year in a contest."

"I hope you spent your winnings wisely," Kate said.

"Aye, mistress. That I did. Sent back to me home fer a wife."

Pride laughed. "Now whether that's wise or not will have to be seen." He slapped the man on the back. "I've set Simon to work in the stables. I'll keep a close watch on him there."

"He's a bad'n. No honor to the man. A runaway if I ever saw one. And a fighter! Near killed Zeke with an iron wedge."

Kate pretended to tighten Meshewa's cinch. So the man Simon was tough and a runaway. He might be a man she could use, someone as desperate for freedom as she was. He would bear watching.

She and Pride watched as McBane chopped down a young oak. The Scot stripped to the waist and took up a broadax. His strokes were sure and even, a steady rhythm of blows. Chips flew like snowflakes and the tree groaned and then toppled, landing exactly where he had said it would.

Then they rode to the sawmill and Kate patted the muzzle of a roan-and-white ox as Pride gave instructions for the week's lumber. Two brawny men were using a pit saw to cut the square logs into boards. Pride yelled orders over the sound of the saw. Then he showed her how the wood was stacked under a roof to dry.

"The men seem to work well," Kate admitted.

"Most of them are professionals, freemen. Not many bondmen have the strength or intelligence to fell trees or to work here at the mill. I pay them well and they're worth every penny. McBane makes twice the salary he did in Scotland, and I may have to raise that to get him to stay."

They galloped back to the house side by side, riding into the barnyard from a different direction than they had left. The shepherd boy Robin was just coming around the building, a rabbit in each hand.

"Rabbit fer dinner!" he called cheerfully. "Robin's dinner."

"Hello, Robin," Kate answered. "How are you today?"

Pride grimaced and tried to hurry her along. "That's nice, Robin. We can take the horses through this gate." He dismounted and took Meshewa's reins. "You can go on up to the house, Kate. I'll be along in a few minutes."

Robin held up his rabbits proudly. "Miss Kate! Miss Kate like rabbits! You want rabbits for dinner? Robin get Miss Kate rabbits too!"

"No, Robin, that's not necessary," Pride said.

Kate eyed the dead rabbits suspiciously. They had not been shot and there was no blood. How had the boy caught them? "Where did you get the rabbits, Robin?"

Robin grinned. "Rabbit pen. Robin gets rabbits in d'rabbit pen."

"Rabbit pen. What rabbit pen?" Kate slid down from the saddle. "Show me the rabbits, Robin."

"You don't want to see them," Pride protested. "Just a few caged rabbits."

"Uh-huh." Kate followed the boy across the yard and around the chicken house. There was a large wooden slat pen. Inside were dozens of rabbits. Kate turned to face Pride. "*Just* a rabbit pen? And I suppose if someone wanted rabbit for dinner, all they'd have to do was open the door and pick one up by the ears?"

"In a manner of speaking."

"You told me you killed those rabbits with a rock!"

"Well I did, sort of," Pride answered sheepishly. "I just didn't say where they were caught first."

"Mighty hunter!" she taunted. "I suppose the trout came out of a cage too."

"No, they came out of the stream."

She spun on her heel and walked toward the house. "I'll never believe anything you say again, Pride Ashton!

Never!'' She could not stifle the giggles. Killed them with a rock. And she'd believed it! ''Mighty rabbit killer!''

During the evening meal, Kate and Rebecca shared a laugh over the stone-killed rabbits. ''And I believed him,'' Kate repeated. She glared across the table at Pride. ''Great Indian hunter.''

''I can kill them with a rock, if I've got time and if I'm hungry enough,'' he insisted. ''Mother? Tell her.''

Rebecca shrugged. ''I don't remember any rabbits. Wasn't that your brother?'' She and Kate exchanged amused glances. ''I'm sure of it.''

Pride and Kate rode out often after that, sometimes with Rebecca but more frequently alone. They shared laughter and warm companionship but Kate would permit no further intimacy. And if the warm summer days were full of happiness, the nights were hell.

Night after night she awoke in a cold sweat. Pride Ashton was winning. Against all her determination, he was making her love him again. How easy it was to forget England, to forget Queen's Gift and her brother Geoffrey. How simple it would be to settle into life here in the wilderness as lover of this determined and charming man.

In the dark hours before dawning, Kate often walked the herb garden alone. The net was tightening. No matter that the strands of the net were golden. She, Kate Storm, was being caged. Once she gave in, either sexually or by consenting to become Pride's wife, she would give up all control of her own life.

How often she had seen it at home. One gay intelligent girl after another wed and immediately lost not only sense of identity but status as a human being. A woman could not come or go without permission from her husband. He could beat or starve her, shut her away in some lonesome country house, or even have her put to death, without fear of retribution.

Kate was not sure if any of her father's estates or wealth had escaped confiscation by the Crown. But if it had, then she certainly was an heiress. Kate's mother had left vast holdings to go to her daughter. Now that her father was dead, these would be hers. With wealth she could surely buy her pardon. And if she married Lord Ashton, all would come under his influence.

No answer had come of her letters to Geoffrey. Not knowing where he might be hiding, or even if he had left England, she had written to several of his closest friends. Had Pride sent the letters? How could she be sure? They could have been lost in the long journey or his friends might have been afraid to trust her and reveal Geoffrey's whereabouts. A hundred things could have happened to prevent her receiving an answer, and fifty of those things began and ended with Pride Ashton.

It came around again to trust. He expected her to trust and believe in him, to hand over the rest of her life to him. A man who had lied to her how many times? A rogue who had deceived her from the first moment she met him!

As a child she had been raised on tales of kidnapped maidens who had come to love their captors. Even then, the stories had not rung true. How could one love a man who held you prisoner? Who committed rape? Her own case was not rape; the word was too harsh. But under other circumstances she would never have succumbed to his advances.

Her own great-great grandmother had been captured by a Scottish brigand and carried off into the wilds of his own outlandish country. The plan had been to force the lady to wed him. But she had held strong. Her brother's men had made a daring rescue and the lady, honor bright, had come home to make an honorable marriage. Could she, Kate, do any less?

Perhaps Pride Ashton did care for her. But he could not see she was his equal, no possession but a human being. He could not comprehend *honor* in a woman! He would soon find another, a female more easily dominated.

For her, there was only one answer. She was too far away to expect rescue. Geoffrey could have no idea where she was. She must escape and she must do it soon. While she still could . . .

It was only natural that Kate go often to the stables to see to her pinto, and only natural that she speak kindly to the stableboys. It was easy to make Simon's acquaintance and to observe his behavior.

The man was sullen, but not stupid. He was well-spoken and did not have the look of an ordinary thief. By his speech Kate guessed he was from somewhere near the Welsh border. She had never heard of the village he named when she asked. He had been in the Colonies for two years before coming to Ashton Hall. So much the better. He should have learned something of the land and its people. As a candidate for an accomplice, Simon seemed ideal.

As the crops ripened on Ashton Hall, Kate's plan followed suit. Pride would learn he was not the only one who could practice deception.

Chapter 10

A violent summer thunderstorm gave Kate the opportunity to take shelter in the barn. She stood just inside the big double door until her eyes adjusted to the dimness of the interior. Meshewa smelled her and whinnied a greeting. "Hello, boy," Kate called. "Good boy." She went to the roomy box stall and hugged him.

A figure at the far end of the barn was mucking out a stall. There seemed to be no one else in the barn. Kate waited a few moments, soothing the pinto, flinching when thunder cracked overhead. Storms had never been a favorite.

She was wearing the loose shirt and breeches. They had become a habit when she was riding. The comfort was overwhelming. They gave such freedom in walking that it seemed natural to wear them more and more. Pride and Rebecca humored her and there was no one else to shock with her unmaidenly behavior. Rebecca had produced several more shirts and had set the maids to sewing. If Kate wished to wear boy's clothing she could, as long as she appeared properly dressed for dinner.

When she was certain they were alone, Kate went to the tack room for a currycomb. Cautiously, the man followed.

"Sure you weren't seen comin' in here?" Simon questioned.

"The way it's raining outside it doesn't matter. Have you thought more on what I said?" Kate stared at him arrogantly. If Simon were to help her escape, he must remember his position. She couldn't have him think she was afraid of him or that she wasn't the one in control. Pride was right. He was untrustworthy. But one could hardly choose a church deacon for what she had in mind. She had dealt with tougher men than him before.

His eyes narrowed, and he scratched at his beard. "I don't know. I could be hanged if I'm caught. We know where you'll end up." He laughed unpleasantly.

"I can provide the horses and the supplies. Once we reach Philadelphia I know of a banking house where my father has friends. They'll provide us with funds to take passage on a ship home." She folded her arms and leaned back against the door, pretending a coolness she didn't feel.

"And what's to keep yer fancy friends from turning us in fer the reward? There's always a reward for runaway bond servants. Never saw a banker yet wouldn't sell his own mother fer two shillings."

"Not these men. They've reached the position they have by keeping confidences. Besides, my family did them a favor a long time ago." There was no need to keep her voice low. The drumming of the rain on the cedar roof and the howl of the wind were enough to lose their voices in the emptiness of the stable.

"You'd trust them?"

"With my life. The Storms and the . . . Never mind. There's no need for you to know their names. Your job is to lead us west and then northeast to Philadelphia without being caught."

"Be a sight easier to ride straight east." He stepped close to her until she could smell his unwashed body. "Be less nights to spend in the woods together."

"And where do you think the search party will look first?" Kate made a sound of disgust. "You're getting your freedom and you'll be well-paid. But don't think for a minute that I won't blow your brains out if you forget who you are and who I am. You're being hired to do a job. If you can't do it, I'll find someone else who will."

"What's to keep me from carryin' the tale to Ashton? He'd pay well to hear it."

"Try it. And I'll tell him you tried to rape me. Who do

you think he'll believe?'' Kate's chin went up. ''I've no
doubt you feel the same toward me as I toward you. But
we need each other. What say you? Are you game?''

''When?''

''On Friday morning, Pride's riding to Annapolis. We'll
give him a few hours' start and then head out in the opposite direction. I won't be missed until nightfall if I give
reason for skipping the dinner hour. I want to reach Philadelphia in plenty of time to sail for England in good
weather. Friday?''

Simon nodded. ''Friday. But I warn you. Once I'm free
of here I'll not be slowed down by a woman. You'll keep
up with me or be left in the woods. Clear?''

Kate laughed. ''I wouldn't worry about it.''

The following day, the weather cleared and she and Pride
rode out to investigate a report that a squatter was building
a cabin south of Ashton Hall. They traveled fast and hard
for two hours, following first a faint trail and then cutting
across a rocky meadow and over a series of hills. Kate had
lost all sense of direction and the trees overhead kept her
from taking a bearing by the sun.

''Are you sure you're not lost?'' she asked finally. A
blackberry thicket had tangled her hair and left Meshewa
with bloody scratches down his sleek sides.

''No.'' He reined in the chestnut and motioned her to
silence. ''Thought I heard something.''

Kate listened. There was no sound at all, no birds, nothing. Puzzled, she stared hard into the woods around her.

''Get down,'' he ordered, slipping from his saddle.
Wrapping the reins around his waist, he pulled the long
rifle from the saddle holster and checked the priming.
''Keep your horse quiet.''

Kate held Meshewa's head and waited. Sweat trickled
down the back of her neck. Her legs cramped from standing still. What was it? What had he heard or not heard?
What danger were they in? Her mouth felt dry and she bit
at her lower lip.

Minutes passed. A bird whistled and Kate nearly jumped
out of her skin.

Pride's hand clamped over her mouth. He pushed her

down to the ground, and she crouched there, terrified. The bird sound came again from a different direction. ''Deet-dee-dee.''

Meshewa moved restlessly and Kate pulled a handful of grass to pacify him. The chestnut stood like a statue, not a muscle moving.

A squirrel chattered directly above them, and Pride relaxed. He helped Kate to her feet and then onto Meshewa's back. ''We've got to go back,'' he said. ''Right away.''

''Why? What was it?''

''It sure as hell wasn't a towhee.''

Kate frowned. The little bird was one of her favorites. ''But it sounded like—''

Pride swung into the saddle. ''If it was, he was near six feet tall and wore Iroquois markings. Let's ride!'' He turned his stallion's head in the direction they'd come.

''Iroquois? Is it safe?''

Pride ignored her. There was nothing to do but follow. Once out of the thick woods, he urged the chestnut into a hard trot. His rifle lay across his saddle, ready.

''You saw them? Which way were they heading?'' Kate reined Meshewa close, and for a moment their legs brushed. She ignored the little thrill which ran through her whenever she touched him. The fear was receding, overridden by a sense of adventure. She hadn't seen or heard anything that indicated Indians. How had Pride known they were there, if they really were?

''I saw them. Ten, maybe fifteen, not counting scouts.''

''On horseback?'' Kate asked, disbelieving. She'd heard no animals either.

''On foot. The main war trail's farther west along the Blue Ridge Mountains. They shouldn't be here. That's why we're heading home.'' The stallion turned onto a deer trail and Pride pushed him into an easy canter.

The August sun was hot. Meshewa's sides were soon streaked with sweat. He gave no sign of tiring, though, as he followed willingly in the chestnut's path. Kate rode on, trying to ignore the dryness of her mouth and wishing they'd cross a creek soon.

When they did reach a river, she didn't have to be told

to water Meshewa first, or to allow him only small sips. It was a relief to dip her head completely under and to splash water over her sweat-soaked body. Pride kept an uneasy vigil as they rested the animals and shared the food in their saddlebags.

"I should have brought Jonas with me, or Bill," he admitted, breaking the silence. "But I wanted a day alone with you."

"Jonas? I haven't seen him since I arrived at Ashton Hall."

"He's been up in Pennsylvania for me, acting as scout for the military. He just got back last night. That's why I didn't ask him to come. He was worn pretty thin."

"What do you mean, scouting for you? You mean the King's regulars?" Kate took another long swallow of water. It was heavenly.

"His Majesty's advisers don't have the faintest idea what's going on north of here. Jonas knows his business. He can help a few British soldiers keep their hair without starting an all-out war. I sent him, along with a letter of recommendation. He was of use to Colonel Ayers-Smith as well as to me. The news he brought back was all bad." Pride ran a hand through his dark hair. "You're to stay close to the house while I'm gone, Kate."

"If it's so dangerous, why are you going to Annapolis?"

"It's urgent that I be there for the governor's conference." He tightened the chestnut's cinch strap and mounted. "Let's not waste any more time."

They were crossing a rock-strewn meadow when Kate spied a movement in the tall grass. "Oh, look! What's that?" She reined in the pinto to get a better look.

A black furry ball waddled toward her. "Pride, look! It's a bear cub!" It was hardly bigger than a pup, with a little pink tongue and coal-black eyes.

"Get—"

Pride's warning shout was lost in the savage roar that emitted from the throat of the mother bear as she hurled herself toward Kate and the pinto.

Meshewa screamed and reared, panic-stricken by the musty scent of bear. Kate rose in the stirrups, fighting to keep control of the horse. Pride brought the barrel of the rifle down across the pinto's rump and he bolted toward the woods. Pride fired the rifle over the head of the charging bear and wheeled the stallion far to the left.

The sow hesitated. The squeal of the cub drew her attention, and she ran toward it, snarling defiance toward the intruders. She raised on hind legs, peering about with red shot pig eyes, then dropped to nuzzle the crying cub. The hated scent of man drifted away.

Kate clung to the mane of the terrified pinto as he plunged through the trees. Branches caught at her face and hair, threatening to tear her from the saddle. She sawed at the bridle futilely. She didn't know that the horse had survived a grizzly attack as a colt, and nothing could dim the memory of that terror, renewed now by the smell of angry bear!

"Whoa, Meshewa!" Kate cried. "Whoa!"

Pride galloped up a steep bank and into the woods in an attempt to cut her off. "Pull him in a circle!" he yelled, but his words were lost in the crash of brush and snapping branches.

The ground fell away before the pinto, and horse and rider tumbled head over heels down a gully. Kate was thrown clear of the thrashing legs and rolled to a breathless stop. Meshewa's cry of pain cut through her like a knife and she scrambled down the incline, oblivious to the cut on her forehead or her throbbing shoulder. "Meshewa!"

The pinto was a tangle of reins, saddle and underbrush. Tears ran down her cheeks as Kate stripped away the broken saddle and tried to pull free the branches. "Good boy," she soothed. "Good Meshewa. You're all right. You're all right."

Pride appeared at the top of the hill. "Kate? Are you all right?"

"I'm all right! I can't get him up! His legs are tangled!"

"I'll be right down!" Cautiously, Pride urged the chestnut down the edge of the gully.

The pinto gave a low whinny and staggered up. "Good boy," Kate murmured. "Good boy." She felt the slender forelegs anxiously for broken bones, then led him forward a few steps.

Pride reached the bottom and threw himself from the saddle, grabbing Kate by the arms. She flinched. "You're hurt," he said. "You're bleeding." He pulled her against him. "My God, you could have been killed!" Tenderly, he touched the cut on her head.

"Ouch! Leave it alone."

He took her chin, tipped it up, and kissed her. Kate's knees went suddenly weak and she leaned against him, unable to resist the kiss. "Oh, Katy, I thought I'd lost you." His hands were in her hair, stroking her, and his body molded against hers.

"Ouch! Stop that." She rubbed the back of her head. A bump was rising. "Let me see how bad Meshewa's hurt."

"Damn the horse. It's you I care about," Pride whispered hoarsely. He kissed her again. The kiss deepened as she warmed to his touch.

Kate's arms went up to pull him down to her, all caution thrown to the winds. It's the last time, a voice within her cried. The last time. His hand was inside her shirt, covering her swelling breast. She felt her nipples harden and a familiar moistness seeped from the core of her womanhood. Her mouth opened to his searching tongue and then everything went black.

"Kate! Kate!" Pride knelt over her. "Kate!"

She opened her eyes. "What happened?"

"I think you fainted. That blow to your head must have been worse that I thought." He helped her to sit up. "How do you feel?"

"Dizzy. Did we . . ." She blushed as memories flooded through her. They had been . . .

"No. You passed out on me. I've never had a woman do that, one that wasn't drunk, that is. Do you think you can stand?"

"Of course I can stand up." She got to her feet unsteadily. "I couldn't have fainted. I never faint." She rubbed at her aching head. "Meshewa? Is he all right?" She turned to look at the pinto. He stood, head down, with one leg up.

Pride examined the animal carefully. "Nothing broken. Probably pulled something in the fall. It needs wrapping and care when we get back to the stable. Do you think you can ride?"

Kate nodded. She couldn't remember fainting. But if she had, perhaps it was best. Why start up something that could never be finished? She had no resistance to him. In another moment they would have been making love right here on the ground. "I can ride."

"Between the bear and that damn horse we made enough noise to alert the French up in Canada. We'd better head for Ashton Hall. You'll ride with me. He can't carry any extra weight on that leg."

"Is it safe for him to walk on it?" She patted the sleek neck and withers. "Poor Meshewa. Poor boy."

"We can't leave him here. That mother black bear may decide to have him for supper. It might be better for him to walk the stiffness out anyway."

It was long past dark when they arrived at the plantation. A worried Rebecca had waited supper. "Jonas and Bill rode out to look for you two hours ago," she said.

Kate watched as Simon led Meshewa toward the barn. "I'll be out with a hot compress soon," she said.

"You'll do no such thing. You'll go straight to bed," Pride ordered. "I'll tend to your pinto." He looked at his mother. "She fell down a hill and took a knock on the head."

"Kate! You must let me see to it. Pride's right. A bath and bed for you."

"But I'm starving." Protesting, she allowed herself to be fussed over. A bath did sound heavenly, and her shoulder was killing her. "We saw a bear," she told Rebecca. "And Pride said—"

Pride motioned her to silence. "Later, when we're alone." His eyes moved toward the servants. "I'll see to Meshewa first, and then we'll tell Mother."

Rebecca stiffened and she mouthed an unspoken word. Pride nodded and she turned back to Kate, her lovely face a mask of stone. "Come, child," she murmured. "You look like you've had the worst part of a bear fight."

In the morning, Kate was sore but clear-headed. She'd half-expected their encounter with the Iroquois to cancel Pride's trip to Annapolis, in spite of what he'd said, but it soon became evident he was still going.

"No riding out while I'm gone. I shouldn't be more than a week or two at most. I'll leave Bill here to look after things."

"You don't think they'll come back and attack the plantation?"

Rebecca poured another cup of tea. "If they were going to hit us, they'd have done it on their way south. I'm sending a rider to my people. They should know of this. Who and why and if we need be concerned."

"I could hardly ride Meshewa with his leg swollen like that." Kate had been to the stable before breakfast. The injury was painful but she didn't think it would leave him with permanent damage. The worst thing was, she would be unable to take him with her when she made her escape.

"You're not to ride any of the animals. I'll leave word with the stableboys."

"Then I'm to consider myself under house arrest."

"Damn it, Kate! You see, Mother, what I told you. She's impossible."

"Maybe you'd better lock me in my room." Kate stood up, trying to keep her voice soft. "Either you trust me or you don't."

"It's got nothing to do with trust," Rebecca soothed. "I won't be riding out either. Until we know whether there's a state of war, we'll live cautiously."

"It's your safety I'm thinking of and you know it," Pride insisted. He came around the table and put out his hands to her. "Let's not fight before I leave."

Kate brushed him aside and fled to her room. This time she was the one lying, the one deceiving, and she didn't like it at all! It was what she had to do. She had to. She kept repeating that to herself as she wept bitter salt tears into her pillow.

She didn't answer the knocks at her bedroom door or the urgent voice that called her name. Eventually, it stopped and she heard his footsteps receding down the hall.

"Goodbye, Pride Ashton," she whispered. "Goodbye."

Pride rode out at dawn with Jonas and four other armed men. Kate watched from her chamber window, ignoring the lump in her throat. There was no turning back.

The servants were all outside to see the master off. It was easy to slip into Pride's room. She needed a gun and that was the best place to find one.

The floor of Pride's chamber was strewn with animal skins, bear and wolf. The simple pieces of elegant Chippendale furniture were augmented with Oriental paintings and strange wooden masks Kate assumed were American Indian. A bow and quiver hung over the fireplace, the beaded quiver a thing of rare beauty. Books filled the shelves along one wall. A desk held an unfinished map of the colony. A quill lay forgotten on the fine parchment.

Again Kate was struck by the diverse nature of the man. He was as many faceted as a precious gem. She pushed thoughts of Pride Ashton from her head. She would not think of him at all. She began to search the room.

In a desk drawer she found a key. It looked familiar. Had it been the key he used to unlock the iron-bound trunk on the ship? The trunk stood at the foot of the bed, battered and out of place next to the lovely dark wood of the four-poster. She tried the key; it turned easily in the lock.

Two pistols lay inside, along with shot bag and lead. Guiltily, she snatched them up. A folded paper caught her eye. She opened it and scanned the writing. Her indenture. That would do to start her first camp fire. She tucked it into her shirt. She could not resist fingering a leather drawstring bag. Silver coins spilled out on the wolfskin rug.

Kate dropped the bag and fell to her knees. Beneath a cloth were bars of gold. How they glittered, even here in the semidarkness. She let her breath out with a gasp. No wonder Pride was nervous about her touching the trunk. She lifted one in her hand. Gold. A lord's ransom! What might their lives have been worth if anyone had known what they concealed in their cabin?

Well, Pride could keep his gold. She was no thief. The pistols she would borrow, and a little silver to get her to Philadelphia. She would tell no one of the gold, least of all her partner Simon. She closed the trunk and locked it, returning the key. She started for the door, then stopped. Returning to the desk, she dipped the quill in the ink and scratched a message across the corner of the parchment: *Please try to understand. I must be free. Sorry. K.S.*

He would be furious, of course. He might even search for her. But by the time he returned from Annapolis, it would be too late to stop her. She would send his pistols and money back once she was safe in England.

If she could not take a horse openly from the stable, it was simple enough to catch two in the pasture. Only Robin saw her as she saddled a dun gelding for Simon and a rangy black mare for herself. Robin did not approach, but only waved as she rode off into the trees leading the dun. If he remembered which way she had gone, it would mean nothing. She deliberately made a large circle to the place where she and Simon had arranged a meeting.

Kate had almost given up on Simon when the bushes parted and he stepped into the clearing. "I thought you'd lost your nerve," she said. Simon was carrying a long rifle. "Where'd you get the gun?"

"Did you get the pistols?" He held out his hand.

"You're armed. I'll keep these." She handed him the dun's reins. "We'd better ride. I don't think they'll search for us for hours. But the farther we get from the house, the better."

They pushed the horses hard, galloping where there was a trail to follow and keeping to a brisk trot in the woods. Kate kept one pistol thrust into her waist and her eyes on Simon. She let him ride ahead, she didn't trust him at her back.

Kate dug her heels into the black's sides and grabbed a handful of mane as the animal scrambled up a steep hillside. It would be dark soon, but they'd keep a cold camp. No fire tonight and no hot food. It was too risky to build even a small camp fire. There'd been no sign of people, white or red, and that suited Kate fine. She didn't care to see anyone until she reached Philadelphia.

Rebecca's face kept flashing before her inner eye. She would believe Kate a thief and a betrayer of friendships. Maybe she was . . .

They halted the horses when it was too dark to see. Kate spent the night with her back against a beech tree, the horse's reins knotted about her wrist and the loaded pistol in her hand. They took turns standing watch, but Kate hardly slept a wink. If she slept, she might awake alone and on foot.

The second day was much like the first. Simon seemed to know what direction to take. He rarely spoke and Kate held her own tongue. Still there seemed to be no sign of a search party from Ashton Hall. Kate passed the time by trying to identify the trees, those she knew from home and others new to her in the colony. She recognized oak and ash and beech, red cedar and different kinds of pine. It helped to relieve the boredom.

By afternoon, she was catnapping in the saddle. Her eyes just would not stay open. Clouds scudded over and it began to drizzle. Even the rain hitting her face could not shake her drowsiness. When a game bird broke cover almost under the black's feet, the animal started and Kate was nearly thrown.

The fright did the trick. She was wide awake and alert as they swam the horses across a river and then waded a swampy area beyond.

"We're beyond catchin' now," Simon said. He turned to look over his shoulder at Kate. "We've crossed over into the Pennsylvania colony, or close enough. We'll turn east soon."

Kate had to admire the toughness of the man. Coarse he might be, but she could never have made it this far without him. She made an effort to treat him fairly. "There's a little meat left and some bread."

"Tomorrow I'll hunt for fresh meat. I'd rather not risk a musket shot just yet. We'll have a fire tonight. I'm soaked through."

It was the most Kate had heard him speak at one time. "I'd just as soon dry out myself," she said.

It was one thing to decide on a fire and yet another to light one. Everything was damp. Simon struck spark after spark that sputtered out when it touched the wood shavings. At last a small feather of smoke snaked upward and flames licked at the twigs. Kate watched over the fire carefully until the bigger sticks began to burn.

The warmth of the fire seeped through her aching bones and she nodded, jerking upright foolishly. Kate rubbed her eyes and took another bite of the dry biscuit. Shadows were deepening beneath the trees and the sun had already set behind the hills. "Want me to take the first watch?" she offered.

"I'll do it. You sleep." Simon leaned the rifle against a tree and wrapped himself in a blanket. His shirt hung on a forked stick beside the fire. It had stopped raining, but the twilight air was cool and damp.

"No. I'm awake now." She might as well take her turn now. In the long hours of the night it would be impossible to keep her eyes open.

He shrugged. "Suit yerself."

An owl hooted from the stillness of the trees and the black mare cocked her ears to listen, then returned to her grazing. Kate added another branch to the fire. She shivered, wishing for something dry to sit on. Even her moccasins were wet. How good the fire felt. She stretched out her hands to it. There was no sound but the low, even hum of an insect. Without realizing it, Kate drifted off to sleep.

Rough hands seized her and threw her to the ground. Kate opened her mouth to scream and a hand smashed across her face! Dazed, she threw up an arm to protect her head and clawed for the man's eyes with her hands. A shrill cry escaped her lips and Simon cursed.

"Shut up, damn you!" He grabbed her hair and slapped her face hard.

Kate brought her knee up and rolled away. He caught her shirtfront and ripped it away, throwing himself on her and pinning her to the ground. The horses snorted in fright and tried to pull free of their tethers.

"Feisty bitch, ain't you?" Simon backhanded her again. "Don't be high and mighty with me! You been givin' it away to him all along." He laughed. "You didn't think I was ridin' clear to Philadelphia with my britches swole tight, did ya?"

Kate's breath came in ragged gulps and she tasted the salt bite of blood in her mouth. Simon's face loomed out of the darkness inches away from her own and she struck out at him with balled fists. A blow to her left cheekbone stunned her and she fell back.

His weight pressed her to the ground. One hand roughly pawed at her breasts, the other clutched at her throat. He was choking her, cutting off the air! Frantically, she pounded at his face, using precious breath. Black spots danced before her eyes. She felt like she was falling . . . falling.

Suddenly the weight was wrenched away. Simon cursed. Two struggling forms fell into the embers of the dying fire. Gasping, Kate struggled to a half-sitting position. Sparks flew and the horses neighed in terror. The dun broke loose and ran past, trailing a rope. Kate cringed at the thud of flesh against flesh. She staggered to her feet and leaned against a tree.

"Pride," she cried, recognizing the man fighting with Simon. A knife flashed. "Be careful!" Remembering her pistols, she knelt down and felt for them.

A man screamed and Pride fell back. Simon stood over him. Kate grabbed a piece of firewood and struck him across the neck. He took a step toward her and she backed away. Pride was motionless! Simon stretched out his hand.

"No!" Kate yelled. "No!"

Simon fell facedown in the ruin of the fire. Kate began to scream.

"Hush, hush," Pride said. His arms were around her. "It's all right. Hush, now. It's over."

The smell of burning hair filled her nostrils and she bent over, suddenly sick. "Please . . ." She motioned toward the body.

Pride pulled it from the coals and rolled it aside. "He

feels nothing. He's dead.'' Kate began to sob and he pulled her against his chest.

He waited until she had cried herself out and then asked the question she knew was coming. ''Why?''

''I had to. I thought I had to.'' Kate took a deep breath and looked up into his face. ''I didn't want this to happen. I . . .'' She pulled the torn pieces of her shirt together. ''He tried to rape me.''

''And you didn't lead him on . . . promise him . . .''

''No! I didn't!'' she protested. ''I promised him money to help me get to Philadelphia. That's all. Money. I thought I could handle him.'' She was shaking. ''I just wanted to be free . . . to go home to England. You wouldn't let me go.''

Pride's voice hardened. ''So you ran off with a man like Simon Girt, a killer.''

''I didn't know he was a killer. I thought—''

''I don't give a damn what you thought!'' Pride seized her shoulders and shook her. ''You couldn't be that stupid! Not even you!''

''I'm sorry. I'm sorry.'' Kate began to cry again. ''You could have been killed. I didn't mean . . .''

''And Bill? You didn't mean for that to happen either?'' he said icily. He bent and pulled a knife from Simon's body.

''What about Bill?'' Puzzled, she watched as he took the long rifle from Simon's blanket and threw it to her.

''Look at it. Look close. Does it look familiar?''

''No.''

''It should. It's Bill's. Simon killed him to get it. He cut his throat.''

Kate buried her face in her hands and sank to her knees. ''No. No,'' she protested. ''I didn't know.''

Pride kicked dirt over the fire. ''I can't listen to your pleas of innocence now. You can try again tomorrow. Saddle up your horse. We're getting away from here.''

By the time Kate was mounted on the black, Pride had caught the dun and brought his own horse from the woods. He swung up and motioned for her to follow. ''You're just going to leave him here like that?'' she said.

"You're damn right! Let the wolves have him. He's not fit to bury." Pride's hawk face was illuminated by a splinter of moonlight. "Stay close," he warned. "If I have to chase you any farther, I may forget you're a woman and just remember Bill Bennet."

Kate slumped forward in the saddle. Bill was dead and she was responsible. Pride would never forgive her. She would never forgive herself. Bill had been a good friend. She couldn't believe he'd been murdered so senselessly.

They rode for perhaps two hours without speaking. Heavy clouds piled up and the wind began to blow. The rumble of thunder threatened a storm.

Abruptly, Pride reined in ahead of her. "Get down," he ordered. He led the way up a steep, brush-covered incline.

Lightning flashed, revealing an overhang of solid rock, and farther in, the mouth of a cave. Efficiently, Pride hobbled the horses and left them under the shelter and walked to the mouth of the cave. Rain was already beginning to fall.

"There's dry firewood inside. I'll start a fire. We'd best spend the night here. We'd not get far in this storm anyway." He pointed to a spot and Kate sat down.

"How did you know this cave was here?" Kate stared into the blackness, thinking of bats and spiders. The woods in the rain seemed preferable to a forbidding cavern.

"The Shawnee use it for hunting parties. There's a spring back in the rocks. A bear usually winters here, but there's no danger in August. I've been here lots of times." He began to strike a flint. In a few minutes, he had a small fire going.

Kate was grateful for the light, even if it meant seeing the hard set of Pride's features. "You have to believe me," she said quietly. "I didn't know about Bill. He was my friend too. I wish I was dead instead of him."

"Don't talk like a fool. No one wishes they were dead instead of someone else." He leaned his rifle against the wall and began to clean the bloody knife. "Bill deserved to die better."

Outside the rain fell in sheets. Thunder boomed overhead and the wind ripped at the trees. Pride took a clay trade pipe from his saddlebag and filled it with tobacco. He lit it, leaned back, puffed slowly, and let the sweet smell drift across the flames.

Kate stared into the fire. The warmth heated her skin, but nothing could warm the chill she felt within. "Whatever you do to me," she said finally, "I deserve it."

He took another deep puff on the pipe. "I know that."

"Well?"

"Well what?"

"What will you do? No, it's not what you're thinking. I'm not asking for mercy." Kate's back straightened. "It's my fault. Running away was my idea. I killed them both and I'll take my punishment. It's just hard not knowing."

"What do you think?" he said hoarsely. "I'm taking you back, Kate. Back to Ashton Hall. It will be the same as it was before. Except . . . except I won't deceive myself anymore that you feel the same way about me. I've offered you all I have to give. It wasn't enough."

"Offered me? What did you offer me? A chance to be your leman? Your whore?"

"I wanted you to wife and well you know it!"

"Didn't you say I was nothing? A bondwoman. Not Lady Kathryn Storm but Katy, your servant?" Hot tears scalded her cheeks. "You can have me hanged as a runaway, but I'll still be Kathryn Storm when they put me in the grave!"

To her shame, she couldn't stop the tears. She buried her face in her hands and began to hiccup. "Damn it." Her nose was running, and she wiped at it with a corner of her shirt.

"You'd do better to cover yourself with that shirt." Amusement surfaced in his voice.

"What difference does it make? You've seen it all before anyway." Futilely she tried to hold the shirt together with one hand and wipe her eyes with the other. The hiccups came faster.

"Katy Storm, sometimes I think you're older than Eve and other times about ten years old." He came around the fire and took her, protesting, into his arms. "Who said anything about hanging you?" He kissed away the tears.

"You'll probably end up cutting my throat, but I believe you. I want to believe you." He held her against him and rocked her like a child.

At his touch, her resistance melted. There was no fight left in her. He rubbed the back of her neck and stroked her hair. "Did I ever tell you what beautiful hair you have," he murmured. He brushed his lips against hers and then brought them to rest on the faint pulse at her throat. "I was wrong to try and curb your pride, Katy. I've the same damn fault." He kissed her quivering mouth.

She pulled him tight against her, so close she could feel the beat of his heart. The world outside was black and wet and stormy. Here, she was safe. This man would keep her safe; he would hold off the terror.

He kissed her again, and the comfort of his touch pushed away the guilt and fear. Her fingers touched his brow, traced the strong nose, the rugged line of his cheekbone. "You're a fine figure of a man, Pride Ashton," she whispered. "And more at home here than in a drawing room in England."

He laughed. "Praise from you? Ah, Kate, do I love you, or do I lock you away for a hundred years?" Distrust warred with the emotion he felt when he touched her, looked into her eyes. "You're not to be trusted. You never were. But you weave a spell of magic about you, girl. Are you a witch? The Shawnee would call you so."

"The only spell is the one you've put on me," she answered softly. Kate wrapped her arms around his neck and pulled him down to capture his lips in a searching kiss. Desire rose in her brain, and she strained against him, molding her body to his.

"Woman," he threatened. Her tongue teased his lips.

"Love me," she begged. "Love me."

"Ah, Katy." His voice deepened. "Kate."

Pride brushed away the torn shirt, letting the rosy firelight play across the soft round lines of her breasts. His fingertips found her nipples and teased them until they stiffened. Kate moaned and moved against him. He bent his head and kissed each nipple, then flicked it lightly with his tongue.

"Yes . . . yes," she murmured. "That feels so good." A trickle of fire ran from each nipple down across her belly to light hotter fires in her loins.

He cupped each breast in his hand and suckled it until Kate thought she would go mad with longing. She clung to him as he rested her back against the stone. He paused an instant to pull his own shirt over his head and lay it under hers. Kate's hands stroked the broad, hairless chest, lingering on his nipples and gently teasing the scars which crisscrossed the tanned skin.

"Let me," she begged, unfastening the belt at his waist and stripping away his pants.

Pride leaned over her, naked in the firelight, and she gasped at the beauty of his virile male body. A faint sheen of moisture coated his tanned skin, accentuating the superbly muscled frame. "Velvet steel," she teased, running her fingers down the length of his manhood.

"Two can play this game," he groaned. Slowly, deliberately, he slid her breeches down and tossed them aside, revealing her own soft curling fleece. His lips brushed it and Kate arched her back and gave a little cry of joy. "I've waited too long for this to play a boy's game," he laughed. "Sweet, sweet Kate." His fingers touched, explored, found the source of her passion.

"Take me," she begged. "Now." The fire in her blood was a sweet agony. She felt her senses building. She was swept up in a conflagration of desire, rising higher and higher until all control was swept away. She pulled his head up to hers and they kissed. She opened her mouth to him as she welcomed him inside her.

She felt him enter her, filling her with strength, with a wonderful oneness. Slowly, delightfully, he moved within her. She moved her hips against him, taking and giving.

Pride rolled over on his back, pulling her up on her knees so that she could direct his thrusts. "Love me, Kate," he begged. "Love me, *ki-te-hi*." Joyously, they joined their bodies, uniting flesh and soul in a way they had never done before.

They slept away the remainder of the night locked in each other's arms. When Kate awoke there was no guilt left, only joy. Still, when he laughed at her, she hung her head and blushed like a virgin bride. He teased her and their laughter led to another romp on the floor.

"Enough, enough Kate," Pride pleaded. "You'll ruin me."

She laughed. "And now, in the cold light of dawn, tell me, am I to be wife or mistress?" She kissed him soundly. "It doesn't matter. As long as I can be with you. I love you so much."

He pulled his shirt over her head and tied a rawhide lace about her waist. "I'll not have you showing those lovely breasts to all the world." He kissed each one in turn and her nipples rose beneath the material. "Wife, Katy, if you'll have me. And I swear, I have never asked another."

Wife! The word sang in her ears. "Yes," she whispered. "Yes."

"I'll send to Annapolis for a minister. We'll be married as soon as he arrives." From his saddlebag he took a crumpled parchment. "We'll not be needing this." He threw her indenture into the coals and it blackened and burned. "I picked it up by Simon's body. You must have taken it from the trunk."

She nodded. "I would have sent back your pistols."

"I know you would. I never thought you a thief." He raised her chin tenderly and kissed her. "I must share the blame for your running away, Kate. I'm used to having my own way. But it will be different, I promise."

The morning was overcast, but the rain had stopped. There was no reason to linger in the cave, but both hated to leave. Here they had found joy neither was willing to share with outsiders. "I'd keep you here if I could." Pride grinned. "We could live on rabbits and trout."

"If you didn't run out of rocks." Kate's eyes danced with mischief as she curled herself in his lap and laid her head against him. "I've never seen a grown man with skin so smooth."

"And how many grown men have you examined so closely, wench?"

She kissed his lower lip and traced a finger across the haunting cheekbones. "You're like a statue hewn of oak," she murmured. "At least parts of you are oak." She looked down meaningfully.

"God, woman! The Iroquois could use you. You'd torture a man to death." He cupped a warm breast in his callused hand. "I can't get enough of you, Kate." His voice deepened and they kissed, a deep soulful kiss of passion. "I want to give you everything, to make up for what's been done to you . . . to make up for what I've done."

"What I want most is your love," she whispered, "and your respect. I must be me, Pride. Can you understand that? It's in my blood and I can't change." Her eyes begged him for understanding. "And I'll probably never learn to cook."

"You warm my bed and we'll hire a dozen bakers to warm the ovens." Reluctantly he stood up. "We must go, Katy. Mother will be worried. There is bad news from the north. The French . . ." He picked up his rifle. "No need to spoil today with that. We've wedding plans to make, woman."

Together they saddled the horses and strapped on the saddlebags. Pride looked over the stallion's neck at her as she slipped on the black mare's bridle. "You're going to look beautiful pregnant. I want your children, a full dozen of them."

Kate grimaced. "Would you have me slack-hipped and shapeless?"

"If you'd gotten that way carrying my babes." Pride took her waist and swung her up into the saddle.

"And am I suddenly too frail to mount a horse?" she teased.

"Can you not understand? I want to touch you. To know you're real and not a dream. God, how I've dreamed of you, of having you like I did last night."

"Me too," she admitted shyly. "I'll try to be a good wife to you, Pride, although I'm a bit long in the tooth as you say."

"And just how old are you?"

She laughed. "You'd not believe me if I told you."

"Older or younger?"

"What difference does it make? Have I asked you how

old you are?'' Kate bit the tip of her tongue. She was doing it again. Would she never learn to act womanly, even to her lover? Her voice softened. ''I'm twenty-two.''

''When's your birthday?''

She laughed. ''That you'll never know, for I'll not be taunted every twelve months about becoming an aging matron.''

''And how will we celebrate your birthday if . . .'' He broke off and dismounted to look at a sore on the dun horse's side. ''I'll have to treat this when we get back to Ashton. Remind me, it's infected.'' He fingered the swelling where a strap had rubbed. ''Flies can get to an animal this time of year.''

''Shouldn't we be leading them back down the incline?''

''We're not going down; we're going up. There's a game trail over there, hidden by those trees.'' He pointed. ''There's an easier way back, over the ridge. It's steep, but they can make it at a walk. We'll save an hour or two.''

Kate ducked as they passed under the trees. The black's feet knocked loose small stones and gravel as they climbed the hill, but she was surefooted as a goat. They came out on a rocky knoll. ''Oh look,'' Kate cried. The valley spread before them, green and soft in the misty morning. As far as the eye could see was green, interspersed with brown and the gray of stone. A river twisted like a ribbon far to the south. ''I think we crossed that,'' she said. There was no smoke, no sign of human activity. ''It's like Eden.''

''Just don't forget about the snake. Let's ride. This is too exposed to suit me.''

Pride led the way down a nearly invisible trail and across a rocky stream. Kate's hands held the reins, her body molded to the familiar sway of the horse, but her eyes and mind were fastened on the man ahead. Her lips curved up in a smile as she remembered their lovemaking and waited for the night to come.

''You'll not tell me your birthday?''

''No.''

''Then we'll celebrate it today. What do you want for a present? Don't ask for Williamsburg. I can't afford it. Other than that, Kate, whatever you want." He smiled at her and winked. "It's my guilty conscience."

"Let me think about it. No, wait!" Kate kicked the mare and reined in beside him. "I know! Oh, Pride! Find Geoffrey for me! Find my brother. I've been so worried about him. He must be still in hiding, but I know you can locate him. Perhaps we can bring him to Maryland. He'd love it here, and I'm sure he could help you with the plantation." Her blue eyes sparkled. "Geoffrey. That's what I want."

The dark eyes chilled and his features hardened. "We'll talk about it." He urged the chestnut ahead.

"But why?" Kate demanded. "You'd like him, I know you would. Pride, Geoffrey's all I've got left. If I had him here in America, I wouldn't even think of home . . . of England. What's wrong?" The back ahead of her was stiff and unyielding. "Pride? You can't be jealous of my brother."

"I said we'd talk about it later."

"I want to talk about it now."

"Damn it, woman. Must you always have your own way?" He kicked the stallion into a hard trot.

"Pride!" An uneasy feeling crept up her spine. What was wrong? Did he know something about Geoffrey he hadn't told her? "Pride, please!" she called. "We have to talk about this."

He yanked the chestnut up hard. The animal half-reared and blocked the path. Kate's black nearly ran into it. Kate caught her breath as she saw his stricken face.

"Pride! What is it? What's wrong?"

"I wanted to spare you. Geoffrey's dead. He was killed in the coach robbery." Pride leaped from the saddle and caught her reins. "He was shot. He rode away, but the shot took him through the lungs. He bled to death."

A red mist filled Kate's line of vision. She heard words coming from far off, but they were impossible to believe. What was he saying? Something about Geoffrey being shot? "No!" she screamed. "No! I won't believe it. You're lying again. Geoffrey can't be dead! He can't. I saw him ride away. Geoffrey got away. He got away."

Pride pulled her from the horse and held her against him,

pinning the flailing fists. "I'm sorry, Kate. I didn't know him. He was just a highwayman. He would have shot me."

"You? You shot him? You killed Geoffrey?" Her stomach turned over and heat rushed over her body. "I'm going to be sick," she cried.

"Sit down. Put your head between your legs," Pride ordered. He held her as her body wracked with nausea. "Take deep breaths."

Bitter bile rose in Kate's throat. She took slow, even gulps of air. Slowly, the dizziness passed. Pride's words echoed and reechoed in her brain. *Geoffrey was dead. Geoffrey was dead.* She saw his laughing face before her. Geoffrey teaching her to angle for trout . . . Geoffrey leading her pony . . . Geoffrey . . . Geoffrey! she screamed silently. The pain was too great to bear, too great for tears.

Kate stared at the chiseled features before her. "You knew. All along you knew and you let me go on hoping . . . planning."

"I didn't want to hurt you, Kate. I love you and I wanted to protect you."

"He bled to death?"

"There was nothing to be done for him. He died while I was chasing you. He was dead when my man found him. He's buried at Queen's Gift. Dead he was of no interest to the authorities, so I had him taken home when I found out who he was."

"I suppose I should be grateful for that." A coldness spread through Kate, a coldness that forced back the pain, numbed it so it couldn't hurt so much. "All the Storms are buried there. I hope they sent my father there."

"Yes. Kate, look at me! There was nothing I could do. He killed the coachman. I didn't know he was your brother, and if I had . . ."

"If you had, you would have shot him anyway."

"Under those circumstances, yes. I know I should have told you, but I couldn't. I know you were close." He helped her to mount the mare and handed her the reins. "I'm sorry, Katy." His dark eyes begged for understanding.

"Close? Yes, we were close. He was my teacher, my

friend, my idol." Who would inherit the Storm title? she wondered. Had the King given it to another already? It should have gone to Geoffrey's sons. But now he would have no sons. The Storm name would die with her. Mechanically, she followed Pride. The aching inside her gnawed like a live thing. How could you have so much pain and live? They were gone, both of them. First her father and now Geoffrey. Dead. The horses' hooves picked up the sound and beat it into the earth. Dead . . . dead . . . dead.

"It was a dangerous game the two of you played," Pride said. "You must learn that if you gamble for high stakes there is a price."

"You should have lied," she answered flatly. "You should have let me go on believing." Her hands and feet were numb; her mouth tasted like blood. She had bitten her inner lip until it bled. She welcomed the sting. "I would have married you."

"What do you mean would have? This doesn't change things between us, Kate. What's happened between you and me happened since Geoffrey's death. I regret it, but I can't change it. And you can't blame me for it for the rest of your life." He reached out and patted her leg and she flinched. "Your brother knew the chance he was taking. You told me he'd been riding with your father for years. They were outlaws, Kate."

"But not then. You don't understand. It wasn't real. It was only to free my father, to give him an alibi." Her voice was clear and unwavering. If she kept talking, she couldn't hear the *word* echoed by the horses' hooves.

"It's a shock to you. You've had a rough time these last few days. Once we're home, you'll be able to accept it," Pride reasoned. They were crossing an open meadow; the grass was stirrup high. He rode close beside her. "There's a stream ahead. Water will clear your head."

Kate's eyes narrowed. She *had* accepted it. Geoffrey was dead and Pride Ashton had killed him. Everything was hollow and burned away. There could be no wedding. There could be nothing between them anymore, nothing. She could never look at his face and not remember.

They dismounted at the stream and led the animals to water. Pride tried to take her in his arms, tried to soothe her hurt, but she would have none of it. His pleas were greeted only by stony silence. And then, when he knelt to drink from the stream, Kate took a rock in her hands and struck him on the back of the head.

Chapter 11

Pride crumpled forward into the water with a groan. Kate plunged in after him, catching his arm and dragging him to the grassy bank. Had she hit him too hard? No, he was breathing. But the back of his hair was turning an ugly rusty brown. She examined the cut; it was fast swelling, but not too deep. She held it shut until the bleeding stopped.

"I'm sorry, Pride," she whispered. "But it had to be this way. It had to." She laid the rifle and his saddlebags beside him. He would be awake soon. She had to be gone before he came to. If she rode fast and hard, he'd never catch her on foot.

Tears were flooding her eyes, making it hard to see, as she swung up onto Pride's saddle. She would lead the other horses. "Goodbye," her lips moved without sound. She slapped the reins and forced the chestnut stallion into the stream.

Branches slashed at her face and body as she urged the horse into a gallop. Faster! Faster! He would hunt her like a wolf. She knew it. But he'd not catch her, not this time. She'd ride and ride until she reached the sea. She'd put the ocean between them.

She rode until the red hide of the stallion was white with sweat and his sides heaved. Then she reined him in, just long enough to mount the black and gallop on. Somewhere, the dun's reins had pulled free. The animal followed for a while, then stopped to graze and was left behind. Kate didn't care. She had her head start. Once before she had raced Pride Ashton. This time would be different. This time she would be the winner.

Darkness caught her unaware. She had lost all track of time and direction. For the past hour she had been riding in a circle. Now, without the light, she could not identify the lightning-struck oak she had passed before.

Both horses were exhausted, the black near to dropping. When the mare stumbled for the second time, Kate slid from her back and began to lead them. She only knew she must keep going.

An owl hooted just ahead and Kate jumped. She slipped a pistol from the saddlebag and checked the priming. She was so weary she could hardly walk. Her legs were stiff and her back ached. Stubbornly, she put one moccasined foot ahead of the other. If her body hurt enough, she could not think.

A chilling cry rent the air! A form hurled toward Kate from the trees above and she screamed. She squeezed the trigger of the pistol. The muzzle roared and the form fell with a moan. The black pawed the air and galloped away. Frantically, Kate tried to mount the chestnut in the darkness.

A hand closed on the back of her shirt and yanked her around. She brought the empty gun up to use as a club, and something struck her wrist. A cry of pain escaped her lips, and the pistol dropped from her useless fingers. The odor of bear filled her nostrils. Indians! Kate flung herself backward under the hooves of the stallion. The chestnut reared and struck out at the man.

Kate grabbed on to the animal's mane and was dragged back along the trail, desperately trying to pull herself up on his back. Two shots rang out and the chestnut stumbled. Kate lost her grip and rolled. Before she could catch her breath, a heavy weight landed on her back, and her head was yanked from behind. Cold steel kissed the base of her throat.

"Matchele ne tha-thai."

"Do it, you bastard, if you've got the nerve!" Kate was long past terror. Better to die quickly than by torture.

The Indian laughed and eased the pressure on the blade.

With one motion, he pulled her to her feet and stared into her face. "What have we here? My brother did not tell me you were a she-panther."

The mocking voice was familiar. "Tschi?" He back-handed her across the face, and she rocked with the blow but made no outcry.

"Silence, woman! You will speak when I say!" He laughed again, a cruel, hard laugh. "What penalty for a woman who has slain one of my warriors and wounded another?"

Other voices came from the darkness. She did not need a translation to understand their meaning. They meant to kill her. She would provoke a quick death if she could. She lowered her head and rammed his stomach, knocking the wind from him. Tschi fell sprawling and Kate scrambled for the trees.

She covered five feet before he tackled her, wrestled her over on her back, and knocked her unconscious with one blow of his fist. When she opened her eyes, she was bound upright to a tree, a tight band around her throat. In the firelight she could make out six men, all painted, half-naked and ghoulish. Her mind scrambled for something solid to cling to.

Tschi! Pride's brother. He had been the one to capture her. They could not be Iroquois then; they must be Shawnee. Would the Shawnee dare to torture her, kill her?

"Ahhh." Tschi grabbed her chin and lifted it to glare full into her face. "The woman of Chobeka Illenaqui. Where is your lover now?" His hand trailed down her neck to cup a breast cruelly. He said something in Shawnee and the others laughed.

Kate spat into his face.

With a cry he pulled the tomahawk from his belt and brought the steel blade crashing down toward her head. Kate closed her eyes, and it missed her flesh by a hair's breadth and sunk into the tree trunk beside her. He brought his face close to hers so that she could smell the paint on his face, smell his breath. "Are you mad, Englishwoman? That you do not fear me?" His nails dug into her shoulder. "You will learn to fear me, mad or not."

"Pride will kill you for this," she lied. Her mouth was dry. If she had not been tied to the tree, she could not have stood alone. "You'll be the one to fear, you red devil!"

"Let him come if he dares. He is a traitor to his people. If he comes here, he will find death." Tschi stalked away.

The Indians were cutting strips of meat to roast over the flames of the small fire. Kate watched helplessly as they ate, joking and talking together. One man, she could see, was in great pain. They had bound his arm and shoulder with leather strips. No, it was a saddle cinch. Had the chestnut broken his arm in the struggle?

Kate would not have believed it possible to sleep in such a position, but finally she did, until a blow brought her full awake. A knife sliced the rawhide. She fell to her knees and was kicked and dragged toward the fire. Tschi put one knee on her chest and tied a thong around her neck. Her wrists were tied behind her back, and they set off single file through the woods.

In the early morning light, she could make out differences in the men. Two were no more than boys, sixteen or seventeen; another was graying at the temples. The wounded brave was in his prime, slim but muscular. He looked at Kate with pure venom in his eyes.

From the corner of her vision, Kate saw something which made her blood freeze. The chestnut stallion, or rather what was left of him, lay on his side in a grotesque pose. A large section of flesh had been cut from his hindquarters. Kate gagged. That magnificent animal to be shot and eaten! She stumbled and was rewarded with a blow across her shoulders that brought tears of pain to her eyes.

"If you fall, you die," Tschi warned.

The pace of the war party was grueling. More than a walk but not quite a run, it was all Kate could do to keep up. If she slowed or took a misstep on the uneven ground, Tschi was quick with blows and curses to drive her on. Soon, she ceased to think. She set all her will to put one foot in front of the other.

Her shoulders ached. It was hard to hold her balance with her hands tied behind her back. The rawhide rubbed raw spots on her wrists, and the raw places became sticky

with blood. Insects buzzed about and bit her. She was helpless to drive them off.

It was mid-afternoon before they crossed a creek. Kate
fell facedown in the water and drank. She didn't care if
they killed her for it. The cold water numbed her swollen
face and she twisted to get her wrists under.

Tschi pulled her up and undid the rawhide, freeing her
hands. "Do not try to run. If you run, you die." He motioned to the ax at his belt. From a skin bag he took a twist
of leather. Inside was a strong-smelling grease. He took
some on his fingers and rubbed it on Kate's face and neck.

She wrinkled her nose at the smell and glared at him.
"What is it?"

He ignored her question and rubbed some on his own
neck. "You are strong woman. Good." He offered her a
dirty chunk of meat from his bag. She shook her head.
"Go hungry then. You will learn to eat horse and be glad
of it."

Kate's mind seized on the last sentence. He did not mean
to kill her right away. Was he afraid of Pride? If only Tschi
knew . . . Pride would hand her over to them willingly
after what she had done. Was he all right? She winced at
the thought of his bloody head. She could have killed him.
He had murdered Geoffrey, hadn't he? His gun had sent
the ball that . . . No, not murder. She could hate him for
taking Geoffrey's life, but it was not murder. Yesterday
she could deceive herself. Today was different.

Tschi pushed her back into line, and they began the trek
again. Kate's mind followed the same course. She had
killed that Indian and it meant nothing. He might have a
wife, family. But she had pulled the trigger in self-defense.
They could hate her for it, but they could not call her
murderer. She wished she had killed Tschi. She would kill
Tschi. The idea formed and crystallized. She had no illu-
sions about escape, but she would not go lightly to the
stake. She would give good measure for her own death.

The trail Kate had left was as clear as if she had painted
signs along the way. Pride followed, cursing the pounding
headache that blurred his vision and slowed his step. He

had trusted her again, and she had betrayed him. He'd known she was distraught over her brother but he'd been too stupid to realize she would run.

That she had taken the horses and left his rifle and supplies meant she hadn't wanted him to die. It was small consolation. Kate Storm was exactly what he had first surmised: a highwayman. She was a thief and a liar.

He had been the fool. He had created a woman in his mind and given her qualities she'd never possessed. And to think he'd come so close to marrying her, to giving her all he had. She would have done well to finish him off while she had the chance. When he caught up with her . . .

Pride wept over the chestnut's body. Those strong legs had carried him many a mile. He stroked the cold neck and closed the sightless eyes. The wolves would have him soon enough.

The ashes of the campfire were cold. They had been gone for hours. A rustle in the trees brought his rifle to his shoulder. He froze and listened. The birds chirped undisturbed. Pride melted into the woods and moved cautiously in a circle toward the spot the noise had come from. Fifteen minutes passed before he reached it and laughed.

The black mare whinnied anxiously, her reins tangled in a tree stump. The smell of a dead horse was in her nostrils and she welcomed a familiar voice. Pride's practiced hands moved over her. She was scratched, but sound. He led her into the clearing and tied her to a tree.

The area had been brushed over with branches. He knew a party of Indians had passed this way and had probably taken Kate. But what Indians? He searched the clearing again, foot by foot, until he found the shallow grave covered with leaves. He dug at the loose soil until he uncovered the body. "Shawnee, by God," he said. He even knew the warrior, a man by the name of Crow Eyes. He had been killed by a pistol ball at close range. Kate? Damn her for a lying whore, but she was tough. Pride had seen Crow Eyes take on three Mohawk warriors and walk away from it. Now the death chant would sound for him and his children would weep.

Pride covered the warrior over and dragged a log over

the spot. The wolves and scavengers would have enough to feast on without disturbing the man's rest. He mounted the black mare and turned her head toward Ashton Hall. He knew where to find the Shawnee. There was no hurry. If they had not killed Kate immediately, he would have time to do what he must.

There was no doubt in his mind that he would find Kate Storm and bring her back. She would serve her years of bondage if he had to keep her in chains.

This time, there would be no commutation of her sentence. She would be his possession, to be used as he saw fit. He spoke gently to the mare, but there was no mercy in the haunting obsidian eyes.

On the third day, the war party attacked a farm and murdered four settlers, taking a pregnant woman and a boy about five years old as prisoners. Tschi ordered the cabin and barn fired and the Indians dropped their victims' bodies into the well before they left.

The young woman prisoner screamed hysterically, throwing herself to the ground in utter desperation. Kate watched in a strangely detached manner, wondering at the uselessness of the gesture. She's wasting her strength, she thought. She tried to convey the message, but the girl just stared at her and jabbered in a strange tongue. Kate pointed at the girl's swelling middle. "Think of your child."

Her wails were cut short by a blow from her captor, the gray-haired warrior. He pulled her up by her yellow hair and tied her to a horse. The child was put up behind her, his waist secured with a length of rope.

Kate smiled at the little boy. He rubbed his dirt-streaked face and stopped crying. His eyes were large and pale blue, his hair the color of corn silk. He was a sturdy child, despite the mosquito bites that dotted his arms and face. Kate laid her finger across her lips and he nodded. He said something to the girl, but she kept sobbing.

"What will happen to them?" Kate asked Tschi. Fresh scalps dripped from his belt.

He shrugged. "What will happen to you, Panther Woman? Weep for yourself."

"Never!" she spat. The blood and gore sickened her. The settlers had never had a chance. She had seen it all from the edge of the woods where they'd bound and gagged her. "What will happen to you when Pride finds you?" He struck her from force of habit, but there was no strength in it. She forced a laugh and was rewarded by a gleam of respect in Tschi's dark eyes. I'm alive, she thought, on the whim of a madman. She would stay alive until she brought about his death.

Tschi took the other horse. Kate walked with the rest. Within an hour, she had lost sympathy with the weeping blond. The stupid chit didn't have sense to know when she was well-off. If she wasn't careful, she'd earn her own death and that of the boy.

Her feet were aching. The moccasins had worn through in two places, and blisters had formed and broken. She picked up a stick to use in walking. Tschi had argued with her about it, but had let her keep it. It would have made a poor weapon in any case. Without it, she might not have been able to keep pace.

Tschi had given her smoked bacon and a piece of flat bread from the cabin. She chewed gratefully as she walked. The bacon was rank but at least it wasn't horse. She shared the bread with the little boy. He grinned and said something in his own language. Kate pointed to her chest. "Kate." She motioned to him and then repeated the action.

Tschi turned in the saddle and snarled at her. Kate lowered her eyes and walked on, but not before she heard the child's reply.

"Sven."

Kate winked at him when Tschi turned his attention to the trail ahead. They were traveling uphill now, and she was having trouble. She breathed deeply and tried to think of her footing. The man behind her was right on her heels.

That night the girl miscarried her baby and died. They left her beside the trail. Kate took her place on the sway-backed gelding with the little boy. There was no saddle, but Kate was grateful for the relief it gave her bleeding feet. The child's arms around her waist were comforting.

Sven chatted in her ear in what she decided was Swedish

and she pointed out simple words like "horse" and gave him the English equivalent. As long as they did not become too loud, Tschi ignored them.

They were heading due west now; Kate could tell by the sun. The weather was hot and humid. Tschi had given her more of the grease and she'd rubbed it on herself and on Sven. She soon grew used to the smell, and it was better than being eaten alive by insects.

Kate was not sure if it was the fifth or sixth day when the band split up. A dark-skinned warrior took the sway-backed horse and the boy and headed out with one companion. Kate sighed. She had come to care for the child; now she would never know what happened to him.

"Kate!" he cried. "Kate!" The man said something to him. Sven turned and waved, the pale face growing smaller in the distance.

Kate forced her expression to indifference. She would not let them know what she was thinking.

Tschi gave the rope a vicious tug, and Kate fell to her knees. She grabbed the tether and held it while she got up. She made a rude gesture, and he laughed and offered her his hand. She took it and scrambled up behind him on the horse.

"Good," he said. "You proud but not too stupid to ride."

Kate stiffened, trying to hold her body away from his. The trail grew rough, and she was forced to put her arms around him to hold on. It was like touching a snake. Not too stupid to kill you, she vowed. This journey would end some time, and when it did . . . She smiled. Let him think what he would, she would have the last laugh.

She heard the dogs long before the village came in sight. She had suspected they were close when the warriors had reapplied their paint and quickened their stride. There were welcoming shouts, and a band of children ran from the woods. Dogs barked and circled underfoot, and a young woman threw herself into a warrior's arms. Kate steeled herself for what would come in the village. Would she be tortured as Tschi had threatened? Just how much courage did she possess?

The village was a large one, and all the people turned out to greet the returning war party. Laughter turned to wails of mourning when the realization came that one man had not returned. Kate shuddered. She had been responsible for that death. What mercy could she expect here?

The houses were little more than bark huts, scattered about the clearing in no particular pattern. Kate was surprised at the cleanliness. Tschi passed through the houses until he reached a bare piece of ground before an oversized building. He shoved Kate off the horse. A circle of curious faces soon surrounded her.

A woman shoved her way through the crowd, her face contorted with grief and rage. She let out a scream when she saw Kate and leaped at her with hands outstretched like claws.

Kate sidestepped her and blocked her with one arm. The woman seized a handful of Kate's hair and scratched at her face. Tschi roared with laughter. It was too much. Kate doubled up her fist and struck the screecher full on the chin. She tumbled backward into the dirt. A half-dozen women swarmed over Kate, punching and kicking.

Kate went down under their blows, but the women scattered when a musket shot exploded. Bleeding, Kate staggered to her feet. The screecher still sat where she had fallen. Tschi waved the rifle and shouted an order; the women backed off. He pointed toward a hut with the rifle barrel.

Kate had to duck her head to enter. It was dim inside. She stepped down into a dug-out floor. The frame of the hut was made of bent saplings with a covering of bark sewn together. There was a fire pit in the center of the dwelling, and bags and baskets hung from the wooden supports.

Kate had taken no more than a few steps when Tschi came in behind her. He said something in Shawnee, laughed, and seized her wrist. She tried to twist away, and he tripped her and threw her to the dirt floor.

"Let me go, damn you!" she cried.

He twisted her arm cruelly and bound her hands behind her back again, then bound her ankles. Finally, he took a strip of leather and wrapped it around her eyes and head.

"No! Don't!"

"Silence, woman, or I will find cloth for your mouth," he threatened.

Kate lay panting, holding back the tears.

"Tonight much sing! Much dance! Burn Iroquois captive. Maybe burn white woman too." He gave her a savage kick and she gasped in pain. "You not be brave long under the knife, English." Animallike, he padded away, and Kate was left in darkness.

She pressed her face against the dirt and tried not to panic. To be sightless was almost more than she could stand. Her heart felt like it was going to burst through her shirt.

Tschi was trying to frighten her. Trying to? He had frightened her. She was petrified. If she didn't get control of herself soon, she'd have no chance to survive long enough to kill him. She forced herself to breathe slowly. She must think rationally.

Was it possible they had brought her back to the village to burn her at the stake? She had seen no Iroquois captive. If he was lying about that, perhaps he was lying about the rest.

The smells of the hut were strange but not unpleasant. There was a musky smell of animal hides and a lingering odor of mint. A dog must make its home here, too. Bread had been cooked in or over the fire sometime recently. Identifying the various scents helped to dull the fear.

She heard shouting outside and a drum began to beat. Someone stuck a head inside the hut and shouted to her. It was meaningless. She tried to rub the blindfold away, but she couldn't. There was laughter, and someone entered and poked her with a hard object.

"Stop that!" she yelled. "Untie me."

Giggles. Then a gush of water poured over her.

"Damn you!"

A barking dog came into the shelter and began to growl and snarl at her. The giggles came again.

"Who are you?" Kate demanded. "Let me see you." Her hair was yanked. "Ouch!"

The giggler poked again. A stern voice, a woman, called

something and Kate's tormenter ran from the hut, followed by the dog. Kate lay and waited.

Hours passed. The merriment outside had risen to frenzy level. The drumbeat had become a throbbing, interspersed with musket shots. Kate's mouth was parched. Moist heat pressed about her. There was not a breath of moving air in the hut. Her mind was filled with memories of the cool running stream they had crossed. Then, above the laughter came the scream.

Kate jumped, and the shrill cry came again. It was inhuman. No, all too human. It was a shriek of agonizing misery. "No," she murmured. "No." She wanted to cover her ears, but there was no way. She held her breath and waited for it to come again.

Tschi's laughter filled the hut along with the strong smell of rotgut whiskey. "You like? You come and see!"

Strong hands pulled her upright and jerked away the blindfold. "Give me my pistol," Kate begged. "And we'll see who laughs." A blow rocked her head and she would have fallen but he held her.

"Outside, woman!" A knife cut the bonds at her ankles and she stumbled outside.

Tschi pushed her through the crowd to the edge of the open space. A stake had been set into the ground and a man was tied to it. His contorted face was lit by the dancing flames of a half-dozen fires. "See what the Shawnee do to enemy!" Tschi boasted. "Maybe you next, Panther Woman."

The Iroquois was naked, his body blackened with paint and charred flesh. Arrows stuck from his legs and arms and his feet were heaped with burning coals.

Tschi pulled Kate's head up. "Look well," he ordered.

The hellish flames, the tortured warrior, the screams, all blended into one spinning ball and Kate fell backward into a bottomless pit.

Someone was carrying her. She tried to scream and a hand clamped over her mouth. Tschi? "No!" she tried to cry, but her words were muffled. She struggled and he laughed. Her efforts were useless against his sinewy bulk. "I'll kill you!" she screamed silently. "I'll kill you!"

He threw her to the ground and dragged her kicking inside the hut. She crouched there, her eyes wide with terror. "Pride will kill you," she wept. "He will."

"Let him come. He will find only death here. You are my woman now."

"No. I'll kill myself first."

Tschi pushed her to the floor. "Do you think I am fool enough to let a slave escape me?" He dropped beside her and pinned her against his body. "Your flesh is soft, English." He brought his mouth down on her neck and she twisted away. "You are wild like the panther." He laughed. "Good. I will enjoy the taming."

Kate strained against her wrist straps, and one hand slipped free. She lashed out with it and clawed his face. His first blow knocked her back, and she brought her knee up into his groin with all her strength. He groaned and doubled over, and Kate rolled away. Her hand closed on a wooden object and she threw it at him.

"*Aye yea! Tschi!*" An amused male voice. "*Oui-shi-cat-tu-oui!*"

Tschi got to his feet and took an iron collar from a bag on the wall. Stealthily he approached Kate. She tried to dodge away from him, but he threw her and snapped the collar around her neck and tied it to a rope. The other end he fastened to an overhead sapling. "Stay, Panther Woman. Tschi will come back soon."

The other man laughed, and Tschi followed him out of the house with a sharp remark, leaving Kate alone.

She tried the limits of her tether and pulled uselessly at the knot. It was at the back of her neck and too tight to undo. She sat down and rubbed at her aching jaw. "Damn his foul soul to hell."

A little feeling of satisfaction crept through her battered body. If he'd looked for an easy rape, he'd gotten a surprise. She was alive, and the fear was beginning to retreat. If they'd meant to burn her at the stake, they'd have already done it.

She thought of the tortured Iroquois, and her stomach turned over. That bloodthirsty mob had spared her. She didn't know why, but it gave her hope. If she'd had to face what he did . . . She had looked into the face of hell and survived. Kate straightened her back. "You'd be proud of me, Geoffrey," she whispered. Tears formed in the corners of her eyes and she blinked them away. A Storm was a match for a naked savage any day.

"Englishwoman?" A woman put her head in the door. "Do you wake?"

"Yes." Kate eyed her suspiciously. The voice was not unkind, but she'd had no reason to expect anything but cruelty from these people.

"I bring you water." The woman entered the hut and held out a gourd container.

Kate took it and smelled the liquid, then tasted it carefully. It was water. Gratefully, she took deep swallows. "Thank you."

"You are hunger?"

Kate strained to see the speaker in the dim light. She sounded young, but no longer a child. "No. No food."

"No eat, you weak." The English was heavily accented but comprehensible. "What call you, English squaw?"

"Kate Storm."

"Katstum?"

"Kate."

"Kat." She offered the water gourd again.

"Close enough." Kate poured the water over her swollen face. "What is your name?"

"Name? Name . . . Ah, me Wabethe."

"Thank you, Wa-bethe."

"Wa-be-thee," she corrected.

Kate repeated it and the woman clapped her hands and laughed. "What does it mean, Wabethe?"

"Ah, you say English. Big bird. Goose. No. No goose. Swan. Me Swan. Wabethe."

"That's a lovely name."

"Lovely?" She made a sound of satisfaction and began to apply a soothing ointment to Kate's face.

Kate winced. "You don't hate me, Wabethe? Like the rest?"

"Wabethe no hate. Me be Englisher, long time, long

time go. You. Me. Sister. No tear. Shawnee good man. Good woman. No tear.''

"You're English? You're a captive too? How long have you been a prisoner here?" Kate caught at the bare arm. "What's your name? Where are you from?"

The woman giggled. "No Englisher. Shawnee. Shawnee long time. No member white name. No captive. Shawnee squaw.''

"But you're white. You're a civilized woman. Not like them. Did you see what they did to that man? The Iroquois?" Kate's voice trembled and she held tight to the woman.

"I see. You no see! Iroquois brave. Enemy. Good to see enemy die on stake.''

"No, Wabethe. It's not good. They tortured him, burned him. It was horrible.''

"Iroquois enemy." Wabethe shrugged. "Dead enemy. You woman of Chobeka Illenaqui?''

"No. Yes. Well, in a way I am.''

"You his wife?''

"No, not his wife. I was running away, going back to my own people. English people. Tschi captured me in the forest," Kate explained.

"You be wife to Tschi?''

"No!''

"Tschi bad man. Chobeka Illenaqui good man. You fool run from Chobeka Illenaqui. He much man . . . great warrior.'' She let out her breath. "No let Tschi make you tear. He hit, kick. No kill. He want white English for wife. No kill.'' She patted Kate's shoulder. "Maybe you be Shawnee. Choose husband. Is good.''

"No. I don't want to be a Shawnee. I want to escape. I must go home to my own people. Can you help me to escape?''

"You be Shawnee by'm by. You like. Shawnee good man, good woman. Englisher bad. You brave woman, Tschi say Panther Woman, Meshepeshe Equiwa. Kill warrior. Make good Shawnee woman.''

"No. I am English. I must escape.''

"Wabethe go now. Sun come, you eat. Make strong. No tear."

"No, wait. Don't go," Kate begged. The woman ducked out of the hut. For a long time, Kate crouched, waiting for Tschi to return. Eventually, she slept, her body too weary to mind the bare dirt floor.

In the morning, Wabethe came to untie the rope and lead Kate outside. The village was quiet. Only the dogs and a few children were about. In the daylight, Kate got a clear look at her benefactor.

She was perhaps twenty, a tall, slim girl with gray eyes and hair so dark Kate would have taken her for an Indian. She wore her hair in one long braid down her back, secured with a beaded strip of leather. Copper bracelets jangled on one arm, and around her neck was a silver crucifix. Bright tufts of feathers dangled from her ears. A narrow strip of red trade blanket was twisted about her narrow waist. She wore nothing else but moccasins.

Kate blushed and turned her eyes away from the firm pointed breasts that bounced when Wabethe walked. The girl must have been a captive since she was a small child to have forgotten all sense of decency. "I need to . . ." Kate fumbled. "To relieve myself."

Wabethe nodded in understanding and pointed toward the woods. "I take you. I give food. You no run. No hurt Wabethe." She waved a tanned hand. "Braves there and there. Watch. All time. No run. You run, die." She made the gesture of a knife across her throat. "No run, Englisher," she repeated.

"No, I won't." Kate lied. Not now anyway. Not when this girl might be blamed and punished. Not without taking her revenge on Tschi. She glanced about the village.

The coals of the torture fires were dead, the charred post empty of its prey. Two little girls sat on the ground near the big house playing with a doll. It was hard to believe such an obscenity had taken place there the night before.

A dog snapped at Kate and Wabethe threw a stone at it. The animal cringed and slunk off, belly dragging. "No afraid dog," Wabethe said.

"No, I'm not." To the left was a cornfield. The corn

was shoulder high and several small boys stood guard with tiny bows. "Are they playing?" Kate asked.

"No play. Shoot crow. Crow no eat corn. Shawnee eat corn."

"Oh."

Wabethe smiled at her as if she were a simpleminded child. "Corn good." She made eating motions. Kate nodded and Wabethe grinned. "Eat crow."

I probably will, Kate thought, before I get out of here. It can't be any worse than horse. She found, to her surprise, that she was hungry. "Eat?" she said to Wabethe.

A few minutes later, Kate was sitting outside a bark hut eating a bowl of corn mush sweetened with honey. "This is good," she said.

"Dame," Wabethe explained. "Dame . . . corn." She looked at Kate expectantly.

"Dame." She was grateful that the food was soft. Her jaw was swollen, and she was certain two teeth were loose where Tschi had hit her. "Tschi did not come back last night. Do you know where he is?"

The girl laughed. "Tschi sleep another woman." She made a motion with her hand that was impossible to misunderstand. "Another woman be good Tschi. No hit. No bite."

"Let him stay with her. If he comes near me, I'll . . ." Kate's blue eyes hardened. "He'd better stay away."

"No stay away. You slave. Better be wife. Wife strong. No hit." She pointed to the house behind them. "Wigwam. Belong Wabethe."

"Your house? Do you live there alone?" The girl looked puzzled. "Do you have a husband?"

"Husband. Yes," she answer proudly. "Great warrior, Muga Ki-lar-ni. Bear . . ." Wabethe pointed to her tongue. "Muga Ki-lar-ni."

"You have an Indian husband?"

"You stay. No move." She ducked into the house and came out with an infant in her arms. "Wabethe son," she said. "Wabethe wigwam, Wabethe husband, Wabethe son."

God help me, Kate thought. I'd rather be dead than in

her shoes. Trapped here for the rest of her life! She touched the baby's dark hair and forced a smile. "He's beautiful," she said. "A beautiful baby. You must be very proud of him. What's his name?"

"No have. By'm by give name. Son." She unwrapped the chubby infant and put fresh padding of dried grass under him, then laced him into a deerskin and wood cradle board. She hung the cradle board from a tree branch and the baby swung slowly back and forth until he fell asleep. "No beautiful," Wabethe cautioned. "Sick. Ugly. No beautiful son." She winked at Kate to share the deception.

Other people were coming out of the wigwams now. Most looked as though they had been up most of the night. The men ignored Kate, going about their daily business as though she were a natural part of the village. A little boy, no more than three, came and stared at her until his mother called him away. She glared at Kate and said something in Shawnee. Wabethe shouted back.

"That one Tschi sleep," Wabethe whispered. "She want make wife. Tschi sleep. No make wife. That one sleep too much warrior. Paaah!"

"She can have him for all I care." Kate kept her eyes down. Most of the adults were in the same state of undress as her friend. The young children were naked.

Tschi came out of a wigwam across the way. He stretched and called out an order. The child's mother hurried to bring him food. Unconsciously, Kate's hand went to the heavy metal collar. He saw her and laughed. The woman made a remark and gestured in Kate's direction.

"No good be slave Tschi," Wabethe muttered. "Quick you be Shawnee. Take good man husband. No tear Tschi."

"Afraid? No, I'm not afraid of Tschi." She turned her back to him and tried not to feel his slanting eyes boring into her.

"Slave work all time. Wife better." Wabethe stood and looked at Kate's dirty clothes and scraggly hair. "You come river. Make clean. English all time stink bad. Shawnee woman clean. You like."

"Yes, I would like a bath," Kate admitted. She followed the slim woman back through the village, trying to ignore the comments of onlookers. Dogs growled and children ran after them. One even threw a stone.

Wabethe turned and reprimanded the boy, shaking her fist. The child laughed and ducked behind a wigwam. "No tear . . . no afraid, Kat. By'm by no rock."

Several women were already swimming in the river. They put their heads together and giggled as Kate and Wabethe made their way down the muddy bank. "You make swim?" Wabethe asked. Kate nodded, then whitened as the girl pulled off her cloth wrap and dove in. She surfaced and waved to Kate. "Come!"

Kate looked at the other women apprehensively. She had no intention of swimming nude before this audience. If she took anything off, they'd probably steal it. Reluctantly, she slipped out of the moccasins and set them aside, then waded in.

The women pointed at her, giggled, and whispered together. Wabethe frowned. Was Kat so stupid she would wash in her clothes? "No. Off," she called. "Off."

Stubbornly, Kate dove under and swam, hindered by the heavy iron around her neck. The water felt wonderful. She coiled the tether in one hand to keep from being tangled in it. She kept her eyes on the surface of the water, trying not to see the naked swimmers around her. Why was it that she was so embarrassed and they showed no shame at all?

Wabethe called to a child on shore, swam in, and returned with a handful of sticky substance. She divided it, handed half to Kate, and proceeded to wash her hair. Kate did the same.

When they emerged from the water a few minutes later, Kate felt a hundred times better, despite the dripping clothing. She would dry soon enough in the August heat, and her clothes were much improved by the dipping. A jerk on the tether pulled her around, and she looked into the taunting eyes of Tschi.

"Why are you here, slave? There is work to do in my wigwam." He would have cuffed her but she ducked. Tschi contented himself with shoving her in the direction of the village.

Kate glanced at Wabethe, who shrugged helplessly. If

Tschi desired something, there was nothing she could do. Her eyes signaled caution.

Tschi pushed her inside the hut and tied the tether overhead. From the floor he picked up a bloody deerskin and threw it at her. "Scrape this. Take care. If you tear the hide through carelessness, I will beat you."

"I don't know how." Kate pushed the deerskin aside. Bits of fat and matter clung to it and the smell was foul.

Tschi grabbed her arm, his fingers twisting her flesh. "Do not defy me, woman. I will send a squaw to show you how. You will obey."

"You can kill me, but you can't make me your slave!" Kate spat. "When Pride comes—"

Tschi grabbed the leather and pulled Kate against him. "When he comes, he will find death! I have no brother." He seized the front of her shirt and ripped it until the heaving tops of Kate's pale breasts were exposed. "I saved you from the stake once, woman. Next time I may not." His hard body pressed against her and he touched her possessively. "You are my slave! You do what Tschi say. If you do not . . ." He pulled a razor-sharp knife from the sheath at his waist and held it in front of her eyes. "Maybe I cut your face so no other man will look at you. Or . . ." He laughed. "Maybe I cut out your eyes." He drew the point of the knife down her cheek until it drew blood. "What do you say now, English?"

Kate froze, not daring to move a muscle lest the blade cut deeper. Tears formed in her eyes but she would not cry out. "I say," she panted, "I say give me the knife and then we will see who is the brave one."

Tschi threw back his head and roared. "Meshepeshe Equiwa! Panther Woman!" He wiped the knife on his breechcloth and put it back in his sheath. "Your tongue is like a snake, quick and sharp. I can see you will be great trouble." He shrugged, and the bulging muscles of his arms rippled. "But it does not matter. I am a patient man. You will give your white body to me, woman. And you will give me a son . . . a son with the courage of his panther mother."

Chapter 12

Kate's knees felt suddenly weak, and she leaned against the supports of the wigwam. She stared at the man disbelievingly. When she spoke, it was in a calm, detached voice. Her blue eyes, hidden in the semilight, burned with an inner fire. "You're less than a man, Tschi; you're a beast. I'll never lie with you willingly. And I'll never, never, bear you a child."

The loathing in her voice lay between them like a tangible presence, and for an instant, something like fear was visible in Tschi's fierce glare. It faded into the ebony depths and was replaced by a sadistic humor. "Tschi will tame you to his touch, Panther Woman, or destroy you." He thrust the stinking deerskin at her. "Remember, a blind slave can do much work and will not run far."

"Even a blind slave can drive home steel into a man's ribs."

"Talk is cheap, English. And nights are long." He turned abruptly and stalked from the lodge.

Kate fell to her knees and buried her face in her hands. If Pride did not come . . . and soon . . . No! She must not let herself believe in him, or trust in his coming! She must look to herself. He'd have no reason to come after her. No reason but revenge! And despite her brave words, if he did come, he might well leave her with his brother. Her fingertips brushed across her closed eyes. Tschi had threatened to blind her. What chance would she have to escape in darkness? If he did it, death would be her only escape.

She rocked back and forth in utter despair. Her eyes

184

were dry; there were no tears left to shed. "Pride," she whimpered half-aloud. "Please come. Oh, please come."

Dressed only in breechcloth and moccasins, Pride ran steadily along the ancient war trail. His thick hair was braided and held back from his hawklike face with a leather thong. In his right hand, he carried a long rifle made in Germany. It was shorter than the English rifle by more than a foot, but deadly accurate. At his waist was a twelve-inch, double-edged hunting knife and a French-made tomahawk. Powder horns and a small leather bag were the only other things he carried. He must travel fast and light. Extra pounds on the war trail could mean the difference between life and death.

Pride's worst fears had been realized. A Nanicoke runner had brought the word to Ashton Hall. A peaceful village of Lenni Lenape, or Delawares, had been attacked without provocation by a force of English Regulars. Men, women, and children had been slaughtered without mercy. Their cornfields had been burned, fields full and ripe with summer's bounty, and the village leveled by fire and steel.

The fact that many of these people had become Christians had not slowed the British charge; it had not kept the women and girls from being raped. The log chapel the missionaries had built so lovingly was ashes. Even the horses and livestock had been put to the sword in the killing frenzy.

The village had been a small one and isolated. The British troops had been weary of chasing hostiles and eager for action. The two actualities had come together and had set in motion an irrevocable holocaust of blood and destruction.

The Shawnee were cousins to the Delaware. They would rise in retaliation against the British settlers. Ashton Hall was a symbol of English claim to Indian land. In the face of war, Pride must be brother to the Shawnee or enemy. There would be no middle ground. The Shawnee nation would be lost to the French cause, and Pride could not become a French ally. If there was any chance of his recovering Kate alive, he must act swiftly. He must act before the Shawnee war drums began to sound.

He had considered long and hard about the wisdom of going on foot instead of by horse. But a man on horseback was an easier target. A Shawnee in the forest was less than a shadow. And Pride, from the moment his moccasined feet touched the war trail, had become pure Shawnee.

Rebecca had watched his departure stoically. Her two sons had been bound lightly by the ties of blood and clan. Now that tie would snap. Tschi would not forgive his younger brother the shame of English lineage. He would give no quarter. By staying at Ashton Hall, she had relinquished her Shawnee heritage. Menquotwe Equiwa, the Sky Woman, was dead. And in her place was only Rebecca Ashton. She would wonder the rest of her life if it had been the right decision.

The muscles in Pride's right calf had begun to cramp. He was growing soft. As a boy he had been taught to run all day without stopping for food or water. He had not received his first medicine until he had run a deer to earth. He ignored the pain and continued to run, listening all the time to the sounds of the forest around him.

If the Shawnee took arms against the English soldiers, the Iroquois would consider it open season on the Shawnee and their allies, the Delaware and Nanicoke. The Iroquois had claimed sovereignty over the Lenni Lenape nation. It was a one-sided claim and dubious at best. There was no love lost between the two peoples. They were of different races and spoke a different language.

The corners of Pride's mouth turned up in a wry smile. Any human that crossed his path would be a potential enemy. The Shawnee might shoot him for being white, the English for being a red savage, and the Iroquois for fun. The center of his back itched as he imagined an arrow sinking to the bone. Damn Kate Storm to hell! The little blue-eyed bitch had ruined his life. No matter what happened when he caught up with her, he was bound to lose.

The dead Shawnee brave had been of his brother's band. Pride knew where the summer camp had been a year ago. He hoped they had not moved. If Kate wasn't there, he was certain some of the tribe would tell him where to find her. At least she'd had the good sense to be captured by Shawnee instead of Iroquois. He wondered if she realized just how lucky she was.

Trying not to gag, Kate took a handful of mashed deer brains from the birchbark container and smeared it on the hide. The deerskin was stretched out and pegged to the ground. Kate knelt beside it, following Wabethe's instructions. Pride had once told her that each animal, including a human being, had just enough brain matter to tan its own hide. She'd doubted his story. Now it seemed somewhat more plausible.

The brains must be rubbed into the skin now that it had been scraped clean of all blood and flesh. It was a slow, tedious job. The smell sickened her, and once, to the delight of the children crowded around, Kate had had to run into the woods and vomit. Using a piece of wood, she worked the brains deep into each section of the deer hide. Her clothes were soaked with the greasy mess, and she'd probably never get the smell out of her hands and hair.

The next step was to pull the hide back and forth over a tree branch, breaking up the stiff nature of the green skin. It would require hours of rubbing, twisting, and pulling to turn it into a soft beautiful leather. Kate was beginning to value her beaded moccasins.

Wabethe worked nearby on a spotted fawnskin. It would provide a wrap for her baby. The hide was much thinner and more delicate than the one Kate was doing. It took a light hand so the skin would not be torn and ruined. The baby, tied safely in the cradle board, hung from a tree branch overhead, asleep.

"You make much anger," Wabethe said. "Tanning skins must be done. Is squaw work. Why you anger? English squaw no work?"

"Englishwomen don't do this kind of work," Kate grumbled. "They sew and cook and tend the children. This makes me sick."

The children giggled. A girl reached out and tugged at

Kate's hair, then said something in Shawnee. Kate frowned at her and she jumped back.

"She want know how you make hair color of winter grass," Wabethe explained. "She think it not be real."

"A wig? No, it's not a wig. Tell her I was born like that."

Wabethe translated. The girl retreated and yelled something back. "She say she glad she have proper hair, not grass on head."

Two other women moved shyly nearer to sit under the tree. One brought a basket she was weaving, the other beadwork. The basketmaker had gray streaks in her dark hair. The younger woman looked as though she might be pregnant. They spoke to Wabethe softly and she nodded.

"Tell them I won't bite," Kate said.

"They friend. Unsoma my sister." She pointed to the girl with swelling breasts and round stomach. "Methotho me . . ." Wabethe shook her head and shrugged. The degree of kinship was too difficult to explain with her limited vocabulary. "Methotho."

The older woman smiled at her name, and Kate smiled back. Despite the language and racial barriers, these women did not seem so very different from those she had known at home.

Unsoma called to a chubby little girl about three. She came running, a handful of broken flowers in her tiny brown hands. She wore nothing but a string of silver beads. Unsoma took her on her lap and nuzzled the back of her neck. The child giggled and snuggled down.

"Unsoma want boy baby," Wabethe explained. "She lose son. Lose man. Iroquois."

"They killed her husband and child?"

"Kill man. Take scalp. Steal son. No see no more." She pointed north. "Iroquois country. Much cold. Bad."

"That's terrible," Kate said sympathetically. "At least she has the little girl. Does she have a new husband?"

Wabethe nodded. "New man. Squithetha. Squithetha born Wabethe. Sister no man, no baby. Much tear. Wabethe sister. Wabethe give Squithetha."

"You gave her your child?" Kate looked at her friend

in disbelief. "Squithetha is your daughter and you gave her to Unsoma?"

"No Wabethe. Unsoma."

Kate continued to rub at the deer hide. She would never understand these people. To give away such a beautiful child . . . Wabethe seemed to dote on her son. Perhaps girl children were worth little among the Shawnee.

Two boys ran by with a pet crow on a string. Methotho waved toward the cornfield and scolded. She got up and took a few steps in their direction. They nodded and ran back to the field. The woman turned to Kate and asked a question.

"She wants to know are you woman kill Shawnee brave?" Wabethe chattered on in Shawnee for a few moments then said in English, "I tell her yes. She say you have strange eyes. You stupid. No do hides good. She say brave woman. She no care you stupid. She like."

"She doesn't care that I killed a man from this village?"

"Methotho care. Methotho sister son. You kill."

"I killed her sister's son and she likes me?"

Wabethe sighed in exasperation. "You Englisher." The other two women understood and nodded in agreement. "You Englisher. Shawnee come. You fight. Shawnee fight. Kat kill Shawnee." She accompanied her speech with hand motions. "Englisher come Shawnee camp. Shawnee fight. Kill Englisher if can. You see? Kat warrior woman. Shawnee no hate brave woman. Like."

Kate looked away. Nothing here was as it should be, as she thought it would be. How could these gentle, laughing women condone the torture she had witnessed with her own eyes? She pushed the wooden tool back and forth across the deerhide. No wonder she had been unable to comprehend Pride Ashton. His heritage was as foreign to hers as though he had been born on some distant star. How could she ever have believed that they might live together as man and wife?

She was startled from her musings by Tschi's hard grip on her shoulder. She whirled to face him, coming to her feet like a cat. His open-handed slap caught her across the face and brought tears to her eyes.

"Lazy squaw! I send you to work and you do nothing!" he accused. The woman beside him laughed, then her eyes narrowed and she pointed to Kate's moccasins. She spoke rapidly to Tschi in Shawnee and he nodded. "Take those off," he ordered.

Sullenly, Kate did·as she was bid. Her face stung from his blow, and this was not the place to challenge his authority, in full view of the village. She recognized the woman. It was the one Wabethe had said wished to be Tschi's wife.

Eagerly, she snatched up the beaded moccasins and put them on, discarding her own worn ones. Smirking, she held out first one foot then the other.

"She says it is not fitting for a slave to have better moccasins than a true Shawnee woman," Tschi translated. "What say you, Panther Woman?"

"I say let the slut have them if she wishes. If she must rely on the castoffs of others, I can only pity her."

Wabethe gave a little coo of approval and whispered to the watching women what the Englisher had said. There was a twitter of laughter and Tschi's features hardened.

"Have you nothing better to do than to pry into the affairs of others?" he snarled.

The three gathered up their work quickly. "Why is it?" Wabethe asked innocently in Shawnee, "that a man will often take on two women, when he cannot handle one?" Her friends covered their faces to hide their amusement. Kate could not understand the language, but the meaning was clear.

"Such a man," Methotho added, "shows a fool's face to all the world." The three women walked off, giggling.

Kate forced a straight face. If she were here long, she must learn the tongue. It was certain these women were not the obedient drabs she believed them to be.

Tschi shouted at the remaining woman angrily and she burst into tears and ran off toward her wigwam. "What have you done with my deer hide," he demanded of Kate. "If you have ruined it . . ."

"I have not ruined it." She stood beside the skin defiantly. If he hit her again, so be it. He could never crush her spirit. All it did was to give her more reason to take Tschi's life.

"Fetch wood for my fire! My belly is empty and I find you gossiping with idle women. You forget your place, slave!" He gave her a shove. "You will cook my food quickly or I will beat you for all to see."

"I'll cook your food," Kate agreed meekly. Her skill in cooking over an open fire was such that Tschi's would be the greater punishment this night. She kept her eyes downcast.

"Hmmpt," he grunted. "See you move swiftly, lazy one! I am a man who does not like to wait." He jerked at the tether. "You are taming, Englisher, as I said you would. Soon you will crawl to my robe in the darkness."

"Like hell I will," she whispered, between clenched teeth. It would not be enough for Tschi to die; he must die slowly. God, she thought, I am turning into a savage!

She was returning to the wigwam with an armload of firewood when a strange brave stepped in front of her and held up his hand. She looked at him uncertainly.

"Peace, English squaw. I mean you no harm. I am husband to Wabethe. She sends a message she had not words to say. Be strong. Tschi may beat you. As a slave you may be beaten . . . or he may take your life. But he may not take you as a man takes a woman. It is not the Shawnee way. A woman must give herself." He stepped back to let her pass. "I hear you are the woman of Chobeka Illenaqui. If this is so, pray he does not come. There is no welcome for him in this camp. He will find only death."

Kate stumbled and would have fallen, but he caught her. "Thank you," she murmured. Wabethe had sent the message to ease her heart. Instead, it had terrified her. She had not believed that Pride would be in danger coming here. These were *his* Shawnee, his mother's people. If Wabethe's man spoke the truth, she might now be the cause of Pride's death.

Tschi threw two rabbits at her when she entered the dwelling. Both had their heads and skin. Kate dangled the limp bodies distastefully. "What am I supposed to do with these?"

"Cook them, stupid woman." He raised a hand threat-eningly and Kate flinched. Tschi laughed. "You learn quickly, English. Soon we begin lessons in how to please your master." He caught at the tether and pulled her to him. She could not control the trembling. He pulled his knife and slashed the leather knot at the back of the metal collar. "Do not run. If you run, Tschi's knife will cut here." He brushed the blade across the back of her left knee. "And you will never run again."

Kate's mouth was dry. The fear tasted bitter. She backed away from the man slowly, the rabbits clutched in her hand. Somehow, even when the Indian had threatened to blind her, she had not believed him. *This* she knew he was ca-pable of doing. If he cut the tendons in her knee, she would be a cripple for the rest of her life. That he could say it coldly, without anger, was even more terrifying. She had prided herself all her life on her bravery, on fearing no man. Ashamed, she backed from the lodge.

She carried the rabbits toward the woods, then realized he had given her no knife. How was she supposed to clean and skin them? To return to the wigwam and ask for a knife would be humiliating. Tschi would laugh at her again. Unable to decide what to do, she kept walking.

It was beginning to get dark. Cooking smells were drift-ing from the houses; mothers were calling their children home to eat. A village cur barked halfheartedly at Kate, then turned to chase another dog. Was she beginning to smell like a Shawnee? She looked around for a familiar face. If she saw Wabethe, she could explain her problem.

Something glinted from a ridge above the village; Kate caught a brief glimpse of a sentry. No wonder Tschi was not concerned about letting her roam the camp. There were armed guards posted in a half-dozen spots. Wabethe had pointed out two to her the day before. Within the camp, no one was visible but a strange warrior wrapping his horse's foreleg and an old woman.

Kate entered the trees near the cornfield. Even the crow hunters had gone home for the day. She pushed through the low-hanging white pines until she came to a fallen log and sat down. What the hell was she going to do now? She threw the rabbits to the ground and kicked them.

A hand clamped over her mouth. Kate panicked and lashed out wildly at her assailant. She was dragged over the log and thrown to the ground. A man's body pinned her down with the full force of his weight and a low voice hissed in her ear. "Hold your tongue, Kate! I'll cut it out if I have to!"

The pressure on her mouth eased and she tried to speak. "Pri—" The hand tightened and fingers pinched her nose, cutting off all breath.

"I said shut up."

She made what she thought was an affirmative mumble and he took his hand away. "Pride? What are you doing here?"

"What the hell are you doing here?" he demanded angrily.

Kate stared at him, wide-eyed. No wonder she had not known him. Naked but for a breechcloth, his dark skin tanned by the sun to a tawny hue, Pride looked as much a savage as any Shawnee warrior. "I was captured. Your brother brought me here." She tried to pull free. "Well, are you going to let me up or not?"

"Should I? When we last parted you were less than gentle."

"I could have easily killed you!" she flared. "But I didn't."

"You may well live to regret it." He lifted her to her feet, keeping one iron hand around her wrist. "You've endangered both our lives and put Ashton Hall in jeopardy by your treachery. You've had your chances, Kate. They're all used up. From now on the game is mine," he said bitterly.

"You shouldn't have come. They'll kill you. Tschi—"

"My big brother has overstepped his bounds. No one steals from me, not even Tschi." Pride drew her farther into the pine grove, then pinned her to a tree with his powerful arms. He stood barely inches away, not touching her, using his body as a barrier. "No man could do what you did and live!"

Kate could not see his eyes in the shadows, but she felt their intensity and mentally retreated. "I'm sorry," she whispered.

"Sorry you did it, or sorry you were caught?"

"I'm sorry I hurt you. I didn't want to, but I didn't know any other way to get free." A chill seeped through her as she realized how similiar Pride's voice was to his brother's. "When I found out you'd killed Geoffrey, I . . ."

"Enough! We've no time to listen to your excuses."

"Are you taking me out of here?"

Pride laughed. "And how do you suggest I get you past the lookouts?"

"How did you get past them in the first place?" Kate bit at her lower lip. He had come to rescue her, hadn't he?

"Have you slept with him?"

"Who?"

"Tschi. Who the hell do you think I'm talking about?" Pride laid his hand on her throat, almost tenderly. Kate clenched her teeth to keep them from chattering. "If you have, you'd better tell me."

"No!" She shook her head. "No, of course I haven't! He's . . . he's an animal!"

"Tschi?" Pride forced a sarcastic chuckle. "I've heard him called a lot of things by women, but never an animal. I'd think his *charms* would be attractive to *you.*"

"No. I wouldn't let him. He threatened me but . . ." She began to weep. "How could you think I'd . . ."

"Save the tears, Kate, for someone who cares." His fingers tightened around her neck. "You've deceived me from the first minute I laid eyes on you. Well, I learn slowly, but I eventually catch on."

"If you feel that way about me, why did you come here?"

"Because you're mine and I don't let go of what's mine!"

"Let go of me, you're hurting me." Pride stepped back and released her. "I don't know how you got here or why you're dressed like that, but I'm still damn glad to see you," Kate admitted. She rubbed her neck. "Can you get this thing off me?"

"Why? I should have thought of it." He examined the metal collar. "It will have to be unlocked or filed off. I don't have time to bother with it now." He pulled her around to face him. "How many braves are in the village? Has there been war talk? Are the men meeting at night in the big house?"

"Yes, they've been meeting every night. I could hear them arguing. There were drums, but not drums like the first. When Tschi first brought me here, they had an Iroquois captive. They murdered him. It was terrible!"

"It usually is." He shrugged. "The Iroquois and Shawnee are bitter enemies—this year. You'd see worse in an Iroquois village."

"No. It couldn't be. They burned him and shot him full of arrows."

"Did they cut him open and roast his heart? No?" Pride snickered at her shudder. "The Iroquois are eaters of men. It's no tall tale, Kate. I've seen it. The Iroquois believe they can take on the qualities of a brave enemy by eating his vital parts. Perhaps they're right. The Iroquois are as fearless as they come."

"I don't know how many men are in the village. Tschi doesn't tell me anything."

"You're no better at spying than you are at women's work. I'll have to find out for myself, before I confront Tschi. Go back to the wigwam and don't let on you've seen me. That way." He pointed.

"You can't leave me!"

"Can't I?" Pride picked up his rifle.

"No. Wait. I can't go back. He'll beat me again." Kate grabbed Pride's arm and explained about the rabbits.

"And what do you expect me to do about it?"

"Couldn't you clean them for me, take off the heads? Please, Pride."

"You want me to risk being seen to skin rabbits? For God's sake, woman! Where are they?"

Kate ran back and picked up the discarded animals. She brought them back, half-expecting him to be gone. "Pride?" Her voice was near breaking. "Please."

"Give them here." He stepped from the shadows, knife

in hand. Squatting, he made quick work of the job and handed back the rabbits. "Wash them at the river, cut them into pieces, and broil them over the flames."

"Thank you. When will I see you again? Pride?"

He was gone, moving into the darkness without a sound. Kate stared after him. There hadn't been a rustle, not a snapped twig. She waited a few heartbeats, then hurried to the river and back to the village. Pride was angry, and he had a right to be. He'd get over it. She'd make him see why she had done it. As soon as they got away from this awful place, things would be all right.

"You are slow, woman," Tschi said.

Kate noticed that he had built a fire while she was gone. If he hadn't, it would have taken her forever to start one. Quietly, she went about the task of cooking the rabbits. Wabethe had given her some corncakes and a container of berries earlier in the day. They could be served with the rabbit. Kate used a flat stone to warm the bread near the flames. The rock was hot, and she burned her finger and instinctively stuck it in her mouth.

"You not only slow, you clumsy. Why my brother want you, Panther Woman? You know tricks to keep man happy?" He laughed. "Tonight I must go to council fire. When I return, you will show me these tricks. Yes?"

Kate concentrated on the rabbits, turning the green spit so the meat wouldn't burn. Despite her fear, she could feel her stomach growling. She was hungry, and she wasn't going to let Tschi bluff her out of her dinner. "It is not the Shawnee way for a man to force a woman," she whispered.

"Shawnee way? Shawnee way?" he roared. "What does an Englisher know of Shawnee ways?" Tschi leaped to his feet catlike, and crouched over her menacingly. "You are not a Shawnee woman. You are slave!"

Kate lowered her head and bit the inside of her cheek until it bled. If he touched her, she would seize a burning stick from the flames and stab his eyes out. It grated her to pretend fear, but she would not press a confrontation, not with Pride hiding in the woods nearby. "Yes," she whispered.

Mollified by her seeming acquiescence, Tschi grunted and returned to what he had been doing. Using a small French trade mirror and a feather brush, he resumed painting his face in black and yellow patterns. "You stay in wigwam this night," he ordered gruffly. "Not go outside. Lenni Lenape warriors come. Make talk. You stay hidden."

"How many warriors?" Kate looked at him expectantly. "Why should I be afraid of them?"

"You Englisher," he said slowly. "Englisher burn Lenape village. They Jesus Delawares, but Delaware all same. Englisher kill, take women, shoot horse. Lenni Lenape mourn dead brothers. See blood. You show white face . . ." He shrugged. "Have much anger. Maybe I give you to them."

"I won't go out," she lied. "Will you go to war?"

"Why you ask question? No ask question before. Why this night, Panther Woman?" He added a series of yellow dots down one cheek. "Slave woman no ask why. Slave obey. *Eie?*" Kate nodded. "No go war! War come to Tschi." He admired himself in the mirror. "Many scalps. Many rifles. Tschi great warrior! Great war chief! *Nenothtu oukimah!*" He grinned at her wolfishly, showing his even white teeth. "Perhaps one of these scalps will be that of your lover."

Kate kept her eyes on the broiling rabbit. She would not lose her temper this time. He'd eat and be gone. She'd hold her tongue a few more minutes.

"You smell bad, woman. Why keep ugly shirt on?" In an instant he was behind her, stripping the shirt off over her head!

Kate exploded into a fighting, clawing storm of fury. She used all her strength against him, and it was useless. All she succeeded in doing was being slapped around and tearing the shirt. Panting, she backed away from him on hands and knees. Her bare breasts glowed with a faint sheen of moisture in the firelight.

Tschi tossed the useless garment aside. "I like better. Now you look like Shawnee squaw. Give food, now!"

Tears rolled down her flushed face as Kate pushed the meat off the stick into a wooden bowl. She set it and the bread on the floor near the man and retreated to the opposite side of the fire. Crossing her arms over her breasts, she tried to hide herself from his leering eyes.

"Do not sleep, Panther Woman. Tonight you will teach me your tricks," he promised, stuffing pieces of meat into his mouth. "Wait for me." He grinned and reached for another corncake. "Tschi much warrior, you like."

Kate lowered her head and tried not to cry. Pride must come before Tschi returned. He must! She knelt there, watching him intently, until he finished eating and picked up his weapons.

"Remember, English. Do not leave wigwam." He ducked his head and disappeared through the low doorway.

"Bastard," Kate mouthed silently and made an obscene gesture after his departing back. When she was certain he was gone, she went to the fire and took the rest of the rabbit and began to chew. It was overcooked, but tasted wonderful just the same. She was starving.

When she had eaten the meat and a corncake and the berries, she examined the shirt to see how serious the damage was. It was torn badly, but she put it on and tied the pieces in the front. It just covered her, and she felt better. With a stick, she scattered the coals of the cooking fire. It was hot in the lodge and they didn't need a fire. It was easier to hide in the darkness.

Two gunshots brought Kate to the doorway. Had Pride been discovered? Her heart was in her throat as she waited. Men and women poured out of the wigwams, shouting. It was more a cry of greeting than alarm, and she began to hope again.

A line of painted warriors filed into the village. They were small men, for the most part, sinewy and hard, heavily armed and unsmiling. Kate counted more than forty; they ranged from graying veterans to boys in their teens. They wore the dust of a long journey lightly; such men would not know the meaning of fatigue. Their eyes were the eyes of hunters, and the steel tomahawks gleamed wickedly in the light of the council fire.

Drums began to sound. One was the deep hollow sound of a summer thunder; the others small and quick. The beating was repetitive; its message seemed to summon ancient memories in Kate's blood. She felt her breathing accelerate as she watched the Shawnee join the Delaware before the big house.

A full moon hung low over the village; the yellow orb seemed close enough to touch. The night was hot and humid and a ghostly mist crept over the cornfield to embrace the Shawnee town. Kate longed to leave the wigwam and creep closer to the council fire, but she dared not. She sat crouched, slapping at mosquitoes, straining her eyes to see what she could.

There seemed to be speakers; Kate couldn't tell if they were Shawnee or Delaware. Pride had told her the language was so similar she wouldn't be able to tell the difference. One voice would go on and on, then there would be general cries of agreement and shouting. Then another would begin to talk. Once, she saw the flash of metal as a tomahawk was buried in a black-painted post.

As the night wore on, the drumming came faster. The pitch rose to a frenzy and the yells increased in direct proportion to the cadence. The cries became fiercer and Kate noticed the women slipping back to their houses. Soon after, the dancing began. The hair rose on the back of Kate's neck as the first sounds of the war screams reached her ears.

Repelled, yet drawn by the primitive ritual, Kate crept from the wigwam and inched around the edge of the houses to the darkness behind the big house. There was so much noise she didn't have to be afraid of drawing attention to herself by an accidental crackling twig or barking dog. Slowly, on her hands and knees, she worked her way as close as possible.

Shawnee and Delaware warriors merged as one force. Painted faces, thudding moccasins, and flashing blades swirled before her eyes. Tschi stood before the council fire, a feathered lance raised high in his right hand. With a cry, he threw it, and the steel spearpoint stuck in the black post and quivered there. The war cries rose to a fever pitch!

Kate pressed her body into the soft grass, ignoring the mosquitoes that buzzed and whined about her, needling into every exposed inch of skin. If she were discovered now, she had no doubt what her fate would be. She would join the spear against the torture post!

She strained to understand what the speakers were saying, but it was useless. She could only comprehend a quick word here and there, mostly "Englisher." There were also repeated shouts of "Tschi! Tschi!" She thought they were calling out his name until the fact sunk in that Wabethe had told her that the word meant killer or kill. Where was Pride? Had he crept away in the night? She couldn't really blame him if he did. It would take a madman to walk into this hell without a full battalion of British Regulars!

Then, abruptly, the scene blurred. The council fire shot up, sending flames and smoke erupting in all directions. For seconds, pandemonium reigned as a thick white smoke hung over the meeting ground. Then, as the rising wind lifted the smoke, a man stood beside the fire!

There were cries of anger, and one warrior ran toward the apparition with raised tomahawk. The black-faced giant lifted his long rifle and fired a volley over the charger's head. The warrior ducked, dove to the ground, and rolled to safety, still clutching the hatchet in his hand. The crowd drew back a step and hesitated for the space of a heartbeat.

A strong voice rang out through the night. *"Shawnee Neethetha! Lenni Lenape! Oui-shi e-shi-que-chi!"*

It couldn't be, but it was! Kate half-rose from her hiding place in awe. She couldn't understand what he was saying, but she knew the voice. It was Pride! She watched mesmerized as challenges were screamed at him and he riposted.

"Atchmolohi, Chobeka Illenaqui!" came the soft command from a white-haired elder. As if by magic, the warriors stilled their cries. The old man rose unsteadily to his feet and pointed to Pride, then to himself. *"Atchmolohi!"* he repeated.

Pride leaned his rifle against the post and brought his right fist against his heart, nodding to the speaker deferentially. He began to speak again, more slowly, his authoritarian delivery carrying to every man in the circle. Kate cursed her inability to understand the language!

What was he saying? The black paint on his face had deluded her momentarily. He looked as much a savage as any of them. The only difference between Pride and Tschi was Tschi's hideous shaved head.

Suddenly, Tschi rushed at his brother, murder in his eyes! Pride stood unmoving, and Kate could not contain a scream. He was not an armspan away when the white-haired man lifted his arm, palm outstretched. Tschi halted his charge, unable to hide the uncontrolled rage in his contorted face.

The old man began to speak. He paused and looked expectantly around the circle. The response was immediate. War cries rent the air. The drums began again and the warriors danced, their screams echoing out through the hills and meadows, filling the land with a sense of dread premonition of bloody years to come.

Pride took his rifle and walked from the circle. A few called out against him, but no one raised a hand to strike. He stopped to talk with the old chief, then squatted before the big house to watch the war fever build. It was evident to Kate that the decision had gone against him, but he seemed unconcerned. He sat, stony-faced as any Indian, only his size making him visible among the painted warriors.

Kate began to breathe again. She didn't know how she had screamed and not been discovered. She considered it a miracle. Perhaps the Indians had taken her scream for that of one of their women. It didn't matter how or why; what mattered was that she hadn't been dragged to that damn post and murdered. Drenched in sweat, she began to creep backward to the edge of the woods. It took forever to cover the few yards. A stick jabbed into her knee and she winced. Her knee breeches were hanging in rags anyway; another tear would hardly show.

Once she reached the trees, she moved slowly back around the village and dashed the last fifty feet to the safety of Tschi's wigwam. She pressed herself against the floor and chuckled. Since when did she feel safe here? She was becoming as mad as the rest of them.

The war chanting showed no signs of letting up. Hours

passed. Kate waited, afraid to sleep. Reluctantly, she had stirred the coals, found a live one and started the fire again. Better to be hot. The smoke would keep away the worst of the mosquitoes and insects.

She drew her knees up and wrapped her arms about them. What had Pride said to the Indians? Was he joining them, going to war against his own kind? Had he become an enemy too? She'd thought, at first, that he'd come to rescue her. He showed no signs of it! Instead, he'd become one of *them*. He'd left her to whatever Tschi had in mind.

The more she thought about it, the angrier she got. Tschi had threatened to kill Pride if he came here. Whatever had transpired at the council fire had changed everything. The old chief had welcomed him. Pride had deceived her from the first. Was he now a traitor? Not to the Shawnee, but to the British?

Like a dark shadow, Tschi pounced on her. She was too startled to scream. Only a little moan escaped her lips as he threw her to the floor and ran his brutal hands over her body. "No," she protested, struggling. "No!"

His foxlike teeth nipped at the soft part of her throat, and he whispered huskily in Shawnee. He burrowed his face into her breasts and caught a nipple between his hard lips. Kate pounded at his face and muscular shoulders. "Let me go!" she gasped. "Damn you. Let me go!"

"Brother." A low voice from the entrance cut through Kate's struggle. "I've come for my woman."

Chapter 13

Tschi sprang into a crouched position, skinning knife in hand. The blade gleamed wickedly in the firelight. "Is it a woman you seek, or death? I have no brother, Englisher! Here you will find only steel for your heart!"

Kate scrambled away. Tschi was between her and the entrance. Pride was only a shadowy outline. "Be careful," she warned.

Pride laughed, and the sound raised the hair on the back of Kate's neck. "He has a knife," she cautioned. "Don't come in."

"He has a knife," Pride agreed sarcastically. "One I brought him from London."

"You are a traitor! Our ways have parted. I am Shawnee. You are white. Go now, and I will spare your life. The woman is mine, and I keep her," Tschi declared.

Pride eased through the doorway and stood up, his hands outstretched and open. "When I was six, I had a puppy. You took him away from me and broke his head open with a rock. When I was ten, you took the bow Grandfather made for me."

"I remember well; I fought you for it and won."

"You were twelve and almost a warrior. I was still a boy. I'm a boy no longer, Tschi. Kate is my woman and you stole her. I want her back."

"A dead man needs no woman." Tschi clutched the knife lovingly.

"My brother speaks the truth."

"Pride, please!" Kate cried. "He'll kill you." She tried

203

to sneak past Tschi on the far side of the fire. With the speed of a snake, he spun toward her. The blade nicked Kate's arm and she froze.

"Stay!" Pride ordered. He moved not a muscle and Tschi turned back to him. "This is between us. We will settle it in the circle."

Tschi nodded. "The circle. At dawn. The man left alive takes the woman."

"No!" Kate protested. "I'm not goods to be bartered off."

"One condition," Pride insisted. "That man must make her his wife. She is not to be a slave."

"Agreed."

"I'm not going to be anyone's wife!" Kate looked from one to the other. "That's barbaric!"

Tschi sheathed the knife and followed Pride out of the wigwam. "We must prepare the circle of death."

Kate ran after them. "You're not listening to me!" she screamed. "You can't do this! I won't let you!"

Pride turned a granite face. "You have nothing to say about it, woman!" He weakened as he saw her features crumble. "As a slave you have no rights at all. As wife, even to my brother . . ." He shrugged. "You'll be better off, Kate, whether you realize it or not. You'll survive."

"But you're a civilized man! You can't fight that savage to the death over me like . . . like some pagan gladiator."

"That savage, as you call him, is my brother." Pride couldn't quite disguise the pain in his voice. "He taught me to fight. When the sun comes up over there"—he pointed to the east—"I'll try to kill him." He sighed. "I don't know if I can. He's good with a knife, damn good. And he's fast, and he's strong. The hell of it is, I'm going to try and kill him . . . over you. And he's going to do his damnedest to kill me."

"But I don't want—"

"Shut up! Shut up and let me finish," Pride snapped. "Right now, I'd just as soon not look at you. Because tomorrow I'm going to try and kill my brother for a woman who's not worth the powder to blow her to hell."

* * *

Kate clutched at Wabethe's thin hand. The entire village had gathered to watch the contest between the brothers. The Lenni Lenape warriors stood together on one side of the circle, the council members and important Shawnee braves on the other. Women and children packed tightly close to the white chalk line.

The circle was empty, its center marked with colored patterns, crisscrossing the hard-packed dirt. Wabethe's hand moved slightly. "The circle," she explained. Her forehead wrinkled in exasperation as she tried to recall the language of her childhood. "Like Jesus house of white man."

"Not like a church." Kate shook her head. "That would be blasphemy! A church is a sacred place, a house of God." She tried to make Wabethe understand. "This . . . this is violent, an act of bloodletting. It's wrong."

"No! You do not see. Shawnee all brother. Not Tschi, Chobeka Illenaqui. They brother too. All Shawnee. Men . . . women. Shawnee no kill Shawnee. Very bad medicine. Shawnee, Delaware, all same people, same brother. No kill brother. White man no same. White man . . . Frenchman, Englisher, Dutchman all kill. No brother. No same blood. Shawnee, Delaware, same blood." She pressed her open palm against her heart.

"But Pride and Tschi are brothers. They are Shawnee and they're trying to kill one another in your damn circle!"

Wabethe sighed and began again, patiently. Her baby fussed, and she removed it from the cradle board on her back and offered a round breast. The infant began to nurse greedily, giving little contented squeaks of pleasure. *"Some time* Shawnee brother much anger. No can . . ." She clasped her hands together. "Must fight. Must kill. Old ones make circle. Brothers enter. Fight. No one help. Shawnee watch, remember. All Shawnee have pain. Much sad. Strong medicine. One brother live." She made the motion of wiping away tears. "Long time no circle. Circle much tear Shawnee."

"You can't make a sacred act out of this!" Kate protested. "What they're doing is wrong. I won't marry either one of them! I don't care what anyone says."

"If brother fight brother over woman, woman must be

wife of man win. His medicine stronger. Woman no wife, circle no fix anger. You see? Shawnee law. Must be husband, wife. Long time, many winters, when grandmother small child, two squaw fight for man. Man must marry woman win. Shawnee law.''

"It's barbaric," Kate said incredulously. "I'm not Shawnee. If it is your law, it can't mean me. I'm English.''

"No Englisher long. You be Shawnee."

"I don't want to be a Shawnee."

Wabethe shrugged and continued nursing the baby.

Pride and Tschi came from opposite ends of the village, walking proudly, heads up and shoulders back, like Oriental princes. For an instant, Kate didn't recognize Pride and thought there had been some substitution. Then she realized his head was shaved in the same manner as Tschi's. Each bore a single spot of blue paint on his cheekbones, and each wore only a white deerskin breechcloth. The crowd grew silent.

A strange Shawnee in a wolfskin head covering and black robes stood before first one, then the other. He murmured softly in the Indian tongue and sprinkled cornmeal over their heads. Then, he too stepped back, and they entered the circle.

Each man carried a knife. In the center of the circle, a steel tomahawk was stuck, the blade partly buried in the dirt. They faced each other in a half crouch, moving like dancers to some silent rhythm.

Without realizing it, Kate strained forward. Wabethe held tightly to her arm. "Make no sound," the girl warned. "Sound bad."

A drumbeat began, so softly that Kate thought at first it was her own heart. She could not see the drummer; perhaps he was hidden in the edge of the forest. The beat was urgent, disturbing. It throbbed, stirring her blood, and she found her breath coming in deep gasps.

Pride looked into his brother's dark eyes. Tschi laughed and beckoned with his knife hand. Control your anger, Pride told himself. Don't let him use it against you. He stepped sideways, his bare feet lightly brushing the earth.

The morning sun rose bright and hot over the trees. In

the early light, the two men looked like bronze giants, their knife blades glimmering. Tschi's back was to Kate, broad and muscular, oiled to keep Pride from getting a grip on him. He was three fingers' width shorter than his half-white brother, but thicker in the waist and thighs. His skin was but a shade darker.

Pride's body had been oiled, too. He circled, his face a granite mask, his eyes expressionless. The sinews in his tanned back strained like braided cords.

The crowd was silent. For years men had watched the brothers and known this day would come. They were evenly matched in strength and speed. Whichever man fell, the Shawnee would lose an epic warrior. Wishemenetoo alone knew who would walk from the circle of death, knew which man's medicine was more powerful.

With the speed of a diving falcon, Tschi lunged for the tomahawk. His hand closed on the handle, and he swung it at Pride. Kate screamed. Time slowed, and the deadly ax soared through space toward Pride's undefended face. She would have thrown herself into the circle, but Wabethe and another woman held her fast. Unable to watch, she shut her eyes, then opened them. Pride was a full two yards from the spot he had occupied not a second before.

Wabethe elbowed Kate hard in the ribs. "No scream!" she ordered. "Look! Your man no be trick like child."

Kate covered her mouth with a hand, vowing she would not shame Pride by crying out again. She bit down hard on a finger, tasting blood, as she saw Pride rush at his brother and slash with the knife, barely missing a blow from the tomahawk by twisting aside. The blade drew blood; a thin trickle ran down Tschi's left thigh.

Bile rose in her throat as Kate tore her gaze from the red stream. Tschi seemed not to notice the blood. Her eyes fastened on his face; his white teeth gleamed wolfishly, and he let out a shrill war cry. Kate gasped as the tomahawk left Tschi's hand and flew through the air, cutting a crimson furrow across Pride's shaved head.

Stunned, Pride stumbled and went down on one knee. Tschi leaped on top of him, and they rolled across the hard-packed ground. Tschi was on top, his knife poised, frozen

in the air. Pride's hand was locked around Tschi's wrist;
his own knife lay a few feet away. A *hooo* went up from
the watching Indians; the man on top held the clear advantage. It took raw power to hold back a descending blade.

Sweat beaded on Tschi's face. Kate couldn't see Pride's.
Blood ran down his head and pooled on the earth. The wound
must have hampered his thinking! "Pride!" she cried.
"Fight!" Wabethe elbowed her again, and she pushed her
back. "He's hurt," she whispered to her friend. "Can't you
see he's hurt?"

Tschi's knife hand wavered and moved, inch by inch
toward the man beneath him. Then, almost too fast to see,
Pride's other hand let go of Tschi's left wrist and drove
upward into his brother's face. Tschi groaned with pain;
his knife hand was pushed back, and Pride rolled free.

Shaking his head, Pride scooped up his knife and hurled
it. It struck Tschi full in the chest, and the warrior crumpled backward. Like a panther, Pride was on him, pressing
his brother to the earth, and raising the tomahawk for the
coup de grâce.

"No!" Kate cried. "Don't!"

Tschi's head lay to one side, his hand tugged futilely at
the knife. He opened his eyes and he whispered in Shawnee. "Strike, brother."

Pride's face contorted with emotion. Muscles twitched
in his upraised arm as he balanced the steel ax. A savage
war cry sprang from his lips, and the tomahawk plunged
down.

Kate twisted free of the women and ran toward him.
"No! Pride! Don't kill him!"

The tomahawk buried in the earth beside Tschi's head.
He shuddered and tried to raise his head. *"Tschi . . .
tschi,"* he begged. He lay there panting as Pride leaped off
him and raised both arms in the age-old symbol of victory.

Kate ran to Pride and threw her arms around him, oblivious to the dirt and blood. "I was so afraid he'd kill you,"
she cried.

A murmur of approval rose from the onlookers, and
women hurried to see to Tschi's knife wound. Pride walked
from the circle, head high, his arm possessively about Kate.

"You shouldn't have entered the circle," he murmured. The stern expression did not hide the light in his eyes.

"I thought you were going to kill him."

"I should have." Pride placed his hand over her heart and nodded to the old chief. He said something in Shawnee, and the old man nodded back.

"What did he say?"

"You'll find out soon enough. Wabethe! Take my woman and see to what needs to be done." Pride pushed Kate in her direction.

Wabethe grinned. She and a half-dozen women ran toward Kate, shouting in Shawnee.

Kate tried to shake off the clutching hands. "Pride! What are they going to do to me?" She began to struggle, half-heartedly at first and then in earnest. "Stop! What are you doing?" she screamed.

Chanting, they dragged her to the river and proceeded to tear off all her clothing. Kate fought in desperation now, despite Pride's laughter from the riverbank. She landed a few good punches, but ended up swallowing half the river before she was finally pulled ashore. She spat water and shook her head like a drowned rat.

"This isn't the least bit funny!" Kate yelled. "Stop laughing, damn you, Pride Ashton!"

Wabethe threw a mangy bearskin around Kate's naked body, and the women surrounded her again. Laughing and shouting, they dragged her toward the edge of the village where a low bark-covered structure stood.

"What's that?" Kate demanded. "Where are you taking me?" The women pushed her into the darkness. To her surprise, the hut was dug into the ground. Wabethe and two older women followed her inside, stripped off the bearskin, and threw it out the door.

"Panther no afraid," Wabethe giggled. "No tear. Shawnee no hurt baby."

"Baby? What baby? Ouch!" Kate swore as she stumbled over a large round stone. The floor was covered with them. "There's no baby here," she protested.

"You baby," Wabethe explained. "We make you good Shawnee. Marry Chobeka Illenaqui. You like, yes?"

"Yes . . . I mean no! No, I don't like to marry."

"No matter. He great warrior. Win you Tschi." A spark glinted in the darkness, then another, as Wabethe struck her firestones together. Soon, a whisper of a flame was spiraling upward. Wabethe blew on the tiny flame and pushed shaved bark into it. Soon a brisk fire was burning, and Kate could see the curving roof of the tiny building.

"Isn't it too hot for a fire? What kind of a wigwam is this?" Kate asked. The fire pit seemed huge for such a small hut.

Wabethe chuckled merrily. "No wigwam . . . sweat house. Make clean for be Shawnee." She pushed stones close to the flames. Then, she and the other two women removed their short skirts. Someone outside opened the skin door flap and handed in buckets of water. Wabethe poured them on the rocks and the hut filled with steam.

Kate choked, hardly able to breathe in the thick steam. She had been in the steam lodge for hours, maybe days. Water ran off her body in streams. She felt like she was drowning in the steam; the other women moved about the low space like dancers in a dream, chanting.

She clutched at her mid-section. She'd felt queasy since she'd gulped the container of liquid Wabathe had given her. It was bitter, and she wouldn't have swallowed at all, but she was so thirsty. Now, her stomach gargled ominously. "Wabethe!" she cried. Suddenly, it was urgent she get out of here! "Wabethe, I've got to—"

Giggling, the women threw the damp bearskin over her head and pushed Kate out the opening. They surrounded her, leading her blindly away from the sweat lodge and into the forest. Kate was frantic! If she couldn't relieve herself soon . . . Waves of shame surged through her body.

In the privacy of the trees, the bearskin was removed. "Now," Wabethe instructed, barely hiding the merriment in her eyes. "We no watch."

A weak Kate staggered under the dripping skin back to the sweat lodge. Abruptly the ground gave under her feet, and she tumbled through space into running water. Screaming, she began to splash about. The bearskin nearly smothered her, and the water felt like liquid ice. Laughing, Wabethe and her friends dove in and rescued her.

Sputtering and cursing, Kate was hustled back to the sweat lodge. "No more," she protested. "You'll kill me."

"Just like baby," Wabethe chuckled. "Scream. Cry. Kick."

Once more, rocks were heated, and water poured on them. Kate laid her head against the bark wall. She was too weak to fight anymore. She'd be the first English lady ever steamed to death. Maybe it wasn't only the Iroquois who practiced cannibalism. The Shawnee were probably going to serve her as the main course at Pride's victory celebration.

Wabethe was shaking her. "Come. We go now." Tugging at her arm, she coaxed Kate to the doorway once more. "Stay," she ordered. The other women held her arms while Wabethe went through first. "Now come!"

Kate crawled out of the door and was mortified to see she had crept out between Wabethe's spread legs. "What are you doing to me?" she begged. Tears rolled down her cheeks. Stupidly, she felt like giggling and did. Had she lost her mind?

Rubbing her eyes, she peered around. Women and little girls danced around her, faces painted. There were no men in sight, not even boy children. The skins over the wigwam entrances were closed tight.

The little daughter Wabethe had given away, Squithetha, came shyly forward. She covered her face with her hands and giggled. Her mother, Unsoma, gave a gentle shove, and the child uncovered one bright eye. Unsoma gave another nudge, and Squithetha reached up toward Kate with a string of red beads.

Uncertain, Kate looked puzzled. Wabethe cleared her throat loudly, and Kate bent down so the little girl could slip the necklace over her head. There were coos of approval from the women. The child clapped with pleasure, a wide smile spreading over the round little face.

"Thank you," Kate murmured. The child skittered behind her mother to safety.

Wabethe cleared her throat again and pointed toward a

large wigwam. The door skin was moved aside and an old woman stepped out into the late afternoon sunlight.

Kate couldn't remember seeing the woman before. She was so old, the parchmentlike skin was stretched tightly over the bird bones of her face. Snow-white braids hung below her waist. She wore a robe of red fox pelts that left the thin arms bare.

The procession moved toward the wigwam. Kate was captivated by the old woman's eyes. They were huge pools of molten ebony. They dominated the diminutive face. They seemed generations younger than the old body.

"Quaghcunnega Squithetha," Wabethe whispered reverently. "Her name is Rainbow Girl. She is all knowing. Great medicine woman."

The old woman stared into Kate's eyes. A great feeling of peace and contentment crept through her. Kate knew she was in the presence of a great lady, a queen in her own right. She curtsied, no longer realizing that she was completely nude, except for the red beads. "Madam," she murmured. "I'm very pleased to meet you."

Quaghcunnega smiled, showing ivory teeth, worn almost to the gum line. She inclined her head slightly and spoke in the shrill, piercing voice of the very old.

Wabethe translated. "She happy you, much like. You strong woman. Enter circle. Bad. Your heart good. You enter circle for good. Want save Shawnee warrior make you slave. You no like French woman. No like Englisher. You have Shawnee heart. Rainbow Girl say she call you Ki-te-hi Equiwa. Woman of Great Heart."

"Ki-te-hi," Kate repeated softly. "Tell her I am greatly honored."

Wabethe did, beaming at her charge. "You Shawnee, now," she explained. "Born from Shawnee woman." She giggled, remembering Kate's face as she crawled out of the sweat lodge. "You Wabethe daughter. You Ki-te-hi." She grinned. "Now daughter come. We make Shawnee—"

Suddenly, a woman burst through the laughing women. She screamed and shook her fist at Kate. Kate drew back. It was the woman she had fought with when she first came to the Shawnee camp.

Strong hands caught the woman and held her fast. Enraged, she spat at Kate and let loose a volley of angry words. She looked like a madwoman; her hair was chopped off in uneven handfuls, and her face was streaked with ashes. Even the deerskin skirt around her loins was ripped and smeared with filth.

Quaghcunnega went to the woman and laid her palm on the screamer's forehead. She spoke quietly, and the woman went limp and began to weep.

"Rainbow Girl say," Wabethe whispered. "Rainbow Girl say Englisher woman kill her man. Bad Englisher. Duty of wife to kill evil murderer."

Kate paled.

Wabethe continued. "Where is this Englisher? Who can say? No white woman here. Only Shawnee. Eyes see Shawnee woman, Ki-te-hi Equiwa. Sister. Englisher dead. No weep."

"But that won't work," Kate insisted. "She knows who I am."

"She know. Ki-te-hi no know. You no more Englisher. You Shawnee."

One by one, the women pushed forward to pat the grieving widow and offer words of comfort. Wabethe nudged Kate. "You're crazy," Kate said. "I'm not getting near her!" Wabethe shoved her hard. "No!"

Quaghcunnega looked in Kate's direction, an order in the shining eyes. Holding her breath, Kate took a step forward and held out her hand cautiously.

The woman took it and held it against her cheek. She looked into Kate's face, murmured something, and turned to another woman.

Kate stood in shock. "I don't believe it."

Wabethe took her hand. "No worry. No more fight. You sister. Englisher . . ." She shrugged and threw her hands in the air. "All gone."

The older woman who had been in the sweat lodge with Kate came out of the wigwam carrying a deerskin garment. There were coos and cries of approval as the dress was dropped over Kate's head.

It fell to her knees, soft as velvet, with eight-inch fringes

at the hemline and plunging vee neck. Marvelous designs
had been worked into the deerskin, red and yellow and
blue, both quillwork and beading. The delicate decoration
only accented the startling whiteness of the dress.

A child came with beautiful knee-high moccasins to
match the dress. Shyly, Wabethe offered silver earrings,
cunningly fashioned into tiny bells that tinkled as Kate
shook her head. She was glad her ears were already pierced.
She had no doubt that the women would have pierced them
on the spot in order that she might wear the lovely jewelry.

Quaghcunnega removed a silver armband, worked in ancient design, from her own frail body, and slipped it on
Kate's arm. Kate nodded thanks, touching the smooth, cool
surface with joy. The old woman stretched up and rubbed
her frail cheek against Kate's. The cheek was warm and
Kate embraced her gently.

Women rubbed dried flowers and herbs into the palms
of Kate's hands and painted her face with two red dots on
the cheekbones. They brushed her hair until it shone, making thin braids on either side of her face and leaving the
rest flowing free down her back.

Next, she was offered sweet corncakes baked with berries and strips of toasted squash. There was a rabbit stew,
but Kate could only swallow a few bites. Little Squithetha
brought fresh water from the spring in a gourd dipper.
Nothing would do but that Kate eat and drink of each offering.

Gifts were brought for Wabethe's new daughter: a copper pot, a precious steel needle, a knife with an otter skin
sheath, a hoe made from the shoulder bone of a deer, and
a new skirt. Kate thanked each woman with smiles and
gestures.

By now, it was growing dark. Children and men began
to drift out of the wigwams. Some of the women left to
begin cooking the evening meal. Kate noticed large por-
tions of a deer roasting over a fire near the council house.
Drums began to sound, and excitement was evident
throughout the camp.

Wabethe's husband came across the clearing to join
them. Together, they led Kate to a spot directly before the

council house. Kate looked around her; there was no sign of the circle. The lines had been wiped out. Wabethe pointed to a deerskin robe and motioned for Kate to sit on it. Wabethe and her husband sat on each side. Then Wabethe clapped her hands.

A man wearing a false face dashed from behind the council house. Children screamed and shouted, running close to touch him and then dodging away before they could be caught. He wore a furry mantle and huge bear paws with claws over his hands. Another, smaller man, his face painted yellow and blue, danced after the Bear Man, playing a bone flute.

The Bear Man whirled and peered into Kate's face. She jumped back and the gathering crowd laughed. From the folds of his cloak, the performer removed three leather balls and tossed them in the air, one after another. One ball disappeared, then another and another. Kate couldn't see how he managed the trick. Quickly, he bent down and seemed to pull a stuffed bird from a child's ear. The children laughed and begged him to repeat the act.

The man with the flute danced around, blowing and capering. Two women got up to dance and the flute player tried to chase them away. They joked and teased, calling insults to him and asking other women to join them. Soon a dozen or more women were dancing. The step was very simple, almost a stylized walk of step-step-slide. They sang while they danced, and Kate was caught up in the steady, simple rhythm.

She felt strange and wondered if even the water had contained some drug. She was light-headed and confused. Where was Pride? How could she be part of this Indian marriage they obviously intended to force her into? She wondered if Tschi would recover from his terrible wound. He'd lost so much blood. When had the fight been? Kate couldn't remember. It seemed so long ago . . . days, weeks.

The drums changed their beat, and the women stepped aside. Three men danced, and Kate found she could understand their story without knowing the Shawnee words. They were telling about a deer hunt. One man took the part of the deer and the other two told of the chase and the kill. Somehow, in the simple motions and varied facial expressions, Kate felt she was watching the hunt take place. She clapped her approval when it was finished, and the men grinned with pride.

Now, in total darkness, a group came from the trees on the far side of the camp. There was much shouting and laughter. Kate strained to see the tall warrior in the center.

He came directly toward her, head held high. Kate's heart raced! It was Pride. He wore only the scant loincloth, and his cheeks were painted with blue and red. In his hands was a circle of wild flowers. He grinned as he slipped them over her head.

"An old Shawnee custom?" she asked.

"It is now." Wabethe's husband slipped aside and Pride sat next to Kate on the deerskin. Pride leaned close and whispered in her ear. "You make a beautiful squaw."

The touch of his skin made her tremble. Drug or no drug, Kate longed to be cradled in those strong arms. She licked her lips and took a deep breath. "Don't think you're going to get away with this," she challenged. "It isn't a real marriage."

"No? Then why are you so agitated? You look like a bride to me," he teased. Pride gave his attention to a new set of dancers before them.

"I'm serious. Nothing is changed between us. You can't keep me in slavery, and you can't keep me with this farce of a marriage."

The dark eyes turned on her, penetrating. "Are English customs the only ones you recognize?" He shrugged. "The ways of the Shawnee go back thousands of years, before the time of Rome, before the birth of Christianity. This *is* a marriage. You think you've been tricked into it. Maybe you have, but if so, the trick's on me too."

"Then why . . . ?"

"Shut up, woman, and watch the entertainment."

"You don't want this any more than I do," Kate hissed.

Pride looked at her openly and the guests twittered. "Make up your mind. There is nothing you can do but go through with the ceremony and make the best of it. Whether we want it or not, it's fate. We were destined to be joined, *ki-te-hi*. In this life . . . and in the next if we don't fulfill our karma.''

Kate's mouth fell open stupidly. A little girl giggled, and Kate flushed. "What are you talking about?" *Ki-te-hi*. He had called her *ki-te-hi*. The sounds were sweet in her ears. She stiffened. He must not know how she felt, now that he'd admitted he was against the ceremony. "I'll go through with it," she agreed. "But I wanted you to know that it isn't willingly."

"So now I know. Shut up and watch the dancing."

"But—"

The drums stopped and Rainbow Girl came forward, aided by a younger woman. From a birch-bark bowl, she took a round, flat corncake and offered it to Kate.

She looked hesitantly at Pride.

"Take it. Break it in two. Eat one half and give the rest to me." Pride took her elbow and motioned her to stand.

The bread was dry and sweet. She forced her hand not to tremble as she gave a portion to the man towering over her. Had he always been so big?

Next, the old woman poured a tiny bit of white substance into Pride's open hand.

"Salt," he explained, tasting some and placing a few grains between Kate's lips.

The younger woman gave Rainbow Girl a soapstone bowl of water, and she held it out to Pride. He took it and offered it to Kate. She sipped and he did the same, then handed back the precious bowl.

Rainbow Girl raised her withered hands and offered a prayer in Shawnee, then took Kate's hands and placed them in Pride's. Shouts of joy filled Kate's ears.

"That's it?"

"That's it." He bent and kissed her to the delight of the wedding guests. They hooted and called out at the strange custom! "You're now an official Shawnee wife," Pride chuckled, "with all the rights . . . and duties." He leered mischievously.

The Shawnee and Delaware crowded around them, pushing good-naturedly. Kate found herself propelled to the far end of the village. Wabethe caught her hand and pulled her free from the well-wishers. Giggling, she embraced Kate and whispered advice.

"I can't understand a word you're saying," Kate protested. "Speak English, please."

"Wigwam! Belong you," Wabethe repeated. "Here." She pointed to a new hut. "Belong Ki-te-hi Equiwa." She gave Kate a little shove.

Pride was deposited beside the blushing bride. "The sooner we go inside, the sooner they'll go back to the party and leave us in peace," he said. "May I have your leave to enter, m' lady?"

Kate looked at him in bewilderment.

"The house is yours, wife. I may not enter without your permission. Do I have it?" Kate nodded helplessly and he grabbed her hand and pulled her inside. He dropped the skin door flap in place and the crowd roared with laughter.

Kate backed away and sat down on a skin rug by the fire. The wigwam was spotless. Dried meat hung from the saplings overhead. Baskets and bowls of food were stacked neatly along one side. A sleeping platform, covered with soft pelts, dominated the hut. Her wedding gifts were laid out beside it.

Pride squatted by the doorway until the noise outside lessened. A few more shouts and catcalls were heard, and then the voices faded. "See," he boasted. "What did I tell you?"

"You don't have to—"

"Shhh!" Pride held his finger to his lips. "Not a sound," he whispered. His eyes searched the wigwam.

"What's the matter? What's wrong?" she mouthed silently.

He laughed. "Nothing, Katy. Nothing's wrong. I just wanted to enjoy looking at you without hearing your mouth."

"Damn you!" She couldn't quite hold back a snort of laughter. "I thought we were being attacked!"

He caught her hand and pulled her to the sleeping platform. "Be sweet to me, wench. 'Tis my wedding night."

"Be sweet to you? I'll be sweet—"

Pride stilled her threats with a lingering kiss. Kate cupped her hands behind his neck and pulled him tightly against her. "This isn't going to work," she murmured softly.

He sat up and fixed her with an accusing stare. "Is this any way to treat a bridegroom? An injured bridegroom?" He touched the angry wound on his head. *"Heart Woman?* They should have named you Heart of Stone Woman!"

"That old woman seems to have great power in the tribe. Who is she?" Kate drew her legs up and sat cross-legged on the platform, hands folded under her chin. "I like her."

"Quaghcunnega Squithetha? She's my *cocumtha,* my grandmother. Actually, she's my great-grandmother. She's quite a woman. She was born a Lenni Lenape and married into the tribe. The Lenapes are highly spiritual; they have great personal power. She was a medicine woman among her own people as a girl. They claimed she can ride rainbows."

Kate laughed. "Well, it sounds like fun. I wish she'd tell me the secret."

"The Delaware take it very seriously." He shrugged. "When I was a boy . . . Well, who knows, maybe she can. Anyway, she's my mother's grandmother and I spent a lot of time in her wigwam as a child. Among the Shawnee, the mother's people are more important than the father's."

"Why?"

Pride grinned. "Every child has a mother. When it comes to fathers, who can say for sure? There are no illegitimate children among the Shawnee." He ran his fingers along Kate's bare arm. "Am I to spend my wedding night telling folklore?"

Kate pulled her arm away, trying not to admit the thrill she felt at his touch. "Pride . . . I . . ." He laid a gentle kiss just above the silver armband, and she trembled.

"For tonight, Kate, can't we put away the anger and fear? Tomorrow will be time enough for plans and recriminations. This is a sacred night for Ki-te-hi and Chobeka. I'm tired and my head hurts like hell. All I want is you curled beside me. I want you soft and tender, not coiled like a rattler ready to strike. Kate?" he murmured huskily.

The first drops of rain were beginning to hit the bark roof overhead. The fire hissed as water dropped onto the coals in the center of the wigwam. Kate could hear the rustle of the pine boughs in the wind. Suddenly, she too was exhausted.

"If we make a truce for the night, you won't break it?" she questioned. "Promise?"

"I won't break it." Pride stretched out, next to the wall, and lay down, his head propped up on one elbow. In the firelight, he was a bronze god out of some ancient legend, and Kate's blood quickened.

"Swear?"

"Are you going to keep up this nonsense all night? I said I wouldn't bother you." His mouth tightened into a taut line.

"It's really too warm for a fire, but if I put it out the mosquitoes will eat us alive," she hedged, slipping off the beaded moccasins and putting them at the foot of the bed.

"You're not supposed to sleep in the dress." Pride turned his back to her and snuggled down in the bearskin sheet.

"Is Tschi alive?"

"I don't want to talk about Tschi. I should have killed him." The wide shoulders tensed, and the loincloth fell away to reveal the full length of Pride's hip and thigh. "Maybe you'd have preferred to honeymoon with him."

The little-boy slight in his voice made her smile. "No," Kate admitted. "Tschi's worse than you." She slid off the armband. "I hate him."

"You hate me, remember."

"I hate him more than I hate you." She removed one earring and looked for a safe place to put it. "He is your brother. I only wanted to know if he died."

"He's not dead yet."

"Who's taking care of him? That woman who stole my moccasins? The camp slut?"

Pride turned his head and glared at her. "Where did you get that foul mouth? For a woman who *claims* to be a lady, you use the coarsest language. And yes, that's who's patching up his wounds."

"It's a wonder he doesn't already have a wife. And children."

"Tschi doesn't have trouble getting a woman, just keeping them. He's had three." He sat up. "Are you coming to bed or not? If you're not, shut up so I can get to sleep."

"Three wives? You mean I would be number four?" Kate dropped the earrings into a clay bowl and they tinkled together. "Four wives? And how many children?"

"None. That's why his last wife divorced him. They fought over whose fault it was." Pride turned back to the wall.

"She divorced him?"

"The Shawnee recognize divorce. All you have to do to be rid of me—after a suitable period of time—is to set my bow and moccasins outside the wigwam, and announce publicly that you're divorcing me. Of course, you'll have to learn the language first. It wouldn't be legal in English," he chuckled.

"Then I'll start lessons first thing in the morning," Kate teased, slipping the tight buckskin dress over her head.

"Good. I'll teach you."

The corners of Kate's mouth turned up in a smile as she crawled into bed beside him, wearing nothing but her feathered braids. If she had her way, her husband would get little sleep this night.

Chapter 14

They lay back to back, bare skin inches apart. Pride's breathing was slow and steady. Kate was certain he was pretending to be asleep. The rain was falling heavily; the wind brought a relief from the humid heat of August. Kate stretched, catlike, reveling in the soft fur against her body. "Pride?" she whispered. No answer. "Are you asleep?"

Since she was a little girl, rain had affected her this way. It made her dreamy and lazy. She pictured in her mind the wet forest around the snug hut. Here, they were warm and dry, sheltered from the world. "Pride? Chobeka?

"Hmmm?"

Kate rolled over. "Want me to scratch your back?"

"Let me sleep," he mumbled.

Kate drew five fingers across one shoulder and down the center of his backbone. "Doesn't that feel good?"

"Mmm."

Kate began to scratch circles on his back, and then to rub the thick, corded neck. She rubbed a hand across the bare spots on his head and giggled. "You look ridiculous. Why did you let them shave your head?"

"It isn't shaved."

"Don't tell me it isn't shaved. Look at you. It's barbaric." She ran her hand over the stiff crest. "You had such beautiful hair and you let them pluck you like an egg."

"Umm-hmm. That's how they do it. They pull the hairs out with a clamshell. They shave that way too."

"That's why you don't have hair on your chest? You

pluck it with shells?'' Kate ran her tongue down an inch of backbone. ''You are a savage, Pride Ashton.''

''Leave me be, woman,'' he grumbled. ''There's no pleasing you! I promised you I'd not partake of your charms tonight. Now, stop tormenting me.'' He pushed Kate's hand away. ''Damn independent squaw! Three hours a Shawnee and you've picked up all their bad habits.''

''I want to know why a grown man wants to look like a half-starved buzzard.''

''It's a war-lock. The Shawnee warriors wear their hair that way for two reasons. First, they think it frightens the enemy. Two, an enemy can't get a good hold on you to cut your head off. I did it because I didn't want Tschi to kill me.''

''Oh.'' She massaged the knotted muscles of his shoulders.

''Stop tormenting me. Are you possessed by Maté-kanis?''

Kate stopped rubbing and sat up. ''Matey who?''

''Maté-kanis. He's a little brown creature—something like a dwarf—that lives in the deep forest. He plays tricks on people.'' Pride hunched down and covered his head with his arm. ''Please! Let me sleep. I'm sore, I hurt all over. I'm tired. Go find a bear to bait.''

''A dwarf? A brown dwarf? That's what I remind you of?'' She began to tickle his ribs. ''A dwarf, huh? I'll show you dwarf!''

Pride didn't move. ''Demon woman, I'm not ticklish.''

Kate withdrew her hands as though they were stung. ''I thought you were just teasing me,'' she murmured. ''If you really want to go to sleep, I'll go to sleep.'' She turned her back and retreated to the far side of the bed.

Instantly, Pride's long body pressed against her back. The throbbing tumescence against her buttocks left no doubt that he was fully aroused. He lifted her hair and his lips brushed the back of her neck. A wide hand slipped under her arm and captured a tingling breast. His other arm slid beneath her. With a single motion, he turned her to him and pinned her to the bed with powerful legs. ''I'm awake,'' he murmured, between kisses.

"Damn you . . . damn you . . ." Her mouth opened to his, lips full and moist. His kisses were sweet and lingering, drawing her down into a whirlpool of delights.

His hands traced the curves of her breasts, caressing, bringing each nipple to an aching awakening. Kate moaned and pulled him tighter against her. Her fingers moved down to fumble with the rawhide tie that held his loincloth. Pride caught the thong and snapped it, tossing the leather covering aside.

A hand wandered down Kate's hip and brushed at the soft curls. She gasped with pleasure. Her skin seemed on fire; his hands were everywhere, stroking, tantalizing. Kate could do no less than to serve her rugged warrior as well.

They lay, side by side, touching, kissing, drinking in the nearness of each other. "Ki-te-hi," Pride said hoarsely. "I love thee. More than my own soul . . . I love thee."

"I love you too," she pledged. "I love every inch of you." Her teeth nipped at his shoulder.

"Never leave me . . . never," he entreated. "Promise me."

"I won't, darling . . . never again." She pulled his head down and kissed him once more. Her lips were swollen with desire; her inner thighs were moist with the anticipation of love. The tip of her tongue traced the fullness of his lower lip, then explored the honey-sweet riches of his mouth.

"Love me," Kate begged. "Now!"

Trembling, he pushed her back against the bearskin robe and filled her with the proof of his passion. She rose to meet his plunging thrusts with equal fervor, crying out as the fiery spasms caught them, transporting them beyond the bounds of earth. Higher and higher they soared, until . . . together . . . they rode the rainbow.

Secure in his loving arms, she looked down at the green world below and let all her fears and doubts fall free. This man was all she desired in life. England, her brother's death, her own vows of independence seemed insignificant. As long as Kate drew breath, she would walk beside him and entrust her heart to him.

All through the rainy night, they lay close and whispered

lovers' secrets. Kate's inner soul sang with indescribable joy. She could not hold back the tears of happiness. Laughing, he held her and kissed away the salty drops.

"You are Shawnee," he teased. "All squaws weep when they are happy and laugh in anger."

"Women," she retorted, between sniffs. "Is it any wonder, when we have men to contend with?"

In the misty hours before dawn, they bathed together in the river, splashing and pushing one another under like mischievous children. Pride showed Kate how to swim with her eyes open, and they explored the river bottom with its sunken logs and moss-backed turtles. Incredibly, in this Eden-like setting, a few hundred yards from a Shawnee Indian village, it seemed completely natural to swim naked as silkies from the watery depths.

They walked together, hand in hand, back to the wigwam, letting the cool air dry their bodies. Kate built a fire and broiled the fish that Pride had cleaned and pegged to a hickory slab. She watched while he molded cornmeal and berries into flat cakes and laid them on a stone to bake.

"You'll have to learn to cook, woman. You'll not always have me to do it for you."

Kate mouthed a dare, and the corncakes burned to a crisp while they were lost in each other's embrace. They made love fiercely, possessively . . . and then a second time, in slow, gentle tenderness.

"Maybe being a Shawnee isn't so bad," Kate admitted, stretching catlike. "I suppose we have to go outside and play Indian now."

"No, we don't. We are supposed to make love for the next two weeks, nonstop. Someone will hunt for me, and someone will gather wood for you."

"Two weeks?" Kate made a face. "I thought we'd be leaving for Ashton Hall today, or tomorrow at least." She sat up and wound the skirt around her. "Isn't there any top to this thing?"

"No." Pride grinned. "And we're not going home, not for a while anyway. We're prisoners."

"Prisoners?" Kate whirled on him. "What do you mean?"

"I tried to convince the tribe not to go to war against the British. They didn't buy my argument. I'm accepted as a full member of the tribe; they'll honor my decision not to go to war with them. But they've got no intention of letting us go back to warn the Maryland colony or His Majesty's troops. We're virtual prisoners until the war is full-scale. Then, they'll only let me go if they're certain I won't fight against the Shawnee. We're in a touchy spot, Kate, and it can only get worse." He lay back, hands behind his head. "You may get your chance to learn Shawnee. With any luck, our first son may learn to speak the language."

"This is another one of your tricks!"

"I wish to hell it was."

"Then we just sit here? And do nothing? While they plan a war against unsuspecting farmers?"

"No. We don't. We figure out a way to escape, without hurting any Shawnee. These are my people, too, and yours." He reached above him to take down a leather pouch and removed a long-stemmed pipe and tobacco. "We can't give them any reason to be suspicious. We'll wait and watch for a chance." He got up, lit the pipe with a glowing coal from the fire, and took a long puff. A pungent odor filled the small hut. "We wait, Kate, until the time's right."

"At least we won't be bored," she answered wryly.

"I like you in that bit of a thing. In time you'll tan to a honey color all over. There'll be no need for me to waste money on gowns for you when we get back to Ashton." The dark eyes twinkled as he squatted Indian-fashion and enjoyed his pipe. He'd not bothered to don the loincloth.

Kate blushed. "It's too warm for the dress inside. But I'll not take a step out of this house without a proper shirt. Find me some cloth, and I'll make something. I'll not expose myself for any buck who cares to stare."

"Kate Ashton offering to sew? This is a morning to remember!"

Kate Ashton, she thought. He'd called her Kate Ashton. She repeated the name in her mind and laughed out loud. "If I'm really your wife, I guess I'm Lady Ashton."

"Aye, Katy. Cream will rise to the top. Although you'll find, in America, the title will win you few friends among the common folk. It's a different place and time. England's ways are not ours, and it's growing more so all the time."

"Will we be wed in the church then, a Christian ceremony, Pride?" She was suddenly serious, her blue eyes large with concern. "I won't leave you. But . . . I would like a real wedding. Please."

"You can have a Chinese wedding, if that would please you." He laid aside the pipe and drew her down into his lap. "Anything that will bind you closer to me, wench. Anything. For I mean to keep the highwayman I've captured." If I can, he thought.

He kissed her, and she snuggled down against his chest happily. "A country parson will do fine," she whispered. "And I must have the shirt. I'll not add lewdness to my other sins."

"In that case." Pride reached for a basket at the foot of the sleeping platform. "I might have something that would do in here." He drew out a fringed vest of spotted fawn-skin and slipped it around her shoulders. "You tie this and this," he explained. "I suppose it will have to do, though I prefer you without it."

Kate fingered the soft leather with delight. The garment covered her breasts, leaving a wide expanse of bare skin between the bottom fringe and the top of her skirt. A design of green leaves and gold flowers bordered the edges of the vest, worked in tiny glass beads. "It's beautiful," she cried. "Thank you." She wished for a mirror to view the pagan outfit from every side. What would London think of her? No Saracen dancing girl would dare to appear in public in such scant attire!

She remembered the red beads and silver earrings, and added them to the costume. "Well, what do you think?" she begged. "Am I Indian enough to suit you?"

"I'm not sure," he growled. "Come a little closer. I need a better look." He lunged for Kate and she giggled and ducked away. He caught her and carried her to the bed. At least when she was in his arms, he was certain of where she was and what she was doing.

"No more," she pleaded. "You're not a young man anymore. You must save your strength." He closed her laughing mouth with kisses.

"Damnable wench," he grumbled. "We'll see who's too old for this sport!"

The first war party left the village three days later. Pride watched tight-lipped as Delaware and Shawnee warriors filed from the council circle. Their faces were painted, their weapons primed. He could not suppress a shudder at the thought of the bloodshed to come.

Kate stood beside him silently, her joy shattered. The sounds of the war dance had penetrated the thin walls of their wigwam, ending her idyllic dream and bringing her solidly back to earth. This was no game; it was war. People died in war. And suddenly, she realized there were people on both sides she cared about.

The days that followed were tense. Pride went out hunting with men too old to go to war. Kate was watched closely and not permitted to leave the village proper. At night, sentries guarded not only the camp but Kate's hut.

"You could get away," Kate suggested, "and carry the warning to Annapolis."

"By myself, but they'd kill you."

She paled. "You said I was safe here, that they considered me one of the tribe." She offered him a gourd of water. "What else haven't you told me?"

"You are Shawnee. And you're my wife. If I turn traitor, you suffer my punishment." He caught her chin and lifted it. "I never told you that you were safe here. The village could be attacked by the Iroquois, or by English troops, or by colonial militia. And if we are . . ." Pride's fingers tightened on her flesh and his eyes held her fast. "You run like hell! Don't try to fight, and don't try to tell them you're English. It won't do any good. If you're here, you're fair game for rape and murder. Run into the woods, find a thicket, and lie low, for days if you have to. Don't scream and don't make a sound."

Kate's blue eyes narrowed. "I'm to fly off into the forest like a frightened quail. A Storm doesn't run, and I don't

think an Ashton does either. If we're attacked, I'll fight
. . . with anything I can. There are babies here and old
people. What about Rainbow Girl? Am I supposed to
scamper off and leave them to the Iroquois?'' she scoffed.

"Damn it, woman! You'll do as I say. You have no idea
what you're talking about. An Iroquois warrior would make
the Tyburn executioner look like an English nanny!''

"The devil himself couldn't be any worse than Tschi,
and he didn't scare me!'' she lied. ''I'll be damned if I'll
play the coward and leave my friends to die.''

"An Indian camp doesn't stand and fight. This isn't a
European battleground with troops lined up in even rows.
The men will try to gain a little time for the women and
children to run and hide. Even the small children know
better than to cry out. For once in your life, listen to me!''

"And what will you be doing if the camp's attacked?''
She glared at him.

Giving her a look of utter contempt, Pride got to his feet
and left the hut. He didn't return until long past midnight.

Kate pretended to be asleep as he climbed into bed.
She wanted to apologize, but the words stuck in her throat.
She lay there, staring into the dark, knowing how wrong
she had been in questioning his bravery.

Pride's hand touched her shoulder, and she turned toward him. "I was a fool," she whispered. "I didn't mean
it when I—"

He pulled her against him. "We're both on edge. I
should have laughed instead of storming off. I don't want
anything to happen to you. You're my wife, and I've put
you in a situation of great danger. I can't even protect you.
I owe you the apology, Kate."

"I'm scared," she admitted. "And I took it out on you.
We'll get out of this together."

He kissed her. "Even when I'm furious at you, it's hard
to stay away." His hands traveled down her arm. "I want
to make love to you," he said hoarsely. "Now."

A shrill cry brought Pride to his feet and scrambling for
his weapons. Answering yells from the village and the
barking of dogs added to the commotion. Kate grabbed for

her clothing. "I don't think it's a raiding party," Pride said. "Wait here." He was out of the wigwam and gone.

Tying the front of the vest, Kate ran after him, hesitating only long enough to pick up Pride's tomahawk.

Two gunshots were heard, and then the welcome shout. "The war party! It's the war party returned."

"What is it?" Kate demanded, coming up behind Pride. "What are they saying?"

"It's our people. The war party's back," he translated. He frowned at her. "Don't you ever listen? I told you to stay put." He took the tomahawk from her hand. "Who did you intend to scalp with this?"

Three warriors came along the path, then two more half-carrying a wounded man. A woman screamed and ran to him, her cries turning to moans as she saw the extent of his wound. Wabethe dashed past them, searching for her husband.

The women and children crowded around, gratefully embracing their men and counting the missing and wounded. Kate saw Wabethe with her arm under a brave's shoulder. A half-grown boy led a horse with a body slung over the saddle. Unsoma cried out and fell to her knees, pounding the ground in her grief.

"No prisoners," Pride said. "They met an Iroquois war party a day's march north. We have two dead, five wounded."

"And the Iroquois?"

"Six killed, that many wounded, but they got away. They also wounded a German that was traveling with the Iroquois. The Delaware took him to trade for one of their people the British took earlier."

"I don't see any of them." Kate looked around. These braves all seemed to be Shawnee.

"They joined up with a larger war band of Delaware from the Ohio country. They're going to hit the Lancaster Valley." Pride's face was hard. "There are a lot of isolated farms up there. Damn the British! Don't they realize what they've started?"

"You're British," she reminded him softly.

He shook his head. "I was once. Now I'm Shawnee and

American. And that's enough difference to try a man's soul." He walked her back to the wigwam. "Best you stay out of sight for the rest of the night. Tempers are high. You'll be safe in the house."

"And you?"

"I'll find out whatever I can. The sooner we get out of here, the better." His jawline tightened. "I'm worried about Ashton Hall and my mother."

No one in the camp slept that night. Food was cooked for the returning warriors; groups gathered around fires to hear of the battle. From the doorway of the wigwam, Kate watched, sick at heart for the widows and fatherless children.

She hadn't known the husband of Unsoma, but the woman had had more than enough tragedy in her short life. She didn't need to be left alone a second time. Kate could not shake the thought that it could easily be Pride who was killed. Already, he seemed the most important thing in her life. Fear grew within her until she could taste it.

The following day, the tribe gathered their belongings in preparation to move. Men and women harvested the corn and squash. The pumpkins were not yet ripe. A party would come back for them in a few weeks, if it was safe. Now, it was urgent that the people move to their winter camp, a place more remote and easier to defend.

The wigwams were closed and left. Kate looked back at hers as they marched away. It had been her first home as a wife, and she had grown fond of it. Shouldering her heavy pack, she fell into line behind Wabethe and her husband. The man's shoulder and arm were bandaged, but he seemed strong. Wabethe carried the baby on her back.

Kate could see Pride striding along a dozen yards ahead. The bearskin was slung over his shoulder, and he carried his long rifle and weapons. They'd not been able to take all the bowls and baskets. Wabethe had shown her how to dig a hole in the floor to hide the items she couldn't carry.

"In spring, we come back these field," Wabethe said sadly. "Maybe so. Good field."

Among the warriors, Kate saw a familiar face. Tschi! He walked stiffly, his body unnaturally rigid, obviously in pain. Once, she saw him glaring at Pride. She shivered, despite the heat, remembering Pride's words. *I should have killed him.* Was it only anger speaking? Or . . . ? She vowed to watch Tschi closely. He was not one to forget and forgive.

That night, the women slept together. No fires were lit; the people ate cold food and drank warm water. There was no chance to speak with Pride alone. Wherever he went, Shawnee warriors kept close to his back. Kate was so worn out from the journey that she fell asleep almost at once.

At dawn, they began the march again. The way was hilly, and the woods were thick. At mid-day, Kate offered to carry Wabethe's baby. She could see the weariness on her friend's face. The baby was heavier than she'd thought; she was more than happy when a halt was called two hours before sunset. Again, it was a cold camp.

They reached the new site at mid-morning the following day. Giant oaks towered overhead, shading the remains of an old village. The clearing was sheltered by two rock-strewn hills and watered by a fast-running, white-foamed creek.

The old bark was pulled away by eager hands. Women chattered excitedly and the children ran free. The feeling of strain that had permeated the journey was gone. Sentinels stood guard on the hilltops, and warriors accompanied the women who went to strip fresh bark from trees a distance away. Wabethe talked nonstop, and she and Kate worked to clean out a leaf-clogged hut.

"Tonight you sleep here. Tomorrow we . . ." She shrugged. "Tomorrow Ki-te-hi's wigwam. You like sleep man again, *ayi?*"

Kate nodded. It seemed like weeks since she and Pride had been alone together. Energetically, she dug at the debris, stooping to pick up a handful. A snake slithered away from the pile of leaves and she jumped back.

A man's laughter brought crimson to her cheeks and she whirled to face him. "Tschi!"

"So Panther Woman, you do not like snakes," he said softly. "I will remember." His eyes were shuttered glass, so black as to be almost lifeless. "My brother tells me you bade him save my life. It is good to know the love you have for me."

Kate spat at his feet.

Tschi laughed and turned away. "Walk softly, little sister," he warned. "And beware of snakes."

Wabethe's eyes narrowed. "Tschi snake."

"I agree."

"You watch back." Wabethe's fist tightened. "No trust, ever."

"No trust who?" Pride asked, catching Kate around the waist and swinging her above the ground.

"Stop," Kate giggled. "Put me down. People are staring at us."

He set her down and kissed the top of her head. "Who cares? Let them look."

"No trust Tschi," Wabethe repeated.

"Don't worry about him. His pride is hurt because I let him live, and because you prefer me over him. But he's my brother. He told me this morning that he was wrong. Tschi's hard, but he's my blood. You've nothing to fear from him, Ki-te-hi." He offered Wabethe a plump turkey hen. "For the evening meal, mother of my woman."

Wabethe giggled and put her hand over her mouth. Her eyes sparkled as she reached for the bird. "No worry. I cook. Ki-te-hi no cook. Wabethe let her pull feather."

"Thanks," Kate said. "Just what I've always wanted." She joined in the laughter, hiding her concern. Did Pride know his brother better than she did? Or was Tschi's hate the living thing she believed it to be? She couldn't argue with him in front of Wabethe. Later, when they were alone, she would tell him what Tschi had said. She would make him understand how real her fears were.

By the following night, their wigwam was up. It was wonderful to have privacy again. They could lie in each other's arms and talk far into the night. And they could know the joy of one another. If she tried hard enough, Kate could almost recapture the dream.

The days and nights fell into a routine. In the morning, Pride hunted with the men, and Kate learned the skills of an Indian wife from Wabethe and her friends. She began to understand more and more of the Shawnee tongue, although her attempts to speak it were met with gales of laughter. Tschi stayed away from her, and his threats faded into the background.

A few trees began to turn color; stray leaves drifted on the September wind. The days had dissolved into weeks, almost without Kate's realizing. Somehow, the upside-down world of the Shawnee had begun to seem normal. The time before . . . the time when she had not belonged to Pride Ashton, body and soul, seemed to belong to another century.

There had been a sort of harvest dance that night, with feasting and games. The men had played at gambling and Wabethe had taught Kate the dance step. Even the children had stayed up late, marveling at Rainbow Girl's stories. Kate and Pride had been among the last to leave the dying camp fire for the snug privacy of their wigwam.

A few words and kisses had sent Kate off to sleep. The day had been long, and she was content to cuddle close to Pride. "Night," she whispered.

"Good night, little dancer."

She didn't know how long she'd slept when a hand over her mouth and Pride's calm voice in her ear woke her to total blackness. "Shhh," he warned. "It's me. Don't make a sound. We're getting out of here, tonight."

"But how? The camp guards?" She pushed his hand away and rubbed at her eyes. She was barely awake and not thinking clearly.

"It's all right. Tschi's on duty. He's letting us escape."

"I don't believe it." Kate grabbed his arm. "Don't trust him. He hates me. Why should he help us?"

"Shhh. Sound carries easily," Pride warned. "He's as worried about Mother as I am. He knows she needs me there to look after her. Once I'm gone, the people will stop talking about the circle, and he can get back to being a war leader." He handed her a bundle. "There's food in there to last us a few days. Get dressed." No need to tell Kate that he didn't trust her or Tschi any farther than he could throw them. Pride's Shawnee half insisted that a brother would not—could not—betray another brother. It went against all Shawnee law. Family was sacred. A man who would do such a thing risked his immortal soul. And yet . . . The English half remembered the hatred in Tschi's eyes, remembered the old hurts and angers.

"Hurry," he whispered to Kate. A wave of shame passed over him. Tschi always said it was Pride's white blood that made him different, made him distrust. What kind of man would suspect his brother of treachery? This chance might not come again, and to refuse it would sever any chance he and Tschi would ever have of making peace between them. It would be an unforgivable insult to his brother's honor. They would have to risk it.

Kate interrupted his thoughts. "No. I won't go. I'm afraid, Pride."

"I'm going, and you're coming with me. If he tries anything, I can handle him. It's the first chance we've had, and I've got to take it. He loves Rebecca. She's probably the only person he's ever loved. Now, get dressed, or I'll drag you out of here the way you are."

Kate pulled the deerskin dress over her head and fumbled for her moccasins. "I don't feel right about this."

"Do you want to be a Shawnee all your life?"

"No . . . but . . ."

"No buts. Come on."

Cautiously, she followed him out of the wigwam. There was no moon. It was so dark she could hardly see Pride inches in front of her. He took her hand, and she clenched her teeth to keep them from chattering.

Every step she took was terrifying. Twigs snapped beneath her moccasins and dry leaves crunched. She could hear the pounding of her own blood in her veins. A baby cried and Kate almost jumped out of her skin. She clenched her teeth and tried to follow in Pride's footsteps.

A shadow loomed ahead of them, materializing out of the haze. "Chobeka?"

"Tschi?"

He grunted and motioned for them to follow him. Three horses were tied in the trees. They mounted in silence and rode off single file down the twisting path.

When they were a mile as the crow flies from the camp, Pride broke the silence. "Why?"

"I'm more familiar with the country than you are. There's a Lenni Lenape camp a half-day's journey away and I want to make sure you give it a wide berth." He switched from Shawnee to English. "You have Panther Woman to slow feet. No good you escape Shawnee, leave scalp Delaware lodgepole."

"He was supposed to be on guard duty," Kate said suspiciously. "Leaving his post demands the death penalty. Even a white squaw knows that." She guided her horse close to Pride's. "Why are you being so good to us, Tschi?"

"Your woman thinks too highly of herself," Tschi said in Shawnee. "She does not believe we left our anger in the sacred circle. H'kah-nih took my place tonight. He is known as a fool. None will doubt you slipped away without his knowledge. It is believed that I went to hunt a bear with three of my friends. My absence will cause no alarm in the morning." To Kate he said, "Chobeka my brother."

"Brother be damned. Pride, he—"

"Enough, Kate. We're too close to the camp to be sitting here. I want to put miles between us and them, and I want to do it before daylight." He kicked his horse into a stiff trot. If they got out of this with their hair they'd be lucky.

They pressed hard for several hours. Kate had no idea of the direction they had taken. Most of the terrain was wooded and hilly. She was grateful for the horse, knowing how hard it would have been on foot.

A false dawn sent halos of shimmering fuchsia spilling across a star-sprinkled sky. The growing light brought trees and rocks into focus, and Kate breathed in the dew-drenched air. An owl gave a final hunting cry as it swooped on a scurrying rodent almost in her path.

With a snort of panic, Kate's horse reared and she fought to hold her seat. Pride turned in the saddle, and a blow from Tschi's rifle barrel knocked him to the ground. Kate screamed, and a form hurtled from the tree overhead on top of her! The force was too great; horse, Kate, and attacker fell backward in a jumble of thrashing limbs.

Kate tried to struggle free. The horse's weight pinned her right leg; only the thick brush kept the bone from snapping under the strain. Cursing, she struck out at the Indian with her fists. He struck her on the face and the sting changed her terror to a white-hot fury. She dragged a knife from the brave's waist sheath and attempted to stab him with it.

The horse scrambled up, and Kate rolled and caught a handful of mane. The animal pulled her to her feet. From the corner of her eye she counted at least three men, all closing on her. Pride lay motionless, a dark stain spreading across his face. "You've killed him!" she screamed. She lunged at the astonished warrior with the knife, slicing a crimson streak down one copper arm.

Iron arms went around her, twisting her wrist cruelly until she cried out in pain. The knife fell from her numb fingers; she was thrown violently to the ground. Tschi kicked her several times. Kate seized his bare leg and sank her teeth into it. A blow knocked her senseless.

As she came to, her arms were being bound behind her back roughly. The blue Storm eyes fastened on Tschi's smirking face and darkened to gray slits of hate. A string of curses rolled from her lips until she had exhausted every foul name and oath she had ever heard. "May God strike you," she gasped, "and put the mark of Cain on you that you deserve. A man who would betray his own brother is yellow scum! What will you tell your mother when she asks? Will you lie to her too? Or will she see through you?"

Tschi backhanded her across the mouth and signaled to the brave behind her. A leather gag was tied over her protesting mouth. Tschi grinned wolfishly. "You talk too much, woman." He slung her up on the horse, tying her legs together under the animal's belly. "My brother is not dead," he said softly. "Not yet." The cold flame in his eyes struck her like blow. "He will die slow. You?" He shrugged. "You may wish for death."

Kate's mind fastened on Tschi's words, "My brother is

not dead.'' If Pride were alive, it would be all right! He'd find a way to save them. She watched as they tied his unconscious body to the horse in front of her. The wound was still bleeding. It should be stitched. He moaned, and she strained helplessly at the leather thongs that held her. It was maddening to have him hurt, only a few feet away, and to be unable to help.

As the light increased, Kate recognized the braves with Tschi. Two were still in their teens. She knew none of them well enough to remember their names. They were Shawnee, from the village, and, she assumed, friends or followers of Tschi.

To her surprise, they did not turn back along the trail they had come on. Instead they turned west. She could get some idea of direction now, by the sun. It was rising in the east. Where was Tschi taking them if not back to the Shawnee village? She fought against the gag, succeeding only in rubbing a raw spot on her lip. I'll get even with you, Tschi, she vowed. On my brother's grave, I swear it!

There was no stop for food or water all through the long day. By the time night came, Kate was reeling from exhaustion. The leather gag was soaked with her own blood; her wrists had long since become fiery wounds. Only the bonds on her raw ankles kept her from falling off the horse.

Still, they pressed on. Kate's mouth felt like a desert. She would die before she would beg water from Tschi. In any case, she had seen no water. They had crossed no streams or rivers. Foggily, she began to pray for rain.

She was worried about Pride. He had drifted in and out of consciousness all day. Even when he was awake, he didn't seem lucid. He was talking crazy, half in English and half in Shawnee. He didn't seem to realize they'd been betrayed and captured. He kept talking about a bear hunt; Kate's fears grew with every passing hour.

The horses stopped, and Kate slumped forward. If they made camp, she might have a chance to get water, to see to Pride's injuries. Tschi fired his rifle in the air. Kate's horse jumped and she grabbed at the mane to keep her balance.

Two shots answered from the woods ahead. Tschi and

the men dismounted. Figures began to appear in the trees. Kate soon lost count. They were not Shawnee. She didn't know who they were. The language they called out was totally meaningless to her. Tschi waved, and they walked forward, leading the horses.

Strange braves closed about them, fierce and hard-eyed. It was too dark to see clearly, but most wore their hair like Tschi's and seemed to be tattooed. They carried modern rifles and painted war clubs with vicious balls on the end. Kate had seen nothing like them before.

Tschi spoke with them in the strange tongue. A warrior took the reins of Kate's horse and they moved quickly down a tree-studded hillside. Kate heard the welcome sound of running water. When they rounded a bend, she saw a circle of camp fires.

"Ho!" Tschi called. "I come! Tschi of the Shawnee! I bring the man you want! I bring Pride Ashton!"

A white man stepped into the firelight. He wore fringed buckskin clothing and pistols at his waist. Cradled in his arms was a French long rifle. *"Bon soir,* my friends."

Waves of nausea washed through Kate as the man's accent sounded in her ears. *He was French! Tschi was turning them over to the French!*

The gray eyes appraised her thoroughly. "Madam," he said, coming forward to stand by her horse. "Permit me to introduce myself. I am Captain Andre DeSalle." He smiled and inclined his head slightly. "Be at ease." His English was stilted, but letter-perfect. "You are under my protection."

"I bring prisoner; you give guns," Tschi said. He lowered his own rifle menacingly.

DeSalle looked at Pride, saw he was still breathing, and nodded. Two Indians came forward carrying a heavy box. They put it on the ground and slid back the lid. It was full of rifles. "I keep my word, Tschi," DeSalle reminded him. "Tell your brothers, the Shawnee, the French are their friends. We will give them fine weapons, powder, and shot. The French King is generous to all his allies."

A brave pulled Kate from the horse, cutting the ties at her ankles and removing the gag. "Please," Kate cried.

"You're a white man! For the love of God, help him. He's badly hurt."

Tschi's men began to remove the guns and tie them on Kate's horse. Tschi cut the thongs holding Pride and he tumbled to the ground. Kate would have run to him, but the Frenchman stepped in front of her.

"Leave him to me, madam." He was not much taller than she was, but stocky. His white-blond hair was caught in a queue at the back of his neck. He smiled at her kindly. "You are in need of care yourself." The handsome young face was smooth and without blemish, his beard freshly shaved.

"You don't understand," Kate pleaded. "You must let me—"

The Frenchman's hand cracked across Kate's face. "It is you who does not understand, madam. I will have no trouble from an English whore. When I speak, I expect to be obeyed." He turned to an Indian and gave an order.

Hands grabbed Kate and pulled her away, struggling. "Damn you!" she cried. "Damn you! You're a white man! You're worse than they are!"

DeSalle rolled Pride over on his back with a booted foot. *"Bon soir*, Monsieur Ashton." He laughed coldly. "I told you we would meet again."

Chapter 15

Her captor had unfastened her hands and thrust her into a tent. A lantern on the table filled the interior with faint light. Kate picked herself up from the floor and reached for the bottle of wine on the table. A few slow swallows took the edge off the greatest part of her thirst. A little more went over her chafed wrists; the wine stung, but Kate knew it would keep the raw places from becoming infected.

A plate lay on the table. Tschi had interrupted the French captain's dinner. *Good.* Kate ravenously devoured the bread and meat, then washed it down with more wine. The wine was thin and sour, but it didn't matter. It tasted like nectar.

A quick search of the tent turned up clothing, a large map, and a round of sharp cheese—no weapons, to her disappointment. She broke off a piece of the cheese and ate it, then tucked another piece into the small bag at her waist.

She must get to Pride! He would die if something wasn't done for him soon. She tugged at the bottom of the tent. Perhaps she could slip under the—

"Ah, madam." DeSalle's smooth voice cut through her plans. "Are you a thief as well as a whore?"

Kate's face flamed. "I'm no whore! Pride Ashton is my husband. It's Lady Ashton to you, Captain."

He laughed, dropping the tent flap behind him. "So the Englishman's slut fancies herself a lady? You amuse me, *fille*. Tschi told me you went through some pagan Indian rite with the man."

"I'm his wife!" Kate insisted.

DeSalle's eyes took in the empty plate, the overturned wine bottle. "Mother Church recognizes no common-law liaisons. Neither do I. You're lucky I haven't seen a white woman in months or I'd turn you over to my Hurons."

Kate got to her feet stiffly. "You can go to hell, you pious French bastard! I ate your supper because I was hungry."

"A practical woman," he said, taking her arm and pulling her to him. "Just how practical are you?"

Kate slapped him as hard as she could. He shoved her back and hit her across the face. She fell back against the table, seized the lantern, and threw it at him.

The lamp shattered in a hundred pieces, and Kate dodged past the Frenchman as he frantically tried to stamp the fire out. Outside, she looked around for Pride. He lay in a heap where he had fallen.

The Indians stared incredulously at her. She glared back at them. One man was drinking something from a gourd. She snatched it from his hand and ran to Pride. Behind her rose the sound of laughter and catcalls. A tiny question formed in her brain. What had the Frenchman called them? Hurons? She'd never heard Pride mention Hurons; they must be insignificant. None looked as fierce as Tschi, although most were bigger.

She knelt beside Pride and lifted his head, shuddering at the sight of the wound. If he lived, he'd carry a scar the rest of his days. She brought the gourd to her own lips and gasped. It was rum. For the lack of anything better, she dribbled a little into his slack mouth.

A cry of alarm went up as the Hurons saw the flames from the tent. Kate ignored them. One crisis at a time was all she could handle. She poured a little more whiskey into Pride as he choked. She lifted his head higher. "Pride? It's me, Kate. Can you hear me?"

The brown eyes flickered. His lips moved. "Kate?" he murmured hoarsely. "Where are we?"

"Tschi betrayed us. He sold us to a Frenchman and his Indian allies. The man's name is DeSalle. Captain Andre DeSalle. Do you know him? Pride? Do you know him?"

He had passed out again. Kate heard movement behind

her and quickly poured the rest of the whiskey over the open wound. Pride cried out and went limp. She lowered him to the ground and faced DeSalle, who had approached them. "He's my husband. We were married in England before we sailed," Kate lied. "You'll not make me a whore for any reason!"

The Frenchman swung at her and she ducked. He laughed. "Whore or goodwife, you have spirit. I like that in a woman. In any case, madam, you will be a widow soon enough." He prodded at Pride with his foot. "Tend him if you like. There's not enough left of him to provide good sport for the stake."

Kate turned her attention back to Pride. Let the man ramble on. He was of no consequence at the moment. As a captain, he must be of good breeding. Too bad he had the manners of a swineherd.

"Have you medicine? Bandages? How am I to look after him? I need a needle and thread to sew this cut. He must have hot food, something he can sip like broth."

"That, madam, is your problem. If you venture from the camp area, my Huron will fetch you back and roast you over the fire. You'd make a tasty meal," he said sarcastically. "We camp here until I rendezvous with a comrade, no more than two days at most. After that, we move out. If he can't travel, I'll shoot him."

"At least help me move him closer to the river. I need water to wash the wound."

DeSalle shrugged. "You seem quite resourceful, Lady Ashton. I'm certain you'll think of something." He turned on his heel and strode away.

The arrogant French bastard! He was so sure she was helpless that he wouldn't even bother to confine her. If she could get a gun . . . or steal a horse . . . He'd see who was helpless!

The Huron watched curiously as the white squaw dragged her man inch by inch toward the river. They talked among themselves and joked, and made bets as to whether Chobeka Illenaqui would live to give entertainment. He was an old and hated enemy. Whoever ate of his heart would gain great courage. Whoever took his man parts would know a hero's virility. Whoever won his scalp lock would receive much honor.

Again and again, Kate had to pause for breath. She hadn't realized Pride weighed so much. He groaned when she moved him. She was sorry to bring him more pain, but she had to have access to water. She leaned against a tree to get a second wind. The tree was old; a large section at the base had rotted away. Then she remembered that Wabethe had said spiderwebs were good to heal wounds. Cautiously, she felt inside. Her skin crawled. What if there were spiders in there, or even a snake?

Quickly she drew out a handful of sticky spiderweb, balled it together, and tucked it into her pouch. First, the wound would have to be cleaned. With renewed strength, she pulled Pride the rest of the way to the riverbank.

Scooping handfuls of water, she washed his face and head, then laid the spiderweb in the gash. The washing had started the wound bleeding again, but it didn't seem too bad. He stirred and Kate warned him to lie still. Leaving him for a minute, she went to the tent. On a bush beside it, a white linen shirt was draped to dry. It undoubtedly belonged to DeSalle. Kate took it without hesitation. He'd told her to be resourceful, hadn't he?

Tearing the shirt into strips, she bandaged Pride's head. Then, she used more of the shirt to drip water into his mouth. He coughed and opened his eyes. "Hello," she said.

"I feel like a horse kicked me."

"A snake. Tschi hit you with his rifle. It should be stitched, but I don't have a needle." She bent and stroked his damp hair. "I was worried when you wouldn't wake up."

"Don't you get near me with a needle. I've seen you sew."

"Pride," she whispered, "we're in trouble, big trouble. Do you remember what I told you before?"

He touched his head and winced. "No. Can't it wait until morning?"

Kate looked at the Huron warriors around the campfires, and then at DeSalle's tent. A light burned inside. "No, I don't think so.'' She told him again what she knew of their captors. ''Do you know him? DeSalle?''

Pride shut his eyes. ''I know him. We're not what you'd call friends.'' He fingered the wound again. ''Did you pull this thing tight?''

''Yes. And I put cobweb in it. Wabethe said—''

''Make the bandage tighter. I'm seeing double, but I think that will remedy itself in time. What kind of warriors did you say DeSalle has with him?''

Kate offered him more water. ''Just Huron.''

Pride's eyes flew open. ''Huron?''

She took his hand and brushed her lips against the callused fingertips. Pride's hands were solid and square, the nails cleanly pared. Kate forced a chuckle. ''It's not so bad,'' she quipped. ''At least they're not Iroquois.''

He opened one eye. ''Kate, Hurons are Iroquois.''

''But they can't be,'' she whispered. ''DeSalle's French. The Iroquois are British allies. You told me that yourself.''

''The Five Nations were friendly to the Crown the last I heard. But the Huron are French allies. The Huron—oh, hell, Katy! Just take my word for it. If you get a chance to escape, take it. Don't worry about me.'' He pushed himself up on his elbows, then sank back. ''Are there any other whites here? Any other Frenchmen?''

''No, I haven't seen any. There are about twenty Indians. DeSalle said he was meeting with someone in a day or two. Then we'd be moving out. He said if you couldn't travel, he'd shoot you.''

''Stay clear of him, Kate. He's dangerous. I don't know who he's meeting, but if you get the chance to go with him, take it.''

''You know I won't leave you. Why does DeSalle hate you?''

''We fought. I cut him bad . . . in a place no man wants to be cut.''

Kate paled. ''You're not serious.'' She glanced over her shoulder at the tent. ''I told him we were married. He wanted me to . . . Well, he called me a whore, so I lied. I said I was your wife.''

''You didn't lie, Ki-te-hi. I am your husband, before

God and man, in every way that matters. I want you to know that, and to know how much I love you.''

"Shhh, don't talk now. You're still weak. Sleep if you can; I'll be here with you." She cradled his head in her lap. Pride's talk of double vision frightened her more than the Indians. What if it didn't get better? What if . . .

"No, Kate. You've got to understand! DeSalle mustn't know that I consider you my wife. If he had any idea how much you mean to me . . ." His muscles tensed, and he tried to rise. Dizziness and nausea overcame him. "I think I'm going to be sick," he admitted sheepishly.

Kate held his head, then washed him with fresh water from the river. "It's no more than you did for me," she whispered. He drifted off into a fitful sleep.

The camp fires died down, and most of the Huron braves lay down to sleep. Trying not to show the fear that surged through her, Kate walked casually to the nearest fire. A grizzled warrior glared at her. She glared back, hoping she wouldn't disgrace herself by wetting her pants like a child.

The remains of an animal were suspended over the coals; it looked like a goat or a small deer. Kate knelt beside the fire and stared at it. There was plenty of meat left on the carcass, but she had no way to cut it. Her eyes met the Huron's again. A twisted scar ran from the corner of his left eye to his lip, giving him a terrifying appearance.

"May I borrow your knife?" she asked in Shawnee. He stared at her as though she were a bug; not a muscle moved in the copper mask. Kate repeated the question in English.

He grinned and drew his skinning knife from the sheath. He rose to his feet, catlike; he was well over six feet tall, and his chest and arms were covered with tattoos. The blade glimmered in the firelight as he brought it close to Kate's throat.

"Cut the meat, not me," she snapped, without flinching. Another second and she would shame herself. The Huron looked like an ogre from one of her father's fairy tales. She could well imagine him devouring human flesh.

With a chuckle, he sliced off a hindquarter of the animal and threw it into the dirt. He stood over it, daring her to reach and pick it up.

"Merci," she said, snatching up the bone. She turned on her heel and walked slowly back to Pride, praying the knife would not bury itself in her exposed back. Pride would need food when he woke again. She couldn't depend on *them* to feed him. She must find the courage to do it herself.

Her knees turned to jelly as she reached Pride and dropped down in the dirt beside him. He was still asleep. Methodically, she began to tear the meat into tiny pieces.

Through the long night, Pride woke and slept, tossed by fever and wracked by shaking chills. When he was himself, Kate urged bits of meat and water into his mouth. When he wasn't, she bathed his face and chest with water, or lay close to warm him with her own body.

The Indian guards paid her no more attention than a camp dog; DeSalle never stirred from his tent. Her eyes burned with weariness, but she dared not sleep. As long as she kept her vigil, she convinced herself, Pride would be safe.

"Fille!" An accented voice woke Kate from sleep. The Frenchman stood over her. "What have you done with my shirt?"

"What do you think?" She turned her attention to Pride, touching his head to reassure herself that he was breathing naturally. The fever was gone. She got to her feet. "I am, as you said, sir, a practical woman."

"Stir your ass, and make me some tea." He motioned to the tent. "There's a kettle inside. Can you cook?"

She laughed. "No."

"Believe her, DeSalle," Pride said weakly. "She's good for only one thing, and precious little good at that."

"Not a very gentlemanly way to speak of your wife, Ashton."

Pride scoffed. "Did you tell him that? The slut fancies herself highly. It's not likely I'd hunt a wife in Newgate where I plucked her."

Kate flushed crimson. "He lies! I—"

DeSalle shoved her toward the tent. "I thought as much.

Have you a name, woman? Or does he just whistle when he wants you?'' The bland face smirked.

"My name is Kathryn.'' He slapped her backside, and she stiffened, fighting back the urge to hit him with anything she could pick up. "And I come to no whistles!''

"Make me some decent breakfast, and then wash this shirt.'' He thrust a soiled linen shirt in her face. "Find whatever laundry there is and clean it. Don't touch my buckskins.''

"I'm no kitchen maid!''

"You'll be whatever I choose, or Ashton won't live out the day. You've loyalty for a whore, but it's misplaced. Ashton and I have an old score to settle. If you're smart, you'll stay out of it.''

"He's lying. I am his wife. I can pay any ransom you demand. Name your price.''

DeSalle shook his head slowly. "I'm fast losing patience, madam. The price I want is there.'' He jerked his head in Pride's direction. "Have you ever seen a man begging to die? The Huron will cut his scalp from his head and pile live coals over his brains.''

"Stop it,'' Kate begged. "That's inhuman. You can't let them—''

"Let them?'' He laughed. "I'll pay them to do it, as long as I can watch. Ashton will take a long, long, time to die . . . and he'll be in hell long before he does.''

Pride was bound hand and foot, although Kate protested that he was too ill to attempt escape. DeSalle permitted her to feed him and to dress the wound on his head. A quick death was not what he planned for Pride. Kate lived hour by hour and tried not to think of what might happen in the days to come.

At night, she slept beside him, without blanket or fur, even on the night it rained.

"It's your own choice, madam,'' DeSalle had mocked. "You are welcome in my tent.''

She had chosen the cold mud gladly. Pride was regaining his strength, although they went to great pains to keep their captors from realizing it. Kate continued to brave the Hurons to obtain fresh meat. She knew Pride must eat, no matter the risk.

On the third morning, Kate was at the riverbank, rinsing out DeSalle's remaining shirt, when a party of horsemen emerged from the forest. A Huron brave called out, and DeSalle came from the tent to greet the visitors.

A man about fifty with gray hair, wearing the uniform of a French officer, dismounted and shook Andre's hand. The stranger looked in Kate's direction and asked a question. DeSalle answered with a shrug, and they went into the tent. Kate noticed that the older man limped when he walked.

An olive-skinned man in buckskins remained on his horse, as did the four Indians with him. Kate couldn't tell what tribe they belonged to. They wore their hair long and affected a mixture of white and Indian clothing. Their skins were darker than the Hurons, and they seemed somewhat apprehensive.

Kate shook out the wet shirt and started back toward the tent. A Huron brave blocked her path and shook his head menacingly. "DeSalle wants his shirt," Kate said stubbornly. The brave raised the butt of his rifle, and she backed off. "It's nothing to me." She tossed it on the ground and returned to the river.

With the gourd full, she carried it to the trees where Pride was tied. He was bound to a hickory at the neck and waist, with his wrists and ankles tied in front of him. His back was to DeSalle's tent. Kate described the newcomers as best she could.

"Did they see you?"

She nodded. "He asked Andre who I was."

Pride frowned. "You two are on a first-name basis now?"

"For God's sake! Would you prefer I called him captain?"

"I'd prefer you not wash his laundry! Or cook his meals! He's a pig! Stay clear of him." He cursed under his breath. "Damn it, woman. Don't be fooled by a pretty face. He's a killer."

"You're jealous of DeSalle? Pride! Listen to you! Have

you forgotten I'm his prisoner? Just because I'm not tied . . . How can you think . . . ?'' She shook her head. ''You'd be dead now if I hadn't . . . Ohhh!'' She balled her fists tightly and tried to realize how he might feel, bound hand and foot, helpless, while she seemed to have the run of the camp.

''I'm sorry,'' he admitted. ''If I could see them, I might know who they are. Anything you hear, remember—no matter how insignificant it might seem. See if you can find out who the half breed with the Frenchman is or what tribe the Indians are from. The French are raising the hostiles against the settlers all up and down the Ohio valley. Maryland and Virginia will be hit hard. You can write off western Pennsylvania if the Colonies don't send out their own militias.'' Pride leaned back against the tree. A muscle jumped on the side of his jaw; the blood drained from his tight lips. ''If we get away, Kate, we might save a few lives.''

''What do you mean *if?*'' She forced a laugh. ''How many people walk off the platform at Tyburn? My father said I was born lucky.'' She tried to keep her tone light.

''A man's luck doesn't last forever . . . or a woman's either. If you get a choice, go with the Huron. The Iroquois are devils, but they don't rape women or torture them. You'd be better off dead than with DeSalle.''

''Why did you do it?'' She crouched close to him. ''Cut DeSalle? You must have had a reason. Was it over a woman?''

''Yes. And that's the last you'll hear about it. Never ask me again.''

Kate recoiled from the naked pain in his eyes. ''You expect me to deal with the man, but won't tell me. It's not fair.'' She noted fresh blood seeping through the bandage. ''Your wound has reopened. Let me see it.''

''Let it be.''

''But it was healing so well! What did you do to—''

''I didn't do anything. One of DeSalle's playmates hit me.'' Kate jumped up. ''No! Sit down and shut up. Keep your head, woman. You'll get us both killed by acting like a fool. A cuff on the head's not worth confronting them over. The Frenchman's the one to worry about.''

"You keep saying that, but he hasn't treated me so terribly. He may have changed since . . . since then. You're not yourself, Pride; you're hurt. Hurt bad. Maybe you aren't thinking straight. I could try to convince him to ransom us. We're civilians, not military,'' she reasoned.

"Damn it, woman! If I could get my hands on you, I'd throttle you. You're making judgments on something you are totally ignorant of. I know what I'm talking about!'' He twisted his wrists against the leather straps until blood ran down his arms. "If you could just get me a knife . . .''

"Don't.'' Kate caught his wrist and held it. "Don't hurt yourself anymore. I'll try and get a weapon.''

"What have we here?''

Kate whirled at the voice. It was the light-skinned man who rode with the French officer. She glared at him. Whoever he was, he made her skin crawl. His buckskins were filthy with grease and dirt, and his long hair looked alive with vermin. Tobacco juice dribbled down the scraggly beard.

"Are you DeSalle's private stock or free for the takin'?'' He leered, showing a broken front tooth. "It's been a while since I seed such quality as you, gal.'' He slid down from the pinto horse and came toward her.

"Run!'' Pride warned. He threw himself against the rawhide ropes.

Kate stood her ground until the man was an arm's length away from her, then ducked past him and grabbed for the rifle on his saddle. Pulling it free, she turned and raised the barrel. The half breed caught the rifle and twisted it from her grip. Kate kicked at him and ran. She covered a dozen yards, and he was on her, throwing her to the ground.

Cursing, she clawed at his eyes, and he cuffed her violently alongside the head. Kate tasted blood as her tooth sliced the inside of her cheek. His weight pressed her to the ground; a rough hand pawed beneath her skirt. Terror seized her as the realization set in; he meant to rape her, here and now. Fear lent her strength, and she drove the palm of her hand upward to smash against his nose. He hit her with his fist, and her head slammed back, jarring her senses. From a long ways away, she heard Pride screaming. A harsh mouth ground against hers, and the stink of the beast clogged her nostrils.

Pinning her wrists with one muscular arm, he fumbled with his trousers with his free hand. She tried to bring her knee up to strike him in the groin. It was impossible to breathe! The broken tooth gouged her lip; a thick tongue forced its way into her protesting mouth.

A grotesque hardness pressed against her thigh. He pulled the deerskin dress up over her hips and she screamed, "No!"

An explosion, inches from her head, rocked the ground. "Let her up," a quiet voice commanded. "Or the next shot will not miss."

The weight rolled off, and Kate lay there, sobbing. Rolling into a tight ball, she pulled the dress down to cover her nakedness. She couldn't control the spasms of ragged weeping.

"Back to your master, dog." A second shot rang out.

The half breed fell, clutching his shattered knee. Blood poured over the leaves, and the man's screams shocked Kate to silence. "My leg!" he howled. "My leg! You killed me!"

A hand pulled Kate up. "My regrets, madam. I assured you that you were under my protection here."

She caught her breath and wiped at the bleeding mouth, her eyes drawn to the writhing man on the ground. Pieces of bone and muscle protruded from the ruin of his leg. She covered her mouth and tried to hold back her nausea.

Straightening, she wiped away the tears. "Thank you," she said with as much dignity as she could muster. A strangled sob caught her attention, and she turned to look at Pride.

His face seemed carved of granite, the hawk eyes fierce with blood lust. She ran to him and threw herself against his chest.

Tears ran from the blue eyes. "I was so frightened," she cried hoarsely. "Oh, Pride." She drew back. He might have been part of the tree. There was no gentle comforting, no word of love.

"Get away from me," he snarled. "I can't help you. Go to your hero, DeSalle."

Kate recoiled from the bitterness in his eyes. "What would you have me do? Spread my legs for that animal, rather than take help from DeSalle? What do you want of me?" She turned and walked to the river to wash her swollen face. There would be no more tears. She locked the pain and terror inside. Her happiness was coming apart thread by thread. If Pride didn't love her anymore, nothing mattered.

She waded into the water. Loud voices in French came from the edge of the trees. DeSalle and his fellow officer were arguing, probably about the shooting. She wished he had shot him in the head. From the looks of his knee, this was probably worse. If the leg wasn't amputated, and soon, the man would die a slow, painful death.

She wanted to strip off her dress and scrub her body with wet sand and water. She felt dirty. If that creature had raped her, she wasn't sure she could have stood it. The bruises on her face and body were nothing. They would heal. The real hurt was inside. She had done everything she could, fought with every ounce of her strength, and it had been useless. Without DeSalle . . . She shuddered at the thought.

They were on the trail within an hour. DeSalle's tent and belongings were carried on packhorses. Kate rode close behind the Frenchman, hands free, ankles tied beneath the horse's belly, with a lead line on the animal. Pride walked, a rope around his neck, arms bound behind him. Kate's pleas that he was too badly hurt went unheeded.

"Let him ride with me, please," she begged. "If his head starts bleeding again, he'll die."

"He will die anyway, Kathryn. To bleed to death is not an unpleasant way to go, believe me." DeSalle slowed his horse and leaned out to touch her arm. "It is time to reassess your loyalties. You are badly in need of a protector. You could do much worse." His face hardened. "I could have let that breed have you. Are you free of disease,

madam? I can assure you that you would not have been
after he was finished with you.''

Kate turned her face away. To give him the reply she
wished would only put Pride in great danger. "I love him,''
she said quietly. "I can't forget him so easily.''

"Love!'' Andre scoffed. "You are too old for such foolishness. I tire of brown-skinned maidens. You interest me.
I prefer my women willing, but I am not a man of great
patience.'' His gloved hands stroked the leather reins. "I
won't be in these godforsaken woods forever. Eventually,
I will return to France. It is not beyond possibility that I
might take you with me, if I was pleased with you.''

"I am English. I have no wish to see France,'' she dared.

"A whore has no nationality.''

"This one does.'' Kate kicked the horse's side and the
animal leaped ahead. She glanced back at Pride. He staggered, and she bit her lip to keep from crying out.

The Huron brave who held the lead line to Kate's horse
glared at her and shouted a threat. She returned his arrogance with a haughtiness of her own. His gaze turned to
one of careful appraisal. Kate lowered her eyes. All she
needed was an amorous Huron on her hands.

Pride dragged his feet as he walked. He noticed a Huron
watching him from the corner of his eye. The bastards were
sharp. It wasn't easy to outfox a fox, but he was trying.
He must give the impression of being weak. He'd have a
better chance of jumping one of them if they believed he
was helpless.

From under hooded lashes, he scrutinized Kate. She'd
been talking to that pig DeSalle again. He wished for the
thousandth time he'd killed the Frenchman when he had
the chance. He'd give half of Ashton Hall for the opportunity to sink his fingers into DeSalle's throat. Kate had no
idea how much danger she was in. Pride was certain she
hadn't believed him.

He leaned against a tree and breathed hard. The horseman jerked the rope around his neck, and he stumbled and
let out a little moan. He'd have to take a chance soon. If
they got him back to DeSalle's main camp, he'd be so

much chopped meat. Or fried . . . The Huron were big on burnings.

Pride was no stranger to Iroquois torture. He'd run the gauntlet when he was no more than fifteen. They'd clubbed and knifed him nearly to death. The women were more vicious than the men. He'd seen . . . Pride closed his mind against the chilling memories, shutting them away in the shadowy recesses of his brain. He'd escaped that time by the grace of God. A man couldn't expect two miracles in a lifetime. If he and Kate were to make it, it would have to be by their own efforts.

DeSalle wanted Kate; Pride could see that clearly. But the Frenchman was still unsure of what she meant to Pride. If he had any conception . . . *Don't think about it!* He won't find out. Kate wouldn't die the way . . . *Damn!* The bastards were getting to him. He wasn't thinking straight. His head ached, but it was an ache he could deal with. Damn Tschi to hell! If he ever got him in his rifle sights . . .

Kate was so vulnerable. He'd told her why he had to pretend. Told her that it was to save her life! Why did she have to get that hurt-puppy look in her eyes when he'd called her a whore? Of all the women he could have had, he had to set his sights on her. She was as prickly as greenbriar! A proper woman . . . Pride tried to keep from smiling; his eyes were fixed on the doeskin dress in front of him. Damn, but she was tough! Her back was as straight as hickory! She would probably lift the scalp off Captain Andre DeSalle if he came too close. Pride would have to watch his own. God! What sons a woman like that could give a man!

Children had always been something he knew he'd want someday. He had none living that he knew of; there might be a few in Indian camps, but no woman had claimed him as father to her babe. Just that one, and she was gone . . . they were both gone, long before their time. Now, he wanted a child of Kate. No, not a child, children. He wanted sons and daughters, a full dozen of them. They'd fill the rooms of Ashton Hall with their laughter and deviling. They'd till the land and hold it against all odds when he and Kate were dust.

Pride's eyes softened as he pictured a tiny Kate toddling across the lawn, blue eyes large with wonder. He'd teach his daughters to ride, and hunt, and shoot. On second thought, their mother could teach them to ride. Kate was second to none on a horse! He'd give his girls an education; he'd give them land of their own. They could marry or not, suit themselves. Or, if they wanted, they could go back to England. There were titles and gold aplenty for those who carried the Ashton name.

And for his sons . . . he'd give them all he could. A boy needed love, and discipline, and responsibility to grow into a man. He'd try to listen when they spoke. God willing, he'd be better at it than his own father! But they would find their own paths when they were grown. A father had no right to choose for his son.

Step by step, Pride spun a shining future in his mind, knowing full well that he might not live to see tomorrow's sunrise. Knowing that the woman he cherished above all else on the face of this earth might well meet the same fate, and there was precious little he could do about it.

Kate's mind was on DeSalle. Was he really the madman Pride had insinuated? What was a gentleman, a man of breeding, doing in this wilderness? He was obviously educated, cultured, a man who would have been at ease in the courts of Europe. Duty could not explain this assignment. What secrets did the charming smile hide? He had made terrible threats. Were they real? Or was he just trying to frighten her?

Her nipples brushed against the buckskin with the movement of the horse. She was sore and aching. Her breasts felt full and tight; she must have been battered more than she realized in the attempted rape. She pushed the heavy braid aside and rubbed at her neck. What she needed was a bath and a bed to sleep in, a bed with real feather mattresses. She looked back with longing on the quiet days at Ashton Hall. She must be getting old. All her life she had longed for excitement, for adventure. Now, all she wanted was—

A Huron whooped and Kate's horse reared, tangling one front leg in the lead line as he dropped to ground. Kate caught at the mane, cursing DeSalle for the ties at her ankles. If the animal fell, she'd be caught beneath it. Eyes rolling, the gelding threw himself back, one leg sliding on the damp leaves. The horse snorted, throwing his head. Kate fought to control him, unable to jump free.

Pride threw the neck rope over one shoulder and darted forward to catch her horse's head. "Whoa! Whoa, boy," he commanded. He wrestled the tossing head down and slipped the lead line off his foreleg. Trembling, the animal stood still. "Are you all right?" Pride demanded of Kate.

Two Indians leaped from their horses and closed in on him. Pride kicked one in the groin and whirled, charging into the other's mid-section with his head, knocking the brave flat. With furious cries, they poured over him, pinning his arms and striking him with fists and gun butts. Kate screamed as he fell, his face covered in blood.

DeSalle reined his horse in close. His gray eyes narrowed. "A good recovery, Ashton." He motioned, and they dragged Pride upright. "I'm glad to see it. It would be a shame to make a poor showing after they've waited so long."

"Damn you!" Kate cried. "Leave him be!"

The Frenchman rode close to her and put a hand on her knee. "He's not quite as indifferent to your welfare as he pretends, is he, madam?" DeSalle's smile left his eyes cold.

Kate felt as though she were staring into the depths of a frozen sea. She shivered and caught a whiff of pure evil. "I hate blood," she stated flatly. "It sickens me."

"Then we'll have to be certain you're otherwise occupied when Ashton goes to the stake." He inclined his head slightly in salute and took his position at the front of the warriors.

Invisible insects crawled beneath Kate's skin. For an instant, she had glimpsed something in DeSalle that was unclean, satanic. Was she losing her mind? She glanced back over her shoulder at Pride. He was on his feet and walking, a glazed look on his face. He'd been beaten for coming to her aid. He'd thrown away his pretense of weakness, and of not caring, to save her from being hurt. She must find a way to help him, regardless of the cost.

A bitter bile rose in her throat as she glanced sideways at DeSalle. Could one deal with a madman? A devil? She'd seen desire in his face. Would it be enough?

Suddenly, she noticed a change in the Huron braves. They were more alert. They called to one another and laughed; one warrior applied fresh paint to his face.

The horses broke into a trot. A Huron on foot ran past her, shouting. Another fired his rifle in the air. Ahead, Kate saw the log walls of a stockade. The remainder of the Huron braves galloped into the clearing. Pride was dragged behind a horse, struggling to hold on to the rope.

DeSalle turned to Kate and smiled. "You'll want a bath and decent clothing. It should be a big improvement."

"I want nothing from you but freedom."

"And you will have nothing, *ma chère*, but what *I* choose to grant you." He spurred his bay down the hill toward the stockade.

It was a structure built for defense rather than comfort. The enclosed area was small, surrounding a log building, animal sheds, and a well. The Huron camp lay outside the high walls. Pride was tied to a post on the lean-to porch of the cabin. Kate was escorted inside. She tried to speak to Pride as she was hurried past, but he hung against the ropes in a stupor.

The main room of the log building seemed to be a store. A rough counter ran along one end. Barrels and bales of furs were stacked against the walls. Blankets and trade items lined the crude shelves. A fireplace of reddish stone filled one wall; the floor was plank.

To the left of the main room was a kitchen. DeSalle poked his head through the doorway and barked an order. A thin Indian girl, wearing only a greasy skirt, crept into the room. DeSalle motioned to Kate and repeated the command. The girl nodded. "The squaw will see to your comfort," he said to Kate. "Don't leave the cabin." He went into the room on the right and closed the door behind him.

The girl glared at Kate with red-rimmed eyes. She was

hardly more than a child; her half-formed breasts bore dark bruises. One eye was puffed and swollen; green discoloration spread down a pockmarked cheek. Her hair hung in dirty strings about her narrow shoulders. She pushed Kate toward the kitchen.

"What's your name?" Kate asked in Shawnee. The girl made a garbled sound; Kate tried again in English, and then in French. "What tribe are you?" No answer. Kate shook off her hand and stepped into the low-ceilinged room.

There was a trestle table and benches, one chair, and a three-cornered stool. A fire burned on the hearth; the kitchen smelled of baking bread. The room was bare but clean. The girl dragged a half barrel from the corner of the room and picked up a bucket. She waved Kate to sit, then ducked out the low door.

Kate made a quick inspection of the room. She found a small knife and slipped it under her skirt. A sound alerted her to the returning girl, and she jumped back to the bench.

The girl staggered under the weight of two full buckets of water. She poured them into the barrel, then added water from a copper kettle on the hearth. She looked at Kate expectantly.

"I'm Kate Storm," she said, slowly and distinctly in English. "Who are you?"

The girl dropped her eyes.

"No use to look for talk from that one," DeSalle said from the doorway. "She's a mute. She has no tongue."

Kate looked at him in disbelief.

"Show her, Janine."

Obediently, the girl opened her mouth and poked out the stub of a mutilated tongue.

Kate's vision blurred. Black spots spun before her eyes and she gripped the edge of the table. She knew she was going to be sick. Tears welled in the corners of her eyes as she fought the nausea. "Damn you, DeSalle," she whispered. A whirling blackness threatened to drown her; she smacked her fist against the table. The pain gave her something solid to hang on to. "You're no man . . . you're a monster."

Peals of laughter assaulted her brain; the girl had joined

her master. "Enjoy your bath," DeSalle chuckled. He handed the Indian a blue gown. "See she puts this on. That barbarian attire disgusts me." He turned and left the room as quietly as he had come.

Kate leaned over the barrel and splashed water on her face. DeSalle's taunts were nothing. A greater fear had risen, one that drowned everything else in comparison. One that she must come to terms with before anything else.

For days she had denied the signals her body was sending. She had found excuses for the weariness, the sore breasts, the weak stomach. She had pushed aside the questions she hadn't wanted to ask. She had deliberately let the days pass without acknowledging the unimaginable. She was pregnant. For the first time in her life, her monthly time had passed without a showing of blood. She carried Pride's child. She, Kate Storm, was going to be a mother.

Kate slid to the floor, leaning against the damp barrel, and began to laugh silently. Well, old girl, you picked a hell of a time! And a hell of a place!

The mute stared at her as though she were crazy, then dropped the dress over the bench and returned to her cooking. She squatted beside the coals and began to roll out corncakes.

Kate dried her eyes and got up feeling foolish. Going to pieces wouldn't help her, or Pride. If she was pregnant, she was pregnant. And any baby that had held on through rain and beatings and bucking horses wasn't about to be dislodged by hysterics. Like it or not, she was going to produce an heir for Ashton Hall.

She frowned as she stripped off the deerskin and climbed into the water. She and Pride might be wed by Indian custom, but to English society she was no more than his whore. Her child would be a bastard if they weren't legally wed. If DeSalle killed him . . . With a sigh, she sank into the cool water. Her hand went to her taut belly. It wasn't possible. They had been together on the ship without his seed taking root. She had begun to believe that perhaps she was barren.

Kate took the lye soap the girl handed her and scrubbed at her hair. All her life she had sworn she would never marry, never, never have a child. She liked children well enough—other people's. They were cunning little creatures, cute and amusing. But . . . She had vowed never to tie herself down with a squawling brat! And now . . . now . . . She caressed the soft skin below her navel. If it were a boy, she would call him Geoffrey. Her eyes misted and she smiled. Pride's son . . . Geoffrey Storm Ashton. Her jaw tightened. DeSalle be damned! No Frenchman would keep her son from being legitimate! Geoffrey would carry on the Storm name. Somehow she would find a way to save them all.

Chapter 16

Kate slipped from the cabin in the semidarkness. Pride hung from the post, eyes closed. "Pride," she whispered. "It's me. Are you all right?" She took his face in her hands. "Pride?"

"Kate?" His eyelids flickered. "Water. I need water."

"I brought some." She held a dipper to his lips. "Drink slow," she cautioned.

He looked at her, noting the blue gown that had replaced the buckskin. "More." He sipped at the water, then shook his head and she took it away. "You've got to get free, Kate," he warned. "Any way you can. Don't trust him. Not for a second. Don't . . ."

Kate closed his lips with a tender kiss. Her arms slipped around his neck, and she pressed against him. "Oh, darling, I love you so much," she murmured.

"Don't," he said hoarsely. "There's not much time. You've got to get away from DeSalle."

The warm autumn night was filled with the cadence of Iroquois drums from the encampment. Kate looked quickly about and pulled the knife from the folds of her dress. "I'll cut you loose."

"No. It's too late for me. Steal a horse if you can, and ride." His face was hawklike in the shadows. "Get back to Ashton Hall if you can. Mother will look after you. Tell her everything, especially that we were married."

"I can't go and leave you."

"You can't go." A soft voice came from the darkness. "You disappoint me, madam. Have I not shown you every courtesy?'' DeSalle shouted and two Hurons stepped into the light. "Take him. I promised him to you. Now he is yours."

The Frenchman held her as they dragged Pride away. "You said you were afraid of blood," he murmured. "Let us go and see." Holding her wrist, he pulled her toward the gate. "It is really quite interesting. You of all people should appreciate primitive rituals."

High chilling shrieks of glee pierced Pride's brain as the Huron squaws saw him being led across the compound to the torture stake. Rocks and sticks struck his face and shoulders. A half-grown girl ran forward to spit in his face. A pole tripped him and he stumbled, to the delight of the onlookers. A woman jabbed at him with a burning stick.

"May the night devils fly down your throat," Pride cursed her in Iroquois. She paled and back away, making a sign against evil.

From somewhere off, he heard Kate's cry and steeled himself against it. The time for miracles had passed. It was a time to die. Not a good day, as the Shawnee war parties dared, but the allotted day. He must wipe his mind clean of all passion. There were a hundred ways to cause pain; the Huron were master of them all. His woman must tell his mother he went to the stake like a man. Pride threw back his head and began to sing the Shawnee death chant.

DeSalle bound Kate's hands at the wrists and tied the thong to a stake. "Watch closely," he commanded. "And see the wolf turn to a whining cur."

The Huron called out words of praise for the bravery of their victim. He stood erect, chest out, shoulders back, as they tied him to the bloody post. His eyes were obsidian orbs reflecting the flickering fires; his bronzed and scarred body loomed godlike with defiance. He took their threats of pain and death and threw them back in their teeth. This was a mighty enemy, and the Huron loved him for it.

Kate fought the bonds like a wild thing, unable to watch, and unable to look away as knives sliced at Pride's body. He only laughed and sang that blood-curdling chant, that chant that rose above the cries of his tormentors.

"Stop it! Stop it," she begged DeSalle. "I'll do anything you ask. For the love of God, don't let them kill him.''

An arrow sank into Pride's upper thigh. Blood poured from the wound. He didn't pause in his song, or seem to notice. Kate covered her face and wept. The leaping fires, the inhuman cries, seemed a nightmare, a scene from hell. It *could not* be real.

"Surely you don't think they'd let me interfere with their entertainment," DeSalle said. "The Huron are Indians, not men. Animals can be led, but not commanded. You think too highly of me." He regarded her pleading with obvious amusement.

"Please, Andre." Kate raised her hands; the nails were snapped off, her fingers bleeding. "Anything."

He laughed. "Perhaps." He slashed the leather cords and shoved her in the direction of the stockade. "We'll see how truthful you are."

The four-poster bed dominated the bedroom. There was a straight-backed chair, a small desk, and a finely crafted walnut armoire. "One does not have to live like a savage, even in the wilderness," DeSalle bragged, unfastening the buttons of his shirt. "We will play a little game," DeSalle proposed. "Undress. Quickly!"

Kate's hands trembled as she obeyed. In a daze, she laid the blue gown over the back of the chair and reached for the wine goblet the Frenchman offered. It isn't real, she told herself. She felt numb all over. She'd rather die than give herself to this man, but that wasn't the issue. It was Pride who would die—and die horribly. The numbness spread down her arms to her hands and fingers. She felt like a wooden puppet. Perhaps she was already dead and didn't know it.

"A toast to us, madam," DeSalle offered smoothly. He hung the shirt on a hook behind the door. A fresh uniform waited on a similar hook. "Don't look so frightened, *ma chère,* I'm not going to devour you. Well," he laughed, "perhaps not all at once."

"You must promise me his life." Kate was startled to hear her own voice. It sounded strained and far away. If the dead could talk, they must sound like that.

"I promise nothing," he snapped. "Let loose your hair. I like my women with loose hair." He sat down on a chair and held out a booted foot. "Take it off." Biting her lip, she knelt to remove the black leather boots. *"Merci,"* he said. "And now the chemise."

She shook her head. "No. I can't. I can't do it."

He laughed again. "I told you, madam. It is only a little game. You are useless to me as you are. I told you, I like my women willing and eager. You do not have to submit to my attentions, you have only to *pretend* to do so. We will put on a small performance for your lover."

Disbelief clouded her eyes as she stared at him. "Why?"

"For a man of my education and tastes, there is little in the wilderness to stimulate my intellect. I have learned to take pleasure where I find it, in the small things. It amuses me to cause Ashton to suffer the mental anguish of believing you have betrayed him." He dropped his breeches and climbed into bed. "Come. I'm waiting. If you are a good enough actress, I will spare him."

Kate shook her head again. "I don't believe you." She measured the distance to DeSalle's rifle. He saw her glance. She knew it was too far.

"I tire of this. Come to the bed, woman."

"Not until I know you mean to keep your word."

"Your own actions will determine his fate." He patted the bed beside him. "Come, my pretty. I give my word, as a DeSalle and a gentleman. I will spare him the stake and death by torture if you play your part well enough. Make up your mind. What shall it be?"

Kate climbed into the bed beside him and slipped between the sheets. She clenched her eyes shut and lay unmoving. "If you are lying to me, I'll kill you," she promised. Tears forced their way past the closed lids.

DeSalle grasped her arm and squeezed it hard. "Don't lie there like a lamb waiting to be slaughtered! Wipe away those stupid tears. It will be no good if he thinks you're being raped." He ran his hand through her hair and her fists tightened under the sheets until the jagged nails cut into her flesh. His fingers trailed down her bare shoulder and arm. Kate gave no reaction. "For shame, *ma petite.*

If you would fight, at least there would be some sport."
He sat up and threw back the sheet. "Look at me."

Kate opened her eyes. DeSalle gestured. "Satisfy your
curiosity, madam. You called me inhuman! That breed
Ashton did this to me. Look at it, damn you!"

Kate's eyes dropped to the twisted scar.

"He butchered me . . . and for a dirty squaw." He
laughed, an ugly demented sound. "But half a man is better than none, *n'est-ce pas?*" DeSalle's mouth descended
on Kate's and his hands pinned her to the bed. She twisted
her face away, striking at him with her fists.

"Remember the game," he panted, pulling her on top
of him and trapping her with his legs.

The wooden door slammed back. Two Hurons entered
the room with Pride suspended between them. His pain had
dulled to a red haze. Pride shook his head to clear his
vision and stood unsteadily. *The Frenchman. DeSalle.*
"Why did you . . ." Pride's voice trailed off, and he drew
a shaking hand across his face. Why had DeSalle stopped
the torture? He took a deep breath. His hand dropped to
his thigh and tightened around the arrow shaft that protruded from his flesh. "Kate?" He shook his head. "What
are you . . ."

DeSalle pinched Kate's thigh under the sheets. "What
does it look like, Ashton?"

Kate forced herself to lay a hand on DeSalle's cheek.
"I've found a way to get home to England," she said
softly. "I've changed protectors."

Pride blinked stupidly. "You what?"

She swallowed hard and dropped her eyes. If he looked
into them, he would never believe she was betraying him.
"DeSalle promised to take me home," she repeated. "For
a price."

With a cry, Pride drove the arrow through the muscle of
his wounded leg and out the back. The wound gushed
blood, and he fought to keep his consciousness as he
snapped off the arrowhead and withdrew the shaft.

Kate screamed as he tossed the Huron guards aside like
broken kindling.

The red haze deepened in Pride's brain. Kate's screams

. . . her near-naked body intertwined with DeSalle's . . . the Frenchman's sneering face . . . the crimson shaft . . . The images twisted and turned before his glazed eyes. Pride fought for sanity and lost.

"Pride! No!" Kate screamed.

Pride's lips drew back in a feral snarl, and a Shawnee war cry rent the room. He lunged toward DeSalle, the arrow clenched in his bloody fist. Kate screamed again, and an explosion dissolved his world into a gray haze. There was no pain, no pain, only the curious sound of a woman weeping . . . and then blessed nothingness.

Kate threw herself on Pride's fallen body, futilely attempting to halt the terrible bleeding from his chest. DeSalle's pistol lay on the floor, useless now that its single load was fired. DeSalle moaned and tried to pull the arrow shaft from his side where Pride's fury had driven it.

"You half-breed bastard!" DeSalle howled.

"You lied to me," Kate screamed. "You lied! You said you'd save his life." She cradled the ashen face against her breasts and kissed his hair and slack lips. Her tears ran down and washed away the blood. "You shot him," she murmured. "You told me you'd spare his life. You let him think I . . . He thought I betrayed him with you. And then you killed him. Damn you to hell, Andre DeSalle!"

"You stupid bitch," he hissed. "I told you I'd save him from the torture stake. I kept my promise." He worked the arrow shaft free and held the sheet against his side to stem the bleeding. "Cover yourself," he ordered.

Sobbing, Kate laid Pride's head on the bunched-up chemise, then pulled on the dress and pantaloons. She thought she saw a movement and ran to Pride, pressing her cheek against his chest. Nothing. He lay as still and unyielding as stone. She put her fingertips to his nostrils. There was no hint of breath.

Kate curled into a ball beside the fireplace, her arms wrapped about her knees, and watched, dry-eyed, as the Hurons dragged his lifeless body from the room. She did not move when DeSalle called her to bring water and bandages for his wound. She shut him out and retreated to a cavern of grief, deep within the recesses of her tortured soul.

He's dead. He's dead. The words fell like drops of rain. But he can't be dead. The rain fell harder, drumming out the finality of the truth. DeSalle shot him through the heart. No one can live without a heart. That's a lie! I can.

Kate rocked and hummed a wordless lament. DeSalle's threats held no power to frighten her. If he killed her, she would be with the man she loved. His curses and orders bounced off like hailstones. She watched with unseeing eyes as the little squaw bound cloth strips about DeSalle. Without emotion, she saw the blood seep through the bandages. What was DeSalle's blood? She wished it was her own.

Vaguely, Kate was aware of DeSalle screaming about a physician. She made no protest when a Huron carried her over his shoulder and threw her onto a horse. They could do with her as they liked. Pride was dead. Dead. Dead. Her body sat upright on the animal, her knees gripped the bare sides of the horse. How did they know to do that? she wondered. Her fingers held the reins as though she were alive.

Only one incident pierced the invisible barrier she wrapped about herself. One image was etched in her brain, an image that would destroy her sanity if she dwelt on it.

DeSalle was on a horse beside her; his face was like tallow. His hands were stained with blood. He shouted an order; he was demanding something. "Bring it here!" he screamed. "Now. I want it!"

A runner had come with a small object; he handed it to the Frenchman. DeSalle held it up triumphantly. Kate's eyes fastened on it. DeSalle leaned from the saddle and slapped her across the face with it.

"Look at it! It's Ashton's scalp!" he cried.

Kate's hand went to her cheek. She drew it away and stared at the damp stickiness.

"It's his scalplock, you stupid English bitch!" DeSalle laughed.

Kate pitched forward over the horse's neck in a dead faint.

The days that followed would always be a blur. There

were memories of green trees, of someone lifting her from the horse and pouring liquids in her mouth. She could remember the camp fires and DeSalle's moans. Little else.

And then there was a log fort; there were white men, men who spoke French. A man in black led her to a room. She slept; she woke and swallowed soup. She slept again.

"You are feeling better today, my child?" A white face hovered over hers. The words were English, heavily accented.

"I think . . . I think so." She tried to sit up. The man pushed her back. "Where am I?"

"There now, no questions today. You have been very sick. Lie back. Rest. There will be much time for questions."

Kate realized the man wore the robes of a priest. He was right. She was tired, so tired. "DeSalle?" she asked.

"Tomorrow. Tomorrow we will talk. I brought you some soup. Eat this and then sleep some more."

"Who are you?"

"I am Father Sebastian. You are Catholic, my child?"

She shook her head. "No."

"Are you a Christian?"

"Yes."

"Good. Good. Now have some of this soup. It's fresh today, a good soup with beef and turnips."

"DeSalle. I must know about DeSalle."

"He has been very sick. His wound had to be cauterized. You must pray for him." The dark eyes were gentle as he spooned soup to her mouth.

"I will," Kate agreed softly. "I'll pray for his death."

As the days passed and she grew stronger, Kate realized that she was still a prisoner. From the bars at the tiny window, she saw French troops, Indians, and bearded men in buckskins. The fort was much larger than DeSalle's. Guards stood on the walls with rifles. A French flag flew overhead. There were even a few Indian women.

The priest came daily. He was a break in the monotonous days, even if he did try to convert her to Catholicism. DeSalle had evidently told him that she was a whore and that he had rescued her from a savage half breed.

"God will forgive you your sins, if you will confess them and make a resolution to live a better life," he explained. "You must cleanse your heart of hate. How can you desire the death of the man who saved you?"

"Andre DeSalle is a fiend," Kate answered quietly. "If he goes to heaven, I'll rather spend eternity in hell."

"Captain DeSalle is a gentleman, a Christian, and an honorable man. He has sworn on the Holy Bible that he has not committed fornication with you." The old man sighed. Perhaps the poor girl was touched in the head as Captain DeSalle had said.

"Not from lack of trying. He's a murderer." Kate walked to the window. "I want to get out of here. I want to go home."

"Eventually, my child. You are a prisoner of war. You will be sent to Quebec and held with other prisoners. Many are traded for French citizens held by the British. With God's help you may be one of them."

"I want to go home to Maryland now!"

"That's not possible."

Kate turned from the window, expecting Father Sebastian, when the door to her cell was unlocked that afternoon. Instead, she faced a white-faced and thin Andre DeSalle.

"Bon jour, madam," he said evenly.

Kate stiffened. He looked ten years older. Bones stood out in the once handsome face; his blond hair hung lifeless. Dark circles under his eyes emphasized his wraithlike appearance. "I had hoped you were dead," she answered bitterly. DeSalle had lost his ability to frighten her. When the worst has happened, all else pales. She could hate this human devil, but never fear him again. "If you value your life, Frenchman, you will walk from this room and *never* let me set eyes on you again."

"Riposte!" He smiled, and an unholy light glinted from the dull gray eyes. "You too have recovered, *ma petite* Kathryn. I prefer you sharp and prickly." DeSalle leaned on a polished walking stick. "We will have time to mend your shrewish disposition, a great deal of time." He took a step toward her and she stood her ground, her eyes blue flames of hate. "Due to my—" DeSalle cleared his throat. "Due to my *indisposition*, I am being transferred back to my home province. With a promotion and medals of honor, I might add. I'm not without influence. You are coming with me, madam."

"I won't! You can't make me! I'm a British citizen," Kate declared. "I demand to be returned to my own people."

"As I told you before, a whore has no nationality. I want you; therefore, I *will* have you." He laughed. "It is really quite simple. What you wish is of no consequence. A woman of your sort is no more than goods to be disposed of. *N'est-ce pas?*"

Kate threw herself across the room toward him. The walking stick cracked her sharply across the arm and head, and she stumbled back. "Desist!" he spat. "There will be no more attacks, or I will have you beaten as you deserve."

Kate wiped at the blood that trickled down her face. Silent curses spilled from her lips. "I will kill you," she whispered. "Some night when you least expect it, I'll slip a blade between your ribs."

"I think not." His fingers tightened in her hair. "Others have tried to kill me. Your precious Ashton tried, and where did it get him? I will never let you go, madam, be certain of it, not until it pleases me. It is fitting that I should have the use of Ashton's woman while his body rots, unburied and unchurched." He laughed. "Besides, in time, you will come to my bed willingly enough. You desire me, whether you are honest enough to admit it or not."

"Desire you?" Kate spun away, impervious to the pain of her yanked hair. "If you believe that, you're insane. You murdered the only man I ever loved. I carry his child. He died believing I betrayed him. There is nothing more you can do to me. And if you ever come near me . . ." Her voice dropped to a husky cadence. "I will finish what Pride started."

Rage turned the pale face to burgundy. "You common bitch," he sputtered. "You dare . . . you dare to . . ." A spasm of coughing caught him and his face twisted in pain as he gripped his side. He backed away. "You dare to threaten . . . You'll learn. You'll learn," he promised. "Oh, how I'll enjoy the lessons." DeSalle paused with his hand on the door, gasping for breath. "You carry the bastard seed, do you? Perhaps we can plan some future for Ashton's child? Think on it, madam." He slammed the door and locked it.

Kate flung herself on the bed and cursed herself for being seven kinds of fool! Why had she told DeSalle of her pregnancy? It only gave him another weapon to use against her. Then she'd threatened him. If her father were alive, he would never forgive her if he knew. He'd taught her never to reveal her plans before they were executed. Keeping your opponent in the dark was vital in chess or in fencing.

She lay back and stroked the rounded mound of her belly. Her womb was swelling with Pride's child, all that was left of him on this earth. She would need all her wits and strength to protect him. The time for childish tantrums had passed. DeSalle was insane, but his insanity did not preclude shrewd reasoning powers. He was as dangerous as Pride had warned.

The Frenchman had been right. Public opinion would brand her child a bastard. He must carry the name of Ashton. She must return to Ashton Hall and to Rebecca. Despite all that had happened, Kate knew that Pride's mother would welcome the child. She would acknowledge the baby as Pride's, perhaps even make him her legal heir. If she could give birth to the baby there, Rebecca would see that it was given the upbringing Pride's son deserved.

She must escape from DeSalle before they boarded a ship for France. She would kill him if she could. But escape was primary. Revenge could be set aside if it meant the life of Pride's child. If DeSalle got her to France, it would be much more difficult. She could never let him get his hands on the baby.

Suppose the baby was a girl? All the more reason for her to have the protection of a name and family. All the more reason to have it safe from DeSalle's hands. But it was not a girl; Kate knew in her inner heart she carried Pride's son.

She curled into a tight ball on the mattress, eyes shut. She must find a way to escape, she must! Exhausted, she slept.

"Ki-te-hi." The soft voice wrenched at her heart. Pride's familiar face loomed above her.

"Pride," she whispered. "You're not dead. I thought you were dead."

He laughed huskily; his mouth captured hers. She inhaled the sweetness of his breath; her hands stroked his neck, his shoulders, the bulging muscles of his arms. She let herself be swept up in the utter joy of his embrace.

"Darling, darling," she murmured. "How did you . . . ?"

He kissed her again; he pulled her tight against his warm, hard body. "I've missed you," he groaned, "God, how I've missed you, woman." His fingers found her breast beneath the fabric of her gown; he teased the nipple to rigid passion. The dress parted; his mouth closed on the eagerness of her straining breast. The delicious chills washed through her trembling body, setting her secret places aflame with moist desire.

"It's not safe for you here," she whimpered. "Darling . . . darling. They'll find you." His hand slipped down to stroke her belly; it slid lower to caress the tangled curls.

"I want you, Kate. I want you."

"Yes, yes," she pleaded, rising to meet the hard length of his body, opening her legs to receive his throbbing manhood. She cried aloud as he thrust into her core; she met passion with equal passion, wanting to be one with him, wanting to hold him and never let him go.

Caught in a tempest of spiraling emotion, Kate clung to him, rising with the flames, welcoming the fires in her blood that threatened to consume her in a holocaust of longing. Together, they reached the peak and dropped into the nothingness beyond.

"Pride . . . Pride . . ." she murmured. She reached to pull him against her damp breast. "Pride?" Her hands clasped empty space. She opened her eyes to the barren room. "Pride?" Salt tears scalded her cheeks. A dream

. . . he was no more than a dream. Alone, she wept for tonight and all the nights to come.

Two days later, they came for her. Father Sebastion gave her his blessing and told her that DeSalle would be taking her to Canada.

"He isn't! He's lying!" she protested. "He's taking me to France, with him. I don't want to go. Please help me!" Kate clung to the black robe. "You must help me!"

"I will pray for you, my child. You'll see that all your fears are groundless. Captain DeSalle has given me his word that he will care for you as though you were his own sister." He pulled free of her grasp. "Bless you."

Two white men blindfolded her and led her out of the building. They didn't speak to her. Kate knew it was useless to struggle.

The wood walk gave way to stone. She heard voices and the sounds of animals as they crossed the compound. A horse whinnied, and Kate though of Meshewa. Would her son live to ride him? She held her head high, walking proudly. The catcalls and whistles were as nothing. She could not waste her anger on them.

She smelled the river before they reached it. Strong arms picked her up and waded with her to a fragile boat. Kate clutched the sides to keep her balance. Her fingers explored the smooth surface of the birch-bark canoe. She dipped her hand in the water, then raised it abruptly to rip away the blindfold. She blinked. DeSalle stood on the bank, watching her.

In the bright sunlight, it was even more evident that the arrow wound had taken a great toll on DeSalle's muscular body. His uniform hung on him; he seemed shorter. Streaks of gray marred the blond hair. He leaned on the silver-headed walking stick. "What, madam? No curses? No threats?" He waded through the water to climb into the canoe in front of her.

Kate didn't bother to answer his taunts. She watched as the other two canoes were loaded. One Huron crouched behind her, another in front of DeSalle. A dark-skinned colonial was in the prow. He raised a paddle in salute to a comrade on the shore and pushed off from the beach. The other canoes each carried six; all the men but one were Indian.

"What fort was that?" Kate asked. She had asked the priest and gotten silence for a reply.

DeSalle laughed. "If we had wanted you to know, we wouldn't have bothered with the blindfold, would we?"

"You're a pig, DeSalle." Kate withdrew within herself and watched the shoreline pass. The current was swift; the canoes skimmed along the surface of the sparkling blue-green water. Trees crowded the riverbanks, hanging low to touch the water. The air smelled of pine and mossy stones. Kate felt more alive than she had in a long time.

They rounded a bend in the river and Kate gasped. Two black-and-white hooded mergansers challenged each other with a great bobbing of iridescent green heads and flapping of wings. They rose from the surface of the water, splashing and striking at each other with their bills, sending spurts of foam into the air with the kick of their powerful red feet. They took flight as the canoes approached, joined by a lone female, drab in her muted colors and modest size.

Kate watched them disappear above the treetops, wishing she could open her wings and fly as easily.

The hours slipped by. The Huron struck up a chant; the colonial joined in the song. Bronzed arms moved rhythmically; paddles dug into the water. The three canoes moved as silently as shadows on the water. Once a doe and two half-grown fawns plunged into the forest a canoe's length away, startled by the invasion of humans into their wilderness home.

At dusk, they beached the canoes and built a campfire. Kate feared that DeSalle would molest her, but as she scrambled up the bank she saw the lines of pain and weariness on his face. The wound was troubling him. Good! With luck, the infection would return and kill him.

Two braves left the camp and returned a short time later with two turkeys and a beaver. They cut up the game and roasted it over the fire. DeSalle unwrapped bread and cheese. Kate ate what he gave her, then boldly snatched a turkey wing. It burned her fingers, but the taste was smoky and delicious. She slept undisturbed beside the fire.

The second day was much like the first. Kate had no idea how many miles they had come. The canoes seemed to cover ground much quicker than a horse. She marveled at the paddlers; they never seemed to tire.

In the afternoon, they passed an Indian village. The people waved and called greetings in French. It was a small town with not more than a dozen houses. The women looked much like the Shawnee women, although they wore shapeless dresses of skin that covered them from neck to ankle.

"This river feeds into a great lake," DeSalle had said. "There we board an oceangoing vessel. It will take us to France."

Kate refused to give him the satisfaction of a reply. She might be forced to kill herself, but she would not allow them to put her on that ship. With every passing day, her body adjusted to the burden within it. Each day made her a little less able to defend herself. If she'd had a knife, she would have plunged it into DeSalle's back, and the devil take the consequences.

Dusk was beginning to settle over the river when gunshots rang out from the forest. The Huron behind Kate screamed and slumped forward in the canoe; his paddle fell across her leg.

A hail of arrows fell about them; one pierced the bark by Kate's hand. An Indian war cry rent the air. DeSalle raised his rifle to fire, then let out a groan as a feathered shaft was buried deep in his knee. Puffs of smoke rose from the trees on their left. The men in the canoes were returning fire but the attackers were ghosts.

Kate screamed and slammed DeSalle alongside the head with the paddle, then let herself topple over the right side of the canoe. She took a deep breath and let herself sink to the bottom of the river, praying she had killed him, and cursing the dress that weighed her down. Letting the current carry her, she swam downriver and to the right.

The confusion and fading light were to Kate's advantage. One of the attackers who had seen her strike DeSalle before she went overboard dove into the river after her. A musket ball caught him in the neck, and he died instantly.

DeSalle fell sideways; the canoe overturned, and he slipped into the river.

Kate surfaced only long enough to gulp a mouthful of precious air, then swam under water again. If she could just reach the far shore, she might come up under over-hanging trees and not be seen. Cries and wails of the wounded and dying filled her ears. She reached a tangle of logs and branches, and her skirt caught on it. Panic-stricken, she clawed her way to the top. One canoe was only yards away; the four remaining Hurons were paddling furiously.

Her hand struck something soft. The form moaned and grabbed at her. Kate struck out at the wounded Huron and ducked under. She opened her eyes; she could see only a few feet in the murky water. An opening in the logjam loomed an arm's length away. She pushed herself into it and upward. There was a crisscross of sticks and branches overhead. She pushed her hand into the tangle, gulping in the air trapped in the pocket.

A feeling of terror pressed against her chest until she could hardly breathe. The logs were slimy with mud and rotted debris. Something crawled across her arm; in the semidarkness she saw the outline of a snake. It reared its head and struck at her. Kate fainted.

Chapter 17

The world was dark and wet when Kate opened her eyes. At first, she struck out wildly at the branches around her, not remembering where she was. Then it all came pouring back over her. She was in a logjam. She had swum in through a hole; she would have to swim out. Her heart was pounding. Why was it so dark? She listened. There were night sounds on the river; an owl hooted in the forest. It had been dusk when the shooting started. Now, it was night.

Taking a deep breath, she wriggled down, feeling her way with her bare feet. She forced herself down, holding back the terror with all her might, inching out of the logjam. Then, she was in the river proper. She felt the swift current; she swam away from the logs and surfaced.

The full moon made the night like day. The water was suddenly cold. She shivered, her teeth chattering. A few sure strokes and her feet touched the sandy bottom. Staggering up into the shallows, she pulled herself up the bank. She wanted to lie there, but instinct forced her into the woods away from the river. If anyone was searching for her, they would look near the river.

The branches were sharp under her feet; she bruised her arch on a pointed rock. The underbrush tangled in her hair and scratched her face and arms. Kate kept walking.

Something crashed through the brush; Kate thought of bears. Then there was the sound of an animal running. Only a deer. It must be a deer. The owl hooted again, directly overhead. The forest had never seemed frightening when Pride was with her. Alone, she was terrified. She kept putting one foot in front of another. She must get farther from the river. She had come ashore on the right side; the right side was south, at least she thought so. Maryland was south. She'd just keep putting one foot in front of the other until she reached home.

After what seemed hours, her body would no longer obey. She sank down, too tired to care if they caught her, too tired to do anything but sleep. She wrapped her arms around her knees to try and keep warm. When she opened her eyes again, it was full light.

She was ravenous. Images of the juicy turkey wing teased her brain. If there was anything to eat in the woods, she didn't see it. She was thirsty, too. How could she possibly be thirsty after the river? She'd swallowed half of it. She began to walk again, in what she hoped was a straight line.

She pushed through a thick clump of bushes and nearly toppled into the river a dozen feet below. The river! Was it the same one, or another? Had she been walking in circles all this time?

Carefully, she made her way down the bank and drank. She put her sore feet into the running water and let it wash away the dirt and blood. *Face it, Kate, you're lost!* Some Indian she was! She lowered her body into the clean water and swam a few strokes. Maybe she could catch a fish or something. Although what she'd do with a raw fish, she couldn't imagine.

A canoe bobbed across the surface of the water. Kate panicked and splashed toward the shore.

"Hey!" a voice called. *"Bon jour, demoiselle!"*

She scrambled up the bank and ran into the woods. A quick glance over her shoulder showed the canoe moving swiftly toward shore with two paddlers.

Kate dashed through the trees, dove under a lightning-felled pine, and hid beneath the dry boughs. Her heart was pounding, and her breath came in gasps. She tried to slow her breathing, certain her pursuers would find her by the sound. She clenched her eyes shut and waited, trying not to move a muscle as twigs snapped and leaves rustled.

The leaves parted over her head. 'What have we here?

Come out, little chicken. Etienne will not harm a hair of your head.''

Kate looked up into the grinning face of a bearded woodsman. His voice was heavily accented. He was French. She forced back bitter tears. "I'm not afraid of you," she bluffed.

He took her hand and lifted her up. "Then why do you hide under zee tree like frightened quail?" He looked her up and down with amused brown eyes. He stood not much taller than she, but the long rifle cradled easily in his muscular arm lent authority to his stance.

"I'm unarmed, that's why I ran," she said, brushing the pine needles off the ragged remains of her dress. "Why did you chase me?"

"Ah, you are Englesh. I thought so. I say to Marie, that is my little woman, the startled doe is Englesh. This is no place for you, *petite*. Only yesterday a Seneca war party ambush a French officer and his Huron allies on thees very river. Many men killed. You would not be the Englesh prisoner, would you?"

Kate nodded. Her lower lip quivered. "Do you have anything to eat? Even the condemned get a last meal."

"Bel esprit!" He laughed, showing even, white teeth. "You must not be afraid of me. I am no enemy of yours, *petite*. I am only a poor voyager going downriver for winter supplies. My woman is with me. Come, you will see. We cannot remain here. There may be Seneca scouts in the woods." He motioned toward the river. "Back to the canoe. Quickly, *petite.*" Kate did as she was told.

"How did you find out about the attack?"

"On the river, nothing be secret long. Seneca big news. When Iroquois fight Iroquois, smart man keep head low." He waved to the Indian woman and she paddled the canoe close to shore. "I was right, Marie," he called. "This is lost quail from yesterday. He helped Kate into the canoe.

The woman stared at her. She was young and plump, and carried a baby on her back. "Hello," Kate ventured.

"This is my woman, Marie."

"Wife," the girl corrected.

"Ah, yes. Marie is good Christian Menominee girl. We are legal by priest. What is your name, *petite?*"

"Kate Storm. Kate Storm Ashton," she amended.

"Little one is my son, Louis." Etienne positioned his rifle carefully and took up the paddle. "Safer in center of river." Together, he and Marie guided the canoe into the current.

"Please," Kate urged. "Don't turn me back over to Captain DeSalle. Let me go. All I want to do is to get home. I'm no enemy of yours, either. DeSalle captured my husband and me. I want to go back to our farm in Maryland. I could pay you."

"You do not look as though you could pay for a tankard of beer, madame." Etienne said lightly. "As I say, I am voyager, not soldier." He spat into the water. "I would not turn goat over to that pig DeSalle. He is one bad man, I think." He turned and grinned at her. "I must take you to authorities. But I do not give you to DeSalle." He shrugged. "No one knows where DeSalle may be. Maybe he dances at Seneca stake. Maybe river take him. We can always hope."

"But if you just let me go . . ."

"You starve to death in woods or zee bear eat you. Woods no place for *petite*. You will be traded soon for French prisoners. You have word of Etienne."

Etienne's word was as good as his rifle. At the settlement, Kate received clean clothing and food; she was treated kindly and sent on with another woman prisoner to Quebec City.

Within a month, she found herself in a boat, in the middle of a large river, with a half-dozen sniveling women and children and one gray-haired grandfather. The French soldiers were gentle and efficient as they conducted the prisoner exchange. Kate climbed the ladder to an English boat and was herded below as the boat headed for the south shore.

The rescued captives were transported to Albany and turned over to civilian authorities. The weather had turned bitter, and they arrived in the midst of a snowstorm. Kate was furious at the lack of sympathy the captives received from their own people.

"We'll do the best we can by you," a harried magistrate promised. "But we've exhausted all the funds provided for your care. You must contact relatives to pay for your transportation. We've indigents enough in Albany without you squatters to worry about."

"I'm no squatter!" Kate snapped. "I'm Lady Ashton of Ashton Hall in Maryland colony."

"Sure ya are, sweets. And I'm the Prince o' Wales. I've no time fer yer lies. Ya claim to be a married woman, an' I see no ring on yer finger, nor no mark o' one. Ya look like a common slut to me."

Kate answered him with a sound cursing. Here, with her own kind, she was as much a prisoner as with the French. They were even being held in the local almshouse.

"Shut yer foul mouth, woman, or I'll shut it fer ya. Ya may be a runaway bond servant fer all I know. Fer certain yer no *lady!*"

After two days of poor food, thin blankets, and biting fleas, Kate was given over to a farmer and his wife. "This is Amos Tinley. Yer to go with him."

"I'd not be having trash at my house, but I'm ailin'," the woman whined. She stood just under six feet, with shoulders like a dockhand. "We'll keep her jest till spring. I'll not have her laying round when she drops her bastard, eatin' an' not doin' a lick. Our hired girl jest ran off to get married an' I've got sixteen young'ns to fend fer."

Tinley was a red-faced, dull-eyed farmer. "You'll work fer yer keep at our place," he stammered. "No slackers under my roof."

"Go along, woman! What are you staring at?" the attendant snapped. "Go with the Tinleys."

"In a pig's eye! I'm no servant!"

"You said she'd be biddable," the wife protested. "My back's got the misery. I can't be puttin' up with lip from a uppity wench."

The attendant gave Kate a shove. "No nonsense from you, girl. You'll get plenty to eat, and anyplace'd be warmer than here. Yer in the family way. You don't want to stay round the almshouse in winter. Too many dyin' of the consumption! Use yer head. You'll end up in a pine box here, if they spare one to put you under in.''

Knowing common sense when she heard it, Kate reluctantly got into the open wagon behind the farmer and his wife. It was still snowing, and the wind was sharp. She wrapped a dirty blanket around herself and rolled herself into a ball. She'd have to make the best of the situation until she figured out what to do. It was plain she could go nowhere in this weather.

The Tinley farmhouse was a two-story rambling dwelling of stone and wood. The children ranged from four months to sixteen years. Mistress Tinley was given to producing twins; she was also given to producing the ugliest children Kate had ever laid eyes on.

From before daylight until long after dark, Kate labored to satisfy Mistress Tinley. There were cows to be milked, butter to be churned, chickens to be fed, eggs to be gathered, floors to be scrubbed, and endless piles of dishes to be washed. The woman was too lazy to be cruel. As long as Kate kept busy, she could eat as much as she liked. There were threats, but no physical abuse.

And outside, the snow fell; snowdrift piled upon snowdrift. The wind howled and tore at the windows. Kate's hands turned red and cracked; her nose dripped. Water froze on the kitchen table at night. The dogs had to be driven outside. Winter wrapped the Albany farmhouse in a grip so tight, Kate feared spring would never come again.

By her counting, the baby would be born some time in late May. As March passed without a letup in the cruel weather, she began to worry that she would ever get back to Ashton Hall in time. Leaving now would be suicide; she could never get ten miles in this snow. Each passing week made her less able to travel the distance between upper New York and the Maryland colony.

In early April, the snow turned to rain. As soon as the roads were passable, Kate crept from her room after everyone was asleep. She took food from the kitchen, stole Amos's best riding horse, and headed south.

Hampered by her bulky figure, Kate was only able to

make twenty miles by first light. The horse was up to his knees in mud; a light rain was falling. Kate was cold and damp, but her spirits were high. Ashton Hall lay south, and Ashton's heir was safe under her heart. Nothing and no one would stop her now.

She ate on horseback, pausing only when absolutely necessary. Her body ached, and she felt as if she was coming down with a cold. Kate knew that Tinley would mount a search party for his horse, if not his servant. She must put miles between her and the farm. She drove the weary animal into a teeth-jarring trot.

By dark, the bay was missing a step now and then, his head sagging. She traded him for a roan workhorse grazing in a pasture, and galloped on. She'd have to leave the roads soon enough. Now she could not worry about being seen. She must cover territory. The roan's owner would be surprised, but he had the best of the bargain. Tinley would have to take the loss! She'd worked enough that winter to pay for two horses.

At daylight, she found an abandoned cabin, led the horse inside, and slept the day away. She finished the last of the food and drank from a spring near the cabin. Only a few miles away, she saw the lights of a town. She turned away, across a wooded field, and rode into the forest. An obviously pregnant woman, alone on a workhorse, would be too easy to remember.

She dared not ride at night in the thick trees; she slept rolled in a blanket on the damp ground. At dawn she mounted and rode on, grateful for the saddle. She followed the road until it seemed safe to go back to it. At noon, she met a family traveling to a wedding. She traded Mistress Tinley's split-oak basket for a meal and two loaves of sweet bread.

"How come you be riding by yerself?" the husband asked.

Kate sighed. "My man run off. His sister said she seed him down in Penn's colony, working fer a baker. I couldn't run the farm by m'self, so I'm goin' to look fer 'im. He ain't much, my Harry ain't, but he's the father o' this young'n."

"You ought'n be riding so far along," the wife cautioned. "You might slip it. I slipped one afore Thomas there." She pointed to a large-eared urchin.

Kate nodded. "Yer right, I know. But what's a body t' do? Only right his lawful father do fer a babe."

"What's yer man's name, and where do he hail from?"

"Harry Wiggins," she lied smoothly. "Our farm was in Turpin's Road. Course, Master Elwood took it back now. We was tenant farmers. Good farm, too."

The man nodded sympathetically. "Hope ya find yer man."

"This yer first?" the woman asked. She was stout and puffed when she walked. Her hair was as black as an Indian's and rolled into a knot on top of her head. "What's yer Christian name, Miz Wiggins?"

"Molly. It use t' be Potts. Maybe ye know some of my kin. There's lots o' Potts over t' the coast. I got fourteen brothers an' sisters, most older 'n me."

"Don't say as I do. Listen though, Molly. We're goin' the same way. Why don't you come down off that horse and ride a spell in the wagon? We're goin' to spend the night with his"—she pointed to her husband—"cousin. They'll not notice another. It ain't safe fer a woman alone. We're goin' far as Kane's Crossing. You might come t' Jeannie's wedding with us, if you're a mind. Like to hear the news of your valley. It's been a lonesome winter."

Kate agreed, sliding down from the horse. Search parties would be looking for a woman alone. She'd stay with these people a while, as long as they were traveling south. "I'm no beggar," Kate said. "I got hard coin t' pay m' way." She'd taken a handful of coppers from Mistress Tinley's cream pitcher. Maybe she'd followed the wrong career. It seemed she had outlawing in her blood. It was a lot easier than being honest!

Two days later, she left the wedding party on a fresh horse. She'd traded the workhorse for a black mare, blind in one eye, but sound. The farmer had thrown in a few coins and a good knife. The mare was no more than five years old and had an even gait. She also left with clear directions to Philadelphia.

* * *

Philadelphia was the biggest town Kate had seen since she'd left London. She'd been afraid that people would stare at her, but no one seemed to notice. The streets were thick with farmers, vendors, and travelers. Women carried baskets of eggs and pitchers of milk door to door. A black woman passed with a basket full of gingerbread on her head. She called out as she walked, and children scrambled to trade their ha'pennies for the cookies. Kate's mouth watered for one. She hadn't eaten since early yesterday, but her coins were all gone.

A black-robed Quaker provided directions to the banking house. A few whispered names led Kate to an inner office and the kind embrace of her father's old friend David.

"Whatever I can do, I will," he promised. "We were saddened by word of his arrest and death."

"My brother, Geoffrey, too is dead," Kate told him. "I need enough money from you to hire a guide to take me down to the Maryland colony. My . . . my husband is there," she lied.

The gray eyes were shrewd. "You know you would be welcome in our home as long as you wish. We've had long practice in hiding friends from the authorities."

Kate grinned. "I know. But it's vital that my husband's heir be born at the plantation. I've come so far. Please help me to get to Ashton Hall. It's west of Annapolis, days . . . I'm not sure. But it should be easy enough to find out. It is a great estate."

"Of course we'll help. God go with you, Kate Storm."

The last days of her journey were without incident. The Quaker woodsman and Delaware guides were honest and dependable. If her body protested at the hours in the saddle, Kate kept it to herself. She would tolerate no delay, least of all from her own frailty. On the morning of May 8th, the riders crossed onto cultivated Ashton land.

Kate dismissed her party on the spot. She would brook no argument. They had fulfilled their obligation. She wanted no witnesses to her shame when she confronted Rebecca. Her son's secret must be between the two women if he were to be the legal heir. She rode the last few miles alone.

There were excited cries from the field laborers as they recognized Kate. Robin left his sheep to run after her horse. "Miss Kate! Miss Kate!" he shouted. "Howdy, Miss Kate!"

She waved to him and kicked her heels into the little mare. The house was in view now. She blinked back tears. She'd come so damn far. What if Rebecca turned her away? Would she be forced to deliver her child under a tree like a wild animal?

The horse trotted into the barnyard and whinnied. Another answered the call. Kate let the reins go slack; suddenly she was afraid.

"Kate?"

The hair rose on the back of her neck, and she whirled in the saddle. Pride Ashton stood in the shadows of the barn. "Pride? Pride?" She rubbed her eyes. It couldn't be. "Pride?" He came toward her. Her head began to spin, and she would have fallen if he hadn't caught her up in his strong arms.

"I thought you were dead," she whispered hoarsely, laying her head against his chest.

The dark eyes burned with a cold flame. "You had damn good reason to think so." He stood her on her feet. "Why are you here?"

Kate stared at him; her hand reached up to stroke his cheek. He jerked away, and she flinched. "I . . . I thought you were dead. All that blood . . . I thought DeSalle killed you. How . . . ?"

"Why are you here? What do you want?" he demanded harshly. The scar on his face had faded to a thin white line against the bronzed, glowing skin.

"I came back to have our child . . . here at Ashton Hall," she answered softly. Tears formed in the corners of her blue eyes and spilled down her cheeks. "I thought you were dead, all this time."

"You've come here to have some man's child, that's for sure." He eyed her large stomach.

"Damn you to hell, Pride Ashton! It's your child!" She backed away from him.

"Save your lies and your tears for someone else! You forget where I saw you last," he lashed. The hawk face was hard; his eyes showed no trace of tenderness . . . no love.

"It wasn't what you think."

"No? And it wasn't what I think with Simon? Or with my brother? Tschi told me about you, Kate. Don't waste your talent on me."

"Tschi? I never . . ." she protested. "Pride! You've got to believe me. It is your baby. No one else has ever touched me that way. No one." Her hands curled into tight fists. The child stirred within her and she protected it with her arms. "Deny him if you can, but he's an Ashton."

He laughed. "A great performance, Kate Storm. You really should have made your living on the stage. Actresses and whores are all sisters under the skin."

"You don't know what I've been through, what I've done to get here," she pleaded. She could not hold back the tears; she began to hiccup. "I'm telling the truth."

"Like you told the truth to Tschi? To DeSalle? What is the truth, Kate? Do you even know? Or have you told so many lies you begin to believe them yourself?"

"I'm your wife," she cried. "Your wife."

"No," he corrected cruelly. "You were my wife. I divorced you. A Shawnee does not tolerate an unfaithful woman."

A pain knifed through Kate, clearing her brain. It gave her something to ache for, and she took a deep breath. "What happened to all your great talk about the Shawnee *way?*" she demanded. "You said there were no bastard children among the Indians."

"I guess I've too much of my father's blood in me," he admitted. "I've gotten you out of my system, Kate, for good."

"Have you?" She caught his hand and held it, gripping it tightly as another pain surged through her. The joy of finding him alive had been overshadowed by his rejection. The double shock was almost too great to bear.

His hand should have meant nothing to her, a broad, callused hand, marred by scars and briar cuts. She brought it to her cheek, thrilling to the old familiar sweetness that sent chills through her body. "I love you," she whispered. "I think I've loved you from the first day I met you. Don't do this to us, Pride. Please."

"You still don't listen. There is no us." He stepped away from her; his eyes narrowed. "You're in labor?"

"I . . . I don't know."

He put an arm around her. "Come to the house. You should be in bed."

"Not until we settle this." The old stubbornness surfaced in Kate's voice. "You can't believe I came here to have another man's child. I wouldn't do that." His hair had grown out; she longed to run her fingers through it. "Why didn't you die? I thought . . ." She pounded her fist against his chest. "Pride, I saw your scalp. DeSalle threw it . . . threw it in my face."

"Not mine, obviously. A Huron tried to lift it, after they dragged me into the woods. Jonas saved me. He and some Shawnee tracked us."

"But you left me with him!"

"You seem to have survived well enough. I was more dead than alive when they carried me off. It was a week before I was conscious again." He slipped an arm under her legs and lifted her. "No matter whose it is, I won't let it be born in the barnyard." Pride walked with her toward the house.

"Where's Rebecca?"

"She's not here. She's seeing some of her Delaware kin settled on a piece of ground south of here. I sent men with her. We're at war, Kate. The Shawnee burned out a settlement to the east. Five men were killed, the women taken captive. I don't know how you rode through that country without trouble."

"I had an escort south from Philadelphia. I . . ." She flinched. "I thought you were dead, but I wanted your son to be born here. I came alone from Canada."

"DeSalle paid your passage south, I suppose?"

The servants stared as Pride carried her through the front

doors and down the hall to her old room. "You may as well stay here. No one's used it since you ran away." He kicked open the door. A maid ran ahead to strip back the bed and he laid Kate on the clean sheet. "I'll send for the midwife."

Kate recoiled from the frosty tones. He might have been ordering a fence repaired. "Get this through your thick head," she insisted. "This is your baby!"

The little maid flushed crimson and fled the room. Pride stared at her and shook his head. "I loved you once, Kate. I would have done anything for you, given you anything. But you betrayed me once too often. It's over. There's nothing left. Accept it. I got over you a long time ago."

"No! I won't accept it! You're angry, and you have a right to be." A pain caught her and she bit the inside of her lip. "We created this baby in love. If you don't care about me anymore, at least care about your child. Stay with me, please. I don't want to be alone."

"I said I'd send the midwife." Pride paused with his hand on the door. "When you're well enough to travel, I'll send you and the child back to England. I don't want you in the Colonies. I never want to see you again."

Chapter 18

By the time the midwife came bustling into Kate's room, the pains had stopped, and she felt foolish. "I guess it was a false alarm," she said. Kate's eyes were red from weeping; she wanted to be alone.

The woman examined her carefully. "It happens this way sometimes. You say you have been riding for weeks. Your body is tired. Stay in bed. Eat lightly. Sleep. Some first babies are hard to deliver."

A maid brought milk and bread, and hot soup. Kate ate and then slept for twenty-four hours straight. The pains did not return. Neither did Pride.

On the second day, Kate dressed in a silk dressing gown and walked in the garden. She still felt tired; her head hurt, and every muscle in her body ached. To her surprise, she was hungry. She finished every bite of the noon meal the maid brought.

The midwife had returned, felt the child kicking, and pronounced Kate "fit as a fiddle." "Yer lucky, mistress. It's a fine fat boy, for certain."

Kate was no longer certain of anything. If Pride turned them away, what would she do? Should she claim to be a widow? How would she support the baby until she was strong enough to work? It was so unfair. After all the struggle to get here, and the joy of learning Pride was alive, there might be no haven for the child at Ashton Hall.

A maid came running and dipped a curtsy. "Mistress Kate, Lord Ashton will see you in the great hall. Shall I tell him you'll come along?"

"Yes, I'll come," Kate agreed. She followed the girl, wondering what Pride wanted. Had he changed his mind? Was he about to throw her off the plantation?

He stood by the window, his back to her, as she entered the room. He was dressed simply in a fringed leather shirt and buckskin trousers. She assumed that he had just returned from riding. Pride turned toward her slowly, his face as smooth and emotionless as an Indian's. "You're feeling better today?"

"Yes, I am." Kate's back straightened. If he threw her out, he threw her out. She'd manage somehow. She'd proved she could even do a servant's work if she had to.

"I've behaved badly, and I owe you an apology." He waved her to a loveseat and poured a glass of wine. "This is quite good. It was made here at Ashton Hall. Our grape vines are doing very well."

Kate's hand trembled as she took the goblet. A drop of brilliant ruby red stained the front of her blue gown. It looks like blood, she thought. The coldness of his tone pierced her to the deepest corner of her soul. This wasn't Pride. This was the haughty Lord Ashton she had known in Newgate Prison.

He took a sip of the wine. "The midwife tells me you could deliver the child any day. It could be mine."

"It is yours." Kate's eyes locked with his stubbornly.

"You must have known you had missed your woman's time. Why didn't you tell me then?" He couldn't hide the bitterness in his voice. "It would have meant the world to me, Kate . . . then."

"Should I have told you when we were DeSalle's captives? Would it have made you feel better to know you had a pregnant wife—no! Not wife! A pregnant mistress to worry about? Or should I have shouted it out when the Hurons tied you to the stake? Damn it! I don't care if you believe me or not, but you're going to hear the truth." The anger rising within her pushed back the fear. "DeSalle promised to save your life if I pretended to be his lover. He said he wanted to hurt you, to shame you by taking me away from you. I don't know if I believed him or not. But I couldn't lose the one chance I had to stop him. I had to try! Don't you understand, you bloody fool? I did it for you! I didn't give myself to him. Not then. Not ever.'' In desperation, she stared up into Pride's eyes. They were as cold and hard as chips of volcanic glass. ''Damn you! Believe what you want,'' she cried. ''You aren't fit to be the father of my child!'' She hurled the wineglass across the room and it shattered against a mahogany highboy.

''That goblet was part of a matched set from Venice. It was more than two hundred years old.''

''I should have thrown it at you.''

''Ah, the old Kate. I think I like you better sharp-tongued. You play the injured maid badly.''

''And you play the bastard superbly.''

Pride walked to a window and stared out at the fields. He wanted to believe her; God, how he wanted to believe her! It took every ounce of his self-control to keep from taking her in his arms. Thoughts of Kate and his brother were bad enough—they haunted his dreams, even though he knew she wasn't at fault. But DeSalle? ''Where is he?''

''Who?''

''DeSalle?''

''In hell, I hope. I think I killed him.''

Pride gripped the windowsill. ''If only I could separate your lies from the truth.''

''Do you honestly think I would have come back here if I was carrying his child? Do you think I would have let him . . . I would have died first, Pride. If you know me, you know it's true.''

He held up an open palm in the peace sign. ''Wait. I didn't ask you here to fight with you. I said I wanted to apologize, and I do.'' Pride crossed the room and sat beside her, his rugged frame dwarfing the delicate loveseat. He took her chin in his hand gently.

Kate swallowed hard and blinked back tears. He'd learned torture well from the Huron. It was impossible for her to be this close, to smell the fresh, woodsy odor of the man, to look into those large dark eyes without melting. She still cared for him. Nothing he could do or say would stop her loving him. She wanted to run her finger down the scar, to brush the square, solid chin; she wanted to throw herself into his arms.

"I'll take the child, Kate." He shook his head at the confusion in her clouded blue eyes. "No . . . that's not right. I want the child." He dropped his hand to capture her wrist. "It could well be mine or my brother's. Despite what he did to us, we're the same blood. As an uncle, I'd have the same responsibility to the infant as if it was mine."

"And if it's DeSalle's?" she taunted. She wanted to slap his face, to hurt him. Why? Why didn't he believe the truth?

"What's happened between us has nothing to do with the child. I'll love it and raise it as an Ashton, boy or girl," he continued huskily. "Rebecca will welcome a baby in the house." Pride turned her hand over and traced the bruises on her slim palm. "I'll send you back to England, Kate, a free woman. My people will provide you with a new identity and funds to begin a new life. But I want a promise from you that you will never interfere. I want no contact. You won't see the child again. No letters. It will be an Ashton."

"And what will you tell him of his mother?"

"I'll say she was a brave and beautiful lady who died when he was born."

"And you call me a liar?" She shook her head. "No deal, Lord Ashton. What did you tell me about the Shawnee? Every child has a mother. Every child takes the mother's name. Better this baby should be a Storm. Your son deserves better than you could give."

"I'll claim it as my heir," he promised. "Boy or girl. You can ask no more."

Salt tears blinded her eyes; she dug her nails into her palms. Head high, she turned toward him. "This is one thing that's mine. You can accept the baby, or turn us both on the road. I don't expect you to honor our Indian marriage, or to treat me as anything other than the bondwoman I am. But one thing I promise you." Kate's voice dropped huskily. "You'll not separate me from my child without killing me first."

He laughed wryly. "The field is yours, Kate, as always." He came to her and took her in his arms, kissing her forehead. She might have been made of stone. "A peace treaty, Katy. No more fighting. You are a guest in my home. If we cannot be friends, at least we can no longer be enemies."

"I was never your enemy, Pride, not really." Her heart was beating wildly; surely, he must feel it through the thin gown. The child kicked and she grabbed Pride's hand and placed it on her belly. "Feel that," she ordered. "That's your son. Whatever else you think of me, whatever else you believe, on Geoffrey's soul, that's your son."

"I told you," he repeated. "I accept the baby as an Ashton and my heir. I'll kill any man who says otherwise." It was true, he did want the child. He wanted it even if it was Tschi's. He wanted the child because it would be Kate's child. But even more than the child, he wanted the mother. In spite of everything, he still loved her, God help him. He loved her, but he was afraid to trust her. "I will claim the babe and give you an honorable place here, Kate. You have my word on it."

She pulled free from his embrace. "Good enough. And now, if you'll excuse me, m'lord, I'm weary. I think I'll go to my room and rest."

"As you please." Pride averted his eyes. Perhaps the child would give them time to begin again. He would try. He would have to—or spend the rest of his life alone. Kate Storm had taken his heart, and no other woman would do, not now and not ever.

"I'll keep to my room and the garden as much as possible," she promised. "We might as well make this easy on both of us."

"That's not necessary. Ashton Hall is your home. You must consider yourself mistress here," he answered formally. The cultured tones of the English aristocrat crept into his voice.

"I think not." She swept from the great hall with as much dignity as she could muster. Away from those eyes, that voice, she could gain control of her own mind again.

May in Maryland was glorious that year. The garden burst forth in magnificent bloom; the sweet mingled scents poured through Kate's bedroom windows. Her days were reduced to hours of waiting, waiting for the child.

Her body was still increasing in size, so much that it was alarming. Since Kate had never had a child before, she had not expected to become quite so large and awkward.

The maids had altered some of her gowns and made special garments to go over them. The silks and satins felt strange after the coarse gown of a serving wench. When they were finished, they came to her chambers in the afternoon to sew clothes for the infant. Kate tried her hand, but she was all thumbs with a needle as usual. Her efforts ended up being ripped apart and resewn by the giggling servants.

Gossip aside, Kate could find no fault in the behavior of the servants toward her. They were pleasant and respectful. She supposed even the mistress of Lord Ashton rated loyal service.

She took her meals alone in her chambers. She could not bear to sit at the table across from Pride. His courteous attention was harder to bear than his accusation and shouting.

Kate realized that something was worrying him, something other than the situation between the two of them, something he did not wish to discuss with her.

Even from the house and garden, it was evident that Ashton Hall was an armed camp. Twice, parties of men rode into the yard, some badly wounded. Rumors of war troubled Kate's dreams. She saw again the blood, and heard screams of fallen men.

It was on such a night that she rose from her disheveled bed to walk the garden paths. It was the dark of the moon; the night air lay about her like a mist. Kate walked barefoot on the cool bricks; her thoughts drifting back to those few sweet days she'd shared with Pride in the Shawnee village, those days and nights she'd believed she was his true wife.

"What are you doing out here?"

Kate's throat tightened. She had not seen him in the shadows of the willow. "Walking," she stammered. Her voice sounded like a child's. "I couldn't sleep."

"You're in pain?"

"No. Just restless."

He came toward her, a giant in the gloom. "You should be in bed."

"I'm not an invalid. Childbearing is natural for a woman."

"So you admit you're a woman."

"I never denied it. It was your woman I denied being."

Pride caught her in his arms and she smelled alcohol. She'd never seen him drink more than a glass or two. He held her tightly but gently.

"Are you drunk?"

"Yes."

"Why?" She tried to pull free. It was like struggling against an oak. He brought his face down close to hers.

"You're in my blood," he said hoarsely. "I can't sleep for thinking of you."

"And you think a bottle will solve it?"

"Maybe." He lowered his head so that his hard lips brushed hers.

Her fingers slipped through his hair, tangled in it, and pulled him tighter against her seeking mouth. They kissed, a tender exchange of confused emotion. "Pride," she whispered. "Hold me."

"I am holding you." His lips parted and the tip of his tongue caressed her lower lip, then gently explored the warm interior of her mouth. "I don't want to hurt you," he said.

"You won't." Kate's lips trailed down his neck to kiss his chest. "I've missed you so," she breathed. His touch sent shocks of excitement surging through her body. Her breasts ached to have him touch them . . . suckle at them.

"If I don't let you go now, I won't be able to stop," he murmured. His strong fingers found a swollen nipple and tantalized it. "You're so beautiful. Your breasts are so big, so full. I want to kiss them, Kate. Let me kiss them."

"Yes," she moaned. "Yes."

His arm slipped under her knees. He picked her up and carried her to a bench beyond the willow. It was so dark she couldn't see his face. It all seemed dreamlike. "Oh, Pride, I've missed you so damn much."

"Don't talk, Kate. Just let me touch you, prove to myself that you're real." He held her on his lap and slipped aside the silk dressing gown. His fingertips stroked the warm, hard curve of her belly. He bent his head and kissed it lightly. "You're so beautiful. Like some ancient fertility goddess."

His words slurred and a tiny warning voice shouted to Kate to stop it. He's drunk! He'll hate you for this tomorrow. She pushed it away, refusing to listen. Her skin burned like fire where his lips touched. A sweet moistness filled her. She lifted a swollen breast to his mouth.

"I love you," he groaned. "I love you."

The flames grew within her; she twisted and moaned against him as his hand slipped lower to tangle in the dark curls. "Yes," she cried. "Yes."

"You want me as badly as I want you."

"You know I do." Kate felt as if she was floating on a warm tide. She couldn't think, didn't want to think. She only wanted to possess and be possessed by the man she loved.

Pride fumbled with his clothing, then turned her to face him on his lap. He leaned back, and she felt the full length of his throbbing manhood pressed against her. "I don't want to hurt you," he repeated.

She arched against him, lowering herself on his member, taking it into her body completely. There was no pain, only an overwhelming drive to join with him. Waves of joy swept through her veins, cresting and building again as they moved together. Pride cried out with pleasure, and she clung to him, treasuring this moment out of time, this moment when she was truly his.

Later, he carried her to her bed, and they made love again, slowly, exquisitely. He kissed her tenderly, over and over. He stroked the mound of her belly and listened to the heartbeat of the child.

"If it isn't mine, don't ever tell me," he said hoarsely.

She laughed. "It's yours, Pride, only yours. There's not another man I'd go through this for, believe me."

Finally, he slept. Kate lay awake until the first threads of roseate light spread across the polished wooden floor of her chamber. In the half light, his hawk face was almost

boyish, the lines of tension softened. She could not resist
kissing the firm lips, could not keep her fingertips from
tracing the curves of his scarred chest, his muscular arms.

With full daylight, Kate slept. When she awoke, she was
alone. She reached out for him, murmuring sleepily.
"Pride?" The door to her room stood open. Tears spilled
from the corners of her eyes. She curled around a pillow
and slept until late afternoon.

There was no sign of Pride at the evening meal. Kate
drifted to the library and found a book. She read until late,
then went to bed, her heart troubled.

Two days passed and then four. On the fifth night, Kate
woke in the middle of the night with a severe backache.
As she got out of bed, her gown was soaked with a sudden
gush of liquid. A little ashamed, she changed the garment
for a dry one. She knew the breaking of waters usually
meant the start of labor, but didn't want to call the maid
yet. What if this was another false alarm?

By morning, there was no doubt in her mind. The pains
were coming regularly. Her back ached, and she felt sick
to her stomach. She paced the floor, unwilling to lie still
and let this happen to her body. A restlessness filled her,
and she longed for Pride.

There was a quick knock at the door, and it opened.
Rebecca stood for a moment in the doorway, then rushed
to her side. "The baby's coming?" she asked. She laid a
practiced hand on Kate's belly. "How far apart are these?"

Kate told her, and she shook her head. "How did you
know?" Kate asked. "About the baby?"

"I got back late last night. The servants could talk of
nothing else. I would have come then, but I didn't want to
disturb your rest. Where is he?"

"Pride?" Kate winced as another pain took control of
her body. "I don't know. He's been gone for days." She
clasped the strong dark hand. "He thinks I betrayed him."

"Did you?" The almond eyes searched Kate's soul.

"No. I tried to bargain with the Frenchman to save
Pride's life. I would sleep with the devil to keep him from
the stake. Nothing happened between us! He double-
crossed me and tried to kill Pride. He shot him right in

front of me. I was convinced . . ." Kate took a deep breath and blinked back tears. "I thought he was dead. I wanted his son to be born here; I thought you would want him."

"And you don't?"

"Of course I do, but I don't want him to be a bastard. I want the best for our child. I didn't betray your son, and I'm not lying to you now. I wouldn't lie about something so important." She leaned back against the pillows and wiped the damp hair from her face. "This baby is an Ashton."

"If it were yours alone, I would want it, Ki-te-hi. Pride's father was a fool at times. It seems my son has inherited some of his bullheadedness. He should be here at the birth of his child. Never mind, we will care for you. It will not be long now." She crossed to the French doors. "I'll be right back." Rebecca went into the garden and returned in a few moments.

"The pains are harder now," Kate gasped.

"Chew these leaves." Rebecca held out a strange plant. "It will ease the pain without hurting the little one. My people have used it for centuries." She went to the hall and called for a servant, ordering water and clean clothes. She came back to the bed. "Up with you now. You must walk. You may wet your lips with water. Let mother earth share your burden."

Two housemaids came in with the required supplies. A man followed with an odd-shaped chair. "Where do you want it, Lady Ashton?"

Rebecca pointed to a place near the window. She pushed open the doors so a fresh breeze blew through the room. "Send the midwife and Molly. The rest of you may go."

"A birthing chair? I've never seen one," Kate said. She looked suspiciously at it.

"Trust me, Ki-te-hi. Shawnee women crouch to deliver their children. You are strong and healthy. This will be faster; easier for you, easier for the child, than lying flat in a soft bed."

There was a commotion in the hall, and Pride strode into the room. "You're back, Mother. Good. Now, leave us alone for a few minutes."

"No," Kate protested. She leaned against the Indian woman and tried not to show her pain.

"If I stay out of the room long, you will have to catch your child, my son," Rebecca pronounced wryly.

"Out!" He slipped an arm under Kate and led her to the bed. "You could have waited until I got back."

"Are you serious?" She bit her lip as another pain knifed through her.

"I went to Annapolis."

"Fine. Now will you get the hell out of here and let me have this baby!" She tried to stand by herself, and he caught her.

"That's just it. The child will be my heir. I don't want it to be called a bastard by English law. I've brought a minister. He's going to marry us."

"Now?"

"Yes, now! How else would my son be legitimate?"

"But I haven't said I'd marry you. Right now I can think of nothing I'd want less," she lied. "You made it clear what you think of me. We made a bargain. All that I ask is that you keep . . ." A moan escaped her clenched lips. Sweat poured from her face, and she clenched his arm. "That you keep your promise."

"After what happened in the garden, I can't deny to myself or to you that I still love you. We'll be married, and then if you still want to be apart from me, you can go back to England as Lady Ashton. With the Ashton title, there will be no question of your being sent back to prison. The law forgives much to those who can pay well. We will secure you a royal pardon."

"I can't marry you," she protested. Pride must not have slept the whole time he was gone. White lines of weariness showed in the craggy face. The buckskin clothing was soaked with sweat and dirt-streaked.

"I nearly killed two horses to get back here in time," he said quietly. "I'll have none of your nonsense. Our marriage is already registered at the courthouse. You'll sign these papers, or I'll break your arm." He produced a wrinkled parchment from his shirt. "I'm sure we can find quill and ink."

"Do you believe me about DeSalle?" she gasped. "Do you?"

He sighed and shook his head. "I was a fool. Yes, I believe you. I know the child isn't his."

"And Tschi? Do you still think I made love to him?"

"It doesn't matter, damn it! It doesn't matter about my brother!" Could she be telling the truth? Tschi had lied to him before—but so had Kate. It was best not to think about it anymore. It didn't matter. All that mattered now was Kate and the coming child.

"How can I marry you if you think . . ." Tears welled up in her eyes.

"You're already my wife. We're only protecting the child's interests," he insisted.

Kate doubled up; her breathing quickened. "You can't make me," she protested. Her muscles were beginning to push down. He was out of his mind. They couldn't possibly be married . . . "Rebecca," she screamed. "Help me. It's coming."

Pride seized a quill pen from the desk. He looked about for ink and saw none. Pulling the hunting knife from his sheath, he sliced the edge of his thumb. Blood oozed from the cut; he dipped the end of the quill in it and thrust it at Kate. "Sign."

"With your blood, gladly!" Blindly, she scrawled *Lady Kathryn Storm* and collapsed into his arms. "Bastard or not," she panted. "It's coming."

"Mother!" Pride carried her to the birthing chair. "Get that damn preacher in here!"

Kate clutched the worn arms of the chair as Pride stripped away the dressing gown, then spread it over her. "The baby," she gasped. "I can feel it! Rebecca!"

Rebecca knelt by the chair. "That's it, breathe deeply. Now, push."

"No!" Pride shouted. "Not yet! Damn your hide, man!" He grabbed the shaking cleric and dragged him before Kate. "Say the words! Quick before I rip out your tongue!"

With a squeak of terror, the little man began to stammer out the marriage vows. "Do you, Kathryn—"

"She does!" Pride's hand closed on the man's throat. "Get to the important part."

"By the authority vested in me—" The iron fingers tightened, and he croaked, "I pronounce you man and wife."

Kate let out a shout of pain and triumph, and the infant's head slid into Rebecca's hands. The minister twisted away and fled the room. Pride dropped to his knees beside his mother.

"Careful," he warned. "Be careful with him."

"One more push. Good girl," Rebecca soothed. "Now the other shoulder."

A shrill cry filled the room; Rebecca deposited a bloody boy-child into her son's hands. "Don't you drop him," she cautioned. "He's fine, Kate. A beautiful boy. Small, but he has all his parts."

"Let me see him. Let me see my Geoffrey," she sobbed, putting out her hands.

"He's as slippery as a trout," Pride protested, holding him up for inspection. The dark blue eyes were open wide. The tiny fists flailed as he screamed with anger. A thick thatch of black hair covered the infant's head. "He's mine, by God!" Pride said. "Listen to him yell."

Kate stroked a minute finger. "He's so small," she fretted. "Give him to me. Let me hold him."

"Just a second until we get him cleaned up," Pride soothed. "What a temper! He may be a mite, but he'll grow."

Kate gasped and gripped her belly. "Oh! Rebecca!"

"No wonder he's so little," she answered hoarsely. "He's not alone. Put that one down somewhere, Pride. He's got company." Laughing, she knelt to deliver the second child.

"What is it?" Kate cried, laughing and weeping at the same time. "Is it another boy?"

"Not unless she intends to grow her male parts later. You've a beautiful little daughter." Rebecca handed the twin to Pride and concerned herself with caring for Kate.

In minutes, Kate was washed, dressed in a clean, soft gown, and tucked into bed with the infants beside her. Both seemed to be healthy and alert, but very small. Both had black hair, but the girl's skin was darker than her brother's.

"She looks like a Shawnee," Rebecca said. "What will you call her?"

"Elizabeth," Kate murmured, kissing the fuzz on top of the baby's head. "Isn't she precious?" she asked over the squawling of the two. "Elizabeth Kathryn Ashton," Pride added. "A mouthful for someone knee-high to a duck." He touched the boy's hand; the little fingers tightened on his large one. "He has a strong grip."

Kate's eyes met his. "He'll hold whatever's his," she said, "like his father."

The infants were christened by the minister before he was sent back to Annapolis. Pride asked him to sign the entries in the Ashton family Bible and to carry proof of the babies' births to be registered in the courthouse.

"But babies are not usually . . ." he protested.

Pride's stare silenced him. "My children are to be listed officially: Lord Geoffrey Ashton, Baron of Kingsley, Baron of Wells, heir to my title, and Lady Elizabeth Ashton. You will deliver my letter to the governor, personally. He will do what is necessary. I hold you responsible for carrying out my orders."

"Yes, Lord Ashton," he stammered, eager to be out of this man's home. "Whatever you say."

"My men will see you safely back to the capital. I will inquire as to the success of your mission when I am next in Annapolis. For your sake, I hope nothing is left undone."

"No, m'lord." Trembling, he accepted the letters to be mailed to London on the first available ship and hurried out of the door. Even his position as cleric would not protect him from this arrogant lord's wrath. He secretly vowed to have nothing more to do with the nobility. Common folk were properly respectful of a minister of God!

Kate held her son to her breast while Rebecca rocked his sleeping sister. "Was it necessary to be so harsh with him?" she asked Pride.

"It was! There must be no blot on the twins. Doubtless

he will have a merry tale to spread about our wedding.''
Pride looked down at Geoffrey. ''Is he taking any?''

''A little. Rebecca says I have plenty of milk. I'm going
to nurse them myself.'' She blushed. ''I know it isn't fash-
ionable. They are so tiny, I'll take no chances of a careless
maid dropping one. Did you know the Crown Prince of
England was once killed in a servants' game of toss-up? I
won't have the same thing happen to my Geoffrey or Elizabeth.''

Rebecca looked at Pride meaningfully. ''The children
are delicate, my son. They need a mother's care. The first
six months are especially dangerous.''

Pride's eyes narrowed. ''Why do I feel you two are con-
spiring against me? Do what you think is best for the children. These matters are best decided by women.''

Kate busied herself with the infant's blanket. Rebecca
handed the girl to her son and moved quickly out of the
room.

''I want to try and make this a real marriage,'' Kate said
hesitantly. ''I want to find what we had and lost.'' She
dropped her eyes. ''For the sake of the children.''

''And are we to live as a married couple?'' he demanded. ''Only for the children?'' His face hardened.
''Now, at least you are honest with me. You don't pretend
it's me you want.''

''Damn your eyes, Pride Ashton! Are you blind you can't
see how I feel about you. I want you. I want you in my
bed. I want you to look at me like you used to.''

''Sex was never our problem, was it?'' he flared. ''The
problem was always trust.''

''The fault is yours, not mine,'' she whispered.

''No, sweet Kate, it is you. You never trusted me.''

''It is useless to try and talk to you. Our marriage is
nothing but a farce.'' Her face whitened to marble. ''I will
go if you want me to, but not without the twins.''

''You are taking those babies nowhere.'' He laid the girl
beside Kate and covered her with the spread. ''I didn't say
I wanted you to go. I only wanted you to know you have
the option. You'll be financially independent, no matter
what you decide.'' He looked grim. ''What happened be-

tween us in the garden changes nothing. I'll sleep in my own chambers. If you want me, you know where to find me.''

The sound of Kate's weeping haunted him as he went about the day's chores. He had taken her offer of peace between them and thrown it in her teeth. The knowledge tore at his heart.

Why couldn't he forget the past and accept the happiness he knew she could give him? The hours and days after his escape from DeSalle were burned into his brain . . . burned into his soul.

Even now that he knew differently, the pain was still there. He had made her his wife, but he was punishing her for that pain. And maybe he was punishing her for what happened between her and his brother. Or what didn't happen.

He threw a saddle on his horse and tightened the cinch. ''I offered her a way out,'' he said, under his breath. ''Money, and the right to return to her damn England.'' She had refused. Why? Could it be she really loved him? Really wanted to be a wife as she had said?

He swung up into the saddle and dug his heels into the stallion's sides. The devil was in his own heart! And they would wrestle until only one remained. She had accused him of being made of stone. Maybe she was right.

Memories of the night in the garden kept Kate from losing hope entirely. He had opened up to her then, allowing her to see into his heart. If it had happened once, it might happen again.

The twins filled her days and part of her nights; they required careful tending. They must be fed every hour. The girl slept and ate without problem, but the little boy cried constantly.

''More of a thunderstorm than a Geoffrey,'' Pride said, picking him up and walking back and forth with the baby on his shoulder. ''Hush now, little storm cloud. You'll wear your mama out with your clamoring.''

Kate watched the two of them with an ache in her heart. Pride would be a good father. His love of both children was plain for anyone to see. Why couldn't he share some of that love with her?

"Too bad he doesn't have a disposition like my little Shawnee," Rebecca murmured softly. They had switched Geoffrey to goat's milk when Kate's didn't seem to agree with him. Rebecca spent hours dripping it into his tiny mouth and soothing his colic.

Kate had recovered quickly from childbirth. She rarely let the twins out of her sight. She would sing to them and carry them into the garden, positive the fresh air would help their appetites. Pride visited with her and the children every day, often helping with the babies' baths or airing.

"I never thought you'd make a nursemaid," Kate teased. "You can quiet Geoffrey when no one else can."

"It seems to me you're a fine one to talk. I remember something about a woman who swore she'd never tie herself to screaming brats," he countered, with a hint of the old mischief in his eyes.

"But these aren't brats." Kate held Shawny to her full breast. Rebecca had referred to the child so often as "her little Shawnee" that they had all picked up the nickname, shortening it to Shawny. It seemed more appropriate for five pounds of wriggling baby than Lady Elizabeth Kathryn Ashton.

"You are the picture of motherhood," he said. "A madonna. If a man didn't know better, he'd think you a sweet and docile lady."

"My claws are still here," she warned. "Don't come too close, you may get scratched."

"Is that a threat?" He laid the sleeping child down.

"I am trying to play by your rules, Pride. But I find it much easier to love or hate you than to be your friend."

His face flushed beneath the tan as he strode from the room, his massive frame tense with controlled anger.

Chapter 19

The shrill squeal of a baby's laughter echoed through the garden. Kate sat on a blanket facing the two dark-haired infants. Geoffrey, his back well-supported with a pillow, solemnly transferred a turkey feather from one honey-coated hand to another. The Storm blue eyes were riveted to the white tip of the soft feather; the tiny mouth pursed in a circle of wonderment.

Shawny wiggled her way across the homespun in hot pursuit of an orange kitten, her chubby hands grasping for the elusive ball of fascinating fluff. Her eyes, like her twin's, were a brilliant blue, lit now with merriment as she giggled and cooed and closed her fingers on the kitten's tail.

"Gently," Kate cautioned, unwapping the minute fingers and cradling the kitten in her own hands so that the baby could touch it. "Like this." She took one of Shawny's fingers and stroked the purring creature's back. "Nice. Be nice to kitty."

Shawny shrieked with delight and grabbed with both hands. The kitten scampered off to safety, taking refuge under a boxwood. A pink lower lip came out and the blue eyes scanned the blanket for the wonderful toy. Kate scooped her up and held her overhead, tickling the round belly with her head. The baby crowed and seized her mother's hair. Kate lowered her to plant kisses on the silken hair and satin skin of her face and neck. Except for the blue eyes, she could have passed for an Indian baby. Her complexion was her father's, the golden-bronze of a fairy child.

She nuzzled against her mother, and Kate lowered the front of the silk wrapper to offer her a round, full breast. Perhaps catching the scent of milk, Geoffrey looked up at his mother and smiled, a wide, breathtaking grin, showing two pearly teeth against the pink gum. "Wait your turn," Kate ordered good-naturedly. After weeks of worry, Geoffrey's system had adjusted to her milk. He'd grown rapidly, catching Shawny and almost passing her in size. It was hard to believe that they had feared for his life. Kate's heart filled with gratitude and joy as she looked from one baby to the other. They were the picture of health, chubby without being fat and clearly bright and inquisitive.

And yet, even as she soaked in the pure happiness of the warm autumn morning, the aura of sadness permeated her inner being. This was October; precious months had passed since the birth of the twins, and she and Pride still lived like pleasant strangers in the same house. She had tried and tried to reach him. If anything, his heart seemed to have hardened even more against her. He adored his children, showering them with love and attention; to their mother, he presented an icily polite facade.

Ashton Hall was an oasis of peace in a troubled land. Tales of killing and kidnappings filtered through to the isolated plantation. Communication between Ashton and Annapolis was almost cut off. Twice, during the summer months, Pride rode off with a party of men to investigate word of war parties crossing Ashton land. Kate worried for his safety and that of her children.

The closest plantation, Tarleton, was raided and the main barn burned. It was enough for George Marshel. He loaded his family and servants in wagons and traveled back to the security of the coast. Some of the livestock was brought to Ashton Hall for safekeeping. With the animals came several half-breed servants who had worked on Tarleton.

Rebecca had assured George that she could provide work for his people. Annapolis was too big a settlement for the mixed-blood Nanicokes, not to mention Philadelphia. "They'll be safe here," she said, "until you return."

Relations between Tarleton and Ashton Hall had been neighborly, if not warm. George and Margaret Marshel were somewhat suspicious of Lord Ashton and his Indian kin. The Marshels were solid squire stock. They had no claim to nobility, but they could trace their bloodlines back to Henry I. They'd not intermarried with lesser folk.

Still, they were neighbors. The unwritten law of the frontier demanded that Pride and Rebecca give whatever assistance they could. In times of war, it paid to have all the friends one could muster.

Kate had met the Marshels only once. She and Pride had gone to the christening of their newest child, a baby girl. Rebecca had remained behind to oversee Ashton Hall while they were gone. The journey had taken a great deal of planning. Because Kate was breast-feeding the twins, they had to be taken along. It required nurses, mounds of luggage, and of course a company of armed guards to protect the family.

Tarleton was a two-story brick dwelling, much like the manor homes of Kent in England. The Marshels had been gracious hosts. Kate was certain stories of her hasty marriage had been relayed to Tarleton. Margaret had plied her with questions about her family and background; she seemed almost disappointed to learn that the Storms were of the legitimate nobility.

"Fancy Lord Ashton capturing a genuine lady in this wilderness," she'd quipped.

"Amazing, isn't it?" Kate swallowed a smile. Captured was a better choice of words than Margaret could ever imagine.

The other guests at Tarleton had been more friendly. The twins were oohed and ahhed over; Pride was congratulated for having fathered an heir at last. George Marshel had three sons already; this infant was his second daughter. Margaret was little older than Kate. The Ashtons were considered lucky to have had the fortune to produce two living children.

"They may not live though," Margaret said cheerfully. "My first one died in twenty-four hours of the fever. He was a healthy child, too; he weighed over eight pounds when he was born. Then we lost two girls, one while I carried her and the other at six months." She stared at Shawny. "She looks a little red. Are you sure she doesn't have a fever?"

"No," Kate answered smoothly. "It's her Shawnee heritage. Her grandmother is full-blooded Indian, you know."

"Oh, really? My little Caroline has skin like porcelain, so white you can see the blue veins under it. She takes after my family." Margaret was a pink-and-white blond with pale blue eyes. She handed Caroline to a black maid. The infant was wrapped in layers of wool although the afternoon was hot and humid. "Put her in for her nap now," she ordered. "An infant needs quiet." Margaret looked again at the cooing Shawny in Kate's arms. "Blue eyes and black hair. Quite . . . quite different."

The Marshels had put Kate and Pride in the same bedroom with the twins. It had been difficult sharing a bed with Pride, lying beside him in the stillness of the night. She had wanted to reach out and take him in her arms. She had wanted the hard feel of his muscular body pressed against hers. Instead, she had wept silent salt tears into her pillow. They had slept, inches apart, with a wall of stubborn anger between them. Kate could still feel the pain.

The leaves rustled and Kate was startled from her memories. Rebecca came down the path. "Here you are. I looked for you in your chambers. We missed you at breakfast."

"Geoffrey was restless last night. I think he has bad dreams." The twins occupied the room between Kate's and Pride's. "I took them into my bed. I'm afraid we all overslept this morning." She handed Shawny to her grandmother. "Here, take this one. It's Geoffrey's turn."

"Your soul is troubled this day, my child," Rebecca said, sitting down beside Kate and spreading out her satin skirt. "I see it in your eyes."

"And shouldn't I be? A few more months and . . . Damn it, Rebecca. I keep having these stupid thoughts. Why couldn't I be a beauty like Margaret Marshel? Maybe then I'd be able to win back his . . ." Kate laughed. "You see what I mean?"

''Such physical attributes are often a woman's downfall,'' Rebecca mused. ''It was my face that attracted Lord Ashton.''

Kate arched one eyebrow. ''Not only your face, I'm sure.''

''That too. I was vain of my beauty. I was proud and stubborn. If I'd given in to his urging, we would have had a few weeks of loving, and then he'd have returned to his world. Rainbow Girl warned me not to try and hold him. But I knew from the first moment our eyes met, I could be his wife. My life would have been very different.''

''You mean you'd have married a Shawnee.''

''And lived out my life in the old ways. To break the pattern is a great step. There's no going back. You too have broken your pattern. It's not too late to glue back the pieces, but you must decide quickly.''

''There's no decision to make. I love Pride; I'll never stop loving him. He simply doesn't want me anymore.'' Kate lifted Geoffrey's hand to her lips and kissed each tiny finger. ''I'd be a bond servant in this house if he'd love me again,'' she confessed. ''If he'd let me, I think I could go back to England with the babies. It might save both our sanities.''

''So you've just given up?''

''There's nothing more to do! He doesn't want me.''

''Pride is angry and hurt. His brother betrayed him, and he believes you did the same, but he still loves you. He is as tortured as you are.''

''I have tried to be his wife. If he put out his hand, I'd run to him. But he's made it quite plain that ours is a marriage in name only.'' Kate moved Geoffrey to her shoulder and patted his sturdy back. ''There you go, love,'' she murmured.

''If you return to England, it will ruin both your lives. And the children will suffer irrevocable damage.''

''Tell that to your son.'' Geoffrey pulled at the scarlet ribbon in Kate's hair. ''Ouch! Let go.'' She untangled his fingers and laid him on his stomach. ''Here, play with your feather.'' She looked up at Rebecca. ''I think what I need is to get out. I feel so cooped up in the house; it's days since I've ridden Meshewa.''

"I agree. Ride with Pride in the morning. I'll tend the babies.''

Kate threw her a black look. "He doesn't want me with him. I'll not force myself on him.''

"I'll give instruction that Meshewa be saddled at the same time as Pride's horse. They'll both be led to the front door; he's too much of a gentleman to make a scene in front of me or to embarrass you in front of the servants. You can fight when you're alone." Rebecca bounced Shawny on her knee. "They need a mother and a father. But most important, my son needs you.''

"If he does, he picks a strange way of showing it.''

Kate was mounted on Meshewa when Pride came down the front steps. She murmured to the pinto and stroked the silken neck, ignoring the angry glare directed toward her. "Good morning," she said sweetly. The blue Storm eyes were innocent. "I've been in the house so long, I thought perhaps I'd ride out with you this morning.''

Pride swung up into the saddle and turned his stallion's head toward the north fields without a word. Kate urged the pinto to follow, trying not to giggle at the crimson neck and granite shoulders. From the corner of her eye, she caught a glimpse of a curtain moving. She smiled and waved to Rebecca.

"Get up, Meshewa," she said, digging her heels into his taut sides. The gelding leaped ahead, bringing her up beside her husband. Pride refused to give her the satisfaction of recognition. "If you'd rather ride alone . . ." she started. The color flamed in her cheeks. "I can . . ."

"I would." The bronzed jawline twitched slightly; there was no tenderness in his glance. "But these are no times for you to ride alone. You're here, you can stay. Next time ask first.''

"I'm sorry," she stammered. An argument was the last thing she wanted. "I thought if we could talk out some of our differences," Kate explained, "that maybe . . ."

"The time for talk is over. You've gotten what you wanted. I've heard about nothing but your freedom from the beginning. Now you have it. And a large settlement from my estates.''

Tears welled up in Kate's eyes. ''I never wanted your money, Pride. That's unfair and you know it!''

''I suppose I do.'' He slapped the reins and the gray broke into a canter.

Meshewa quickened his pace, and Kate guided him sharply to the right. The road split just ahead. To hell with Pride Ashton! She'd ride alone. There was no reasoning with him.

Pride glanced back over his shoulder and yelled.

''No!'' She urged Meshewa into a run. His sure feet found the narrow path. The wind caught Kate's riding hat and blew it away. She leaned low over the pinto's neck and cried out, ''Faster, faster, boy!'' Pride's curse stung her ears. ''You bastard!'' she flung back. He had swung the stallion into a circle and was in hot pursuit.

The stallion was bigger, with longer legs, but he was weighed down by the burden of a large man. Meshewa had been too long confined; the woman on his back seemed a part of him. The slender legs moved with the precision of a dancer. The gallant heart of the little buffalo pony soared.

A tree had fallen across the path; Meshewa soared over it. Kate laughed with pure joy. She turned the pinto downhill; he scrambled and slid down the gully, then plunged up the far side. Beyond the trees was a cornfield. The stalks had been cut and stacked in shocks. Kate reined Meshewa to a trot, carefully guiding him between the even rows.

She didn't feel like the mother of two babies; she certainly didn't feel like Lady Kathryn Storm. She felt as she had the day she'd escaped from her tutor and ridden off on Father's best hunter. Kate heard the crash of brush behind her as Pride's gray broke into the field.

She slowed Meshewa to a walk and rode head high, trying to erase the amusement from her face.

''What the hell do you think you're doing?'' Pride demanded. He charged up beside her, his tanned face white with anger. ''I told you to stay with me!''

''You told me you'd rather ride alone.'' Kate patted the

white neck. "I wouldn't breed that one. He can't even keep pace with a lady's horse."

"Stop playing games, Kate!"

Anger surged through her and she turned on him. "I just wanted to be alone with you, to see if we could work things out. I can see how foolish it was." Her hand itched to slap his arrogant face. How dare he sit there judging her? They'd been wrong for each other from the start. He'd said sex was all they had in common. He was probably right.

"I'm sorry. I wish I could forget. And forgive."

"Forgive me?" Kate seized the quirt hanging from her saddle and lashed it across his face and bare arm. "Damn you! Who asked to be forgiven!"

Pride's hand closed on the whip; he yanked it from her hand. Kate dug her heels into Meshewa's sides and twisted to avoid his grasp. The stallion leaped ahead and Pride pulled her from the saddle. He tried to drag her up before him, and they both went crashing into the dirt.

"Kate?" Pride shook her.

She took a deep breath, and the spinning horizon slowed and slid into place. She spat out a mouthful of dirt.

"Are you hurt? Is anything broken?" he demanded. He was kneeling beside her like some dust-covered scarecrow. A corn leaf fell from his hair.

"No thanks to you." She spat more sand and began to laugh. Lord Pride Ashton! He looked more like a swineherd. His face and clothes were smeared with dirt. He took her arm and pulled her to her feet.

Kate trembled inwardly at the nearness of him. She fought the desire to kiss those muddy lips, to run her hands over his shoulders and down his chest. An ache grew inside. She took a step backward and averted her eyes as he brushed off her clothing.

The two horses stood a few yards away, watching them. Kate called to Meshewa, and he came forward eagerly. "I'll go home," she offered, mounting the pinto.

"There's no need." Pride pushed a lock of hair from his broad forehead. "You look like a blackamoor." A slow grin broke over his face. He caught the gray's reins and put a booted foot in the iron stirrup. "Stay with me, Kate.

It's not safe for you to ride alone. Hell, it's not safe for me to ride out without an escort. The Delaware are up, the Fox, the Shawnee. Tschi's leading several war bands.''

"He wouldn't attack Ashton Hall?" Kate paled.

"Tschi? How the hell would I know? How do you expect me to know what he'd do?" Pride's voice softened. "No, I don't think he would. But I didn't think he'd turn me over to the French, either." The dark eyes were hurting. "I should hunt him down for what he did, but I can't. He's my brother. If he comes against Ashton, I'll kill him. But if he stays clear, he can go without fear of me."

"Does Rebecca know?" Kate had never mentioned Tschi's betrayal to Pride's mother.

"She knows, but I didn't tell her. There are few secrets in an Indian camp for long."

"The two of you are so different; it's hard to believe that you're brothers."

"We're not so different. He's fighting for his home and his people the way he sees it. I'd fight to defend Ashton."

"Tschi and I were never lovers. I slept in his wigwam, but not in his bed."

"So you tell me. He told me different." Pride edged the gray ahead of Meshewa and unslung his rifle. "Be still. Our voices carry a long way on the wind."

"What kind of a hypocrite are you?" Kate demanded, keeping her tone low. "No matter how many times you're proved wrong, you keep accusing me! You almost let your own son be born a bastard because of your stubbornness."

"Damn it, woman, can't you see! We're fighting again. All we ever do is fight. I'll not spend the rest of my life in constant battle!" Pride cradled the gun in his arm. "Now shut up, or I will take you back." He dug his heels into the stallion's sides and the animal leaped ahead. Sullenly, Kate fell in behind.

In the north fields, the men were cutting the last of the corn. It seemed strange to Kate to see armed guards on horseback patrolling the work area. She caught the flash of a mirror on a nearby hilltop. Pride explained that it was a boy in a tree.

"He can see a lot farther from up there. There's a pattern of reflections. If it stops, we know there's trouble."

"But he's in danger. If he's only a boy . . ."

"Boys grow up fast out here, or they don't live to grow up."

"Wouldn't it be easier just to stop the work?" Kate asked. She'd dismounted to tighten Meshewa's cinch strap.

"For how long? This hit-and-run warfare could go on for years. I have to clear the land to plant crops. If you don't rotate corn with tobacco, the soil gets used up. I'd soon have nothing." He motioned her to silence while he conferred with the foreman. Pride returned in a few minutes and mounted his horse.

"Where to now?" Kate gathered the reins and put her foot in the stirrup.

"You wait here. I'm going to ride out and check on two men a few miles from here. They rode for water this morning and didn't get back yet."

"But I—" she protested.

"No buts."

A burly man took Meshewa's bridle. "You rest awhile, missy," he said. "Until the master gets back."

Kate waited for what seemed hours. The cutting of trees went on about her. Two riders had gone with Pride, men she didn't know. It was hard not to worry about Pride's safety, and harder still to admit he was right in leaving her behind. Unarmed, she would be nothing but a burden to him. Next time she rode out, she would carry a pistol at least.

She dozed and was awakened by the sound of hoofbeats. Three horses came tearing through the woods; Pride was in the lead. She got to her feet and ran to him.

"What happened?"

Ignoring her, he began to shout orders. "Jake, you take three men and escort Lady Kathryn back to Ashton. Alert the patrols! The rest of you come with me. And Jake, signal the boy in. Take him with you."

"What is it?" Kate demanded, untying Meshewa.

"They're both dead. I don't know who did it, but I'm sure as hell going to find out. They've got barely an hour's start on us. You get back to the house and watch after the kids. No nonsense, Kate," he said hoarsely. "I've no time for it."

She nodded, swinging up on Meshewa's back. "Be careful, Pride, please."

"If I can."

There was no word for two days. She and Rebecca slept in quick snatches. The shutters were closed and barred; the house was secured like a fortress. Kate carried a pistol wherever she went.

"White or Indian?" Rebecca had demanded.

"He didn't say. All he said was that the men were dead. Jake said they'd heard no gunshots. But I'm not sure the sound would carry." Kate slipped Shawny into a clean wrapper. It was insane to think of Pride in danger of being murdered on such a beautiful October day. Shawny had just cut a new tooth, and Geoffrey was learning to crawl. How could such madness exist at the same time? He belonged here with her and the children, not off in the wilderness. For the first time in months, Kate longed for the tranquillity of England.

They carried him in just after dusk with a musket ball in his left shoulder. "You've got to dig it out," Jonas said, matter-of-factly. "I'd of done it myself, but I didn't want to start it ableedin'."

Despite his protests, they'd dosed him with rum, and Rebecca had removed the lead from his wound. Kate sat by him and held his hand, grateful when he fainted from the pain. Pride's lip was bitten through, but he'd made no outcry until he passed out.

"It didn't hit the bone," Rebecca said, washing her hands. "If infection doesn't set in, he'll heal well enough. I've seen him hurt worse."

"It were a long shot that caught him," Jonas explained. "Close up, a ball that size will blow a man to kingdom come! Pride's lucky, I reckon. 'Twere a band of renegades, some white, some mix-bloods. They killed them two fellas fer their guns and horses. All kinds of folks in the woods nowadays." Jonas winced as Rebecca poured rum into the wicked gash on his arm. "Seems a waste of good liquor, ma'am. Do me more good in my gut.'' He flushed. ''I mean my belly. Nothin' but a scratch. Little son of a bi—'' The red darkened to crimson. ''I mean he were small,'' he stammered. ''The dirty breed what cut me.''

''How many were there?'' Rebecca asked.

Pride regained consciousness; Kate wiped the sweat from his forehead and covered him with a clean sheet. ''Eleven,'' he whispered. ''One we left alive to spread the word.''

Jonas guffawed. ''Sort of. Pride—'' He broke off at Pride's fierce glare. ''What I mean is, well . . . guess I'll see to the men. See ya in the mornin', Pride.'' Hastily, he backed from the room.

''And I don't suppose we'll hear the rest of that story,'' Rebecca commented.

''No.'' Pride sank back on the pillow. ''Are the kids all right? I suppose they're asleep.''

''Yes,'' Rebecca answered. ''And you should be, too. I'll mix up something to relax you. The longer you sleep, the quicker your body will heal. Kate can sit with you.''

''That's not necessary,'' he protested. ''I'll be all right.''

''I'll stay,'' Kate agreed. For a few minutes, Pride had let his guard down, had seemed almost glad to have her touch. A sense of bitter disappointment flowed through her. Nothing had changed, nothing ever would. He let her touch him because he was hurt. Even a wild animal would do the same. Still, she would stay. Just to be near him, to know he was alive, was better than the worry and waiting.

Pride's wound healed slowly. Rebecca's potions kept the infection down. November passed and then it was Christmas. Since it was the first one for Geoffrey and Shawny, they made a special effort to make the celebration a joyous one.

They had made toys for the children. Rebecca had carefully cut and stitched a leather doll for Shawny. The hair was black, braided from a horsetail; the face was delicately worked in silk threads. The tiny dress of doeskin was fringed. It was a doll to delight any little girl.

Jonas carved a wooden horse for Geoffrey. It had a leather saddle that could be removed. Pride made each child a leather ball stuffed with straw. Not to be outdone, Kate had filled two cloth bags with colored stones, woolen animals, and carved blocks of wood. From England she'd ordered expensive toys and clothing fit for a prince and princess, but no gifts would ever have as much love as those Kate fashioned with her own hands, however crude they might be.

On Christmas Eve they lit candles and brought the servants into the great hall for singing and dancing. Kate and Rebecca had trimmed the room in greenery; a great yule log burned on the hearth. The house was filled with the smells of gingerbread and apple cider. For Kate, it was a charade of Christmas.

Pride had given her a velvet box containing a diamond necklace. She had given him a buckskin hunting jacket, sewn and embroidered by a Delaware Indian woman. For just a second, something familiar had flickered in the dark eyes, and Kate's heart leaped. Then it was gone, and she was left with the frost and a handful of cold stones.

When the house was quiet and all had gone to their beds, Kate checked the sleeping twins. Geoffrey was balled on his stomach as usual. Shawny was sprawled full-length, one chubby hand outthrust, the other thumb in her mouth. Kate held the candle over their cribs, marveling at the perfection of the two of them. If she had ever doubted God, it was impossible to do so now. She had only to admire the precious babies created, carried, and brought into the world during the chaos of the past year. If nothing else remained of the love she and Pride had shared, Geoffrey and Shawny would be evidence for the rest of their lives.

Restless, Kate returned to her own chambers and paced the floor. Outside, it was raining. The steady sound of the drops against the windows seemed to disturb her even more. She could stand the waiting no longer; she must do something or concede the war!

With trembling hands, she poured herself a glass of wine. The warmth of the sweet liquid spread through her body and drove back the cold despair. Pride lay only a few yards away. What had he told her? *You know where to find me.*

Could she swallow her self-respect and go begging? It was impossible. A second glass of wine followed the first.

What did it matter if the comfort would only last the night? Wouldn't a few stolen hours be better than a lifetime of regret?

Swiftly, Kate pulled the ivory pins from her hair and let it tumble about her shoulders. She ran a brush through it until it shone in the candlelight. From the armoire she took a gossamer dressing gown of the finest China silk, red as blood, with jade dragons embroidered down the full sleeves and around the skirt. She considered the diamond necklace, then tossed it on the bed. She would wear no jewelry.

The silk felt cool against her bare skin; it was so fine that it was almost transparent in the shadowy light. It clung to her rounded body, emphasized her full breasts. The vee neck plunged nearly to the tie at her waist; the slit sides parted when she walked. If Pride turned her from his door tonight, she would have no regrets. She would have tried.

Her bare feet made no sound on the polished floor as she made her way down the wide hallway past the door to the twins' room. A maid slept within; two guards patrolled the garden paths. The palms of her hands were moist as she reached for the tiny brass knob on Pride's door. It turned easily, and she pushed the door open.

The room was dark. No moonlight filtered through the windows. The wind and rain masked the sound of her movement. She paused and listened to the heavy breathing from the bed, then stealthily approached.

Kate would have screamed if his hand had not clamped over her mouth. One heartbeat ago he was motionless on the bed, and then he had leaped like a beast of prey to seize her, a knife in his hand.

"Kate?" The knife clattered to the floor, and the hand moved from her mouth. "What in hell are you about? I could have killed you!" Still he held her.

She opened her mouth to speak; nothing would come from her throat. He released her. There was the click of flint and then a candle flickered. He held it high, capturing her in the circle of light.

"What do you want?" he demanded.

He knew, damn him. Kate knew he knew. Why did he make her say it? Her lip quivered. "If you have to ask," she murmured, "then I've come on a fool's errand." Kate lowered her eyes. His bronze body was naked in the glow of the taper. She took a step backward. "I . . . I'll leave. I shouldn't have . . ."

He sat the candlestick on a table and caught her in his arms. "No, Kate," he groaned. "I don't know whether you're a dream or if you're real. But I'll not let you go, no matter what." His mouth covered hers, and she tasted the desire on his lips. An arm slipped beneath her knees and lifted her. Her hands went behind his neck without breaking the kiss.

A rush of burning sensation flooded her veins; all reason fled, all shame. She clung to him. "Pride," she whispered. "Pride, don't send me away. For God's sake, don't send me away."

His mouth plundered hers, devouring the sweet dark places of her inner self, driving the devils from his brain. His hands moved on her body, cupping the full breasts, sliding down her soft belly to the dark curls below. Kate strained against him, demanding, driven by a passion fueled by months of waiting. His touch was like fire; his lips set her aflame.

A firefly of thought danced through her mind. He might plant another child in her body tonight; she prayed it would be so. Pride's children were a part of him, a part he could never take away. Kate moaned in ecstasy, moving against him, with him, driving him mad with the wanting of her.

"I want you," she begged. "Please, Pride, I want you."

"Not yet, darling, not yet," he murmured. A flood of joy poured through his veins. The emptiness was gone, the doubts and hates, washed away by the vision of her beauty in the candlelight. "We've waited too long. There are things I've wanted to teach you, things I've longed to share with you." He laughed as he tossed away the silken gown and stretched out beside her. "My little Ki-te-hi. Darling, you have so much about love to learn."

"I need you, Pride. I can't live without you."

"Darling, darling Kate. I've been so wrong."

"Shhh, just love me. Don't talk. Just love me," she said huskily.

Pride's tongue flicked at her nipples until they ached with desire, and she felt the warm moistness between her legs. Slowly, he moved down her body, kissing, nipping lightly, tasting the salt-sweet flavor of her silken skin. He groaned, deep in his throat, repeating her name over and over.

She strained against him, wanting only to be possessed, to be one with him completely. "Please," she whispered. Her body trembled as he continued his tantalizing path of arousal.

His strong fingers stroked her inner thighs, tracing the curves of her womanhood, kissing the silken mat of curls below her navel, promising pleasures she never dreamed of.

"Oh, Pride," she moaned. "I love you so."

"Ki-te-hi. My woman." His breath was hot against her burning skin.

And then, when Kate thought she would die from the sweet, breathless joy of his embrace, Pride rolled over on his back and pulled her astride him. She accepted his love as the green shoots of spring welcome the rain. Together they blended flesh to flesh, heart to heart, and soul to soul, spiraling higher and higher . . . There was no sense of time, no other being on the face of the earth . . . nothing but a shared rapture of all-consuming joy.

Some time in the deepest hours of the night, the candle sputtered and burned out. Neither noticed. There was no need for light when touch and whisper bound them closer than they had ever known, closer than any dream.

And in the darkness, Pride opened his heart to her, salving the hurt he had done to their love. "I don't deserve you," he whispered huskily. "I've been a proud, hard fool. I—"

She shushed his lips with her own, content in the shelter of his arms. And finally, exhausted by the long hours of love, they slept, Kate's head secure in the hollow of his shoulder, his arms tightly about her.

A scream brought them bolt upright in the bed. Kate

gasped for breath; her heart thudded so she thought it would burst through her chest. Another scream and Pride's feet hit the floor, his hands closing about his long rifle at the head of the bed. Kate grabbed for her wrapper. "What is it?"

"Stay here!" He threw open the door. She was only a step behind him.

"Fire! Fire!" The dread cry spread through the house.

Pride threw open the door to the children's room and ran to the closest crib. He scooped up Geoffrey and thrust him into Kate's arms. The maid, Maggie, was half awake. "Get up!" he yelled. "There's a fire!" Grabbing Shawny, he wrapped her in blankets and pushed the two women back to the hall. He tried Kate's door. The hall was beginning to fill with smoke.

Kate's chambers were free of heat. "Inside! Wait by the French doors. Keep them inside if you can. If the room gets smoky, go out in the garden. Don't take them out in the rain unless you have to." He slammed the door behind them and was gone down the hall. Kate scrambled for her pistol in the darkness. If the fire was part of an attack, she would be prepared.

There were shouts and the sound of running feet. The iron triangle rang out, summoning the field hands. Kate coped with two crying babies and a sniffling maid. Surely the pouring rain would keep the fire from spreading through the entire house! When smoke began to seep under the door, she ordered Maggie to put blankets along the crack to block it.

Long minutes passed until Rebecca came to tell them that the fire was out. It had been confined to the kitchen.

"The hearth wasn't properly banked. I vow, some of the kitchen help had too much cheer," Rebecca said. She reached for Geoffrey. "How are the babies?"

"Not even a mouthful of smoke. She's asleep, but not Geoffrey. You know him. Is Pride all right?" Kate asked.

"Of course. He terrified the staff, running about naked. I finally got some pants on him." One eyebrow arched delicately. "Did the fire interfere . . ."

"No." Kate blushed. "But if I find who started the fire, I think I'll strangle them with my own two hands."

"There's a hole in the kitchen roof. It's a good thing it's raining. I rather suspect we'll have a cold Christmas dinner, but it could have been far worse."

Kate shivered as she tucked Shawny back into her crib, the thumb still in her mouth. Fire was always a terrible danger. If it had harmed either of her babies . . . She wouldn't think about it! They were safe; that was all that mattered.

She sent the maid with Rebecca to help with the cleaning up, and waited. When she heard Pride's footsteps in the hall, through the open door, she called out to him.

"Kate? Are you all well?" He was wearing the trousers and rough shoes of a servant. He went to each crib and looked down at the sleeping children. "They didn't breathe any smoke?" She shook her head. "That stupid wench will be back in Annapolis as soon as I can get her there. I'll not have her on Ashton. We could have lost the house. You or the children . . ."

"People make mistakes, Pride. Maybe . . ."

"She'll not make it again." Pride put his arms around her and pulled her against his chest. He leaned down and brushed her lips with his. "Try and get some sleep. Tomorrow is Christmas, Kate. You've had little rest this night." His eyes caressed her. "I want you well-rested before we seek our bed again. If anything had happened now, I could not have stood it. Not now, when I've found you again." He kissed her hair. "I love you, woman, and I fear it is a sickness that will not go away."

"I hope not," she murmured. "In God's name, I hope not."

The winter was a hard one. Snow fell and piled against the windows and doors. Pride spent long hours overseeing the care of the stock. They welcomed the bitter weather. As long as it was not fit for man or beast, the war trails would lie empty.

For Kate and Pride, it was a healing time. They laughed

and joked with each other like children, and in the long winter nights, found joy in each other's arms.

Geoffrey and Shawny thrived. By March, they were beginning to try their legs, walking drunkenly from one spot to another, clutching the fingers of friendly adults. Shawny was still the more easygoing of the twins. Geoffrey reserved his breathtaking smiles for those he especially wished to reward, usually his sister.

Pride would lie on the floor of Kate's bedroom in the evenings while the babies swarmed over him. Rebecca and Kate laughed at their antics, and Kate found a peace in the quiet family life she had never known before.

If Pride still held some twinge of regret or ache in his heart, he did not show it. For her, it was enough. Kate's heart warmed to the returning twinkle in his eyes, and the shared worry over the early birth of a foal, or the planning of the next year's crops.

From time to time, they heard word of Tschi. His warrior band was infamous from the Ohio valley to Lancaster. The Crown had put a two-hundred-pound bounty on his head.

With the coming of spring, war seemed far away. Teams of horses and men plowed furrows in the black, rich earth of Ashton Hall. It was the time for planting, for new life, not for thoughts of death. The twins were toddling now; they dug and played in the soft soil of the fields. Often, Pride took Geoffrey up before him on the saddle and rode to oversee the planting.

"He's only a baby," Kate protested halfheartedly.

"But he'll be master of this and more. He must learn to love the land." Pride tossed his son in the air. "He likes the horsey, don't you?"

"He-he, he-he!" the baby crowed and clapped his hands with glee. "Da-da! He-he!"

Kate laughed, clearly outvoted. "Take him then, but not far. And keep the bonnet on his head. I'll not have him burned."

"He'll brown like an Indian, but he won't burn," Rebecca assured her. "Let him go, Kate. He'll be safe enough."

"And tomorrow it shall be Shawny's turn," Pride promised. "Ashton will be Geoffrey's, but my daughter will be as rich as any princess. We may marry her to some Virginia planter when she's grown."

"She may prefer to go home to England, or not to marry at all," Kate said.

Shawny clung to her grandmother's leg and wailed as Geoffrey rode proudly off in front of his father. The huge blue eyes darkened to thunderclouds and tears streaked the muddy cheeks. She dropped her moccasin on the ground and kicked the bare foot out from under the white lawn gown. "No! No!"

Kate retrieved the fallen shoe and forced it over the chubby brown foot. "Don't cry, Shawny. We'll go and see the baby lamb. Do you want to see Robin's lamb?" Her embroidered bonnet hung by one dirty ribbon. Kate pulled it on her head and tied it under the quivering chin. Shawny stuck her thumb in her mouth and sniffed.

Rebecca dipped a lace handkerchief in a bucket of water and wiped away the dirt and tears. "Go with Mama and see the lamb. Daddy will take you on the horsey tomorrow."

"When she's trained she'll have to go into breeches. We'll never make a proper lady of her," Kate teased. "Look at this dress. Maggie spent hours getting it clean the last time she wore it."

"It would make more sense to let her go naked like a Shawnee baby." Rebecca dabbed once more at the minute nose and Shawny giggled. "I'll bathe her after you bring her from the barn. She should have a good nap after all this activity."

Kate swung her up on her hip. "Say bye-bye to Menquotwe Equiwa. Tell her Shawny's going to see the lamb." The baby waved, then hid her face in Kate's dress and chuckled. "And what does the lamb say, Shawny?" Kate murmured. "Baa, baa!"

Kate walked easily toward the barn, pausing a moment to exchange pleasantries with Jonas. From the pocket of his tunic, he produced a crumbled gingerbread cookie for

Shawny. She stuffed it into her mouth eagerly and smacked her baby lips.

"She's a beauty," Jonas bragged. "Prettier than any baby this side of England. Prettier'n anythin' they got there, too! Ain't ya, puss? Don't know how you and Pride managed to get such beautiful young'ns." He grinned and walked with Kate to the barn.

Neither of them saw the painted brave lying in the tall grass a few feet from the barnyard. And no one saw the signal he gave to the mounted warrior on the hill behind the house.

Chapter 20

Kate tucked her newly bathed and gowned daughter into her crib. Shawny popped up and began to fuss for her doll, her constant companion. "Where's your poppet?" Kate asked her. "Where did we leave it?"

Shawny scrambled to the end of the crib, thumb in mouth. The round face puckered. "Dee! Dee!" she demanded.

"Did we leave it in the barn?" The doll would have to be found. Shawny wouldn't go to sleep without it. "Mama will get your baby," Kate soothed. Leaving the toddler in her bed, she hurried outside to hunt for the missing treasure.

Geoffrey had his blanket. Shawny had the doll Rebecca had given her for Christmas. The twins were devoted to their comforters and to each other. It was bad enough trying to get one asleep without the other being in the same room.

A maid was on hands and knees in the hall rubbing beeswax into the wide pine floor. "Keep an ear out for Shawny," Kate warned. "I left her doll someplace. I've got to go and look for it."

The little girl's cries of anger brought Rebecca from the herb garden. She entered through the French doors. "What's the matter, sweet?" she asked in Shawnee. From the time of their birth, Rebecca had spoken to the twins in her native tongue as well as English, determined that they should learn Shawnee properly. "What's wrong with Grandmother's precious?"

Shawny bounced in the bed, arms up to be taken. "Ma-ma-ma!"

"All right, all right. But you're going to be spoiled rotten and it's all my fault." Rebecca picked her up, and the sobs stopped. A wide toothy grin filled the little face, and she snuggled against her grandmother with squeals of delight. Rebecca looked around. "Kate?" She opened the door to the hall. "Jane!"

"Yes'm?"

"Tell Lady Kathryn I've taken Shawny with me."

"Yes'm." Jane returned to her rubbing. You'd think those two were the only babies in the world the way the two Lady Ashtons fussed over them. And the master too! Jane had two of her own, and half the time they bedeviled the life out of her.

Rebecca tied on her own bonnet and Shawny's and carried basket, knife, and reed-basket outdoors. She had a nice bunch of mint just beyond the garden wall. The baby could play in the soft grass while she cut it. "Then you can come up to my bed and sleep," Rebecca continued. "We'll both have a nap."

She followed the brick path to the wooden door at the end of the garden. The boxwood was growing nicely. Ashton Hall would have a real maze by the time Shawny was old enough to receive gentlemen callers. The Indian woman laughed out loud. She was even beginning to think like an Englishwoman! Regardless of what Kate thought, Rebecca knew that England would be too small to contain the spirit of this small warrior. When she chose a man, red or white, he would be one to match her! She would lead some man a merry chase, through more twists and turns than any garden boxwood maze.

Shawny caught the chuckle and giggled, loving the smell of her grandmother and the escape from the despised nap. She spied a mockingbird on a low branch and waved both hands in excitement. The bird gave off a series of chirping cries, imitating the new-hatched chicks in the barnyard. Shawny's laugh turned to a deep gurgle of delight.

"You think that old bird's up there just to sing for you?" Rebecca teased. "Well, maybe he is." She repeated the mockingbird's name in Shawnee and sat the baby on the grass. An inquisitive ewe wondered over to sniff at her. Shawny crawled after her, and the sheep retreated to sniff and stare in the baby's direction. Rebecca laughed and began to snip choice bits of mint for her medicine chest.

The ewe snorted, and Rebecca glanced that way. A Shawnee brave rose from the shadows of the willow. His moccasined foot crushed a twig, and Rebecca whirled to face him, taking the war club across her head. At the last second she twisted and drove the kitchen knife toward his mid-section. Her stroke fell short, but the movement deflected the blow and softened the impact of the deadly weapon. It struck her head and shoulder, and she slumped soundlessly to the short grass. With a cry of triumph, the man pounced on the wide-eyed toddler.

Less than a mile from the main house, Pride sat Geoffrey in the shade of a pin-oak and squatted beside a bondman to help drop seeds into the wide, brown furrow. Two half-grown children used bare feet to cover the corn. Almost half of the field was planted. Another day would see the end of it.

The day was warm; the sun beat down on the backs of the workers. Pride removed his linen shirt and laid it beside his son. The sight of the master's broad, bronzed shoulders brought a blush to the women in the next row.

"Mother Mary," Agnes whispered. "Wouldn't I like to have a taste of that?"

"If Devon hears ya speakin' so, he'll blacken yer other eye."

Agnes giggled and spilled a handful of seed in the soft dirt. "Who says it wouldn't be worth it?"

Pride brushed a dark lock of unruly hair out of his eyes and grinned proudly at his son. Geoffrey was gathering acorns and dropping them down a mole hole. "It'll take a while to fill that up," he called.

The baby looked up. His dark blue eyes caught Pride's, sending a shiver through the man's body. God, but he was the spitting image of his mother for an instant! Geoffrey grabbed for another acorn, and Pride dug out another hand-ful of seed.

He hoped Geoffrey would grow to be a man with his mother's courage. He'd have given a year of his life to be there when she'd hit Andre DeSalle with the canoe paddle.

Pride had never hated anyone in his whole life as much as he'd hated the Frenchman. Tschi's perfidy didn't even come a close second. The thoughts of Kate in his hands brought a red haze of fury to his brain even now.

They reached the bottom of the seed bag, and Pride walked back to the trees to refill it.

He should have killed DeSalle years ago, when he'd had the chance, instead of just wounding him. But Pride had been young then and full of noble sentiment. At the time it had seemed a more fitting punishment for what the Frenchman had done. For just a heartbeat, Pride let himself envision that other girl's face. He'd loved her with every fiber of his being. *As much as he loved Kate?* That question skittered across his brain unbidden. No, he realized. He'd been so damn young then; they'd both been young and what they'd had was something special. Kate was alive; she was his wife . . . while the almond-eyed girl was long since dust. She and his unborn child. It took nothing away from that dead love to admit that he loved Kate more.

The Shawnee war whoop split the silence of the forest; a dozen painted warriors charged across the open field. A woman screamed above the howling braves, and Pride ran for his son. He unslung the rifle from across his back and raced for the spot where Geoffrey had been playing. Pride heard Geoffrey's cry and pushed aside a pine bough to see an Indian raise a tomahawk over the child's head. Pride dropped to one knee and fired. The shot caught the brave full in the chest, and he tumbled backward, his eyes glazing over in death.

Men with muskets lay in the furrows and fired at the Shawnee. A few yards to the left, a bondman fought hand to hand with a painted savage. Another Indian cut the hair from Agnes's head. Pride scooped up his son and ran back to the safety of the trees. The gray stallion was beyond hope of retrieving. A Shawnee stalked him across the corn-field.

Terrified, Geoffrey lay across his father's shoulder and made not a sound. If he cried, Pride would have to pinch his nose and mouth to quiet him.

Just beyond the woods was an enclosed meadow. Pride peered cautiously out into the clearing. A loud sobbing caught his attention. A boy lay outstretched near a flock of dead and dying sheep. *Robin!* Pride ran toward him.

Robin raised a tearstained face. "Robin's sheep," he cried. "They hurt Robin's sheep!"

Pride pulled the boy upright. "Are you hurt? No? Good." He thrust Geoffrey into Robin's arms. "This is a game, Robin. A game. Take the baby and hide him. Take him into the greenbriar thicket and keep him there until I come for you. Do you understand?"

The wide eyes struggled to comprehend. "Robin take baby?" he stammered. "Play game?"

"Yes. Take him into the thicket and hide him until I come. You must be very quiet. And you must take good care of Geoffrey. Now! Run!" Pride said a prayer in his heart as the boy hurried across the meadow with his precious burden. The Shawnee would find them if they looked hard enough, but the battle fever would have faded. They'd have a better chance. He turned and ran back toward the fighting, rifle in hand.

Kate had just entered the barn when she heard the first war cry. She looked back through the doorway to see mounted warriors pounding across the farmyard. Gunshots split the air and servants screamed. Leading the attack, on a piebald stallion, was Tschi! His contorted face was streaked with bands of orange and black, and his hands were dripping blood.

Pride? Where were Pride and Geoffrey? She must get to the house! Shawny was in her crib in the bedroom. Her pistol was there too. If she could get her hands on a weapon . . . Kate flattened herself against a wall and ran deeper into the shadows of the barn.

She heard Jonas's shout and then the explosion of his big-bore musket. There was one less Shawnee, of that she was certain. If Jonas was armed, he was a formidable opponent. There were more shots from the house. Where was Rebecca? Her first thought would be for the baby.

Kate smelled smoke; something was afire. Caution aside, she ran from one stall to another, unfastening the doors. Meshewa would head for the low spot in the pound fence. The other horses would follow him out of the barn if the fire didn't panic them. She slapped the pinto's rump with a leather strap! "Yaaah!" He bolted from the stall, and Rebecca's mare followed. The dun sniffed the air suspiciously and tried to go back into the box stall. Kate smacked him sharply and pulled him out into the passageway. There was one horse left.

Kate approached the black slowly. He belonged to Tarleton. The animal was big, over sixteen hands, with the sleek lines of a thoroughbred. He rolled his eyes and danced nervously as Kate ran a hand over him. She'd never attempted to ride him. George Marshel said the beast had killed one of his stableboys. He was a breeding stud, not a riding horse. Bad treatment on the voyage from England had spoiled his temperament. He shied and the whites of his eyes showed; powerful muscles rippled under the satin hide.

Another war whoop! A bondman and a Shawnee appeared in the open door, locked in mortal combat. Kate backed the big horse into the corner of the stall. He struck at her with a front leg and bared his yellow teeth. "Nice horsey," Kate soothed. "Nice bastard." She leaped and forced the bit between his teeth. He reared, striking the side of the stall with iron hooves. Kate grabbed a handful of black mane, threw one trousered leg over his back, and let out her own war cry!

The stallion lunged against the unlocked gate; then he was down the hall and through the doorway, nearly running down the two struggling men. Kate lashed him with the ends of the leather reins and clung to his neck like a burr. A warrior ran to meet her, a war club raised in one fist. The black left him dying in the dirt with a crushed chest.

Kate reined the animal in the direction of the house. Puffs of smoke came from the windows. Someone was still putting up a fight. She had to get inside. A musket shot whistled past her head; another cut a bloody furrow in the black's rump. Terrified, he reared, pawing the air. Kate leaned into his neck, clutching the streaming mane.

A horseman rode straight at her; the orange-and-black face was grinning. *Tschi!* His own animal reared. For an instant they were so close Kate could have reached out and touched him. His eyes locked with hers; he lowered his musket to shoot. Kate threw all her weight hard against the left rein. The black crashed into the piebald, and both animals were down in a flurry of hooves and churning limbs.

Kate let out a gasp of pain as something struck her shoulder; then she was rolling free. She scrambled to get to her feet. Tschi grabbed her ankle, and she went sprawling. Kate rolled and kicked. One booted heel caught him in the face, and he released the grip on her ankle. She ran for the house.

"Kate!" It was Jonas's voice from the smokehouse.

She veered, narrowly avoiding a brave on foot, and ran toward Jonas. The big-bore musket spoke and the Shawnee went sprawling. The heavy board and batten door opened a crack, and Kate dived in.

"I've got to get to the house," she gasped, when she could catch her breath. The interior of the log building was dim and smoky. Jonas leveled the weapon, resting the barrel on the edge of the air vent. The gun boomed, nearly deafening the three people inside.

The groom, Tom, fired through the doorway and then ducked back to safety as answering volleys slammed against the logs.

"Have you got another gun?" Kate demanded. She tried to remember how many Indians she had seen in the yard. Too many! "Jonas?"

"Nope." He spat a wad of tobacco on the floor and pulled a wicked-looking throwing knife from his belt. The blade was more than a foot long. "Best I can do fer ya, Kate." He rammed another ball down the smoking barrel. "Wasn't plannin' on makin' a stand here."

"It's Tschi."

"Yep, seen him. Shawnee and Delaware. Seen a Fox in my gun sights. Pride shoulda lifted Tschi's scalp a long

time ago. Blackhearted since the day he was born.'' He
raised the musket to shoot again. ''Three of our people
dead, at least. Delaware an' Shawnee don't usually kill
women. This is Tschi's doin' fer sure. Spitework again'
his brother.'' Jonas sighted down the barrel with a practiced eye. ''Come on, Tschi, cross my sights.''

''I've got to get into the house. Shawny's in there.
Pride's got Geoffrey. God knows where they are,'' Kate
said hoarsely.

''He ain't here, which means he's got trouble aplenty of
his own.'' Jonas spat and the big gun roared. ''Damn!
Missed the bugger! There ain't but one way outta here and
that's the door. I'd go myself for the little puss, but Tschi
fancies you. He may not blow yer head off. You make a
break fer it and we'll cover you best we can.''

Kate planted a kiss on the sweaty cheek. ''I'm sorry
about Bill,'' she whispered.

Jonas grunted. His eyes were on the powder horn as he
measured the next charge. ''Bill woulda understood.''

At Jonas's signal, Tom opened the door and Kate ran.
An arrow ripped the back of her shirt; dust flew in small
eruptions as bullets plowed into the dirt around her feet.
Jonas's musket cracked, and Tschi's piebald skidded and
somersaulted. Kate didn't look back to see if his rider was
dead or alive. She was only a few yards from the house
when a warrior leaped to bar her way. He raised his rifle
to strike her with the butt; Kate feinted, then kicked him
in the knee. He bent over with a cry of pain and she ducked
past him.

Kate's head was yanked back savagely, and a blow struck
the side of her face. Tschi pulled her around and held her
at arm's length. ''Enough!'' he commanded. ''Will you
see them all die?''

Fighting back tears of rage, Kate swung at him with a
clenched fist. He laughed, and the salt anguish spilled from
her eyes. ''Let me go!'' she insisted. Her hand went to her
waist for the knife. His eyes led her to it. It had fallen in
her struggle with the warrior.

''You are beaten, Panther Woman,'' he hissed. ''Know

now that Tschi is your master!'' His fist descended and the
world dissolved in inky blackness.

Kate choked. Smoke stung her eyes. She blinked and
gasped for air. Flames shot from the windows of Ashton
Hall. A few feet away Pride was tied to a fence post. She
staggered up and ran to him. ''Pride? Where's Geoffrey?''

Tschi's laugh came from behind her. ''Even now my
braves search for the boy-child. I do not think they will
hunt him long.''

''Damn you!'' Kate cried. Curses spilled from her lips.
''If you hurt my children, I'll follow you to hell!''

Tschi snorted. ''You think I will hurt your son? The son
of my brother? I will make a Shawnee warrior of him. I
told you that I would have sons of you, Panther Woman!
You will give me many others.''

Pride strained at the ropes. Blood stained his bare chest
and legs; a bloody gash ran down his face. The black eyes
shot bolts of pure venom. ''Why? Why, brother?'' he demanded.

''Because you have had what I wanted! Always! Always
Pride, the light-skinned son! Our mother . . . women . . .
and now a son. You are no longer Shawnee, no longer my
brother.'' Tschi spat in Pride's face. ''Your house will be
ashes, your woman will lie beneath me. Your son will call
me Father.''

''I have loved you all my life,'' Pride said softly. ''Even
when you betrayed us to DeSalle.''

Tschi laughed. ''I have enough hate for both of us.''

Kate looked wildly about. Where was Jonas? A gunshot
from the smokehouse answered her unspoken question.
Several braves carrying straw moved back out of range of
the musket. They were trying to burn him out, but the
heavy log walls would take a lot of heat before they would
catch. It had rained recently and the wood was still wet.

Tschi motioned and a warrior carried Shawny across the
yard. She screamed and kicked. Kate started to run to her,
but Tschi shook his head.

''No! Stay where you are, Panther Woman!''

''Shawny!''

''Give her to Kate,'' Pride said. ''This is between the

two of us. Leave the baby out of it.'' He threw himself against the bonds and the gash began to trickle blood.

''How do you know the children are not yours, my son?'' Rebecca called. Kate turned to stare at Rebecca, who seemed to materialize from the smoke. The older woman held herself proudly erect despite her head wound. ''You held Kate in your wigwam for many nights.''

''This is not your affair!'' Tschi said harshly. ''You have become white. You too are the enemy.''

Rebecca continued walking toward her granddaughter. ''Give me the child,'' she ordered. ''Yours or Pride's, she is of my clan.''

''Stand back, woman,'' Tschi warned. ''Your brains can spill as easily as the panther kit's.''

''You would harm your own child? What if she is yours, Tschi? What punishment for a man who sheds the blood of his own daughter?'' Rebecca moved still closer to the baby.

''Seize her!'' A Delaware brave grabbed Rebecca's arm. ''Break it if she moves.'' Tschi's face darkened. ''Do you think me a fool, Mother? Am I a god that I can father children without knowing the woman? I have not taken her yet!''

A triumphant cry escaped Kate's pale lips. She turned the Storm blue eyes on her husband. ''I told you,'' she said. ''You didn't believe me.''

Blood drained from Pride's face until it was the color of wheat. ''You said . . .''

''As always, Chobeka Illenaqui, I told you what you wanted to hear.'' Tschi pulled Kate against him and ran a hand over her breast. ''She will be mine in every way. Mine alone.''

''If all this is over a woman, take her and go!'' Rebecca cried in Shawnee. ''Do no harm to your brother or his children, or I will call down the wrath of the Supreme Being, Moneto, upon you and all who follow you!'' She raised a hand toward heaven.

A baby's cry sounded and Kate whirled around.

A half-dozen braves rode into the yard. One man held Geoffrey before him. Kate ran and took him in her arms, soothing him against her bosom. "Shhh, shhh sweet. Mama's got you." She raised hard eyes to Tschi. "Do you make war on children?" Geoffrey wrapped chubby arms around her neck and held on tight.

"Once we fought, brother," Pride said. "Will you fight me again or have you lost your courage?" He raised his voice and called in Shawnee to the watching warriors. "This is a war chief who admits he lied to his brother! A war chief who threatens helpless babies and women! A war chief who shows no respect for the woman who bore him! Is this the man you follow? A man without honor?"

"Pride, don't," Kate cautioned. "He's not sane."

"Once the Delaware and the Shawnee were men to be reckoned with!" he continued. "Now they become scavengers to prey upon their own blood!"

"You wish to fight me?" Tschi answered. "I need to prove nothing to the warriors who follow me! The scalps that line my lodgepole speak for my bravery." He brought his contorted face close to Pride's. "This time there will be no more tricks. This time you do not escape me."

"Choose your weapons, Tschi!" Pride taunted. "I will fight you bare-handed if you wish. My hands against your scalping knife. You dare not! You are afraid! I beat you last time, and you've lost your nerve!"

"Make the circle," Tschi hissed. "I will prove who is the greater warrior. I will silence your English tongue forever!"

There were low cries of approval from the warriors. A Shawnee marked the hard-packed earth with his tomahawk. Rebecca knelt beside Pride and freed his arms. "Be careful, my son," she warned.

"You're hurt," Kate murmured.

For an instant he drew her into his arms. "I've wronged you," he said hoarsely. "From the first. If we get out of this, I'll make it up to you, I swear." He kissed the soft dark hair on Geoffrey's head. "Take care of the little ones."

A seasoned Shawnee warrior threw him a knife. Pride caught it and stepped into the circle, facing his brother.

Kate handed Geoffrey to Rebecca and edged around the crowd to where Shawny was being held.

"Give her to me," she demanded. The brave's eyes widened. "Are you deaf?" Kate took the baby from his arms. "You are frightening her," she lied. Shawny had been playing happily with his bear-tooth necklace.

The two men circled each other in the ring. Kate could not bear to watch; she could not bear to look away. Pride was wounded. Suppose Tschi did win this time. He would kill Pride. She knew it.

Across the yard, the servants who survived the attack were under heavy guard. Many had died. Kate tried to count the familiar faces. The Indians had taken heavy losses, too. Bodies lay scattered about the once-peaceful farmyard. Several of the braves were badly wounded. She wanted desperately to take the children to a place of safety, but there was none.

Tschi rushed at Pride and slashed his knife at his brother's mid-section. Pride sidestepped and countered with his own blow. Their eyes were locked together. They lunged and grappled together. Tschi's foot hooked around Pride's ankle and they went down and rolled; first Tschi was on top and then Pride.

Rebecca pushed her way forward and took Shawny from Kate. "She should not see this."

"Where's Geoffrey?"

"Maggie's got him." She covered the baby's eyes with her hand and carried her away. Kate's hands gripped into tight fists; she bit her lip to keep from crying out.

Tschi was on top. His knife was poised, pressing downward. Pride's hand gripped his wrist. They strained in silence; only their breathing could be heard. Pride twisted and the knife drove down, jamming into the earth. Pride spun away and crouched. Tschi retrieved the knife and rushed in again. Pride met the knife with his own steel. There was a loud crack and Tschi's blade snapped.

He stared at the useless hilt, then hurled it at Pride's head. Pride dodged it easily.

"Come, brother," Pride called. "Where is your bravery now?"

With a cry of fury, Tschi whirled and seized the musket from a Shawnee brave. He dropped the barrel to sight on Pride's heart.

"No!" Kate screamed. She threw herself in front of the gun. A bolt of lightning ripped through her, searing her body with excruciating pain. She put her hand down and touched the spreading wetness. From far off down some echoing valley she heard Pride call her name.

"Kate!"

She staggered and turned toward the man she loved, her breath coming in quick gasps. "Pride . . ." she murmured. "I . . ." She knew no more.

He caught her as she fell. The knife dropped from his fingers. "Kate!" he screamed.

Tschi backed away. His eyes were the eyes of a madman. "You tricked me!" he cried. "You tricked me out of my woman again!" He turned to his mother and his eyes narrowed as he saw the child she cradled.

Pride knelt on the ground and laid Kate in the dirt. He picked up the knife and began to stalk his brother. The warriors walked away muttering angrily among themselves.

Tschi grabbed Shawny by one arm and tore her from Rebecca's grasp. He threw her screaming to the ground and lifted the musket butt to crush her head. Pride launched himself across the space. Tschi hesitated; his face took on a puzzled look. He half-turned and stumbled. Rebecca drove Jonas's throwing knife into his back again. Blood trickled from his mouth. "Mother. Why?" he begged. "For *that* you kill me?"

Rebecca's eyes were as wild as his. "I gave you life," she whispered. "Now I take it away." She threw down the weapon and gathered up the weeping child. "A hair on this baby's head is worth more than your black soul!"

Tschi fell to his knees and held out his arms to her. "Mother."

Rebecca looked down at him with contempt. "May Inumsi-ila-fe-wanu take pity on you in the land beyond the river. I have none to give." With a terrible finality, she turned away.

Tschi sprawled facedown and the earth soaked up the last of his life's blood. He gave a final gasp and lay still.

"Heed well!" Rebecca shouted. "The man you followed! The war chief you chose! His shame is yours! Go from this place and never return, lest you meet the same fate and your soul wander forever between earth and sky!"

One by one, the warriors gathered their weapons and melted away, carrying their wounded and their dead. The servants let out a cheer and ran toward Pride. Jonas and Tom came cautiously from the smokehouse.

Rebecca handed Shawny to a woman and crouched beside Kate's body. "Does she breathe?"

Pride cradled her head in his lap. He was weeping openly. "She took the ball meant for me," he sobbed. "She offered her life for mine."

"She's no different than she's ever been," Rebecca chastened. "I had two sons; one was a fool and one a mad wolf. If Moneto takes her from you, it will be no more than you deserve." She bent and laid her ear to Kate's chest. "Fetch water and cloth for bandages. She can't be moved until I stop the flow of blood."

Later, when Kate, barely breathing, had been carried to a bed of straw in the barn, Rebecca returned to the barnyard to kneel beside the body of her dead son. Tears dropped from the sorrowful brown eyes to mix with his blood. "The fault is mine, Tschi," she whispered. "I did not love you enough." Then she rose and hurried toward the main house to see if her box of medicines had been saved from the fire. Tschi was dead, and Kate still lived. Her tears could wait.

The kitchen wing was burned out. Damage was done to the floors and furnishings, but the stone and brick had acted as a natural firebreak. Much of the beauty of Ashton Hall was ruined, but the walls stood. Rebecca's chambers and those beyond the main hallway were intact.

It was the medicines that saved Kate's life. Pride would not have believed that a woman could lose so much blood and live. The musket ball had gone completely through her shoulder. It had been a small bore; the wound was bad enough as it was. For days, she hovered between worlds;

Pride dripped broth and milk between her lips as she had done for the twins when they were small.

One day she opened her eyes and smiled at him. The next, she spoke his name. By the end of the week, she was sitting up and calling for her babies. Rebecca nodded at her son, and Pride knew that Kate would recover.

She remembered very little about the day of the attack; Pride didn't remind her. "You're better and that's all that matters."

"Tschi? I dreamed . . ."

"He's dead, Kate. He'll never harm you again."

"Did you kill him? With a knife?" she demanded.

Pride smoothed back her hair and tied it with a crimson ribbon. His lips brushed hers tenderly. "No, I didn't kill him. Now eat your soup and stop asking questions. You've lost a lot of weight. I don't like skinny women." He grinned at her boyishly. "Not too skinny."

"You'd rather have me fat?"

"Only if you were swelling up with another child."

Kate flipped the bowl of soup into his lap. "The next one you carry! Then we'll see how eager you are to have a dozen babies." Her eyes sparkled with merriment. "Ask me next year." Her voice dropped to a husky tremor. "Will we have a next year, Pride?"

He tipped her chin up gently and kissed her lips. "A lifetime of years, Ki-te-hi. If you want them."

Kate pulled his shaggy head down and answered with another kiss, one that promised more than teasing.

"You keep that up, and I'll be in that bed with you," he warned. His hand cupped her breast and caressed a swollen nipple.

Kate lifted the sheet. "I'll let you do all the work," she tempted. "I've nothing to do all day but lie here. A girl gets lonely."

Pride slipped out of his clothes and slid in beside her. She felt like a fragile wild thing; he was afraid of hurting her. "Kate," he said softly, "I've wronged you. I know better now. I know you told the truth about Tschi. Can you forgive me? Ever?"

"No."

"No?" He moved away and leaned on one elbow to look down at her. "You can't?"

"No. But I love you anyway." She nestled against him. "Ask me again in twenty years."

"You little witch. You'd make me wait that long, wouldn't you?" His mouth covered hers and they kissed, a deep kiss of passion. Kate's hand slipped down his taut, muscled thigh to brush against his growing desire.

"Or in the morning," she whispered.